MISSING

MISSING

A DETECTIVE RAVN THRILLER

MICHAEL KATZ KREFELD

Translated from Danish by Lindy Falk van Rooyen

Published in 2023 by Podium Publishing, ULC
www.podiumaudio.com

Podium

MISSING

"All along the watchtower
Princes kept the view
While all the women came and went
Barefoot servants, too."
                    Bob Dylan

1

Hohenschönhausen Prison
East Berlin, 11 July 1989

It was the dead of night. The rain pounded onto the corrugated iron roofs, but other than that, Hohenschönhausen was shrouded in silence. In the first watchtower that was mounted on the outer perimeter wall, the guards' silhouettes seemed to glide past the frosted-glass windows. Another four soldiers from Division XVI were posted at the foot of the tower, but their carabines hung loosely from their shoulders; it was a quiet night, no more incoming prisoner transports were expected, and the men chatted amongst themselves as they protected their cigarettes in the cup of their hands.

Colonel Erhardt Hausser emerged from the elevator on the first floor of cell block B. He glanced up at the red light in the ceiling and stopped abruptly at the entrance of a long corridor. Dressed in civilian clothing, the colonel was almost two metres tall and drenched to the bone; his pale overcoat clung to his kneecaps. Hausser was only in his midthirties, but the hard lines on his face made him look much older. Obviously restless and impatient, the colonel wriggled his fingers into his soaked black leather gloves as he shifted his weight from one foot to the other.

The entire prison was regulated by the lights in the ceiling; a carefully planned and systematic principle of isolation that ensured the inmates would not come into contact with anyone else when they were transferred from their cells to one of the interrogation rooms. Even though he very much approved of the system, Hausser did not appreciate being kept waiting.

At last the light switched to green. Hausser took a left and continued along the corridor. Upholstered, hermetically sealed doors on either side; Hohenschönhausen had 120 interrogation rooms spread over three floors, but despite the lateness of the hour, almost all of them were in use. For this was another principle strictly adhered to at Hohenschönhausen Prison: Never let the inmates sleep through the night.

Hausser withdrew a key from his pocket, let himself into the room at the very end of the corridor, and flipped the light switch. The room contained nothing but the bare essentials: a large desk, which took up most of the space, two chairs on either side, a filing cabinet in the corner; an interrogation room that was identical to the other 119 of its kind in the prison. But Hausser was not here to interview a prisoner, nor had he done so in the past six years; the colonel had his own interrogation methods, and this room was merely staged as his office.

He edged past the empty desk and made straight for the filing cabinet, which he opened with another, shiny little key. In the top drawer he found a bunch of keys. He dropped the keys in his pocket and turned on his heel.

Less than five minutes later, Hausser was back in the courtyard. He flipped up his collar against the rain and made a dash for the prison's former administration buildings, which had been converted into a warehouse for storage. A soldier was guarding the top of the stairs to the cellar. The minute he recognised Hausser, he greeted the colonel with a smart salute.

Hausser ignored the soldier and hurried down the steep stairs. In the cellar, two men from Hausser's division emerged from the dark as he passed. He nodded briefly in greeting, and the three of them continued along the corridor, which had a row of cells on either side. The cells were now used for storage, except for the one at the end, which belonged to Hausser's department, Division Z. Only a select few knew about this room and what it contained. Not even comrade Erich Mielke, head of the Stasi, nor comrade Erich Honecker, knew of its existence; they were merely informed of the results that it produced. Occasionally, that is.

Hausser retrieved the bunch of keys from his pocket and unlocked the cell. Leaning hard on the steel door, he pushed it open. The rusty hinges squealed in protest.

A naked bulb hung from the ceiling, casting a pale-yellow glow onto the damp walls. The room had neither windows nor other forms of ventilation. Back in the day, they kept about twenty prisoners in this cell at a time, but now it contained nothing but a large black metal container that was placed in the middle of the room. The container was made out of four ship's doors encased in metal, including the frames, which were welded together. Hausser himself had commissioned a man, hand-picked from the shipyard in Rostock, to fabricate what in DZ was known as "the Chamber" here, on location. The top door, which served as the lid, had a porthole; in the dim light, it appeared to be staring at Hausser as a dull and dreary eye. A thick rubber hose fixed to a tap mounted on the nearest wall was attached to the right side. The connection was not watertight, and a large puddle of water had gathered on the floor just below it.

Hausser stepped over the puddle, walked up to the Chamber, and leaned over the rusty lid, where the black paint was peeling off in large flakes. He rubbed the fist of his gloved hand against the porthole and banged on the glass.

There was a violent surge of movement inside and water splashed up against the inside of the pane. Hausser banged on the glass again, and this time, a large swollen face emerged from the dark, and bloodshot eyes stared at Hausser in blind panic.

"Only the innocent sleep, Leo," mumbled Hausser.

2

Mogens poured the remains of his porridge into the kitchen sink. Turned on the cold-water tap. Using the brush to mash the lumps, he watched the flakes dissolve and disappear down the drain. He glanced at his watch. Ten minutes to seven. Next door, the neighbour's little boy was sobbing. Mogens dried his hands on the dishcloth and looked down to make sure he had not spilt any of his breakfast on his shirt. Satisfied, he yanked open the fridge door and started emptying the contents into a plastic rubbish bag. Then he went out onto the landing to toss the rubbish into the chute.

Once he was back inside, he went to the bathroom to put his toothbrush and half a tube of toothpaste into the toiletry bag that he had packed the night before. The bare essentials. He caught a glance of his reflection in the mirror. His hair was thinning. He brushed a few erratic wisps off his forehead. Removed his thick glasses. Rubbed his tired eyes. He was only forty-two years old, but he felt as if he had one foot in the grave. Chubby jowls and a sallow complexion revealed his unhealthy lifestyle: too much fast food and a complete lack of exercise. And he was at least twenty kilogrammes overweight. The suit he was wearing today was much too big, making his bulk even larger in the unflattering light. But, starting today, things would be different. He'd quit eating junk food and get some exercise; starting today, everything was going to change.

Spinning on his heel, he went into the bedroom, where his suitcase lay open on the bed. He stuffed his toiletry bag into a gap between his clothing and the plastic bag with the blond wig and dark glasses he had bought at a second-hand store in Christianshavn. Five minutes later, he was at the main entrance door downstairs, holding his soft leather satchel in one hand and trailing his suitcase behind him with the other.

He cast a last look over his shoulder. Whatever happened today, he knew he would never return to his flat. Then he shut the door behind him.

Along the canal, rush-hour traffic inched along Overgaden Oven Vandet. An assortment of sailboats were tethered to the quay in a neat row. The plastic wheels of his suitcase bumped noisily over the cobblestones, waking an English bulldog from his nap on the deck of the nearest boat. The dog stared at Mogens and growled. Mogens started and hastily crossed to the other side of the road. At the soup kitchen on the corner, a homeless man drinking his morning coffee gave him a toothless grin.

"*Bon voyjasse*," the man slurred, nodding at the suitcase clattering at his heels.

Mogens made no reply and picked up his pace. Moments later, he walked over the zebra crossing to Christianshavn Square and joined the queue at the bus stop in front of Lagkagehuset. The smell of freshly baked bread spilled onto the pavement and Mogens took a deep breath. Few people knew that the bakery and the building behind it used to be the local prison house, and he dared not think about it. Instead, Mogens looked at his watch impatiently, but the 9A bus wasn't due for another two minutes.

A crowd had gathered at the bus stop and Mogens was feeling claustrophobic. Beads of sweat appeared on his forehead. Mogens had enlarged sweat glands and started to perspire at the merest exertion. He told himself to get a grip—today of all days he *had* to exude calm! Thankfully, the bus arrived, and the doors slid open in front of him. He could feel the other passengers bearing down on him and hastily stepped into the bus, which was already packed with commuters into the city.

He elbowed his way to the area in the middle, as close to the door as possible so he could get some fresh air on the short trip into town. But ever more passengers got on board, and he was forced to move further and further back, where the air was sticky. He could hardly breathe. He felt as if the other passengers were glaring at him and his huge suitcase, as if they knew what he was up to, and it was only a matter of time before they alerted the police. Panic rose in his chest, and he had a violent urge to get off the bus immediately. But he pulled himself together. Closed his eyes and tried to control his breathing.

It felt like a very long time till they finally reached Copenhagen Central Station. Mogens stepped off the bus with relief and followed the trail of other passengers up the broad steps in front of the main entrance. Nausea from the bus trip gave way to adrenaline pumping through his veins as he made for the left luggage room at the back entrance on Reventlowsgade. He slipped past the guard's cubicle, which he knew would not be manned before eight o'clock.

The long row of aluminium doors of the lockers reflected the pale neon lights above; *it made the room look like a morgue*, Mogens thought. He kept his eyes down, avoiding the cameras mounted just below the ceiling. He knew that the police would probably be able to identify him later, but by that time he would be long gone.

He deposited his suitcase in the nearest empty locker and paid the 60 kroner required for twenty-four hours' storage; if all went well, he would be back within five . . . *if* all went well.

His ticket was still valid, so he simply used the one he had and took a seat near the front of the bus. The 9A heading back to Christianshavn was almost empty. But the morning traffic had increased and the trip through the city centre took much longer. He glanced at his watch. Twenty minutes to eight; in six minutes he would be back on Christianshavn Square. From there, he would have plenty of time to walk the circa eight hundred metres down Brobergsgade. At precisely 7:59 a.m. he would punch in for work; exactly as he had done for the last twenty years at Lauritzen Enterprises. None of his colleagues would have cause for suspicion; everything would appear perfectly normal. He smiled at the thought . . . The bus stopped at the edge of Knippelsbro Bridge. Surprised, he looked through the windshield and saw the red-and-white boom lowering, blocking the road. The warning signal seemed to howl in his ears as the bridge raised straight up into the air before them, as if it were a direct passage to the overcast sky.

No, no, nooo, this cannot be happening . . .

Mogens could not believe his bad luck; this eventuality was not included in his meticulous plan. He stared at his watch in blind panic. It was already quarter to eight. He looked out over the canal. An old three-masted schooner was inching towards the bridge. He damned the beautiful old ship to hell—and all the members of the crew who were waving at the curious bystanders and cyclists waiting patiently on the bridge, admiring the beautiful spectacle on the water.

At 8:04 a.m., Mogens sprang off the bus the moment it stopped on Christianshavn Square. Clutching his leather satchel under his arm, he dashed over the road to Dronningensgade. He continued on the pavement along the canal at a run. Mogens couldn't remember when he'd last broken into a run. Judging from his awkward, uncoordinated movements, his body had forgotten how. When he finally reached the corner and turned onto Brobergsgade, he had to stop to catch his breath. Leaning against the nearest wall, he quickly straightened his clothing and dabbed the sweat off his brow. Then he entered the courtyard that led to the main entrance to Lauritzen Enterprises.

The firm's carpenters had long since dispatched to their various building sites about the city, and the parking lot was deserted. Mogens could see the master craftsmen going about their business. He opened the door to the staff entrance and snatched the punch card bearing his name from the pigeonhole shelf under the clock; Lauritzen Enterprises was an old-fashioned business, steeped in old traditions and outdated systems.

A hollow clunk sounded as his punch card was stamped: 08:19 a.m.

Mogens had *never* been late for work in his life.

"Hard time getting out of bed this morning?"

Mogens snapped his head round.

Carsten Holt, the sales manager, was regarding him with a snarky smile. He was in his midthirties with a suntanned complexion and rather short legs, as if they had stopped growing when he turned twelve, leaving his torso to go it alone. Carsten owned an old Camaro that he never grew tired of talking about, so everyone called him Camaro Carsten—or just CC for short; something that didn't bother CC at all.

"You're all sweaty, Mogens. Are you sick?" Carsten said, pointing at him.

"Sweaty?" Mogens said, swiping the back of his hand over his forehead as he returned his punch card to the allocated pigeonhole. "Not at all. What you are talking about, CC?"

"The rain in your face."

Deciding to simply ignore CC, Mogens shook his head and hurried down the corridor to his office. But he could feel Carsten's eyes on his back.

A pile of invoices and accounts had been dumped on his desk. Invoices were not his responsibility. It was actually the girls in the Accounts Department who were employed to do the paperwork. *His* job was to maintain overall order in the financial matters of the company and balance the books, as it were; Mogens made sure that the books—if not absolutely accurate—were presented to the Danish tax authorities in perfect order. To this extent, he had always been a member of the creative industry. He dropped into his battered chair, which protested loudly under his weight.

Mogens sighed heavily.

All his careful planning scuppered by a bloody bridge! *Was Camaro Carsten really suspicious of him, or was it just his imagination?*

Mogens thought about the bulldog he'd seen on the boat by the canal. That bloody dog had given him the evil eye. It was a bad omen, as if sent from hell. But he had to press on.

If he did not complete his plan today, he would never get away.

3

Hohenschönhausen Prison
East Berlin, 11 July 1989

Hausser gripped the wheel on the Chamber's door and turned it anti-clockwise. Putting his back into it, he pulled hard on the lid. With a scrape of the metal bolts and hinges, it swung open slowly and thudded against the side. The rancid smell of urine filled Hausser's nostrils as the corpulent figure that had been sitting semi-submerged in the filthy water lunged at Hausser. But his neck and wrists were restrained with chains that were fastened to the bottom of the Chamber. Hausser regarded the fat man quizzically. He was about sixty years old. His skin was so pale it appeared almost translucent, as if it were about to dissolve after soaking in water for several days. Like a scoured animal hide, the black hairs on his body clung to his limbs and back.

"P-p-p-please l-let me go," the man stammered through his blue lips.

"Prisoner, identify yourself," barked Hausser.

The man looked at Hausser with pleading eyes. "Number 1-6-6 . . . please, I'm begging you . . . to-to l-let me go . . ."

"I'd love to," Hausser said. "Do you think I *like* spending my time down here?"

The man shook his head.

Hausser retrieved the bunch of keys from his pocket. As if hypnotised, the man stared at them and tried to reach out to Hausser with one hand.

"First, I need you to tell me the truth."

"But . . . but I already have . . ."

Hausser shook his head. "No. For the last three months you have lied to our people. In every interview, you were caught in one lie or another. They gave you cigarettes and coffee, they treated you with kindness, and yet—or precisely for this reason—you chose to lie. So, they sent for me."

"But I'm innocent. I don't even know what I am being accused of. No one has told me."

"You know what you are guilty of; we don't need to explain it to you. But instead of repenting and confessing your sins, you stubbornly choose to lie. And just look what this has brought you . . ."

The man tried to change his posture and stretch his legs, but the confined space and chains held him fast.

"I have told them the truth."

"So, you are calling me a liar?" Hausser asked, letting his eyes drift from the bunch of keys to the man's face.

"N-no! I . . . I don't know what they have said to you. But I answered their questions truthfully. Told them everything. I swear to God. I have nothing to hide. I'm begging you . . . I can't take it anymore . . ." he said, and began to sob so hard that his man breasts started to hop up and down.

"Leo!" Hausser yelled.

Shocked by the unexpected use of his Christian name, Leo took a sharp intake of breath.

"You and I are in this situation entirely due to your own actions. If you had told the truth from the start, we would never have ended up here; I would be fighting the cause elsewhere, and you would be home with your wife, Gerda, and your boys, Klaus, Johan, and baby Stefan . . . If you had only told us the truth, Leo, none of this would have been necessary; we would have known that we could trust you, that you were willing to help us crush the Fascists' spies, weed out the traitors to the party. We would have known that you were faithful to the motherland. You alone, Leo, have made everything more complicated than it needs to be . . ."

"But I *do* want to help—"

"Do *not* interrupt when I am speaking!"

Leo bit his lip and looked down into the turbid water.

"The only reason I am still talking to you now—the only reason I have not let you drown in your own excrement—is that you have not yet lied to *me*. I am willing to overlook all the lies that you have told my colleagues. All the time that you have wasted. All the trust that you have abused. Now is the time to consider your options, Leo, and choose your words very, very carefully . . ." Hausser said. His eyebrows gathered in a frown like a dark thunder cloud over the bridge of his nose. "I simply cannot tolerate dishonesty, Leo. I detest lies; they make me feel dirty, every single time that I hear them," Hausser went on, gripping either side of the doorframe. The little bunch of keys clattered against the metal bolts, drawing a brief, desperate glance from Leo's eyes.

Hausser lowered his voice. "Do you understand, Leo? Do you really understand what lying does to me? How . . . unpleasant it makes me feel?"

"What . . . what exactly do you want to know?" Leo stammered, nodding so energetically that his chains rattled.

"The people you are helping to flee. What are they paying you?"

Leo's gaze faltered. "I . . . I . . . don't know what . . ."

"Be careful how you end that sentence. If you lie to me, I will close the lid and drown you in your own piss."

"One thousand dollars!" Leo yelled. "Sometimes more. It depends on the expenses."

"Where are your men digging the next tunnel?"

Breathing heavily, Leo hesitated.

"Where, Leo?" Hausser made to close the lid.

"Ruppinerstrasse, Number 8! The auto workshop . . ."

Hausser nodded and looked up, staring into space thoughtfully. "Yes, I think I know the one you mean. They take care of the cars belonging to the Department of Internal Affairs, is that not so?"

Leo nodded enthusiastically. "The workshop provided a good cover when we started. Several men in high places in the Party helped us set it up; they all want to flee now . . ."

"How far have they come with the tunnel?"

Leo shrugged. "I don't know. But it's the longest one we have planned so far—a hundred forty-six metres," he added with a hint of pride. "When

. . . when your men picked me up, they still had about forty metres to go. If the boys haven't given up and split, I would imagine that they are almost through to the other side . . ."

"How many traitors do you reckon you can smuggle out?" asked Hausser.

"Five hundred defectors, perhaps more. These days, people are keen to get out . . . I'm sorry to say so, but this is the reality of the current political climate . . ."

"There is no need to apologise; I can appreciate a man who takes his work seriously. Even if he's in the human trafficking business. A smuggler and paedophile like you."

Leo's jaw dropped.

"Ah, yes, Leo, we know everything. The Stasi has eyes everywhere. In the bedrooms, in the courtyards and lonely parks . . . on the sports fields and empty schoolyards. All the places where you have satisfied your pleasures with the Young Pioneers All those children you baited with sweets from the West."

Hausser dropped the keys back into his pocket and grabbed onto the lid of the chamber.

"Wait! What are you doing?!" yelled Leo. "I've told you the truth now . . ."

"Well, we'll see about that, shan't we. But till then, you're staying put," he said, smacking the lid shut.

When he turned the wheel clockwise, the screech of the bolts and hinges blotted the sound of Leo's sobbing inside the Chamber.

No more than three hours later, the sun had almost risen, the rain had stopped, and Hausser returned to Hohenschönhausen. He yawned as he stepped into the cell, visibly exhausted from working all night. Together with a unit from Division VII, which was in charge of the Stasi's special operations, he had set up a surveillance team of the auto workshop on Ruppinerstrasse; it soon became apparent that, despite Leo's sudden disappearance, his men had continued digging the new tunnel. During the course of the night, several people came in and out of the building. And, just before dawn, a truck left the premises; the load on the back was covered with a black tarpaulin, but Hausser was almost certain that it concealed the soil displaced by the smugglers' digging operations. So Hausser reckoned there was no reason to keep Leo waiting any longer.

He took a seat on the edge of the Chamber and peeked through the porthole. Leo's pleading eyes rose up to meet his. "It seems you were telling the truth, Leo," Hausser said in a voice loud enough to penetrate the lid. "This must have been a liberating experience for a man who has lived his whole life on the telling of lies. I promised not to drown you. I intend to keep my promise. The problem, however, is that Müller here," he added, pointing to the man standing by the tap against the nearest wall, "is not happy . . . he hates to see people leaving the Chamber alive."

As if on cue, Müller turned on the tap and water immediately gushed through the thick hosepipe that led to the Chamber. When Leo felt the cold water rising, he began to sob and desperately strained against the chains that held him fast.

Hausser shook his head. "Hush, Leo, I'm afraid it could not be otherwise. The Chamber is our secret, you see; the best-kept secret in the empire," the colonel said, watching the water slowly rise up over Leo's head. The prisoner was thudding his shoulder against the lid, but his strength was no match for the massive metal door. Soon, the last of his strength was spent, and all was quiet inside the Chamber; it was full now, the water starting to leak through cracks in the lining on the sides, so Müller turned off the tap at the wall.

Hausser cocked his head, watching in fascination as the last few bubbles rose up from the corner of Leo's mouth; a freshly tapped Berliner Pilsner came to mind, and all at once he was terribly thirsty. He'd love to have a beer. It had been a good night's work. One more traitor had been eliminated. And new ones would soon take Leo's place in the Chamber.

4

The clock showed nine minutes past twelve. Mogens was sitting in his office chair, impatiently drumming his fingers on the desk. His door was always open, and he was keeping an eye on the clock with roman numerals in the front office. When the large hand slid over onto the II, he pushed to his feet, as if the "play" button had been pressed in his brain, and he picked up the transparent plastic folder at the ready on his desk, selected a midsize paper clip from the stationery mug, and popped it into the breast pocket of his suit. There was no going back now; his coup against Lauritzen Enterprises had already been put in motion. He'd been dreaming about this day, which he had planned down to the smallest detail, for all those years that he had worked like a dog for his boss, Axel Pondus Lauritzen. He had suffered countless insults and humiliation. The time for revenge had come. Mogens was no longer the "fatso," the "nitwit," or the "moron who cannot add two sums together." If nothing else, right now he was a man who was determined to execute his plan.

Mogens walked out the door and continued through the spacious open-plan office, which was deserted at this time, as expected. There were six cubicles in total, and he knew that every Wednesday, three of the girls who worked here always had lunch together at Café Oven Vandet, and they would not be back for at least twenty-five minutes. The fourth accounts' office girl had called in sick, and the last two, Karen, and Ellen Thyregod, who was his own secretary, always ate lunch in the staff canteen upstairs on the second floor. Ellen, who was punctual to a fault, would be back in her seat when the clock struck half past twelve, so there was no time to waste.

He rushed to the stairwell and went down to the workshop on the ground floor. Stefaniak, the carpenters' supervisor, had his back turned, bent over a workbench. A loud noise filtered through from the courtyard as a large crate was manoeuvred into the freight elevator. Both doors to the elevator were left open. The driver, in his yellow jacket, closed the elevator and reversed away from the doors.

Mogens knew that Lauritzen Enterprises received a crate of office supplies every six weeks. And it was the office messenger Rune's job to collect the crate from the freight elevator and bring it to the storeroom on the second floor. But Rune always ate his lunch first. All Mogens had to do now was rely on Stefaniak's weak bladder, which habitually sent him to the bathroom at least three or four times an hour. And judging by the way the supervisor was shifting his weight from one foot to the other, Mogens would not have to wait long for the inevitable to occur. Sure enough, no more than five minutes later, Stefaniak straightened up from his workbench, and Mogens passed through the workshop and slipped into the freight elevator unnoticed. He pushed the button for the second floor and the doors closed quietly.

When the doors slid open, he stepped out onto the landing of the second floor. He was greeted by the faint smell of fried food, and further down the corridor he could hear his colleagues chatting in the canteen. He craned his head round the corner and caught sight of Pauline, who was talking into her headset at Reception. He noted that Lizette, the other receptionist, was not at her desk. But Lizette's absence was accounted for in his plan; Mogens knew that at this particular time, she would be busy elsewhere in the building.

He continued past the large window into the studio, where the engineer's assistant Lasse—completely absorbed by a game of *Counterstrike* on his computer as usual—took no notice of Mogens as he headed towards the office right at the end of the corridor. He stopped in front of the mahogany door with a brass plate that proclaimed it was from here that director Axel Pondus Lauritzen manned his business.

Mogens laid an ear to the door and listened. Hearing nothing, he tried the handle; it was locked. But he knew that it would be. He cast a glance over his shoulder. Then, in a practiced motion, he bent down and deftly slid the transparent folder he had brought with him halfway in under the door. Satisfied, he retrieved the paper clip from his pocket, straightened it out, and carefully inserted it into the keyhole. He wiggled the clip a couple of times until he heard a little thump on the other side of the door. Mogens bent down, carefully withdrew the folder under the door, and picked up the key resting on top. Then he quietly let himself in.

Pondus Lauritzen's director's office smelt vaguely of cigarette smoke. Naturally, Mogens had been up here many, many times before; as a rule, upon summons to the director's office for an earful. But he had never been here on his own. The austere mahogany desk and chesterfield chairs. A row of portraits on the wall; four generations of Lauritzen, each with an expression grimmer and more determined than the last.

Mogens moved silently across the thick carpet to the safe, which was placed right next to the desk. His heart was hammering in his chest, and he held his breath. The door to the adjacent meeting room was ajar, and he caught a glimpse of Lauritzen inside. His back turned to Mogens, the director was standing at the end of the conference table, his pants round his ankles and his blue dress shirt only partially covering his enormous white backside. A pair of shapely legs stuck out on either side of him; the toenails resting on the edge of the desk were painted pink, but apart from that, there was no way of identifying the person on the table. But Mogens knew all about Lizette and Lauritzen's affair, which was conducted during lunch hour on Wednesdays. They'd had a sexual relationship for six months now and, according to Mogens's calculations, it lasted for approximately eight or nine minutes every time. For his own sake, Mogens hoped that Lauritzen would stay the distance today as well, despite the director's sixty-six years of age, and he lost no time in punching in the safe's code. Left 19, right 47, left 12, right 05; a combination no harder to remember than Lauritzen's own birthday.

A click sounded from the safe and it popped open. Mogens cast another hasty glance over his shoulder at the conference room, where he could see that Lauritzen had picked up speed; time was of the essence now. The A4 binders holding the annual accounts—both the version created for the Danish tax authorities and the actual books accounting for black market projects—were stacked neatly on the top shelf. Next to the binders lay a modest pile of property deeds and three small jewellery boxes. The shelf below was overflowing with cash; stacks of 1000- and 500- kroner notes. The sight of the cash was overwhelming, and Mogens's breath caught in his throat—it was a lot more money than he had estimated, perhaps as much as a million kroner!

Mogens unbuttoned his jacket and began stuffing the bills into the lining, which he had undone at the top seam so he could transport the cash inside his suit.

"Yes!"

Mogens started and jerked his head over his shoulder, dropping a stack of 1000-kroner notes on his boots in the process.

"Yes! Yes! Yes!" Lauritzen yelled again, obviously close to the finish line.

Mogens could not fit any more bills into the lining of his jacket. In a sudden brainwave, he bent down, tucked his pantlegs into his socks, and started shoving money under his belt. When he had taken the last pile off the shelf, he glanced down at himself; he looked like a stuffed scarecrow. For a split second, he regretted his greed, but the money tickled all the way down his thighs.

"Yeeeesss!!" Lauritzen emitted one final and exhausted victory cry. His eyes bloodshot, the sweat dripping from his nose and face onto Lizette's bare breasts, he swayed on his feet for a moment. "Bloody hell, Lizette, you're killing me," he said. Then he bent down, pulled up his pants, and fastened his braces. Before Lizette could reply, he turned on his heel and went back to his desk. As if he could sense something was awry, Lauritzen looked around his office, but the room was empty.

Back in the freight elevator, Mogens leaned heavily against the crate of office supplies. He could feel the sweat pouring down his sides. The last thing he'd done before leaving Lauritzen's office had been to put the key back in the door. He hoped that Lauritzen would ascribe the unlocked door to his own forgetfulness, but he had no guarantee of that; his boss might smell a rat and check his safe immediately. When the doors slid open on the ground floor, Mogens slipped out and headed into the work-shop. Hard at work, Stefaniak had his back turned and seemed oblivious to anything going on round him.

All he wanted to do was run, but Mogens just hurriedly made his way past Stefaniak and headed for his office to fetch his leather satchel, which contained his tickets and passport. The money stuffed down his pants hindered his movements—he felt as if he were walking like Charlie Chaplin!—and he was terrified that everyone could see that his clothing was lined with cash. Luckily, no one had returned from their lunch break yet. In his office, he snatched his faithful leather satchel from his desk, and seconds later he was back in the corridor, heading for the stairs and his freedom beyond.

"Mogens!" a voice called out from the landing above. "Not so fast, mister."

Mogens froze. Took a breath and slowly turned his head.

Camaro Carsten was coming down the stairs towards him. "Where do you think you're going?"

Mogens was acutely aware of the beads of perspiration on his brow. "I . . . you . . . you know where I'm going, CC . . . it's Wednesday . . . I'm going down to the kiosk to drop off my betting slips," he said, tap-ping his satchel with one hand. To his horror, Mogens noticed the tip of a 1000-kroner note peeking out of his sleeve. *The lining must have split somewhere!* he thought. He was terrified that his pants would start leaking bills right in front of CC.

Mogens swallowed hard.

"Yup, I know that," Carsten said with a smile. "But not without tak-ing mine along with you."

"Of course. I'm sorry, I forgot."

"I hope you haven't laid down your entire fortune," Carsten said, reaching into his pocket for his betting slips.

"No, no, not me," Mogens replied.

"So, you still reckon Everton is a sure winner? Two to one?"

Mogens accepted Carsten's slips and opened his satchel. When he dropped them inside, two 1000-kroner notes slipped out of his sleeve—thankfully, hidden from Carsten's field of vision. "You can just give me the money later," Mogens said as casually as he could muster. He buckled down the flap of his satchel and turned on his heel, but Carsten put a hand on his arm.

"Do you think it's a bad bet?"

"I think it's just fine, CC," said Mogens, carefully extracting his arm. "No pain, no gain, as they say . . ."

Mogens walked along the canal. On the water, a harbour tour came past with a guide giving a description of the area in three languages. The wind bit into his skin, cooling him down, which was a relief. Up until now, his plan had worked just fine. He just had one more thing to do before he could get the hell out of Copenhagen.

5

Berlin
12 and 13 September 2013

At 10:30 p.m., the City Express from Copenhagen pulled into Track 2 of Berlin Hauptbahnhof. The train was thirty minutes late, and the moment the doors opened, passengers spilled onto the platform and impatiently elbowed their way to the escalators. Mogens was one of the last passengers to exit from the final carriage. He was wearing a pink polo shirt, dark sunglasses, and a blond wig. For good measure, he had covered his face and arms in fake tan, which lent an orange-peel effect to his complexion.

Mogens walked slowly along the platform and took the escalators from the pit of the Arrivals Hall in a zigzag ascent, keeping his eyes peeled on the galleries on either side. Two police officers stood chatting with each other at the top of the escalators on the first level as they watched the travellers arrive. Mogens had no idea if the police were already looking for him, and in all truth, he was not entirely pleased with his disguise. In the planning phase of his escape, he had been inspired by the bright and colourful attire of international tourists who milled about Christianshavn in the summertime. But here in Berlin Hauptbahnhof, he stood out like a sore thumb in a sea of grey and anonymous travellers; it had seemed like a good idea at the time, but now he sorely regretted his decision to disguise himself as a tourist.

But the police officers did not give him a second glance, and Mogens resisted the temptation to look back, no matter how much he wanted to.

He continued all the way to the top level of the arcade, where he knew there was a kiosk that sold mobile phone paraphernalia. He bought five SIM cards for his iPhone. Then he made his way to the taxi stand outside.

"*Sohn . . . tagstrasse 15,*" he said to the taxi driver, and showed him the address on the screen of his phone, just to be sure he understood.

The taxi driver harrumphed and turned on his meter. Two minutes later, they were driving through the city night. Despite the lateness of the hour, the traffic was intense, and Mogens already felt carsick, but also a budding excitement. He had always wanted to visit Berlin. The city's history fascinated him; the particular role it had played during the Cold War—and the Wall, which had divided not only Berlin but Europe itself in the aftermath of the Second World War.

He took out his iPhone and checked his Yahoo mail. No messages. He scrolled through his contacts till he found "Schumann48."

"I made it. I am here. When shall we meet?" he wrote in both English and German. He felt as if he was a tourist guide trying to make himself understood.

A quarter of an hour later, the taxi dropped him off in front of Sonntag Strasse 15 in Friedrichshain. The bars and restaurants on either side of the road were humming with tourists. Mogens was surprised; he would have thought the area would be a quiet one. All at once he heard people speaking Danish, and he turned abruptly to face a flock of middle-aged tourists passing by. Mogens ducked his head and hurried over to the main door of the building. He pressed the button below the name Schmidt. Moments later, he was buzzed in. Mogens slipped inside and mounted the stairs to the second floor, his large suitcase banging at his heels.

"Looks like you've got a lot to carry, hey," said the man standing in the doorway to his left.

Mogens looked up and nodded in greeting; he was too out of breath to do anything else.

The man had addressed Mogens in German. He was wearing a pair of shorts and a tank top that revealed more hair than he had on his head. "Well, I'm afraid you've got to go up to the third," said the hairy-bellied man—Schmidt, apparently. He pointed upwards with the index finger of one hand and took a key out of his pocket with the other.

"P-payment?" Mogens said. He had only understood half of the words Schmidt had said.

"You can just slip it through the door tomorrow," the man replied, pointing at the letter chamber. "You Norwegians always pay your bills," Schmidt added, handing over the key. Mogens took the key, opened his mouth to reply, but closed it again; there was no reason to correct the man's assumptions.

Mogens put down his suitcase in the dark entrance and continued into the lounge area and put on the light. Furnished with the absolute minimum with neither decorations nor knick-knacks on the window-sills, the two-room flat reminded him of his own on Langebrogade in Christianshavn.

He found the place on one of those countless internet platforms, where private owners can offer their flats for hire; most of them rent out their homes on the black market, and they're not interested in seeing your passport or identification documents—as long as you pay in cash. Mogens chose this particular flat because it was available for an extended period of time. On the website, Mogens had informed the owner that he came from Oslo and would be visiting friends in Berlin, but he didn't know for how long. The landlord, who apparently used Schmidt down-stairs as a straw man, didn't have any objections provided Mogens paid fourteen days in advance. He had no idea how long he would need to stay, but he thought this would be the perfect place to hide.

The next morning, Mogens stood on the narrow balcony of his hideout. He had barely slept a wink all night. The crowns of the trees obscured his view, but the sounds of people enjoying their morning cof-fees at the cafés below filtered up towards him, and he could watch the traffic on the road. He took his iPhone out of his pocket and checked his messages for the umpteenth time. Still nothing. The sun was shining from a cloudless sky, and it was already quite warm. Unseasonably warm, in fact. He opened his browser and scrolled through the various Danish daily newspapers online; neither *Politiken, Berlingske,* nor *Ekstra Bladet* mentioned his case with a word; perhaps it wasn't newsworthy enough, or maybe the police were keeping a lid on it, whilst the investigation was underway. He was struck by the thought that, at this very moment, the police might be searching his flat. Interviewing his neighbours and colleagues. Contacting his family. The latter would not take long as he only had his younger sister left, and they hadn't seen each other in more than a year. He wondered what Louise would think when the police knocked on her door out of the blue, asking for him. He winced in shame at the thought.

His phone vibrated, interrupting his thoughts. A message from "Schumann48" was displayed on his screen: "Glad that you're finally here," it said in English. Mogens's remorse dissolved in an instant. *None of it mattered now*, he thought. *His new life was about to begin.*

He opened the email and read its contents.

6

Train line S7 to Potsdam chugged lazily through the Charlottenburg district which basked in the late afternoon sun. Mogens sat in the first carriage, watching out for the name of the next station. Even though the instructions he had received in the email were straightforward, he was still afraid he might miss his stop. When the train pulled into Charlottenburg Station, he noted from the display above that there were still stops to go before Berlin Grunewald, which was where he had to get off. He was relieved that their meeting point was outside town, as far away from Friedrichshain as possible, even if the name Teufel Berg unnerved him; he was almost certain it meant Devil's Mountain.

Mogens had decided to make do with sunglasses and leave the blond wig behind. The Danish newspapers still had not published anything on his coup. Not even the *Christianshavneren*, the weekly bulletin of his district, had gone to the trouble of mentioning it. And if they hadn't done so by now, chances were high that his crime would ever be made public at all. Which would be a huge plus for the new life he was about to embark upon. Even though he had stolen a huge amount, he knew very well that the money would not last forever; it was a decent lump sum, and he had plans—so many giddy plans for his future. As long as he avoided the authorities—the Danish as well as the German ones—he would be safe.

Twelve minutes later, Mogens stepped onto the rail platform of Berlin-Grunewald, passed through the picturesque clock tower station, and trudged up the path to Teufel Berg. Not long after, he came to a little café that, amongst other things, served as a bicycle hire shop and the entrance to the forest area. Right in front of it, a wooden stand propped up a hard-backed poster: devil's festival, painted in black letters below a colourful depiction of a devil's fork in flames, and a list of bands and artists that would be performing during the three-day music festival, which was currently being held at the abandoned radar station on Teufel Berg.

Hardly thrilled about the idea of blaring music and hundreds of people, Mogens set off at a sedate pace, faithfully following the cardboard arrows that were posted in trees at regular intervals. After he had been walking for fifteen minutes, the arrows led him down towards the Devil's Lake, which lay at the foot of the hill. Several people were bathing in the water. Their pale faces and shoulders shone like water lilies floating on the surface. A beautiful green meadow stretched along the bank. At the far end, on the boundary to the forest, he could see a family of wild pigs; a sow and her three piglets were digging in the soft soil in peace. Mogens was surprised to see so many people sunbathing naked on the grass in the late afternoon. He could not help staring at the women with their large breasts and black hair between their legs. A lesbian couple were entwined on the grass right in front of him. Apart from the odd, not particularly memorable, visits to prostitutes, his sex life was nonexistent. But he had always had wild fantasies.

He continued past the nudists and followed the path up the steep climb to the radar station on Teufel Berg. Soon after, he could hear live music, and as he approached the top of the hill, the number of festival-goers increased on the serpentine path. Most of them were much younger than he was, many of them with piercings and tattoos covering their bodies.

When he reached the gate marking the entrance to the old military station, he was irked to have to pay a broad-chested guard a 30-euro entrance fee for the festival; the guard took his money in exchange for a red devil's-fork stamp on the inside of his wrist. Had he known that there was a festival up here and that he would have to pay so much money to get in, he would never have agreed to come. But there was nothing he could do about it now, so he simply carried on past the old army bunker and further up the path to the enormous building with its three white radomes above. The festival scene and large stall market selling a hotchpotch of snacks, T-shirts, and bongs was laid out in front of the building. A foul smell of grilled foods, pot, and urine hung over the entire area.

Mogens stopped at the foot of the main stairs, where they had agreed to meet. He was intimidated by the loud rock music and the crowds; obviously stoned, people were either swaying on stage with their arms raised over their heads, or bopping and jiving like madmen, making Christiania back home seem tame by comparison. Mogens felt conspicuous, entirely out of place. He heard, or at least thought he heard, folks near him whisper the words *Stasi* or *Nazi* and give him dirty looks; perhaps they thought he was a plainclothes policeman. He glanced at his phone, but there was no reception up here; he checked his email to ensure that he hadn't misunderstood the instructions; and he looked round and noticed that the festival grounds were filling up fast. *He had to calm down.*

Looking up, Morgens noticed that the light was fading with the setting sun. He hated the thought of being up here after sunset, just as much as he dreaded the trip back through the forest in the dark. Up on stage, the musicians were taking a break, and the crowd clapped and wolf-whistled enthusiastically. Mogens withdrew slowly. He needed to pee, and searched the periphery for the toilets, but it seemed as if the organisers had overlooked this detail.

He walked round the back of the building, away from the festival grounds. There was no shelter from the wind here—it was a constant omen ringing in his ears—and, towering over his head, the battered screens of the old spy radomes howled like the shredded sails of a ghost ship. *Teufel Berg lived up to its name in every way*, Mogens thought.

He stepped up to the nearest bush, and as he was taking a piss, a strobe light shone into his eyes. He squinted at the mouth of the nearest ventilation shaft that led down into the underground bunker. The light appeared to be coming from there. He finished up as quickly as he could, and when he zipped up his trousers, he thought he heard someone calling his name; a voice like a stretched-out melody blending in with the rush of the wind. He walked over to the shaft, and the voice sounded again.

"Hello?" Mogens said, feeling like an idiot.

"Mooog-enssss," whispered the wind voice.

Mogens hesitated briefly. Then he walked into the shaft entrance and, moments later, he was swallowed in the dark.

Above the mountain, the last rays of the sun coloured the sky red, and the old spy station loomed black and ominous. In the fading light, the three radomes rose in the air, as a devil's fork jabbed into the heavens above.

7

The water level was one-and-a-half metres higher than normal, and all traffic on the canal had been suspended. It was as if the bridges of Christianshavn Canal had been brought to their knees, and it was only the kayaks that could slip in under the low arches above the water. The winter storms, followed by heavy rain, had filled the city's reservoirs to capacity, feeding the swell into the canals around the old town of Copenhagen.

Ravn and Eduardo were sitting on *Bianca*'s rain-washed deck, eating ham and fried eggs. Ravn swung his feet onto the railing, leaned back in his chair, and took a sip of his coffee. It was a raw but beautiful morning, and his breath mingled with the steam rising off his breakfast.

"That's global warming for you," said Eduardo, nodding at the water's surface. "And it's only going to get worse."

"At least we don't have to put up with the harbour tours, as long as the boats can't pass under the bridges."

"It's a high price to pay for a little peace and quiet, *amigo*."

Ravn shrugged, took a piece of ham from his plate, held it between his forefinger and thumb over Møffe's head for a moment, and let go. Møffe snapped it up in mid-air.

"Ravn, seriously?! Are you feeding your dog Iberian ham? Do you have any idea how much I paid for that?"

"Nope, I don't. But it must have been expensive because he likes it."

Møffe slobbered in satisfaction.

Ravn patted his dog fondly on the head. Then he sighed, swung his legs off the railing, and pushed to his feet.

Eduardo looked up in surprise. "Where are you off to?"

"I have a meeting in ten minutes," said Ravn, zipping up his jacket and flipping his hoodie up.

"Have you found a job?" Eduardo asked with a note of irony in his voice.

"I have to go up to my flat. The estate agent has found a buyer."

Eduardo quirked a bushy eyebrow. "Another one?"

Ravn nodded. "Yup. The eighth contender in three months. Folks are standing in line to buy it."

"So why isn't it sold yet?"

Ravn made no comment.

Eduardo looked at him. "Ravn, it's time to move on. Why don't you just let the agent do his job?"

"I *am* letting him do his job. I'm just helping him. He doesn't mind . . ." He picked up his mug from the table and tossed the dregs of his coffee over the railing.

"Shall I come up with you?"

"Why the hell would you do that?"

"Take it easy, I was just thinking . . .

"Well, don't . . ." Ravn turned his head and looked out over the quay. He still had not gotten used to the fact that the tide meant he was level with it. "Is that someone you know?"

Eduardo twisted in his seat and stared at the grey Fiat 500 with a burgundy-coloured rooftop that was parked on the other side of the road. "Nah, but I wouldn't mind if I did."

An attractive woman, perhaps in her late thirties, was sitting behind the wheel. The moment she realised they had seen her, she started the car.

"Has she been sitting there long?" asked Eduardo.

"No idea," Ravn said with a shrug. "But I saw her sitting there a few days ago as well."

The woman revved the Fiat's engine, and Eduardo and Ravn watched her pull away from the kerb and disappear down the road.

"So, your copper instincts are still intact, heh."

"Some things never fade. Come on, Møffe," Ravn said, patting his thigh. Møffe huffed like a steam locomotive, then slowly got to his feet and came towards him.

"Are you sure you don't want me to come along?"

"Who's gonna take care of the dishes, then?"

Eduardo waved his arms in protest and uttered a string of expletives, but Ravn was already on the quay with Møffe cradled in his arms. He wasn't worried; he was pretty sure it wouldn't take Eduardo long to calm down and split for his own boat—leaving the breakfast dishes exactly where they were.

8

Ravn strolled down Dronningensgade, his hands buried deep in his pockets. He took out his keys as he approached the building. The nametag by the intercom caught his eye; their names were no longer visible. All the new owner needed was a relatively sharp fingernail to remove the last traces of the two of them.

He put Møffe on his leash, perfectly aware that he would practically have to drag the dog all the way up to the top floor. True to form, when he reached the second-floor landing, Kitty's front door opened slightly. Coiffed blue hair and thick glasses made her look like an insect. Ravn greeted her politely.

Kitty pursed her lips. "It's like a bus station in here today," she said.

"It's probably my estate agent showing some potential buyers around," Ravn replied.

"Again? With all that stamping about, my chandelier's trembling in its sockets."

"I never knew you had a chandelier, Kitty."

The old woman blinked rapidly a few times. Then she withdrew her head into her flat.

Ravn carried on up to the third floor, hauling Møffe along with him.

The front door was ajar, and Ravn took a deep breath before he nudged it open and went inside, bypassing the huge pile of post on his doormat. He'd long since changed his address, and the few official letters and bills addressed to him were now delivered to the deck of *Bianca*, but there was nothing he could do to prevent the tsunami of advertising flooding his entrance.

He could hear voices in the kitchen. His estate agent, named Kjeld-something-or-other, stuck his head round the door. His salesman smile shrivelled the moment he caught sight of Ravn.

"Tho . . . mas Ravnsholt," he said in half-hearted greeting.

Ravn nodded and stepped over the pile of printed materials in the entrance. Kjeld adjusted his silver-sheen necktie; the tip was resting on his belly as if it were the head of a dead snake. The estate agent lowered his voice: "I thought we agreed that I would show your flat on my own, Thomas."

"Yes, of course. I just popped in to see how it was going."

"It was going just fine, till now," Kjeld said, glancing at Møffe with distaste. "But it doesn't help when you bring that dog of yours along."

"Whaddya mean? Everyone likes Møffe."

"Of course," Kjeld said, gesticulating to Ravn that he ought to keep his voice down. "Your dog is . . . sweet . . . of course. But pets have a negative effect on the price when you're trying to sell a flat to nice folks . . ."

"Is that a fact?" Ravn said, brushing past Kjeld into the kitchen.

The estate agent rested a hand on his arm. "Thomas. Don't take this the wrong way, but perhaps you need to consider whether you're ready to sell. I understand how difficult it can be to let go of a flat that you're very attached to, but—"

"Actually, I'm not particularly attached to it—"

"And yet we've been here before; we've got a buyer who is willing to pay the asking price, and you refuse to sell."

"It has to be the right—"

"The right buyer, yes, that much I've understood. The question is whether that buyer exists . . . for you?"

Ravn regarded the estate agent thoughtfully. "I hear what you're saying, Kjeld, and I'm more than willing to sell—"

A young man in a dark-blue suit stepped into the kitchen, interrupting their conversation. "Well, it needs quite a bit of work," he said. "I think it's more of a fixer-upper, and—with all due respect—I think the asking price is a little inflated."

Ravn stared at the guy, who was a lawyer, an accountant, or a bank manager, he reckoned, maybe even an estate agent, albeit much more successful than Kjeld from the looks of the obvious difference in the price tags of their respective suits; either way, he was one of those pricks with far too much money and not enough manners.

"No one is twisting your arm," Ravn said. Their eyes met, and a frosty atmosphere settled in the kitchen.

"No-no, of course not, no need for that, gentlemen, we live in a free country," Kjeld intervened with a nervous cackle, his salesman-smile plastered on his face. "Why don't we check out the rest of the flat. Have you seen the main bedroom? Wonderful light in here, and there's another room right over here that would be perfect for children . . ." he added, pointing down the corridor and waving the man ahead of him.

Ravn stared after them. He had nothing against folks being different, but there were far too many yuppies moving into the neighbourhood; a shame, really, and he already knew that the minute Kjeld was done with his show-around, he'd send him back to his Rolodex of buyers.

Nudging open the door into the lounge, he was surprised to see a young woman standing by the window. She was looking at the view with her back turned to him, and the little boy at her side was tugging impatiently on her hand. When the boy caught sight of Møffe, he hid behind his mother's skirts.

The woman turned round and smiled at Ravn; her huge belly revealed that she was expecting her next child.

Ravn returned her smile. "Are you sure you don't want to sit down," he said, pointing at the sofa.

"No, thank you, I'm fine," she said. "I thought we were the only ones looking at the flat today. Are you also interested in it?"

"On the contrary. I'm trying to get rid of it," said Ravn. "I've been living here for a lifetime. A short one, that is," he added with a smile.

She nodded, as if she understood, and let her eyes travel through the lounge. "It could be a beautiful living room, if . . ." she trailed off.

". . . if you fixed it up a bit," he said, completing her sentence. "I know it needs some work. But the location is nice," he said, smiling again with a sweep of his arm that included the view. "I mean . . . I didn't mean that to sound like a sales pitch . . . It's just that . . . we've always loved the view of the embankment . . ."

The boy had gathered his courage and reached out his hand to Møffe.

"Magnus, don't touch strange dogs," the woman said.

"He doesn't bite," said Ravn. "The worst thing that can happen is that he drools on you," he added, smiling at the little boy. "His name is Møffe."

"Møf-ffe," the boy said.

The woman let go of his hand and he patted the dog's head. Møffe sat dead still, enjoying the unexpected attention.

"So why do you and your wife want to get rid of the place?"

Her direct manner surprised Ravn. "Because there is no 'we' anymore," he said simply with a shrug of his shoulders.

"I'm sorry," said the woman, colour rushing to her cheeks. "I shouldn't have asked."

"There's no need to apologise. We were happy here. It's a wonderful neighbourhood. An oasis in the middle of the city." As if on cue, the clock tower of the Church of Our Saviour chimed from the embankment.

The woman turned to look out the window again, letting her gaze wander over the embankment, the naked trees, and the water in the canals; a moat around the Old Town in bygone times. "I think one could sit here and follow the change of seasons, maybe go for a walk on the embankment . . ."

"Yes, of course you can," Ravn said, utterly disarmed by her honesty. All at once, she reminded him of Eva, beautiful and vulnerable in the soft light shining behind her. He felt a strong urge to go to her, wrap her in his arms, cling to her, bury his nose in her hair.

Kjeld entered the room with the yuppie on his heels. It didn't appear as if the rest of the showing had changed his mood. "Sweetheart, shall we get going?" he said.

The woman turned to her husband and smiled. "I like this flat, Henrik. It's perfect."

"But, sweetheart, don't you think we should—"

"We would love to live here," she said quietly but firmly.

"All right, absolutely perfect," her husband said, biting his lip. "But it's just that—"

"This is great news, isn't it, Thomas?" Kjeld said, looking at his client with a tight smile stuck to his lips.

Ravn looked at the young man. He still didn't like him. Nor was he thrilled about the idea of this bloke moving into *their* flat. "Possibly," he said, turning to face his wife and son.

"I'm sure that you will be happy here. Congratulations on your new home."

Ten minutes later, Ravn was alone in the flat with Møffe. It hadn't sunk in yet that he had sold the place. He had no doubt that Kjeld would close the deal as fast as he could. Not only to secure his commission, but also to avoid any further contact.

Ravn let his eyes wander over the large, sunny living room. The sparse furniture was covered in a thick layer of dust. It was so cold his breath condensed in a cloud, as if he were in a tomb; Eva's tomb. But he was sure that the young couple would create a happy home for themselves here—this much he could read in the woman's smiling eyes.

Ravn stared vacantly at the oak floorboards in front of the sofa. There used to be a glass coffee table standing there, till it shattered under the weight of Eva's body; it was here that he had found her dead. The back of her head had been smashed by an intruder. It happened more than two years ago. But the memory of the dark pool of her blood, right in front of the sofa, was still there, no matter how much he had scrubbed and scrubbed, sanded and polished the oak wood floorboards.

"Let's go, Møffe," he said, tugging on the dog's leash and heading for the door.

9

Colonel Hausser rolled the driver's seat window down an inch and stuck his ID card through the gap. The guard snatched up the card and skimmed it over, keeping half an eye on Hausser, who kept staring straight ahead. Moments later, the guard returned the ID card. The heavy boom was lifted, and the guard waved the car through. Hausser continued along the road between row upon row of dark, monumental buildings that constituted the headquarters of the GDR's Ministry for State Security, or Stasi. Twenty-two of these buildings housed the lion's share of the Stasi's agents, who worked in twenty different divisions, each with their own special function within the country's security operation. Hausser parked in front of Haus 7, where his own division—Division Z, or DZ to those who worked there—was located. He got out of the car and headed for the main entrance, where another guard checked his identity documents.

Hausser rarely came to HQ—in fact, if he remembered right, five months had passed since his last visit—and every time he stepped through the doors and took the stairs to DZ, the sharp smell of the mustard-coloured linoleum floors stung his nostrils. DZ was a subdivision of Division VIII, which oversaw surveillance, intelligence, and interrogations—but it was classified, and everyone else in the Service thought it was a subdivision of Division II, which was in charge of material operations. Only the inner circle knew of DZ's existence, and they took care of internal political affairs; cases wherein the Stasi's own people or members of the SED

Party were involved in activities hostile to the State. Hausser had been working for DZ for nine years, and during his tenure, he had handled over a hundred cases; most of the people Hausser had interrogated were terminated.

"You look like shit, Hausser," Walter Strauss said in greeting. Hausser's boss ended practically every sentence with a wheezy cough. His eyes were bloodshot, and his chubby cheeks were round as a ball, giving him the appearance of an overgrown baby in a general's uniform. The sleeves of his uniform were too short and rode up his arms as Strauss stuck his fat fingers in the little bowl of brandy liqueur chocolates that always stood within reach.

"Take a seat," Strauss said, pointing to the chair that had been pulled over to the desk.

Hausser understood immediately; this was not a friendly chat. If it were, he would have been asked to take a seat on the sofa and offered a glass of vodka. He unbuttoned his coat, placed his briefcase on the floor next to the chair, and sat down.

"Where have you been hiding? It's been difficult to reach you on the phone."

"I had an urgent matter to attend to."

"Yes, that much I know. Ratalzick is not happy about the rising death rate of his inmates at Hohenschönhausen."

Hausser shrugged. "If Ratalzick's interrogation measures had been more effective, we could have avoided that; the only results achieved by three months of *their* methods was that his boys dug a tunnel all the way to Charlottenburg," he observed sarcastically.

"People are getting anxious. Ratalzick doesn't want to attract attention to his institution."

"Attention?" Hausser drawled. "You know as well as I do that Ratalzick runs a prison whose existence is unbeknownst to the public, Strauss. I don't think he has any cause for concern on that front."

"In the current climate we cannot afford to make mistakes. It is essential that we keep our noses clean," Strauss said, loosening his green uniform necktie. Despite the oppressive heat in his office, he'd made no attempt to open the window behind him.

Hausser leaned forward and extracted Leo Danzig's death certificate from his briefcase. "It says here that Leo died of a lung infection," he said, laying out the document before Strauss. "Signed by the prison doctor in Pommern. His loved ones have received a copy. And they have been notified that the funeral has already taken place."

"*Another* lung infection?" Strauss said, drumming his fat fingers on his desk. "You seem to have started an epidemic of some kind. What about his co-conspirators? Have you arrested them?"

"The case has proved to be a little more complicated than that; our surveillance indicates that several high-standing ministers, including two local SED Party members, were amongst the deserters."

Strauss gaped at Hausser. Then his hand clawed for chocolates in the empty bowl at his elbow.

"B-bloody hell . . ." he stammered.

"Yes, the consequences are not going to be pretty . . ."

"Bloo-dy hell," Strauss repeated simply. "I don't know what is worse; yet another tunnel in the heart of Berlin, or the fact that Party members are fleeing the Republic? We're going to be crucified when this gets out. This is petrol on the Opposition's bonfire, do you hear me, Hausser? Do you understand that this is the first time since 1953 that we have a fucking opposition in this country?" he said, looking at Hausser in horror.

Strauss opened a drawer to his right, pulled out a fresh bag of chocolates, and tore it open. "In light of what is happening all around us—in Poland, Hungary, and the USSR, *glasnost* and *perestroika*—we're sitting on a timebomb," he said, popping two chocolates into his mouth and dumping the rest into the bowl. "The whole world is watching, and everyone is going to point fingers at us . . . the Stasi . . . Can't you see what this means?!"

"I understand completely," Hausser said, taking a deep breath. "But no one will ever know."

"What do you mean? This kind of scandal *always* gets out," Strauss said.

"No, it doesn't."

"You haven't . . . please don't tell me that your men have . . . terminated members of our own Party!" Strauss said, swallowing the chocolate.

Hausser was starting to get annoyed with Strauss for his lack of composure. "Of course not—I'm not about to commit political suicide."

"So what have you done?"

"On 18 July, the first group assembled at the auto repair shop on Ruppinerstrasse. As soon as a border patrol from Division XX took up their positions outside, fourteen deserters, including Leo Danzig's co-conspirators, entered the tunnel."

"So you let them flee?"

"Not exactly. I instructed the men to wait until I figured they would be about halfway through the hundred-forty-meter-long tunnel. Then we sent three of border patrol's trucks out to drive along the outer security fence."

"But . . . what happened to the deserters?"

"They were buried underground; their tunnel collapsed under the weight of the two-tonne-trucks patrolling overhead."

For the first time since the meeting began, Strauss smiled. "I see. Excellent. Good work, Hausser."

"Thank you."

"Any reports on the incident?" Strauss asked, nodding at Hausser's briefcase.

"Why would there be a report on an incident that never occurred?"

"Indeed. So, what now?"

"Now I will turn my attention to the next case," Hausser said matter-of-factly. "There're a few interesting leads I'd like to pursue."

Strauss sank back into his chair. "This isn't the time to open a new case. Don't you think we should wait—"

"For what?" Hausser said, cutting his boss off in mid-sentence. "The traitors are not going to wait for us to make a move."

"The tide is turning, Hausser. Not just beyond our borders, but within the Party—within the inner circle."

"What are you suggesting?"

"Have you considered an . . . advisory position? In intelligence."

Hausser rearranged his long legs and smoothed down the crease of his pant leg. "For one of the other Divisions?"

"No. I was thinking of one of our comrades overseas, perhaps."

Hausser stared at his boss in surprise. "I wasn't aware that we were still sending folk abroad."

"But of course we are. Central America, a few of the new African states—and Cuba, naturally; there are many people in high places who appreciate our expertise . . ."

"Thank you, but I'm not interested," said Hausser firmly. "My work at DZ is more important."

Strauss leaned back and folded his hands over his belly. "I've been to Cuba myself. Many years ago, before DZ was established. I can warmly recommend the country. Excellent rum. Cigars as thick as your forearm. Fabulous climate, and the women are extraordinary, of course. Very amenable . . . have you ever been with a black woman, Hausser?"

"Why this sudden desire to send me to the other side of the earth?"

Lost in his own reverie, apparently, Strauss ignored Hausser's question. "Their women are not created like ours. Their skin is rough. The bush between their legs is pitch black and smells of tobacco. A clitoris the size of plum pip . . . Formidable, I tell you, Hausser, truly formidable . . ."

"Are they going to shut down DZ?"

Strauss rested his sad eyes on Hausser. "I don't know. But it's highly likely. And there's a good chance that heads will roll if they need to find a scapegoat . . ."

"A scapegoat? What on earth for? We're heroes," Hausser said indignantly.

"Yes, we are heroes," said Strauss, without a trace of conviction in his voice.

"It would be a mistake to shut us down."

"It's politics, Hausser."

"As I said: a mistake." Hausser would have loved to wax lyrical about what he thought about politicians, but he bit his lip. "Unless you order me to go, I will stay at my post. I'll find another case to lay before the Party. Something big."

"Excellent," Strauss said, smiling in satisfaction. "But take care of yourself, Hausser."

Hausser nodded and pushed to his feet. He gave Strauss a salute, turned smartly on his heel, and left his boss's dark office.

Hausser returned the way he had come, unperturbed; he had spent half a lifetime looking over his shoulder, and always guarded against the enemy—whether it may be enemies of the State, or those who operated within the Stasi. Reports from his hand were kept to a minimum. And he never, ever put his signature on anything that might implicate him; the less paperwork the better. To his mind, the Stasi's obsession with keeping records on everything was a weakness. It was much better to live in the shadows; this was their best defence, their best weapon.

He got back into his car and took a moment to consider his position. It was unthinkable that DZ would be disbanded from above. Absurd. He shook his head and turned the key in the ignition. If they shut DZ down, they might as well shut down the entire Stasi—and that was never going to happen. He put the car in gear and drove past Haus 1, where the upper echelons of power had their offices.

The sooner he found a new case, the better.

10

Ravn walked along the embankment in the pouring rain. Møffe was at his heels, struggling to keep up, but when they got to The Sea Otter, both of them hurried through the open door. It was before noon, but the old pub on the canal was already humming with guests looking for shelter from the rain, which was a good excuse to grab the first pilsner of the day.

As he headed for the bar, Ravn flipped down his soaking-wet hoodie and dried his face with the back of his hand. In stark contrast to the downpour, Kim Larsen's cheerful "Susan Himmelblå" was blaring from the old Wurlitzer jukebox in the corner. Johnson loomed in the doorway to the backroom behind the bar, a filigree coffee cup clutched in his meaty fist.

"Good day, Ravn," the pub owner said, taking up his post behind the counter.

"I'll have a Hof," Ravn said unnecessarily as a bottle of his favourite beer was plonked on the counter before him. He took a seat on a barstool, unzipped the pocket of his leather jacket, and pulled out a roll of bank notes. "I guess I should settle my tab. What do I owe you?"

Johnson arched his bushy eyebrows but made no further comment. Instead, he tapped out a Cecil from the pack at his elbow and lit up, illuminating his face briefly before it disappeared behind a cloud of smoke. "Have you robbed a bank?" he said.

"Nope. Sold the flat," said Ravn. "The money hasn't hit my account yet, but the bank knows it's coming, so they've been kind enough to extend my credit."

"Are congratulations in order?" Johnson asked.

Ravn took a sip from his bottle. "I'm not sure. But I could use the money."

"Have you found a new place to live?"

"What for? I've got *Bianca* . . ."

Johnson put his coffee cup down and regarded Ravn evenly. "You're not seriously considering living on that tub permanently, are you?"

"Why the hell not? I stayed there all winter; it was absolutely fine. And now I've got some money to fix her up . . ."

"If you're asking me, I don't think you've thought this through . . ."

"I'm not. Besides, when I bought *Bianca*, I used the flat as security for the bank and, now that I've sold it, I'll have to settle my loan."

Johnson tapped the ash off his cigarette thoughtfully. "So, you've traded in a nice flat with a view of the embankment for a life on that old skiff of yours?"

"I guess that's one way of looking at it."

"Each to their own," said Johnson, shaking his head.

Ravn downed the rest of his beer and thudded the bottle onto the counter. "What do I owe you?"

"That was quick."

"I promised the estate agent I'd clear out the last of my things from the flat: I need to hand over the keys today. It's only . . . well, you know, Eva's personal things, clothes and stuff . . . that I still need to . . ." he shrugged instead of finishing his sentence as he got to his feet. The disgruntled licking of chops sounded under his stool; Møffe was clearly not inclined to move an inch.

"Well? What do I owe you?" Ravn repeated.

"That round was on the house," said Johnson, removing the empty bottle. "And as for your tab: I don't think you're going to be sailing anywhere in the near future. Let's just say your credit has been extended here as well."

"Cheers, Johnson."

* * *

Armed with a roll of black rubbish bags, Ravn returned to his flat. It was actually a relief to see the rooms so bare, as if scrubbed clean of any signs of Eva's brutal murder. He had sold his furniture and effects for 4,500 Danish kroner to Flytte Finn, a second-hand dealer from Haslev. Finn didn't try to haggle, so Ravn assumed his furniture had some value and could be sold in the outback of Zealand; he deliberately chose a dealer who lived far from Christianshavn, so he didn't have to endure the sight of their belongings displayed in the neighbourhood's charity shops. The only thing he'd asked Finn not to touch was the wardrobe in the bedroom.

Ravn opened the wardrobe and stared at the shelves and hangers. Eva's jeans, coats, and dresses hung in a row. For a split second, he regretted not asking Finn to take the whole lot with him. But then he couldn't stand the idea of someone else rifling through her personal belongings. Ravn's gaze lingered on Eva's blue summer dress; she had been wearing that dress the first time her saw her, when she'd stopped to chat on the quay above *Bianca*. It felt like a lifetime ago. A different life. He folded the blue dress neatly.

Eva had been dead for more than two years, and he hadn't moved on at all.

He ripped a rubbish bag off the roll and carefully laid the blue dress in the bottom of it. Then he started with the shelves for T-shirts, blouses, and underwear. When he had filled the first bag, he immediately got started on the second. He picked up speed. He started ripping coats, jackets, jeans, and dresses off the hangers and stuffed everything into the bags; he had to get this over with as fast as he could, as if ripping off a plaster.

Ravn brought three full bags to the front door and returned to the bedroom. He knew that it would have been easier to simply dump the bags in the containers in the courtyard downstairs, but he'd decided to deliver them to DanChurchAid instead; this is what Eva would have wanted. As long as he'd known her, she'd worked tirelessly for people less fortunate than herself, she was—to his own mind—almost *too* good-hearted. He knew that it would hurt like hell if he bumped into a woman wearing one of *her* dresses, but for Eva's sake, this was a risk he was willing to take.

As he stuffed that last coat into the final bag, a mobile phone fell out of its pocket and landed at his feet. It was an old Nokia. He tried to switch it on, but the battery was dead. He couldn't recall seeing it before, and he wasn't even certain that it belonged to Eva. Her regular phone had been one of the first iPhone models, which she'd never gotten used to; she kept inadvertently touching the display and ringing him or other people by mistake. He smiled sadly at the thought in spite of himself. The home intruder who killed her stole the iPhone, as well as her watch, wallet, and laptop. None of her property was subsequently recovered, the perpetrator had never been found—despite an intense investigation by himself and the police. All they had been able to find out about him was that he presumably was a member of one of the Baltic gangs that ruled over the neighbourhood back then, and it was highly likely that he'd long since fled the country.

Ravn put the telephone in his pocket. He didn't want to think about the case anymore! He knew from bitter experience that if he didn't bash these thoughts out of his head, he would drink himself into a stupor, and he was sick and tired of resorting to alcohol.

He picked up the black bag and deposited it alongside the others. Perhaps it was her work phone. Maybe it was a telephone she owned before the iPhone. Perhaps he could find a suitable charger that could solve the mystery. If the phone belonged to the lawyers' office where she used to work, he would return it. Then he would be rid of it.

11

The Parliament in Poland established a commission to evaluate the actions of their security police; was it a case of political suicide? The Polish media had had a field day, apparently. Hausser had heard about it from his friends in Division V, where news and propaganda from the West was monitored.

The Polacks didn't waste any time in the wake of their so-called "democratisation," Hausser thought. But there wasn't anything to worry about. Not here. The Poles had always been a nation of cowards, after all, and it was inconceivable that something like that could happen here. *This was Germany! The* right *part of Germany!* But as soon as Strauss found out about the situation in Poland, he'd be rattled; he'd piss in his pants, tell Hausser to lay low—and not even think of starting any new investigations, which was exactly why it was imperative that he, Colonel Erhardt Hausser, find a new case immediately.

By the time Hausser arrived in the State underground archive, it was after midnight. Bar the humming sound of the ventilators that constantly preserved a moderate humidity for the files, the cellar was deserted and dead still. The archive cabinets were all lined in a row, like silver dominoes; more than 100 kilometres of report files on all the known degenerates, agitators, dissenters, and enemies of the State who were under surveillance by the Stasi.

Hausser took a seat in one of the empty offices alongside the cave-like archive. Müller had assisted with the preliminary selection for the colonel's next case, and approximately fifty or sixty thick files were stacked in five neat piles around the edge of the desk, waiting for him, next to a jug of water and a bowl of sugar cubes. Hausser rubbed his tired eyes. *So many bloody traitors, so little time.* Leo Danzig had been a big catch; he took pride in that. Especially because the elimination of Danzig had scuppered the plans of other traitors. But it had taken months to achieve the result; his team had spent thousands of man-hours on Leo. For his own part, Hausser had gone undercover and moved into Leo's apartment building so that he could follow him closely. Adopting the role of the friendly neighbour, Hausser had drunk countless beers with Leo on the bench in their courtyard out back. He'd spent the entire springtime watching the suspect 24/7, who ended his days in the Chamber—indeed, watching Leo take his last breath was a satisfying conclusion to several months' hard work, a victory for the State and, not least—a personal and professional liberation for Hausser.

Hausser opened his briefcase and took out a silver brouilleur, a small glass, and a pint-sized bottle of absinthe; the drink was his only weakness, a crack in his otherwise iron-cast socialist mind. Naturally, absinthe could only be purchased on Unter den Linden, at the Intershop selling luxury products from the West. It might be a decadent drink, but it also helped him do his job.

He poured himself a glass and balanced the brouilleur on top. With utmost care, he placed a sugar cube in the brouilleur and filled it with water from the jug on the desk, then he watched in satisfaction as the sugar water slowly plopped into the green spirit, which gradually turned to a milk-white emulsion. When all the water had filtered into his glass, he gulped it down greedily and poured himself another. Three glasses later, he began to skim the files on his desk. He wasn't sure if it was due to the high alcohol content or the thujone in his drink, but there was a buzz in his head; it sounded like November rain on Karl-Marx-Allee, or the rush of ice-cold water filling the Chamber . . . He needed a significant case, something that would shut Strauss's mouth, bolster morale in the

Stasi, show everyone that justice would be served, that the enemies of the Republic would not go unpunished, no matter how high up they were in the pecking order.

He began to eat his way through the first two piles. But all of these were minor misdemeanours, and it annoyed Hausser that Müller had included them for his attention; granted, several Party members were implicated, but their actions were motivated by dissension in the ranks, a petty power play among Party officials. The buzzing in his head became louder. He massaged his temples, but it didn't help. Sometimes he felt as if their informants wasted the Stasi's time; all these reports only made their work more bureaucratic and less effective—it simply muddied the waters, wasting valuable time that could be spent finding the true culprits.

Exhausted, Hausser glanced at the last pile in front of him. The top file was fat and yellowed with age, bound together by a worn elastic band. Codename "Midas" was printed in red on the cover. He slapped the file onto his desk resentfully and began leafing through the materials, which included an old video cassette. The first page revealed that the suspect was thirty-eight years old with a high-ranking position in the International Division of the State Bank. Married, father to a nine-year-old girl. His wife was a former catalogue model who now worked at the Intershop on Unter den Linden—Madeleine—and Midas had been implicated in dealings with black market Forum cheques that were cashed at the very same boutique. Other reports indicated that there had been several investigations into the bank; Midas was implicated in large-scale manipulation of currency rates and fraudulent transactions with precious metals. Several more reports described how Midas and his co-conspirators operated a long list of companies in the West with straw men; the list was as long as his arm, and Hausser could barely believe that the traitor had never been arrested. Instead, Midas was promoted up the food chain and given positions of increasing power and influence, which could only mean one thing . . .

Hausser poured himself another glass of absinthe. Without water this time; he wanted to enjoy the full benefits of the 70 per cent alcohol level while he watched the video surveillance of Midas. He put the clunky video cassette into the player, and the first pixelated recording flickered on the screen while he sipped on the absinthe, which felt more like small whiplashes on his lips than a taste of decadence.

The video surveillance recorded the meeting activities of the suspect and provided proof that Midas's network branched into the financial sector, heavy industry, and high up the political ladder. This confirmed what Hausser had already surmised, and there could be only two reasons why Midas was still at large: First, he was working for very influential members of the business community; second, he obviously enjoyed the protection of an equally large number of prominent members of the Party who wanted to put the screws on their opposition in the highest echelons of the political hierarchy. This made for a volatile and potentially explosive case. Hausser smiled to himself in satisfaction. Midas could be his white whale; the elimination of Midas would shift the power balance between the Party and the Stasi in the latter's favour; this case was the key to his own salvation.

The surveillance moved on to a hidden camera recording of an expensive hotel room. Midas was in bed with two prostitutes. Hausser took another whipping of absinthe, and he had to hand it to the man; despite his corpulent dimensions, Midas seemed rather adept.

Hausser glanced over the title page of the file once more; the suspect's real name was Christoph Schumann. Hausser smiled again. "Schumann" was about to disappear. He would be picked up and sent to Hohenschönhausen. Allocated a number and new living quarters in the Chamber. He'd make sure of it.

"Sshee you shoon, Schumann," Hausser slurred, raising his glass in a toast to the flickering screen.

12

"Bloody hell!" Ravn swore.

"What happened," asked Eduardo. He was sitting next to the open hatch to *Bianca*'s engine room, and Ravn's legs were sticking out of the hole, as if live connecting rods to the engine block. "Are you okay, *amigo*?"

"Yes . . ." Ravn said through gritted teeth. He gripped the hose clamp with a pair of tongue-and-groove-pliers and tried to turn the rusty screw again, but his screwdriver was much too small for the job. The next second, it slipped out of his hand and sploshed into the bilge water. "Oh, for fuck's sake . . ."

Ravn manoeuvred his body further over the top of *Bianca*'s John Deere motor so he could reach to the bottom of the engine room. His fingers fumbled in the ice-cold bilge of filth, seawater, and diesel oil till they found the shape of the screwdriver in the bottom. Adjusting his grip, he tried again, and this time he managed to fasten the clamp over the hose between the boiler and the fuel tank. "Okay, Eduardo, try firing her up now!" he yelled from the hole.

Eduardo got up and climbed into the cockpit, where the regulator for the Webasto air-conditioning system was hooked up. He flipped the switch of the boiler, which immediately began to hum. Not long after, he could feel warm air pumping out of the ventilation shaft near his right leg. "It's working," he yelled.

Eduardo helped Ravn back out of the gap above the motor room, and together they managed to snap shut the heavy hatch with a satisfying clank.

Ravn dried his hands on a dirty dishcloth. He could already feel the temperature rising in the cabin; it was almost warm and cosy inside. "It doesn't look good down there," he said. "Both fuel tanks are rusty."

"Not a problem, *amigo*," said Eduardo. "That can easily be fixed."

"Really?"

"Yes. I saw this video on YouTube. All you need to do is get the boat on dry land, split open the hull, and get to the tanks from the bottom—"

"Nobody is getting anywhere near *Bianca*'s hull," Ravn said, cutting Eduardo off mid-sentence.

"But, Ravn, it looked like a piece of cake, honestly . . ."

Ravn wasn't listening. His attention had been drawn over Eduardo's head to the woman who had just stepped onto the aft deck. She was wearing calf-height, soft leather boots. He brushed past Eduardo and went up on deck.

He had recognised her immediately, of course. She was the elegant woman who'd been watching him from the safe distance of her Fiat 500, which he had noticed on the other side of the road a few times in the last couple of weeks.

"Louise Slotsholm Nielsen," she said without preamble. Taking off one of her long gloves, she offered Ravn her hand.

Ravn gave his fingers an extra rub with the dishcloth, then took her hand. "Thomas . . ." he said in greeting. "Do we know each other?"

"Not yet, no," she said, shaking her head.

"Okay. What can I do for you?"

Her gaze drifted past him over to the canal. "It . . . I . . . It's a little complicated . . ."

He smiled. "I figured that much, seeing as it took you more than a week to get out of your car and come over to my boat."

Her head snapped back to him. "You saw me?"

"You're hard to miss."

Eduardo came up onto the deck and gave the woman an effusive greeting.

She made a curt reply, clearly very uncomfortable with the entire situation.

"Would you like to take a seat," Ravn said to the woman, pointing at one of his white plastic deck chairs.

"I'm not sure. I shouldn't have come . . ."

"Well, now that you have, you might as well take a seat and tell me what this is all about," Ravn said.

She hesitated. "I . . . I was hoping to talk to you alone . . ."

"Sounds good because Eduardo was just about to . . ."

". . . make some coffee," Eduardo chipped in cheerfully. Clearly, he had no intention of missing a word. "Not too strong, just the way you Danes like it."

Before Ravn could object, Eduardo had ducked back into the caboose, leaving the cabin door open behind him.

Ravn repeated his offer of a plastic deck chair and took a seat on the other. Møffe padded over and curled up beneath his seat. Ravn scratched under his chops and patted his neck, waiting for her to work up her courage.

"I read about you in the papers," Louise said at last.

"Okay . . ."

"I'm really sorry about what happened to your wife, I'm so sorry . . ."

"Thank you, Louise, but I'd rather not talk about it."

"No, I'm sorry, of course not, that's really not what I wanted to talk about at all. It's about the other case."

"What case?"

"The one the newspapers wrote about. The young girl you found, the prostitute, who was held captive in Sweden. You brought her home to her mother, alive."

"You mean Masja. What about her?"

"I was impressed . . . I mean," Louise said. Her cheeks flared, and her gaze dropped to her boots. "That was well done, really . . ." she added awkwardly.

Ravn was starting to feel very uncomfortable with the whole situation, and he regretted inviting this woman to take a seat on his boat. "Thank you, Louise. But if that's all you came to say, then . . . I was actually just in the middle of something," he said, showing her the filthy palms of his hands, and he was about to push to his feet when she spoke.

"My brother disappeared six months ago," she blurted out.

Ravn leaned back in his chair. "Okay. Do I know your brother?"

"No, I doubt that, even though he used to live right over there." Louise twisted in her chair and pointed at the block of flats on Applebye Square. "My brother kept to himself . . . I'm here because I thought you might be able to help me.

"In what way?"

"To find him. Bring him home alive. Just like you did for that girl, Misha."

"Masja," Ravn said, correcting her. "And it was a complete coincidence that I found her at all. I have no intention of being drawn into something similar."

Louise nodded. "Of course, I'm sorry, it was stupid and naïve of me to ask, I can see that now," she said, pulling on the glove she had removed to shake his hand.

"There's no need to apologise," Ravn said. "It's just that I can't help you with this. What about the police? Have you contacted them?"

"The police . . . are involved," Louise said. "My brother is not only missing, they're *looking* for him."

"*Madre mia*, what has he done," Eduardo said, emerging from the cabin. He had two steaming-hot coffees with him, and he handed them each a mug.

Out the corner of his eye, Ravn gave his pal a dirty look. "Would you still like some coffee?" he asked Louise reluctantly.

Louise took a sip by way of reply. Then she said: "My brother stole from his employer. I still can't believe he would do something like that, but that's what the police say."

"And now he's on the run with the money?" asked Eduardo, making himself comfortable against the railing.

"Weren't you about to go back to your own boat?" Ravn said through gritted teeth.

Louise took another sip from her steaming mug and looked up at Eduardo; she seemed glad that he'd asked. "Something like that, I guess," she said. "That's what the police are saying, of course . . . but it's not a huge amount of money that's gone missing from his employer's safe . . . it's only about forty thousand kroner."

"But if he disappeared six months ago, surely that money would be gone by now," Eduardo said.

"Exactly," Louise said, sending a grateful little smile in Eduardo's direction.

"So what do the police have to say about that?" he pushed on, as if oblivious to Ravn, who sat in his chair in silence.

"I haven't spoken to them since they came to my home to question me. That was several months ago. They asked me all kinds of unpleasant questions, as if they thought I was involved."

"The police can be real *maricones* at times, ain't that right, Ravn?"

Ravn wished Eduardo would shut his mouth, and patiently waited for this woman who called herself "Louise" to get the hell off his boat and leave him in peace.

"Yes, they made me very uncomfortable," Louise said. "And this is another reason I hoped that . . ." she paused and glanced at Ravn.

"That what?" Ravn said.

"The newspaper articles said that you work for the Copenhagen Police Department."

"Worked. Past tense. That chapter of my life is over."

"Okay. But I thought that you might still have some connections," Louise said more firmly, raising her chin. "Perhaps you would be able to find out if there was any news on Mogens . . . on my brother?"

"I'm the last person who the police want to see at the station," Ravn said, getting up from his chair. "I think you should approach the police yourself. I'm sure you will find someone there who is willing to help you."

Louise bit her lip and stood up as well. She thanked Eduardo for the coffee and gave him back her mug, which was still half full. "I'm sorry I wasted your time," she said to Ravn. She smiled at him briefly and turned on her heel.

Ravn and Eduardo followed her with their eyes as she daintily stepped back onto the quay and made a beeline for her car.

"Are you dumb or what?" Eduardo said, handing Louise's mug to Ravn.

"What do you mean?"

"A super-hot *señorita* willingly comes onto this rust-bucket of a boat of yours and asks for your help, and you just send her packing. Why can't you pretend to be even a little interested in her problem, Ravn?"

"Because I'm not," said Ravn with a shrug. "Why the hell would I do that?"

Eduardo shook his head in disbelief. "To score . . . to ask her out? *Comprende?* What were you thinking?!"

"Not the same thing as you, apparently."

Ravn brushed past Eduardo and went into the cabin to return the coffee mugs to the sink. Eva's old mobile phone lay on the counter. "You don't happen to have an old charger, do you?" he yelled over his shoulder.

Eduardo came up behind him and looked at the phone. "For that thing? I doubt it. Where did it come from?"

"It doesn't matter."

"It's practically an antique," Eduardo said drily.

Ravn washed the mugs in the sink. Perhaps Eduardo was right; he had been quite rude to Louise. But he had absolutely no desire to dig in the past. Neither his own nor someone else's.

The past could be murder.

13

Prenzlauer Berg, East Berlin
16 August 1989

It was only 7 a.m., but already the air was thick and warm. The first rays of sun broke through the trees on Greifenhagener Strasse. Morning radio broadcasts, the voices of people going about their morning routine, and music spilling out of the open windows of the tall apartment block across the road, where six men were crammed into a Barkas van, smoking. Hausser was sitting on the front seat next to his right-hand man, Müller.

His face obscured by dark sunglasses, Hausser was keeping a watchful eye on the gate in front of Greifenhagener Strasse 9. His team had been sitting on the street for almost three hours without anyone coming in or out. In the van, no one said a word; they were all trained to go the distance during a surveillance operation.

Half an hour later, the first signs of life erupted on the pavement. People came out their doors and hurried on their way to work. Further down the road, the municipal rubbish removal was approaching on its morning rounds; Hausser frowned at the truck that would soon block their view of Number 9.

"We should have parked closer to the house," said Müller. "Shall I tell the men in that rubbish truck to move on?"

"No," said Hausser. "No reason to alert anyone to our presence."

The next moment, Christoph Schumann came through the front gate. A brown leather attaché tucked under his arm, he was dressed in a light flax linen suit. He held open the gate for his wife, who was slim as an eel next to her husband. Frau Schumann cast a glance over her shoulder and called to her daughter. The girl appeared by the gate. She was dressed in the distinctive Young Pioneers uniform: a white shirt, black skirt, and blood-red neckerchief. Frau Schumann took the girl's hand, and they crossed the road to the row of parked cars on the other side.

The agent sitting behind Hausser adjusted his telephoto lens and started taking pictures.

Christoph Schumann opened the car door for his wife and daughter, who jumped into the back seat. As if he could feel the agents watching him, Schumann glanced up at their van, before slamming the car door. The large rubbish truck pulled up to Number 9. Through the thick smoke expelled from the truck's exhaust pipe, the agents saw Schumann's champagne-coloured car drive away.

"Holy shit," said Müller. "That prick drives a BMW. How much you think one of those cars costs?"

"Five- or six-years' salary at least," remarked the agent behind him. "Imported directly from the West, no doubt."

Without a moment to spare, Hausser opened the sliding door and got out of the van. The five agents followed at his heels as he crossed the road and slipped through the gate in front of Number 9. They hurried round to the back of the apartment block, gained access to the main entrance with a key, and hurried up five flights of stairs to the top floor, where the Schumann family had their living quarters. Müller picked the front door lock in less than fifteen seconds.

The sweet smell of Frau Schumann's perfume clung to the air in the entrance, where all six men crowded together in their overcoats. Hausser raised his hand and gestured to his men, who dispersed accordingly and began their search of the flat. For his own part, Hausser went into the living room, which overlooked a convent garden next door. Clearly, the Schumanns lived in a lovely neighbourhood. Only a select few had the privilege of living in a home like theirs: a music system with an impressive record collection on the shelf below; original art on the walls; a large television; a sofa arrangement in soft leather that looked brand new; and, most impressive of all, a bamboo home bar with four chairs and an assortment of spirits lined up against a glass wall—imported brands everywhere. Not even Leo Danzig, the human trafficker, had lived in such luxury.

Hausser went into Christoph Schumann's home office. Apart from a huge desk, there were two chesterfield chairs by a small, polished mahogany table bearing a humidor and a decanter containing a dark liquid. Hausser lifted the lid and sniffed. Cognac, he noted. A floor-to-ceiling bookcase stood against the far wall. Hausser skimmed the titles; the Russian and German masters, including Nietzsche and Kant, sharing shelf space with Baudelaire, Shakespeare, and Hemingway. Crime novels filled another shelf and, hidden in between these, he noted a few titles by the pioneering German authors who criticised the political system, including Werner Bräunig, whom Hausser enjoyed reading himself. Despite the impressive library, Hausser was not convinced that Schumann was the erudite and well-read type; the leatherbound books, the Cuban cigars, the humidor, the imported cognac, the home bar—all of it was for show, he reckoned.

Hausser let the agents get on with their search of the office and went into the master bedroom. He brushed past the double bed and walked over to the cupboard that filled one of the walls. He opened the door and looked inside. An impressive wardrobe: mink coats, cocktail dresses, pantsuits, shirts and blouses. And, once again, judging from the labels and the quality, most of these items must have been imported from the West. The average worker for the communist State would need ten years' wages to afford clothing like this. But the Schumanns were obviously not an average family in the GDR. Hausser opened the top drawer to his left. Frau Schumann's underwear. A hint of the same sweet perfume reached his nostrils, and he couldn't resist burying his nose in the pair of white lace panties that lay on top of the pile. There was something at once vulgar and intoxicating about the smell, and Hausser was aroused and intrigued by the thought that Frau Schumann felt the need to spray her underwear with sweet perfume. He was tempted to stuff the underwear into his pocket but managed to get a grip and stay focussed on the matter at hand.

He closed the wardrobe and walked down the corridor to the

daughter's room. On the walls, a few black-and-white posters of Nadia Comaneci and Karin Janz, both of whom were former Olympic gold medallists in gymnastics. On the small *chatol* in the corner, silver-framed photographs of the daughter performing a floor routine at a gymnastics competition. Next to the frames, three medals, made of gold-painted plastic, strung on a light-blue ribbon.

Müller appeared in the doorway. "Do you want us to search the girl's room as well?" he asked.

"Of course," said Hausser. "But be careful with her things."

He left the daughter's room and went into the kitchen, while the agents systematically took photographs of the rest of the flat. He opened the fridge. A fine assortment of cheese, sliced ham, and salami stared back at him. Hausser reached for an open carton of condensed milk, drank a few greedy slurps, and put it back in its place. He didn't care for condensed milk much, but he utterly despised Schumann; the despicable decadence of his lifestyle.

Müller came into the kitchen. "We've been through all the rooms," he said.

Hausser closed the fridge. "What have you found? Any records? Bills? Documents?

"No, nothing useful," said Müller. "But it looks like Schumann spends more money than he earns at the State Bank."

"What marvellous powers of observation you have," Hausser replied.

Müller's gaze dropped to his feet. "The search strengthens our case and corroborates charges of corruption and abuse of his office."

"I want to get to the bottom of Schumann's network," said Hausser. "We need to get access to his accounts and find out who is protecting him. I want to catch him with his fingers in the cookie jar. We need to initiate a full-scale investigation of Schumann immediately."

"I'm not sure I understand, sir," said Müller. "We have found nothing in the flat that implicates anyone other than Schumann, and only indirectly at that . . ."

". . . which is why we must keep looking. Get hold of the Tech Division. I want the whole place rigged: audio, video in all the rooms, and the rear entrance stairway."

Müller passed a hand over his scalp and regarded Hausser intensely with his good eye. "What does General Strauss think about this, sir? Is he not the one who will have to sanction a full-scale surveillance?"

The other agents had gathered in the entrance behind Müller, and everyone was waiting for Hausser's reply: "If you ever question my authority again, I will personally arrange for you to stamp letters in the cellar under Haus Five for the rest of your miserable life," he said at last. His head turned, and the colonel gazed out the kitchen window. In the courtyard below, an elderly man wearing a blue apron was sweeping the quad. "That caretaker down there. He has a room on the ground floor, am I right?"

"Yes, sir," replied Müller. "It's at the foot of the stairwell. On the right-hand side."

"What do we know about him?"

"Wolfgang Voller. Widower. Sixty-eight years old. Former bus driver. Member of the Party since he was twenty-three years old, sir."

"Have him picked up tonight."

"On what charge, sir?"

Hausser shrugged. "Be creative, Müller. Just make sure he stays in Hohenschönhausen until this operation is over. Oh, and Müller . . ." he added as he brushed past his deputy and headed for the door.

"Yes, sir?"

"Get the guys from Tech Division to set up a command centre in the caretaker's flat. We're going to watch Schumann twenty-four seven, just like the Danzig Op."

"Understood, right away, sir. And . . . who's moving in?"

14

Prenzlauer Berg, East Berlin
18 August 1989

A few days following the search, Christoph Schumann came through the gate at Greifenhagener Strasse 9. It was late in the afternoon, and he was eager to get home. His jacket was slung over one arm, and the large stains under his armpits revealed that he was sweating heavily. As he crossed the courtyard, his hand searching his pocket for his keys, Christoph took no notice of the caretaker who was sweeping the yard with his back turned.

"Excuse me," a voice said behind him.

Christoph turned round and looked at the strange man who was wearing the caretaker's blue apron. "Yes?"

The man smiled, wiped his right hand on the apron, and extended it towards Christoph. "My name is Hausser. I'm the new caretaker."

Christoph looked at the outstretched hand, then shook it reluctantly. "What happened to the other guy? Koehler . . . or Voller, something like that," he said, dropping the hand.

"No idea. He was transferred elsewhere, I think."

"Just as well. You could never get hold of him," Christoph said, giving the main door a good shove and stepping inside the building. "I hope you'll be more efficient," he cast over his shoulder with a thin smile at Hausser.

"I'd like to think that I will be."

"Really? We have a problem with our drain in the bathroom. Can you come up in the next couple of days and fix it? The name is Schumann—"

"Fifth floor, yes, I know. I'll see to it," the caretaker replied, smiling at Schumann, who was already on his way up the stairs.

Hausser returned to his broom with satisfaction; all that remained were the tiles around the dustbins, and he'd be done with the sweeping for today.

Ten minutes later, Hausser let himself in to his new quarters on the ground floor of Greifenhagener Strasse 9, which was hot as an oven. Hausser tossed the apron on the floor of the tiny entrance. A humming sound came from the room beyond, and a dim green light was visible in the crack under the door to the right. Hausser turned left and went into the kitchen to fetch his bottle of absinthe and a bucket of ice. He returned to the entrance with his drink, pushed open the door to the right, and was immediately swallowed by the greenish beam of light.

The guys from Tech Division had been thorough, as always; eight monitors were mounted on the end wall. The humming sound came from the video recording equipment that was kept running day and night. The entire apparatus was connected to the hidden cameras that had been installed in the Schumann residence, so Hausser could keep an eye on all the rooms of the flat from the command centre, including the landing and stairs to the back entrance. In addition, twelve microphones had been planted throughout the rooms.

Hausser took a seat on the chair in front of the monitors. The hint of a smile came to his thin mouth. *The boys at Tech had outdone themselves.* This was not like the old days. Back when he started working at the Stasi, they'd had to make do with small reels of film, which had to be developed afterwards. Now, with the use of video, they could watch a recording "live." And their equipment had advanced as the years passed; now, their bugs were microscopic; you could thread the cables through the walls and hook up the wiring to the command centre.

On the monitor in the centre, Hausser could see Christoph, who was standing at the bar, fixing himself a drink.

"Lena? Can I bring you a martini while I'm at it?" Christoph called to his wife.

"Yes, please, *Liebchen*, that would be lovely," Frau Schumann replied from the kitchen.

Hausser glanced over to the monitor on the left where he could see Lena standing by the stove, preparing dinner.

"Yes, please, *Liebchen*," Hausser repeated mockingly as he poured a generous helping of absinthe into his glass.

15

Victoria's *antikvariat* was a labyrinth, shelves packed with books from floor to ceiling, and the moment Ravn stepped through the door, his nostrils were filled with the smell of Petterøe tobacco, freshly brewed coffee, and dust. The gramophone on the large shopkeeper's counter was blasting Chet Baker's "Moment's in Vermont" from the far corner of the store. Ravn was standing just next to it, sorting through a cardboard box of electrical paraphernalia: extension cables, ancient adapters, answerphones, mobile phones, and calculators that would not have been out of place in a tech museum.

"Are you sure you have one that fits," Ravn yelled over his shoulder.

Victoria appeared in the doorway of her supply room out back. She hugged a tall pile of books in her arms and—as if it were a seaman's pipe—half of one of the cinnamon rolls that Ravn had picked up for her at Lagkagehuset stuck out a corner of her mouth.

"Yum, mmm . . ." Victoria said, appreciatively, and carefully put the pile of books on the counter. She took another bite of the cinnamon roll and answered with her mouth full: "If I do, it will be in that box," she said, munching away. "Are you sure this is a good idea?" she asked, brushing the dust off her tweed jacket.

"What do you mean?" said Ravn, digging deeper and deeper into the concoction of cables.

"Wouldn't it be best if you just threw that piece of crap away and moved on?"

Ravn stared down at the box. "Actually, I am moving on, but I need to know if this is Eva's work phone."

"Why don't you just send it back to her office and let them handle it?"

Ravn pulled a clunky adapter out of the box. "But what if it turns out the phone doesn't belong to them? Then they'll just send it back to me," he said, shaking his head. "Maybe whatever is on the phone is none of their business?"

"Yeah, nor yours," Victoria said. She swallowed the last bite of her pastry and fished her tobacco out of the breast pocket of her jacket.

"What's your problem, exactly?"

"No problems here. But you're not Big Brother. Why snoop around in each other's stuff? Just let the dead rest in peace, for God's sake."

"You've never sugar-coated anything in your life, have you?" Ravn observed drily. He took the mobile phone out of his pocket and tried to hook it up to the old adapter from the box. "It's useless; this shit doesn't fit anyway," he said, dumping the lot on the counter between them.

Victoria rolled herself a cigarette with a practised hand and lit up with her faithful Ronson, which produced a flame that threatened to set her silver-grey mane alight if she wasn't careful. She inhaled greedily and sent a gas-blue cloud of smoke to the low ceiling. "Well, if you really want to revive that mobile—"

"Yes, I do. I need to get rid of it. No more no less."

"Yeah, yeah, of course," Victoria said. She jammed the cigarette in the corner of her mouth and clicked her fingers, her sign to hand the thing over. "Adapter-tyranny is bullshit because every adapter on the market works on the same principle, namely, to convert two twenty volts to twelve volts. The *only* difference between one adapter and another is the plug; telephone companies fabricate a distinct plug so that the consumer is duped into buying their brand," Victoria explained as she reached for her letter opener and deftly cut the adapter cable in half. "In fact, you can use any kind of adapter to charge these old phones." She peeled back the insulation on the end of the cable and held the exposed wires up to show him. "You see? Plus and minus. There's no more to it than that."

"But how do you get those wires to connect with the phone's plug?"

"It's easier than you think," Victoria said. She stuck the tip of the letter opener in the groove along the edge of the phone's casing and pressed down hard. The thin plastic gave and the little screws holding the phone together dropped onto the floor.

"Hey, what are you doing, Victoria? You're breaking it!"

"Nah, just wait and see," she said, laying down the exposed telephone on the counter. Very carefully, she connected the exposed wires directly to the phone's card. "Okay, now you can plug it in."

Ravn leaned down and stuck the adapter's plug in the wall. "Anything?"

"Yes, the display has lit up. Now you can just let it stay there and charge for a bit. Do you have the PIN code?"

"The PIN? Where would I get that?"

"Okay. What about the PUK code?"

"I don't even know what that is."

"You're not a technophile, are you?"

"I never said that I was . . . so, what are we going to do now? Can we still access the messages?"

Victoria stubbed her cigarette in the ashtray as a customer made for the counter with a stack of books balanced in his arms. "You can always make an emergency call without punching in the PIN code," she said.

"How would that help?"

"With some of these old mobile phones, it's possible to gain access to the phone's memory card once you've dialled the emergency number. So, you can't make other calls from the phone, but you can gain access to your contacts and messages. Isn't that what you were interested in?"

Ravn brushed a hand over the stubble on his chin. "You seem to know quite a bit about hacking mobile phones."

Victoria shrugged. "It's common knowledge, that."

"Oh, yeah? Where? In *Vestre Prison*?"

Victoria gave Ravn a tight-lipped smile and turned to attend to her customer.

As if hypnotised, Ravn stared at the lit-up display. The phone beeped, and the text INSERT PIN appeared. He glanced over at Victoria, but she was busy with her customer, so he punched in 112. A voice from the Emergency Hotline answered seconds later. He ended the call and hit the "menu" button instead.

Just as Victoria had said, he now had access to the phone's memory. He scrolled through the list of contents; none of the names rang a bell. The truth was that he didn't know any of Eva's clients, nor anyone she used to work with. He could remember that her boss's name was Richard something-or-other, and that she occasionally mentioned a Pia—or was it Lena?—at the defence attorney's office; none of these names appeared on the phone's contact list.

He realised how little he actually knew about Eva's professional life as a defence attorney. They had never spoken about their work at home; this was a tacit agreement that they had both valued highly. Their home had been a refuge from all the horrors that each of them were faced with at work on a daily basis; for his part, on the streets of Copenhagen; for her part, in court.

He tapped the letter icon, and a long list of text messages came up; the first few immediately confirmed that the phone definitely belonged to Eva: court case numbers, her name and professional title, dates and times when her cases would be heard. He scrolled through the messages leading up to the date of her death. One of them caught his attention, and he read the heading of a message jammed between two case numbers: "Missing our Wednesday meetings," followed by a smiley. He tapped on the message: "Missing, missing, missing, missing, missing, missing, missing, missing, missing you, my beloved Eva . . ."

He tapped his way back to the list and started scrolling through more slowly. The personal messages came up again among the work-related ones: *lovely to see you today; thank you for last night and for the wine; we can't keep meeting like this :-); counting the days until we meet again; I think I'm in love—no, I know that I am; Jesus Christ, you're a wonderful woman, Eva . . .*

Ravn's stomach wrenched in a knot. He bent down and yanked the plug out of the wall and wrapped the phone in the cable to keep the case together. He clenched his eyes shut. *This cannot be.*

"Hey, where are you going?" Victoria called after him.

Ravn had already stormed out the door.

His head felt as if it were about to explode, and Eva's telephone was burning hot in his hand.

16

Hausser stood with his back facing the monitors in the living room, buttoning up his shirt. The last two weeks he had decided to grow a moustache because he thought it suited his new identity as the ingratiating caretaker of Greifenhagener Strasse 9. He cast a bleary-eyed look over his shoulder. The monitor in the middle was sending pictures directly from the master bedroom. Christoph and Lena had just turned in for the night. He had snuggled up to his wife and started caressing her belly.

Schumann had tried before, and Hausser had noted that Lena didn't have the same appetite for sex as her husband. But it appeared as if Schumann might get lucky tonight; Lena submitted to his touch, and soon afterwards, she pulled her silk nightdress over her head and let her husband have what he wanted.

Hausser tucked his shirt into his pants and watched them having sex. Schumann was pumping hard now. Lena tried to hush him, and Schumann buried his head in his pillow. Hausser made for the door, and by the time he had collected his jacket from the chair in the corner, he heard Schumann climax with a grunt behind him. Hausser cast a glance at the monitor to the right. Lena got out of bed and went into the ensuite bathroom to pee and wash between her legs. When she returned to the bedroom, Schumann was already asleep. At 11:37 p.m., she turned off her bedside lamp and lay down to sleep with her back facing her husband.

Hausser found his cap on the hook in the cramped entrance and went outside, locking the door behind him.

Without making a sound, Hausser crossed the courtyard and slipped out the gate. His bicycle was locked to a post in front of the neighbouring building. He unlocked it and, moments later, he was on his way down Greifenhagener Strasse. He couldn't remember when he'd last been on a bike. It must have been when he was a soldier. *Perhaps even as far back as his student days?* The beers and absinthe he had consumed that night did not improve the clumsiness of his movements, which made the bicycle meander down the road, as if the colonel were negotiating a slalom course on skis.

Twenty minutes later, Hausser was on Schulze-Boysen-Strasse, cycling along the high wire-mesh fence of the Inner Wall that cut down the middle of the road. Search lights flickered from the watchtower in the "death strip" between the fence and the concrete Outer Wall. He knew that border patrol guards would already have him in their sights. Apart from the grating sound of his bicycle chain against its metal guard, an eerie silence descended on the road as he headed for the black Lada parked by the kerb up ahead. There were no other cars around. Hausser could see a figure sitting behind the wheel, and he knew that Müller had been waiting for him to show for their meeting for hours. He left the bike on the pavement and opened the passenger door.

Hausser hesitated when he recognised the scowl of Strauss, rather than Müller, sitting behind the wheel, and he tried to hide his surprise as he greeted his boss, climbed into the car, and closed the door quietly behind him.

Strauss did not return the greeting. For a moment, he stared dead ahead in silence. Then his temper exploded. "Why the hell wasn't I kept informed?!" He yelled so suddenly that a cloud of spittle was projected onto the windshield. "You've been watching Schumann for more than two weeks, and I only found about the Midas Operation this morning!"

"Due to the high profile of the people involved, I thought it best not to share this information with others."

"I am not others,' I am your superior officer! And I demand to be kept informed about such matters. This point is not up for discussion."

"I apologise if I miscalculated the situation. I merely thought it best to inform you afterwards—just as I have done in the past, when cases ended in the termination of a suspect."

"Shall I expect to be informed of yet another lung infection in Hohenschönhausen?" Strauss snapped sarcastically.

Hausser fingered his moustache. "I can't promise that you won't. Either way, Midas is sitting on some very important information. Whether he shares this with your interrogators or myself is his choice."

"I've read the reports. Why don't we bring him in now?"

"Because in all probability, he's not the only one involved," Hausser pointed out. "There will be others. People who I want to catch in the act. Party members. Perhaps even a few from our own ranks. A major cleansing operation," he added with a smile.

Strauss noticed the new moustache on Hausser's lip. "What the hell is that? Is it real?" he asked.

Hausser nodded, pleased with himself.

Strauss shook his head and lit a cigarette. "Are you aware of what is going on beyond your own four walls? ZDF is broadcasting the news to us on a daily basis."

"I have other channels keeping me busy now. Am I missing anything good?"

"Good?" he exclaimed. "The world is crashing down around us. In Poland, the Communist Party is finished. In the Baltic countries, people are taking to the streets. More than a million people took part in a demonstration; they linked arms and made a human chain six hundred kilometres long . . ."

"They can keep their chain as long as we have our Wall against the Fascists."

"But . . . can't you see the crack?" Strauss sputtered.

Hausser looked at the Wall through his window. "No, not from where I'm sitting."

Strauss rolled down his window and flicked his cigarette stub onto the pavement. "So tell me, what has your surveillance discovered?"

Hausser bit the inside of his cheek. He didn't appreciate the question. He was neither inclined nor used to explaining his actions. Never mind his methods. "We are still in the preliminary phase of our investigation," he said, not looking at Strauss and staring into the darkness beyond the windshield instead.

"You've been active for a fortnight. Have you procured any concrete evidence?"

"It's mostly the little things, which create a bigger picture. Only an investigator in the field is able to interpret the signs," he said pointedly.

"Tell me what you have, Hausser. Right now."

Hausser folded his arms over his chest. "A pattern that has been broken . . . a shift in the dots . . . things that have been said . . . statements that, as a whole, indicate that something big is about to happen."

"You'll have to be a little more specific than that."

Hausser shrugged. "A few days ago, Midas changed his drinking habits; he used to drink dry martinis, but now he's switched to whiskey and soda. This evening, his wife submitted to her husband's cravings for sex, and the day before yesterday he had an argument with his daughter about a gymnastics tournament in Dresden, which he refused to let her attend. The Schumanns are eating more meat. And their consumption of tobacco products has also increased. Midas does not bathe as often as he used to, but this might be just a coincidence.

Strauss gaped at Hausser. "Are you taking the piss?"

"In what way?"

"Are you—Hausser, are you drunk?"

"Only in a very insignificant degree. But, as I was trying to say by way of introduction . . . you must be in the field to understand what all these changes in behaviour mean."

"I don't know what is more bizarre: What's going on in the world around us or your investigation."

"Nevertheless," Hausser said through gritted teeth, "something big is about to happen. Midas is planning something."

"I'll give you one more week. If nothing has happened by then, I'm shutting down the surveillance of Midas and his family."

"That would be a mistake. It could take longer than a week before something concrete happens."

"*One* week, Hausser. Not a day more."

Hausser watched the black Lada disappear down Schulze-Boysen-Strasse. The moon was low, as if it were spying on him over the Outer Wall. The situation with Strauss was becoming intolerable; his boss was weak and prone to panic when action was required. In the good ol' days, his boss would simply have been removed—*cleansed*, Hausser thought. He would have to pick up the pace of his operation.

17

Ravn leaned back in his sofa on *Bianca*, Eva's old phone in one hand, half a glass of neat Jim Beam in the other. The phone was fully charged, and he had wound an elastic band around the casing to keep it together. Sipping his whiskey, he stared blindly at the display. Out on the canal, a harbour tour came by with a guide yelling information into a megaphone, so he reckoned the water level must have dropped to normal levels. *Bad things always come in groups*, he thought moodily.

In the last twenty-four hours, he had read Eva's text messages so many times he practically knew them by heart; the minute he saw the title, the contents of every single one appeared in his mind's eye. The messages increased in frequency right up to a week before her death and outlined her betrayal in chronological order: from the first, tentative flirtation, the repeated scheduling of meetings that became increasingly intimate, to outright declarations of his love. Ravn could not find her replies; she must have deleted them. But he didn't have to see them—her lover's words were sufficiently explicit for him to connect the dots.

He'd tried to run a search and identify the number's owner in the telephone directory. He wanted to pay this arsehole a personal visit. But no name was listed, and now he had no other alternative but to call the fucker and spell out what would happen if he ever clapped eyes on him.

Ravn put the Jim Beam aside and picked up his own mobile phone. The minute he punched in the number, he felt his anger rise. Adrenaline pumped through his veins, and a bitter taste clung to the back of his throat. The call went through. He waited. After a few seconds, an automated voice from the telephone company informed him the number was no longer in use. He punched the "end call" button and tossed the phone into the far corner of the sofa. He regretted not listening to Victoria. He should have left the damn phone alone. But now that the damage was done, he couldn't just let it go.

His brain went into overdrive. There must be another way to figure out who Eva had been sleeping with. There had to be other clues, alternative ways he could track down the person sending the messages, without relying on the phone itself. He'd never found anything incriminating in their flat, and besides, he'd already thrown everything out. *Eva's clothing!*

Ravn jumped to his feet, startling Møffe, who woke up abruptly and barked.

He'd been so eager to get rid of everything that he'd forgotten to check her pockets. Perhaps there was something that could give him a lead—a letter, a photograph, or a bill from someplace where the two of them had met in secret.

Ravn picked up the glass and downed the whiskey without any appreciation for the taste. It had been a long time since he had drunk Jim Beam as if it were water, and in the midst of his misery, he realised that this was a good thing.

The little bell over the door chimed just once as Ravn entered the charity shop on Amagerbrogade. The air smelled faintly of damp, mothballs, and dust from the clothing that filled every nook and cranny in the store. An elderly woman wearing a red cowl-neck sweater was standing behind the counter, folding clothes neatly. Unfortunately, it was not the same woman who had been on duty when Ravn had come by the day before yesterday. He greeted the woman and immediately spotted the bags, which were still plonked on the floor where he had left them, in large rubbish bags just behind the counter.

"Good day. I was in here with those bags over there the day before yesterday," he began, pointing at the bags.

The woman put on her glasses, which were hanging round her neck on a bead chain. She stared him up and down, letting her glasses slide to the tip of her nose. Then she turned her head slowly. "Those bags over there, you say?"

"Yes, those are the ones," Ravn said. "And I would really like to take a quick look through them."

The woman turned to face Ravn again. "I'm terribly sorry, sir, but you'll have to wait until I've had a chance to sort and price the goods," she said, taking off her glasses and letting them hang round her neck again.

"I don't think you understand. I just need to check to see if there's anything left in the pockets; I forgot to do so before I brought the items over."

"I see," the woman said. She pursed her lips. "Even if the bags did belong to you, as you say—"

"They *do* belong to me, I swear—"

"—they are now, technically, the property of the DanChurchAid Alliance. And I can't just let you rifle through them at your leisure," she said, crossing her arms over her chest.

Ravn took a deep breath and gathered all the calm he could muster. "*Technically*, my dearly departed wife, whose clothing is in those bags, cheated on me before she died. And *technically*, I need to go through her pockets to see if I can find anything that will give an indication of who she was sleeping with. So *technically*, I could really use a little help here," he said, looking at her with a pleading note in his voice.

The woman blinked her eyes rapidly. "Ah, well, it seems that you are indeed the one who delivered those bags to us . . . and in that case—"

"—thank you." Ravn stepped round the counter and immediately started rummaging through the bags, while the lady with the cowl-sweater peered over his shoulder, watching his every move.

Fifteen minutes later, he was back on Amagerbrogade, heading back to Christianshavn with Møffe trailing at his heels.

The trip to the charity shop had been in vain. Apart from a hairclip and fuzz balls, he had found nothing useful in the four bags of clothing. He took Eva's old phone out of his pocket and went through the text messages for the umpteenth time.

There was nothing that pointed directly to the man's identity, but he doubted it could be someone from her office because their meetings had been sporadic. It might have been one of her clients. Inwardly, he damned her to hell. *If she'd been unhappy, why hadn't she just said something?* She could have yelled at him, thrown things at him, anything but this . . . Eva had never given him any indication that she was dissatisfied with their relationship. What was missing? It wasn't sex—ugly images of Eva with someone else were burnt on his retina.

Ravn yanked on Møffe's leash and made a beeline for *Bianca*. He was pretty sure Jim Beam would keep him company, but when he reached the canal, he spotted a grey Fiat 500 with a dark red folding hood parked by the kerb—right opposite his boat. He stopped in his tracks and swore under his breath. He really didn't feel like human company right now— least of all from that nosy woman with her boots. Intending to lay low at The Sea Otter, where he could sulk in a dark corner in peace, he spun on his heel and nearly collided headlong with Louise.

"Hi," she said.

"Hi," he said, taken by surprise. "Are you following me?" he added, forcing a smile to his lips.

"Not really. I went to the boat to see if you were there," she said sweetly, pointing at *Bianca*, "but when nobody was home, I decided to take a walk along the canal. Fantastic weather, isn't it?" she took a deep breath and stared up into the sky, where the clouds were already closing in.

"Hmm, maybe," said Ravn. "Was there something in particular you wanted from me?" he said, regretting the words the moment they came out of his mouth.

"Nope, I just came by to see if I could buy you a glass of wine."

"Wine? Thanks, but I don't drink wine . . . it's not good for my stomach . . . the tannins, you know," he said, tapping his belly for good measure.

She smiled. "How about a beer, then?"

"Louise?" he said, hoping he had remembered her name correctly. "I'm pretty sure you didn't come over here to talk to me about the weather, or invite me for a drink, for that matter . . . so why don't you just tell me what's on your mind?"

"You're right," she said, stuffing her hands into the front pockets of her tight designer jeans. "I took your advice and contacted the police again."

"Okay. And what did they tell you?"

Louise smiled again—this time it was a Cameron Diaz smile, and he couldn't help but notice that she was stunning. "Are you sure I can't buy you a beer?"

18

Prenzlauer Berg, East Berlin
16 September 1989

Hausser leaned one hand on the wall and emptied his bladder. His urine was a dark yellow, and the sour smell that rose from the toilet bowl proved what he already knew: He was dehydrated. Living on booze and cigarettes alone wasn't feasible in the long run. He made a mental note to get some decent food in his belly. Even though the hunger created brilliant trains of thought that enabled him to see leads that no one else did; he knew that the Midas Operation was about to take a major turn. He could feel it in every nerve ending. The only problem was that the extra week Strauss had given him to prove it was over. So it was only a matter of time before Müller or some other agent from DZ knocked on his do—

The caretaker's doorbell rang.

Hausser pulled on the flush chain and stepped out into the entrance. He could hear Schumann's daughter singing "Der kleine Trompeter," one of the Young Pioneers' hymns, on the loudspeaker set up in his living room.

The doorbell chimed again.

Hausser closed the door to the living room and went to open his front door.

"Herr Schumann. Good morning," Hausser said.

Christoph looked Hausser up and down. "Morning," he said. "I would appreciate it if our drain could be fixed today."

"Your drain? I don't understand," said Hausser, stuffing his shirt down the front of his pants.

"The drain in our bathroom. It's blocked. I have mentioned it several times."

Hausser nodded as if he remembered. "I'll see to it later."

"Preferably this morning while my wife is still at home. As soon as possible." Christoph did not wait for Hausser's reply before disappearing from his doorway. As he watched Christoph cross the courtyard and exit onto Greifenhagener Strasse, Hausser idly zipped up his fly.

Half an hour later, Hausser knocked on the Schumanns' front door. He would have liked to come over sooner, but he'd struggled to find the caretaker's tools and workman's belt, which he now wore strapped around his waist. Lena opened the door wearing a black silk kimono with Japanese letters on the front and back. She gave off a sweet smell, but her facial expression was sour. "The bathroom is to the left," she said by way of greeting, and retreated into the flat.

She had left the door open, so Hausser stepped through the entrance and closed it behind him.

"Please don't make a mess, I've just had the bathroom cleaned," Lena yelled from the bedroom at the end of the long corridor.

Hausser turned left and went to the bathroom. *Of course she had someone to clean for her*, he thought. And he knew perfectly well who she exploited for the purpose; her name was Klara, and she lived on the first floor, facing the road on the opposite side of the courtyard. He'd watched Klara cleaning up here while Herr and Frau Schumann were at work and their daughter was at school: She drank their alcohol and topped up the bottles with water so the Schumanns wouldn't notice. Then she danced around in Lena's fur coats and smoked her cigarettes. It was very entertaining to watch, as if she were a clown doing tricks in an interval of the main performance.

A rotten smell came from the water blocking the wash basin. He was neither a handyman nor a caretaker, but he felt confident he could fix the problem. He took the plunger from his belt, placed the nozzle over the drain, and began to pump away, spraying water everywhere. Once he was satisfied that he'd dislodged the blockage, he stopped pumping and peered down the drain; clumps of hair and flakes of soap bobbed on the surface of the filthy water. He put down the plunger, took the screwdriver out of his belt, and started scraping out the congealed hair, which he dumped onto the bathroom floor.

The water in the basin started to filter down the drain slowly, and Hausser dried his dirty fingers on the pink towel that hung on a hook beside the bathroom cabinet above the basin. Then he went out into the corridor again. "I need a kettle of boiling water," he called to the other end of the flat.

"There's a kettle in the kitchen you can use," Lena yelled back.

Hausser went into the kitchen and found the kettle by the sink. He filled it with water and took a look round while he waited for it to boil. On the other end of the counter, he noticed a handwritten note. It was a shopping list! Including six bottles of wine and a reminder to buy something for dessert. *Could there be anything more decadent in a communist state?* Hausser fumed quietly. No one in the household was having a birthday soon, but it seemed the Schumanns had something to celebrate, and he doubted it had anything to do with the 40th Jubilee of the Federal Republic of Germany. The kettle started to whistle, interrupting his thoughts, so he put down the note and walked back to the sink. Picking up the kettle, he went back to the bathroom and poured the boiling water into the wash basin.

Moments later, Hausser was back in the long corridor. "That should do it, Frau Schumann," he said. The master bedroom door was open, and he could see Lena standing in front of the wardrobe. She was dressed in nothing more than a black brassiere and a pair of lace panties, busy putting on a pair of nylon stockings. It surprised him that she made no attempt to cover herself. In fact, she stood right where he had an unhindered view of her body. Once she had pulled on both stockings, she began searching through the wardrobe; the scraping sound of the metal hangers against the rod followed the rhythm of her bouncing breasts, and he could feel the bulge in his pants rising.

All at once his view was obscured by the daughter, who suddenly stepped out into the corridor in front of him. She was dressed in her Young Pioneers uniform. He smiled at her, but she merely stared back at him.

"Hi, what's your name?" he said.

The girl didn't reply but kept staring.

"That's a great uniform. What section do you belong to?"

The girl reached out, and a moment passed before he realised that it was the kettle she wanted. He stretched out his arm, and she snatched the kettle from his hand.

"Goodbye," she said.

That same evening, Hausser sat in front of the monitors in his living room, eating a piece of bread and a small sausage, washing it down with a cool Berliner Pilsner. Unconsciously, it had become a habit for Hausser to eat or drink at the same time as the Schumann family; it had almost become a nice tradition.

The family sat round the little kitchen table. Lena was relating a story from her shopping trip to the Intershop that day. Some elderly American tourists had expressed surprise at the wide array of goods available, and the fact that they could pay in American dollars. Lena had overheard them whispering that socialism wasn't so bad after all. Christoph laughed and said that he would have loved to see them stand in a queue in front of the ever-empty supermarkets on Schönhauser Allee.

When dinner was over, the daughter was the first to excuse herself from the table. Hausser followed her movements on the monitor, which showed her going into her room and taking a seat at her desk to do homework. Soon after, Christoph put his plate in the sink, went into his home office, and closed the door behind him. In the master bedroom, Lena got undressed to take a bath. Hausser could not tear his eyes off her; it felt as if the scene from that morning were being played in reverse, and he was enjoying it all the more for it. In the office, Christoph walked to the far wall and picked a volume off the bookcase. He sat down behind his desk and opened the book. A piece of paper slipped out of the pages, and Christoph smoothed it down on the desk before him. Hausser sat up and took notice, and not even the fact that Lena was now completely naked in the bedroom could draw his attention from Christoph; he only wished the camera had a zoom function so that he could read what was written on the note.

Christoph reached for the telephone, and the tape recorder next to Hausser immediately began to record. Christoph checked his note and dialled in a number. Soon after, someone picked up.

"Köster," a male voice said gravely.

Hausser recognised the name from the Midas file.

Christoph invited Köster to dinner at seven the following night, and Köster accepted. Hausser suspected that the conversation was deliberately brief. In the course of the next fifteen minutes, Christoph called five other people on his list and invited them all to dinner the following evening; all of them accepted. Apart from Köster, Hausser recognised two other names, one of which belonged to a high-ranking official in the Ministry of Foreign Affairs. His patience was rewarded; this was exactly what he had been wating for.

That night Hausser cycled to the telephone box on Rosenthaler Platz. He'd intended to call Strauss and report the good news about Schumann's meeting, but once he got there, he changed his mind and decided to call Müller instead.

"We can expect guests, soon," he told Müller. "Make sure the Chamber is ready."

There was no reason to waste anyone's time in Division . . . at Hohenschönhausen, he would take care of these interrogations personally.

19

Christianshavn
April 2014

It had been a long time since Ravn had been to Café Wilders. He enjoyed going there, but for some reason or another, whenever he went out, he ended up at The Sea Otter.

They took a seat against the far wall, right under the eye-catching oil painting of a naked woman seated on the floor, surrounded by a green sea of empty beer bottles. Louise ordered a glass of Sancerre, and Ravn ordered a Jacobsen Pilsner and a bowl of water for Møffe.

"What's your dog's name?" Louise asked.

"Møffe."

"It suits him," she said. Her smile was nervous, even awkward.

"Could the police provide you with any more information about your brother?"

"Not much," she said, taking a moment to sip her glass of wine. "I'm not sure where to start."

"Try from the beginning," Ravn said calmly.

"Okay, thanks," Louise said. She took a deep breath before continuing. "So, as I said, I plucked up my courage to go back to the police. I know you must think that sounds silly . . . not particularly courageous, but if you've never had to go to the police station before and talk to them about something so . . . painful—"

"Which station did you go to? Station City? On Halmtorvet?"

She nodded. "Not a nice place."

"Yup, that's where I used to work, and no, it's not a nice place. What division did they refer you to?"

"Division? Er . . . I spoke with two officers in Reception. The first guy was in uniform, and he called in another guy, his superior, I think. The second officer was in plainclothes, Criminal Assistant Troels Petersen. Young guy, but terribly formal in his manner . . ."

Ravn shook his head. "Never heard of him. What could he tell you?"

"Enough to confirm that Mogens did indeed commit fraud."

"Any technical evidence? Leads they can follow?"

"Petersen didn't mention anything of the kind, but the police have witness statements from Mogens's colleagues. And my brother disappeared immediately after the money was stolen from his boss's safe. Forty-five thousand three hundred kroner in cash, to be exact." She took another sip of wine. "Who would throw away their whole life for a measly forty-five k?"

"More people than you would think," Ravn said. "I've seen folks commit horrible crimes for much less."

"But Mogens isn't like that," Louise said unhappily.

Ravn took a swig of his beer. "Well, it happens, unfortunately. You think you know someone, and then suddenly they . . . they surprise you."

"Sounds like you're talking from experience," she said gently.

Ravn didn't reply.

"Petersen said that in cases like this it's only a matter of time before people run out of money and turn themselves in. So, if I'm understanding this correctly, I don't expect the police will instigate a search for Mogens any time soon."

"When was the last time you saw your brother?"

"More than a year ago. At my mother's funeral."

"Are you estranged?"

"Not at all, we . . . I'm not sure why we haven't spent more time together . . ." she trailed off, avoiding his eyes.

Ravn could see she was lying; at the very least, there was something she didn't care to share with him.

"And you have no idea where he could have gone?"

Louise shook her head.

"A friend? A girlfriend, maybe?"

"Not that I know of. I've never seen him with female company."

"Does he own a summer house, or a boat where he might take refuge?"

"Hmm. he's not really the outdoor type."

"So where does he generally hang out?"

"Here, I guess," she pointed to the window, as if she meant here, in the Christianshavn Quarter.

"So, you don't really know much about him, do you?"

"I know enough," she said, clearly offended. "Enough to know that he would never steal from anyone."

Ravn nodded. "Do you know if he had any debts?"

"No, he—"

"Did he gamble?"

"No, he . . . I don't think so. It's—"

"Does he drink?"

"No."

"What about drugs? Coke?"

"Certainly not!" she said, shocked by the suggestion.

"Do you know if anyone could have been putting the squeeze on him? Blackmail?"

"He's never said a word of the kind to me, no—"

"But you don't know for sure, do you, Louise?"

She was staring at him as if he'd rapped her over the fingers, and he instantly regretted that he'd been so hard on her. He'd automatically slipped into his role as a cop. Even interrogated her as if she was a suspect. *What the hell had he been thinking?!*

"Sorry. Bad habit. Would you like another?" he said, pointing at her empty glass.

"No, thank you," she said in a small voice. "I know that Mogens is a decent man. He's a quiet, shy person who has always done what was expected of him at work. He kept to himself. He liked to read. History books, the war, stuff like that. And he loved opera, Wagner. That's all I know," she said, close to tears. "I'm afraid something terrible might have happened to him . . . since he's been missing for such a long time . . ."

Ravn picked up his beer and downed the dregs in one gulp. He'd always had difficulties dealing with women who cried. Mostly because when a woman cried, she could persuade him to do anything . . .

Louise wasn't crying yet, but he heard himself saying: "Well, if it would help, I could probably swing by the Station and talk to some of the guys. See if they've heard anything."

She looked at him with tears in her eyes. "Do you mean that?"

"I can't promise that it will help."

"Thank you so much, Thomas. I would really appreciate it."

Ravn shrugged. "Do you have a number where I could get hold of you?"

Half an hour later, Ravn was back on *Bianca*'s deck. Leaning against the railing, he took Louise's business card out of his pocket and looked at it once more: LOUISE SLOTSHOLM NIELSEN. ARCHITECT, (MMA). LECTURER. DANISH SCHOOL OF DESIGN AND ARCHITECTURE, COPENHAGEN.

Her mobile phone number was printed just below the school's address. Her *work* mobile. *A kick in the balls. A well-deserved one at that*, he mused. Because he wasn't helping her for the sake of her pretty blue eyes; he had his own agenda for paying the boys at Station City a visit.

But there was one thing he had to take care of first.

20

Prenzlauer Berg, East Berlin
17 September 1989

At 6:45 p.m., Lena opened the door and came into the courtyard. She was holding a casserole stretched out in front of her, as if afraid she might stain her lovely cream jumpsuit. Her daughter was trailing at her heels. At the other end of the yard, Hausser was sweeping the tiles in the garbage nook.

Lena tossed her hair and yelled at her daughter to hurry.

"Why should I have to go to Klara just because you're having guests?" the daughter said sulkily.

"Because children can't always take part in the grown-ups' dinner parties," said Lena.

"But I'm not a baby."

"So stop behaving like one. You'll have a good time at Klara's place, and I've made a nice casserole for you both. Now, hurry up, will you!"

Hausser saw them disappear into the front house, where Klara lived. He had taken up his post in the yard so that he could watch Schumann's guests arrive. That very morning, Hausser had been to Kollwitzplatz to meet with Müller to collect the information he'd requested on Midas's dinner guests; all of them were members of elite society in Berlin. Three of the men were already known to the Stasi. The three new suspects were: Ernst Kohler, Head of the Department of Financial Affairs; William Braun, Managing Director of the Building Supervisory Authority; and Colonel Heinz Schröder, head of the Stasi's Division O, which primarily took care of the falsification of documents for the Stasi's moles in the West. Hausser had no idea what the men were planning, but it was obviously urgent.

Lena's high heels clattered over the cobblestones once more as she hurried back over the yard and disappeared into the rear building of the complex without taking any notice of Hausser.

Schumann's guests arrived one after the other over the next thirty minutes. None of the men paid any attention to Hausser, who was still pretending to sweep the yard in the fading light. Once the final guest had arrived, he returned the broom to its place next to the rubbish bins and retired to the caretaker's flat. He made himself comfortable at command centre and poured himself a glass of absinthe. Up in Midas's flat, the guests were already assembled around the dining table, enjoying a bottle of wine.

During the course of dinner, the men spoke freely about the tense state of affairs that were threatening their consortium. Hausser listened intently as Lena kept the wine coming, and two bottles later, the collaborators began discussing the various earning possibilities that had opened up in the neighbouring countries where democratisation measures were imminent; Braun explained that democracy would pave the way for privatisation of the entire building and energy sector, and if you were at the right place at the right time, there was a lot of money to be made.

After dinner, the men smoked cigars and drank cognac while discussing the incendiary political situation in East Germany. Opposition to the SED Party was growing in Leipzig, but it wasn't strong enough to effect regime change. Not yet. Not after the Chinese government's recent demonstration to the world of how critics of the communist regime were silenced with military force in Tiananmen Square. Everyone at the table agreed that Erich Honecker would impose the same measures, if necessary. After the popular uprising of East German citizens in 1953 and mass emigration to the West, the communist authorities were prompted to build the Wall eight years later, so if the opposition began to threaten their power, the men feared the Party's crackdown would become much more draconian. It was only a matter of weeks—perhaps even days—before the regime retaliated to protect their power.

Now Köster took lead of the discussion. The only way to maintain their consortium's growth was to leave the country, he explained. They had to get out of East Germany, he said. They had to flee for their lives.

Hausser almost dropped his glass of absinthe in his lap. He put down his drink and put on his headphones so that he could follow the discussion more closely.

The others agreed with Köster's assessment of their predicament and immediately began to consider a concrete plan to flee the country; East Berlin would be their point of departure.

"Not through a tunnel, hopefully," said Braun, patting his huge belly. "I heard the last people who tried that weren't so lucky. The tunnel collapsed, and they were buried alive."

"No, we don't need to go underground via tunnel, nor fly over the Wall in a hot air balloon," said Köster cheerfully. "We're going to drive straight through border control."

"And how do you propose we do that without a visa?" asked Schumann.

Köster paused for affect. Emptied his glass of cognac and smiled at each of them in turn. "With a little help from our friends at the French embassy. It's not going to be cheap, but we've already put into place the essential ingredients."

"Can you be more specific?" Schumann asked.

"Yes, please," Hausser mumbled to himself, staring at the monitors in anticipation.

"The French cultural attaché, who I know intimately," Köster said, rubbing his index thumb and forefinger together, "has promised to provide us with three diplomatic vehicles."

"I can prepare the necessary travel documents and false diplomatic passports for all of us within a week," said Schröder.

"You said it wouldn't be cheap," said Braun. "How much is this going to cost us, exactly?" Braun asked.

"I think the question is rather: How much is it going to cost us if we don't leave, right now," said Schumann, leaning back in his chair. "I vote in favour of the plan."

The others at the table nodded in agreement.

Half an hour later, Hausser heard the men coming down the stairwell. He pulled aside his curtain in the kitchen to watch them cross over the courtyard and head for the road. *Parasites, that's what they are*, he thought. *Men who enrich themselves at the expense of others. And they had to be terminated.*

The evening had exceeded all his expectations; treason and desertion from the Federal Republic was far better than trifling cases of corruption and fraud, cases that were bound to go through legal channels that could ultimately result in an acquittal. No, desertion was something final. And thanks to the West, it was an international matter that disclosed the identity of spies, enemies of the State.

He emptied his glass of absinthe and closed his eyes. His head was spinning, and he felt drunk as a lord. *This could be* the *case that saves the nation*, he thought ecstatically. Somewhere in the recesses of his mind he could hear a choir of Young Pioneers singing "The Little Trumpeter"; he could see a military parade on Karl-Marx-Allee held in his honour. He was standing on a balcony, waving to the crowds, Strauss—no, Erich Honecker himself!—was standing to his right. Hausser was hailed as a hero and, accompanied by cheers from the crowd, Honecker put his arms around him and kissed him as a comrade.

Hausser toppled off the chair and hit the floor, where he remained in front of the monitors, intoxicated with joy and absinthe.

21

Christianshavn
April 2014

Ravn woke up to the sound of laughter from Eduardo's ketch. He'd heard his friend come home with his latest conquest the night before. He knew Eduardo's routine well: First, there was music and wine on the deck; then, after a joint or two and much laughter, you could hear them making love for the better part of the night; the next morning, the conquered girl would get a coffee and a loving smack on the butt as she left his boat. Ravn had long since given up trying to put a number to Eduardo's conquests.

Ravn got out of bed and went to take a leak. Through the porthole, he could see Eduardo standing on the deck of his ketch, dressed in boxer shorts only, as he waved goodbye to the blonde from last night. Eduardo blew her kisses as she unlocked her bicycle where she had left it on the quay. Then he disappeared below deck once more.

Ravn pumped water into his toilet and was heading back to bed when he caught sight of Møffe on the floor, staring at him reproachfully. Ravn sighed; he knew that if he didn't take the dog for a walk now, Møffe would find a place on board to do his business.

"I'm just going to find myself a pair of trousers, if that's okay with you," he said, meeting Møffe's disgruntled gaze.

Ravn strolled down Overgaden Oven Vandet with Møffe. The sun stood high in the sky, and despite the biting cold, people were sitting along the embankment, enjoying their morning coffees and the hint of spring in the air. Further down the road, on the corner of Mikkel Vibes Gade, Victoria's vintage Volvo station wagon, a wine-red PV 544, was parked at the kerb in front of her second-hand bookstore. Victoria was unloading a case of books from the rear hatch.

"Can I give you a hand," Ravn yelled as he walked towards her.

Victoria half-turned and smiled when she saw him. "Yes, thanks. Would be great if you could take the last one," she said, pointing at the cardboard box in the back.

Ravn picked up the box and followed Victoria into the shop. They deposited the boxes on the counter next to the others. "Been to the flea market?" he asked.

"Nope, closing-down sale," Victoria said. "It's a tough branch to be in, my friend, but sometimes, one man's death is another man's poetry collection," she added, picking up a copy of Michael Strunge's *Future Memories*. "And some things are just too good to be sold." She blew the dust off the cover and placed Strunge's collection on her desk.

"Did you bring my adapter with you?" she asked. "I didn't think you'd disappear with it."

"I'd like to borrow it for a little longer, if that's all right."

Victoria started unpacking the boxes. "Fine by me. As long as you remember the return address—and pop in at Lagkagehuset for cinnamon rolls on your way over."

Ravn fished the brown paper bag from Lagkagehuset out of the front pocket of his hoodie and dumped it on the counter between them. Victoria's face lit up at the sight, and she ripped open the bag immediately. "On second thoughts, just keep it. How about a cup of coffee, Ravn?"

"No, thanks, I'm good."

"I'm surprised to see you so soon. At this rate, you'll be spending more of your time with books than beers at The Sea Otter."

"Possibly," Ravn said, his eyes fixed on the box of books in front of him.

"If you're thinking of starting to read, I can recommend either Wittgenstein or Kant," she said, tapping the pile of books in front of her. "But I've also got copies of *The Phantom* and *Lucky Luke* in the Kid's Lit section over there," she said, pointing to the opposite corner of the store.

"Thanks, I'll pass. I'm here about the phone, you know, the one—"

"—yeah, the one you're trying to crack. What about it? Does it belong to Eva?"

"Yes, apparently it does," he said, burying his hands in the pockets of his coat.

Victoria stopped hauling books out of the box and looked at him quizzically. "Apparently? What do you mean? Either it belongs to her or it doesn't . . ."

He felt as if Victoria could see right through him.

"Why don't you just deliver it to her old office?" she asked.

He nodded, keeping his eyes on the books. "Yeah, that's probably what I'll end up doing."

"Sure you don't want that coffee after all?"

He shook his head and picked up two of the books from the pile on the counter. The first was on yoga, the second a coaching manual. *Cognitive Coaching*, he read on the cover. "Eva loved these kinds of books," he said absently. "Our shelves were bulging with self-help literature. She used to buy quite a lot of them from you, didn't she?"

Victoria nodded.

"Did you guys talk about such stuff when she was here?"

"What stuff?"

"You know, self-improvement, personal stuff . . ."

"We talked about all kinds of 'stuff' now that you're asking."

"So, she confided in you?"

"No, I wouldn't say that."

"Not at all?"

Victoria was staring at him again. "When did you start working for the police again?"

"What do you mean?"

"Why are you interrogating me?"

"For heaven's sake, Victoria, just because I'm asking you a few questions . . ."

"No, not just because of that. First you come in with that mobile phone. Then you start asking all these questions about Eva. What the hell is going on, Ravn?"

He took a deep breath. Then he told her about the text messages. He told her he'd tried to find out the identity of the person messaging via the telephone directory. And his vain attempt at the charity shop.

Victoria put the empty cardboard box onto the floor. "I told you it was a bad idea to snoop in other people's business; nothing good ever comes of it."

"You make it sound as if this is *my* fault. If Eva hadn't messed around with someone, none of this would have happened."

Victoria took a seat on the edge of the counter. Smoothed down her tweeds and fished her Peterøes from her waistcoat pocket. "Ravn, Eva loved you. How can you doubt that?"

"How can I not?" he said in surprise.

"Just because you found some messages on her phone?"

"Yes, for fuck's sake—it's clear as day she'd been seeing someone else!" He was acutely aware that he was treading on dangerous ground.

"You can't know that for sure. If you don't have her replies to the text messages, you have no idea how far it went. "Either way, Eva's love for you was real. Whereas what you're doing right now is"—she paused to light her cigarette—"it's disrespectful."

"Perhaps," Ravn said, pulling up a chair. He slumped into it and ran his fingers through his hair.

"Unless the moron had something to do with her death," Victoria observed. "But something tells me you've already deleted that possibility from the equation."

"ANYTHING is possible, Victoria! I've even considered going to Station City. I could have a word with the investigator on her case and submit the phone as evidence."

"So you can find out who this guy is?"

"Exactly. So that bastard can get the kick in his arse he deserves."

Victoria stubbed out her cigarette in the ashtray so ferociously that sparks were sent flying. "You're behaving like a complete idiot, Ravn! Are you telling me that just because of some kind of macho jealousy bullshit you're going to tarnish Eva's memory?!"

"What the hell are you talking about?"

"I know how much damage gossip can do. Believe me."

Even though he knew nothing about Victoria's past, he could tell that she was speaking from bitter experience. To him, she'd always been nothing but a dear friend with a heart of gold under her somewhat eccentric exterior. But he knew that others often made harsh judgements about her, perhaps because of her masculine clothing and her direct—even confrontational—style of communicating her opinions. "You're mistaken, Victoria. That is the last thing I want."

"So what's your problem? Can't you see that you're destroying everything around you? Eva was the most amazing person I have ever met. And you ought to be grateful that she wanted anything to do with you. Why can't you just remember her for the wonderful person that she was?"

He jumped to his feet, sending the office chair shooting backwards till it hit the wall behind him with a crash. "But that's just it! I don't feel like I know who she was anymore! For two years I've been mourning a woman I loved unconditionally, someone I trusted completely. And for what? Only to find out that she cheated on me?"

"You need to move on, Ravn. You seriously need to move on."

"There is nothing I would rather do. But now everything is starting all over again. Her death . . ." he zipped up his coat violently and made to leave.

Victoria looked at him with concern and shook her head. "This is not the way to go about it, Ravn."

"I'll only know that once I've found him. And knocked him to the ground."

22

A black Lada pulled into the parking lot outside a tall concrete block in Berlin Pankow. Moments later, Strauss, Hausser, and Müller tumbled out of the car, immediately followed by three strawberry blondes. The German Schlager music blaring from Strauss's car radio reverberated between the buildings. Strauss was drunk as a sailor on shore leave, but he had still managed to drive them all the way from the restaurant in downtown East Berlin to the suburb of Pankow—with one hand on the wheel, the other fondling the plump girl called Helga in the passenger seat next to him. She lived in one of the flats in the concrete block in front of them, and Strauss was paying her rent. When he slammed the car door behind her, Helga dropped the bottle of vodka she was carrying, and it shattered to pieces. "Helga, *Liebchen,* you're such a klutz," said Strauss.

"Never mind, teddy bear, we have plenty more upstairs," Helga said, starting to giggle.

Laughing raucously, the drunken party weaved up the path in a chain, holding onto one another's coattails till they reached the concrete block. Hausser was in the lead, but when he got to the front door, he doubled over and wretched into the nearest bush; it wasn't so much the alcohol as the fatty restaurant food that made him sick; solid food generally didn't agree with him.

"Can't you hold your drink, Hausser?" Strauss smacked him on the bottom so hard Hausser almost fell forwards into the bush.

Hausser regained his balance and wiped his mouth with the back of his sleeve. "I think it's time I went home."

"Home? Home to what? You should be grateful you don't have a family to take care of. Enjoy your freedom—it's you we're celebrating tonight, after all!"

"I meant home . . . to my post."

"Christoph Schumann is with Braun, who is currently under surveillance; those two aren't going anywhere."

Strauss helped Hausser up the step and bundled him inside where the others were waiting.

Helga lived on the nineteenth floor. "Just like my age," she'd joked as they rode up in the elevator together. But Hausser reckoned she and her girlfriends were probably in their late twenties. As soon as they arrived in Helga's messy flat, which reeked of cabbage and cigarette smoke, the girls went about lighting candles and organising drinks for everyone. He accepted a drink and sat down heavily on the sofa, which was the only furnishing in the living room, apart from two upturned white plastic milk crates with pillows on top. Once Strauss had been served with a drink, he joined him on the sofa. Helga put on a record, and soon Slade's "Run Runaway" livened up the party. The girls wanted to dance but only managed to get Müller on the dancefloor.

Strauss raised a toast and clinked his glass. Hausser sipped his cheap vodka in silence for a moment before speaking his mind. "Why aren't we watching the other men in Schumann's group?"

"I'm working on it. But with all these budding political movements that we're expected to take care of, the entire Service is strapped; even our resources are limited," Strauss said, leaning a little closer to Hausser's ear. "So I'm thinking it would be best if we make a move on Schumann's group now."

"What do you mean, exactly?"

"We should arrest the whole posse. Their escape plans alone are enough to get them fired and thrown in jail for a long time."

"If all I wanted was to remove them from their positions, I would have intervened ages ago. But what they are planning is no less than treason,

Strauss. And their crimes implicate influential people in the West. We can win big on this case."

"Or lose everything if we fail, Hausser."

"But we won't."

Strauss was not convinced. "And Colonel Schröder from Division O is a problem. If our superiors find out that we did not act immediately and eliminate the security risk that Schröder creates it could have fatal political consequences for the Party."

"To hell with the politics. The Service ought to have autonomy in this case."

Strauss put a calming hand on his shoulder and lowered his voice. "I agree with you, Hausser. But we are soldiers, and soldiers have to follow orders. Remember that."

Hausser took a sip of vodka. "I want to catch Midas in the act."

"Don't let this become personal, my friend."

"I'm not that stupid, Strauss. But Schumann is a traitor. Just like all the others I caught red-handed. He's just another rodent that needs to be exterminated."

Strauss emptied his glass and started to chuckle. "Can you believe they actually want to flee over the border in diplomatic cars? That takes balls—you've gotta hand it to them."

"Balls that will soon be cut off."

Helga changed records and now the organ music of Procol Harum's "A Whiter Shade of Pale" got Strauss on his feet immediately. Helga smiled. Strauss took her in his arms, and they started to dance close together. Müller was slow dancing with Helga's friend, one hand under her dress and his tongue down her throat. The last strawberry blonde looked put out, and she came over and straddled Hausser's lap.

He stared at the girl in surprise.

"You look like a troll with all that hair on your lip," she said, caressing his moustache. "But I think it's cute."

Hausser jerked his head away. "I'm not interested," he said, trying to shake her off.

The girl clenched her thighs together and remained seated where she was. "Aw, is the troll in a bad mood?" she asked, pouting her lips.

"I've never fucked a whore and I'm not about to start with you," he slurred.

The girl slapped him hard and slipped onto the sofa beside him. "I'm not a whore," she said, crossing her arms over her chest. "Strauss!" she yelled over the music. "Tell your friend that I'm not a whore."

Strauss had his face buried in Helga's hair on the dance floor. "What? No—no, no, of course you're not. You girls are the most talented dancers I have ever seen. The finest troupe in the Republic. We're going to come to your premiere. Just as soon as I've found a place for you to perform," he said. Then he returned his attention to Helga, put his hands on her flushed cheeks, and kissed her greedily.

Hausser turned to face the girl next to him and extended his empty glass.

She reached for the bottle of vodka on the floor and poured for him. Then she filled her own glass to the rim.

"Forgive me," said Hausser. "I was born an arsehole. There's no more to it than that."

The girl shrugged and they clinked glasses. "We all have our roles to play."

"What are you girls going to perform?"

"*Salomé.* You know, the one with John the Baptist, who—"

"—gets his head chopped off, yes, thanks, I know how it ends." Hausser turned to Strauss. "Hey, is that kind of performance even allowed?" Hausser smiled.

"I guess it depends on who will portray John the Baptist," Strauss said. "I've suggested the head on the platter should be Helmut Kohl's."

Everyone laughed out loud.

Hausser smiled again and looked at the girl. "So what's your name?"

"Call me whatever you like," she said, and climbed back onto his lap.

Hausser stroked her thighs and looked at her large breasts straining against her nylon shirt. "You look like a Lena," he said, without meaning it. But when she kissed him and he closed his eyes, he thought it was true. And he thought that victory was nigh. *The victory of the masses.*

23

A few days after the meeting with Victoria, Ravn arranged a meeting with Mikkel at Café Carlton on Halmtorvet. The café was just around the corner from Station City, an ugly slab of concrete that stared hard onto the square behind them. The waiter arrived with their order: a latte for Mikkel and a Carlsberg Special for Ravn.

"I was surprised that you called," said Mikkel in the slow, drawn-out monotone of his thick Jutlandic accent. He stuffed his hands into his pockets and leaned back in his seat. "It's been a long time . . ."

Mikkel was trying to hide it, but Ravn could see that he was hurt.

"I'm sorry I haven't returned your calls. I've had a lot of things going on . . ."

"You have a new job, perhaps?"

Ravn shook his head. "No, it's not that. But I have managed to sell the flat, and I've been clearing it out."

"We miss you over there," Mikkel said, casting his head in the direction of the police headquarters behind them. "Everyone sends their regards."

"Including Brask?"

Mikkel took a sip from his latte. "No, the chief seems pleased to be rid of you. But you should pop in sometime. Don't you miss us at all?"

"Hmm," Ravn mumbled, keeping his eyes on his beer.

Mikkel looked out the window at the Halmtorvet beyond. "God knows how many nights we spent out there shovelling snow."

Ravn nodded. He knew that Mikkel was referring to the nights their unit had spent hassling drug dealers in the Quarter. It was a shitty job that was only done for the sake of appearances—as a rule, in response to some or other local politician making waves in the media about the rise in drug-related criminality in the city.

Mikkel scratched his crew-cut head. "Do you remember how the pushers used to make a run for it the second they saw us coming? Some of those guys could've made the Olympic team," he said with a lopsided smile.

"Yeah, I remember," Ravn mumbled. It was true. He remembered everything they had been through together. The countless arrests of gang members. Pushers roaming the streets of Copenhagen. The mad car chases, as if the Old Town streets were a Formula 1 track. He remembered all the things they had gone through together; they were pals, but he wasn't in the mood to chat about old times. Which was one of the reasons he had asked to meet at the café, rather than at the station. "Have you found out anything about Mogens Slotsholm?"

Mikkel nodded. "Yes, but I had to look long and hard before I found the report; it's not the biggest case in the world. Why are you interested in this case in particular?"

"I'm not, but his sister is worried about him. So I promised to ask if you guys had any news."

"Is she hot?"

"Who?"

"The sister, of course."

"She's nice-looking, yeah, but this has nothing to do with that," Ravn said, taking a sip of beer; he felt like downing it but got a grip on himself. "What can you tell me about Slotsholm?"

Mikkel shrugged. "It's a classic case of the accountant who dips into the till and disappears with the cash."

"And you're sure he was the one who did it?"

"There's no doubt about that. The guy had worked his arse off for them for half a lifetime. One day he's had enough of the place and decides to disappear with their money."

"How did he do it?"

"Olsen Gang style," Mikkel said with a smile. "While everyone else was having lunch, he cleared out the safe while the boss was having a meeting with the secretary in the room next door . . ."

"Didn't you say that everyone was at lunch?"

"Apparently, everyone except the boss and his secretary." Mikkel shrugged, nonchalant. "So, anyway, as I was saying, while the boss and his secretary are having their meeting, the accountant empties the safe right next door," Mikkel added with a chuckle.

"Did he have a key to the safe?"

"Nope, just the code. Right after, he vanished with about forty-five thousand in cash. One of his colleagues saw him leaving the building. No one has seen him since."

"What about the search of his flat? Find anything useful?"

"*Nada.* Close family and neighbours weren't able to offer any useful information either. He's gone. His bank account hasn't been touched; no credit card transactions either since his disappearance.

"So, why so much trouble for such little gain?"

Mikkel shrugged. "Beats me. Maybe he thought there was more money in the safe. The company made large payments in cash to their subcontractors. It appears Lauritzen Enterprises is an old-fashioned business with a lot of Eastern European workers on the payroll."

"Black market labour?"

"Wouldn't know. Ask the tax authorities."

"So the case is being dropped?"

"Until Slotsholm reappears, yes. What does the sister have to say about him?"

"Not much. They weren't close. She said Mogens kept to himself. He read books. Liked Wagner."

"So maybe he's gone to Bayreuth to hear the *Ring* cycle," Mikkel joked.

"The performances are not till the summer."

"Hmm. That's a long time to wait at the box office—even if you're a fan."

"Even for a fan, yes. Thanks for the help, Sherlock."

Mikkel shrugged again. "You're welcome. He's been missing for quite a long time, so if he does reappear, he probably won't be alive. But you don't necessarily need to mention this in so many words to his sister."

"Yes. I've figured that much myself."

Mikkel downed the dregs of his coffee. "I'd better be getting back to the office," he said.

"There's one more thing . . ."

"Yes?" Mikkel was looking at him as if he feared the answer. "What's that, then?"

"Eva's case."

Mikkel sighed. "I was wondering how long it would take you to bring that up. There's nothing new, Thomas. You know how it is. Unless we get a new lead, some evidence pertaining to the burglary comes to light, or a convict in prison squeals, we can't—"

"I know," Ravn said. He fished Eva's phone out of his pocket and put it on the table between them. "I found this when I was clearing out the flat."

"Who does it belong to?"

"It's Eva's work mobile," Ravn said.

His head dropped involuntarily. He had no idea it would be this hard to tell Mikkel about the text messages. To admit that she'd probably cheated on him; relaying the details to his pal felt as if his balls were being cut under the table. When it was over, Mikkel looked at the phone and spun it round. "That's . . . I'm really sorry to hear that, Thomas. You don't deserve that."

"I don't think anyone deserves it," Ravn said with a grimace. He didn't need Mikkel's pity. "I'd really appreciate it if this could remain between the two of us."

"Of course. My lips are sealed—"

"Even though this will now become a part of the investigation."

"What will?" asked Mikkel, confused. "You're not seriously thinking of handing in that phone to the team, are you?"

"I'd like you to find out who wrote those messages."

Mikkel sat in silence, obviously looking for the right words.

"I understand that you're angry, I get that, but . . . we both know that this phone has nothing to do with Eva's murder case. The whole modus operandi regarding the burglary, and the fact that the murder wasn't premeditated but the result of a fatal blow to the back of the head—"

"There's no need for you to recite the details. I am the one who found her, after all."

"I'm sorry, I didn't mean to pour salt in the wound. But you know the facts of the case indicate with a ninety-nine per cent probability that the murderer was a member of the Baltic Mafia that operated in the area at the time—and he would have skipped the country ages ago."

"Even so . . ."

"What I'm trying to tell you is that it makes no sense to turn the investigation down a blind alley, just because *you* want to know who she was sleeping with."

"What investigation? Nothing is being investigated anymore . . . it won't make a difference one way or another."

"Take a moment to think this through, Ravn. Do you really want this information known?"

"No, I don't. Which is why I'm coming to you—my pal, my partner."

"Like every other time you've needed my help?"

Ravn fell silent and looked Mikkel in the eye. "We're talking about a single call to the telephone company, so we can find out who he is. I would have done the same for you, Mikkel. You know that, don't you?"

"For fuck's sake, Ravn, I could lose my job for this," Mikkel said in a lowered voice. "I'm not like you. I'm not prepared to move to a raft on Copenhagen's canal. Don't you get it?"

Ravn smiled. "*Bianca* is not a raft, and I don't live on Christianshavn Canal, not in Copenhagen's."

"Well, excuse me," Mikkel said, unable to hold back a smile in return. "You do realise that Brask will personally kick my arse out the door if he finds out about this?"

"If he does, it would be the first time he finds out anything."

"I mean it, Ravn. Besides, I cannot figure why you want to know at all. Why don't you just toss the damn phone and move on?"

"Because it's not up to me. And because I want to bash that bastard's head in."

Mikkel pushed to his feet and stuck the telephone in his pocket. "As congenial as always," he said ironically.

Ravn shrugged and leaned back in his seat.

24

Prenzlauer Berg, East Berlin
1 October 1989

Hausser opened his eyes in the caretaker's bed and stared at the brown water stain on the ceiling. He tried to stretch, but with a grating sound his boots came up against the bloody footboard. It was a Sunday morning, and he had a hangover. He was fully clothed and his back hurt from the awkward position he'd landed in when he fell into bed the night before. On the stairwell, someone was trudging up the stairs. The sound continued all the way to the top. A door opened and closed, then all was still. He knew he had to get out of bed and see who had called on the Schumanns at this ungodly hour.

Hausser reached for the stub in the ashtray by his bedside, lit up, and shuffled into the living room. His head was spinning, and it was hard to focus on the monitor depicting Schumann's lounge, but he could identify Braun as the early morning caller. The visit was significant; the team from the night before would have informed Hausser if a meeting had been scheduled over the phones they were tapping. This meant that either their surveillance had failed, or this was a spontaneous meeting.

"I'm glad you could come," Schumann said.

Hausser made a mental note to give Müller an earful and tell him to put a man on Braun twenty-four seven. *They couldn't afford to make mistakes at such a critical juncture of the surveillance!*

Lena and the daughter came into the lounge. Braun gave them a hug in turn and asked the girl how her gymnastics was going.

"Fine, thank you," said the girl.

"She's much too modest," said Lena, stroking her daughter's hair. "She's at the top of her class."

The girl blushed and dropped her gaze. Then she retreated into her room.

"Could you fix us all a drink, *Liebling*?" Schumann said, but Lena was already on her way to the bar.

"Thanks, but I think it's a little early for me," said Braun.

"I think you're going to need one in just a moment."

Hausser lit a new cigarette with the old one and turned up the volume.

"That sounds a little dramatic," said Braun.

The two men sat down on the bar stools while Lena fixed them drinks behind the counter.

"These are difficult times, and difficult decisions need to be made," said Schumann.

"I think we've already made the hardest one. I mean, deciding to flee . . ." Braun began, distracted by the glass of whiskey that Lena was pouring for him.

"The situation is complicated. On the one hand, Honecker and the Party remain firm that the Federal Republic will prevail, and we must assume that they will apply the necessary force to follow through on their words."

Braun nodded. "History has shown that they have the will to do so."

"Exactly," said Schumann. "But, on the other hand, the embassies in Prague and Warsaw have been flooded with our citizens. And even though the Stasi is making every effort to keep democratic movements in line here at home, they continue to grow with every passing day . . ."

"I'm not sure where you're going with this, Christoph."

"I'm saying that the political situation is similar to how things work on the international stock exchange; the fate of the nation has become a question of faith. An instinct for the state of affairs. And making the right choice; I know that when everyone else is selling, you have to buy big . . ." he said, pausing to reach for their glasses of whiskey. "So, when everyone else is making a run for the border, it might be best to stay exactly where you are."

"You . . . you don't want to flee after all?" Braun said, staring at him wide-eyed.

Schumann shook his head. "Between you and me, it has never been my intention to run," he said, handing Braun his glass.

Braun snapped up the glass and took a large gulp. "I must admit that your words surprise me, but I'm also relieved. Personally, I was having a very hard time imagining myself fleeing across the border, masked with a beard and dark sunglasses. I haven't even told Vera about any of this yet. But . . . if we're not going to flee, what is the alternative?"

"That's a good question. The problem is—assuming we made it to the West alive—we'd have to start over from scratch; democracy does have its benefits, but no matter how good our established contacts are, the success of our consortium is not guaranteed, because we would always be in competition with others who have been there longer and know the market better than we do. In contrast, if we were to stay and ride the storm until the communist system collapses, we could engage in various lucrative, as yet unimaginable possibilities that arise in its wake."

"You mean *if* the system collapses."

"Of course, therein lies the risk. But try to imagine, Braun, what would happen if they privatised the entire industry, including the financial sector—we could establish our own bank and finance one building investment after another! Never mind what would happen if Germany were reunited!"

Braun shook his head. "You're dreaming, Christoph; that's never going to happen," he said with a snort of laughter.

"Even so, think it through. Where do you think the capital of a reunited Germany would be?" Schumann said, pointing to the floor with both index fingers. "Right here, in Berlin, of course. Just imagine how many building projects there would be—housing, infrastructure, business complexes—an economic powerhouse would spring at our feet. The industry would be throwing money at us to meet the demand . . . billions of capital from international investors would be at our disposal. These are the possibilities we stand to lose if we vacate our secure positions in the Republic now."

Braun looked at him in silence for a moment. "It seems you've been thinking about this for a long time."

"Day and night," Schumann admitted. "An opportunity like this only comes by *once* in a lifetime. A colleague of mine at the bank joked that at this rate the oligarchs would return to the Soviet Union; I think it might not be as ridiculous as he thinks. And why shouldn't the same be possible here, in Berlin? We could become the latter-day princes of a reunited Prussia. Our flags will fly from every single crane towering over the new capital of the Empire. And this would only be the beginning . . ." he added with a fat smile.

Braun emptied his glass and banged it down onto the bar counter. "What about the others in the consortium?"

"If things turn out the way I predict, they will no longer be our allies but our biggest competitors. And a man like Colonel Schröder could prove to be a dangerous liability at our table if legal proceedings are instituted against us," Schumann said.

"You seem damn sure of yourself," Braun remarked with begrudging admiration.

Schumann avoided Braun's gaze, and for the first time since the beginning of their conversation, he seemed anxious. "To be honest, I think the odds are sixty to forty in our favour. But one thing is absolutely certain: If our country introduces a market economy, our people will be divided into those who secured their power in time, and those who . . ." Schumann trailed off and looked at Braun with a troubled expression. "At first, folks will rejoice in their freedom, until they realise that this is all they will get; those who are left with nothing will be the slaves of a new era in our country. That is not the future I wish for myself and my family. Can we get you another drink?"

Braun nodded with a grateful expression in his eyes. "But . . . but what will we say to our partners?"

"Nothing. We continue helping to plan the escape. But when the day arrives, we don't pitch up. I'm sure they will choose to go ahead with the plan rather than wait for us. Whether they succeed in getting over the border or not is irrelevant; either way, we will be rid of them," Schumann said, raising his glass in a toast.

All three of them clinked glasses, and Braun complimented Lena on the brilliance of her husband, hailing him as a genius with a mastermind for strategy!

Hausser was shocked to his boots. He couldn't believe what he had just witnessed on the monitors before him. More than anything else, he wanted to fetch his service pistol, go upstairs, and put a bullet in Midas's brain. *That bastard was about to ruin everything!* he fumed inwardly. He felt as though Midas had betrayed him, Hausser, the same way he had betrayed his friends—and his country!

The sum of his myriad feelings for Midas crystalised into just *one*: HATE.

25

To the tune of "Unbreak My Heart," Johnson was doing the rounds through the crowd, serving bourbon shots from a tray. There was no way of knowing which one of Johnson's patrons had cast a fiver into the jukebox to choose Toni Braxton's schmaltzy hit for just another rainy Wednesday afternoon at The Sea Otter.

Ravn and Eduardo were seated on barstools at the counter. Eduardo was banging away at the keyboard of his laptop, trying to complete his overdue essay on the macroeconomic challenges facing the African continent.

"Whaddawee celebratin'?" Niels "Bluetooth" yelled from the other end of the bar. Despite the nickname, Niels didn't have a whole lot of teeth left.

"Ravn has settled his debt for *Bianca*, so now he can finally call that sea bucket his own," Johnson replied.

Niels raised his shot glass in a toast. "Well, congratulations on that, skipper. Hey, how about loaning me a couple of hundred, then?"

Ravn winked at him and downed his shot glass with a smile that said it was never gonna happen.

"So, everything is settled?" asked Johnson, sipping his coffee behind the bar. "And you received the money in the bank for the flat?"

"Yup, all sorted. The flat is gone and *Bianca* is mine."

"Is there something left for you to live on?"

"A tidy sum, yes. And I still have my overdraft, so it's fine," he said, nodding at his empty bottle of beer.

Johnson reached into the fridge and plonked another Hof on the counter in front of him. Niels "Bluetooth" flagged him down from the other end of the bar, and Johnson ambled over to collect his order.

Ravn stuck his hand in his pocket, pulled out Louise's business card, and twirled it between his fingers. He had meant to call her for the last couple of days, but he didn't know what to say; the information he had received from Mikkel wasn't anything she didn't already know. He wished there was more he could do. He was putting it off, but all he could do was call her up and admit just that.

Eduardo caught sight of the business card. "What are you playing with?"

"Nothing," said Ravn. He was about to put the card away, but Eduardo snatched it out of his hand. He held it up to the light, and then a grin spread over his face. "Aha. It's her, isn't it? The dame who's been watching you . . ." He read the card. "Ooh la la, Louise Slotsholm Nielsen. Architect."

"Yes. And so what if it is?" Ravn tried to snatch the card back, but Eduardo held it out of his reach, and Ravn decided to let it go. "Very grown-up," he said.

"You guys dating?"

"What are you talking about?! I'm just helping her find her brother. There's no more to it than that."

Johnson returned to their side of the bar. "What's that?" he said, pointing at the card.

"Ravn's new girlfriend. An architect. And hot."

"I barely know her," Ravn said, shaking his head.

"Okay, so if you're not dating, mind if I give her call?" Eduardo said.

This time Ravn was quicker. He ripped the card out of Eduardo's hand and stuffed it back in his pocket. "Don't you have enough to keep you busy?"

Eduardo grinned like a self-satisfied cat and returned his attention to his laptop.

"Is she the sister of that accountant who disappeared?" Johnson asked.

It shouldn't have been surprising that Johnson knew about Louise, but he gave Eduardo a sidelong glance to confirm the source.

"Everybody knows about the case already," Eduardo mumbled, without shifting his gaze from his computer screen.

"Do you know Mogens Slotsholm?" Ravn asked Johnson. "Has he ever been here?"

"Not that I know of," said Johnson. "And it's just as well; you've really got to be a moron if you steal from your employer. Especially if you've been there a long time," Johnson said scornfully. He picked up a dish-cloth and started wiping down the counter.

"Yeah, either that or Robin Hood: stealing money from the capitalists and giving it to the poor. Maybe that was why he did it?" Eduardo said, typing furiously as he spoke.

Johnson gave him a stern look. "Lauritzen Enterprises is a respect-able family-run business."

"Oh, okay. So rather . . . a feudal system led by inbred capitalists, which is even worse. Good for Mogens that he got away in time."

"You've heard of this company?" Ravn asked, looking at Johnson with renewed interest.

Johnson shook his head. "Not from personal experience. But the Lau-ritzen family is an institution for all of us who grew up on Christianshavn Canal," he said solemnly. "For three generations," he added, fixing his gaze on Eduardo, "they helped to renovate half the neighbourhood, and in the process created hundreds of jobs for local folks."

Eduardo snorted. "I'll bet most of their workers are underpaid labour-ers from the Baltic countries. I wrote an article about them a few years ago. Lauritzen has taken a lot of flak from the trade unions; they revile fat cats like him."

"So just because you're not a communist, you deserve to have your name dragged through the mud? Is that what you're trying to say?" John-son leaned both fists on the counter and scowled at Eduardo.

"Hey, take it easy; that's not what I said, *amigo*," Eduardo said with a lopsided smile.

Johnson turned his eyes on Ravn. "Lauritzen had to fire a lot of people after the accountant disappeared with his money. I don't like to gossip, but I did hear rumours about a long line of unpaid bills to subcontractors."

"That's odd," said Ravn. "Considering the report that only forty-five thousand kroner went missing. A firm like Lauritzen's would have a turn-over in the millions, no?"

Johnson shrugged. "As I said, I don't like to gossip. I'm just saying what I heard."

"Yes, we got that. But"—Ravn paused to take a sip of his beer—"something's not right about all this."

"Yeah? What are you thinking?" asked Eduardo.

Ravn helped himself to Eduardo's shot glass, which was still full. Eduardo only made a weak protest, and Ravn downed the bourbon in one gulp.

"What is Mogens's motive?" he asked himself out loud. "Why would he raid the safe?"

"Because he's a nitwit," Johnson replied.

Ravn shook his head. "That might explain his character, not his motive. Why did he choose to run with the money?"

"Maybe he was being blackmailed?" Eduardo suggested.

"Threat and consequence have to be proportional. And the amount is too small to justify blackmail," Ravn said.

"Maybe he dreamt of living a different kind of life—like everyone else living in Denmark," Johnson remarked, nodding in the direction of the crowd in his pub.

"Hmm. If he wanted to get away from Denmark and start over some other place, one would expect the bounty to be bigger. Mogens was not stupid. He must have known how much money there was in the safe. And, in light of your information regarding the unpaid bills to subcontractors, this can only mean—"

"It's not because I like to gossip," Johnson said, interrupting.

"—that Mogens got away with a lot more money than they reported to the police."

"Tax fraud? Hiring off the books?" Eduardo said, looking up from his laptop. "That's a damn good story—"

"Which you're not going to write," said Ravn.

"You know you have a lifelong ban against using anything that you heard in here," Johnson reminded Eduardo.

"Of course," said Eduardo. "What? Why are you guys looking at me like that?"

At that moment, a blonde girl walked into the pub. She walked directly up to him and threw her arms around his neck. Eduardo started in surprise.

"So this is where you're hiding," the blonde said.

She looked very much like the blonde Ravn had seen leave Eduardo's ketch a few days before, but he couldn't be sure, and Eduardo didn't introduce her. Instead, he packed his computer away in a hurry.

"So, shall we find somewhere nice for dinner? Something *romantico?*" Eduardo didn't wait for a reply, merely nodded farewell to the bar, put his arm around the girl's waist, and disappeared out the door with her at his side.

"Isn't it the custom to castrate tomcats like him?" said Johnson idly.

Ravn nodded. "The more we get into spring, the greater the number of Eduardo's conquests."

A few hours later, Ravn slipped into the corridor between the billiard room and the toilets. A group of students had taken over the billiard room, and the pub was buzzing. Ravn felt his legs cave under his weight, and he steadied himself with one hand on the cigarette machine.

He took his mobile phone and Louise's card out of his pocket and called her number.

"Louise Slotsholm . . . Hello?"

"*Hej* . . . Hi, it's Thomas. I hope I'm not disturbing you."

There was a moment of silence on the other end of the line and Thomas tried again. This time, with his full name—and he tried not to slur quite so much.

"Hi, Thomas." It almost sounded as if she were smiling. "You sound . . . festive?"

"I've spoken to . . . some of my former colleagues at Station City," he said, concentrating hard to keep his voice even.

"Okay, thanks," she said. "Did they have any news?"

"Er . . . some. I thought we might meet to talk it over."

"Sure. Great. When?"

He checked his watch. "Have you eaten?"

26

As if a wall of water, the rain was pelting down onto Schönhauser Allee. Hausser had taken refuge under the viaduct of the double carriageway. A passing train roared like infernal thunder over his head. At the intersection by Gneistrasse there was a bright yellow telephone box with a long queue of people waiting. Hausser darted over to the box and shoved his way to the front. "Move aside, please, this is an emergency," he said.

A muscular man in a black leather jacket put a hand on Hausser's shoulder and kept him back. "Same goes for the rest of us in this shitty country—get to the back of the line, pal!"

Hausser flipped out his ID and held it under the man's nose.

When he saw the Stasi insignia on the badge, the man stumbled back.

"Get lost, arsehole!" Hausser snarled, and the queue scattered into the pouring rain.

Hausser yanked open the door of the telephone box. The pimple-faced boy holding the receiver was about to complain, but he too held his tongue when he saw the badge that Hausser held up to his face. "Get out!" Hausser snapped.

The boy put down the receiver immediately and did as he was told.

Hausser fished some coins out of his jacket pocket and dialled the number. "We have to meet," he said breathlessly into the receiver.

"Hausser?" Strauss's voice said on the other end of the line. "Is something wrong?"

"There's been a development in the case."

"Nothing serious, I hope, because I have good news for you . . ."

"Is that so? Can we meet—tonight, the usual place on Schulze-Boysen-Strasse?"

"That's not going to work. Meet me at Ostbahnhof, Lange Strasse 11.

"Why all the way out there?"

"Just be there at eight o'clock," Strauss said, and hung up.

Hausser stared at the receiver in his hand. He had to tell Strauss about Schumann's double-crossing plans. Strauss needed to know that Midas did not plan to escape after all. This was a disaster. He'd been so sure about this case. So sure that Christoph, alias Midas, could be caught in the act; Midas alias the Prussian Prince. Hausser fumed with rage and indignation.

Hausser couldn't face going back to the caretaker's flat on Greifenhagener; he couldn't stand the thought of watching Midas's perfect life that unfolded on the monitors before him. Midas and his beautiful, adoring wife, Midas and his equally decorative and ambitious daughter. And he couldn't bear to listen to that man's nasal voice, his girlish chuckle, so he decided to board the S-Bahn instead, let himself be carried around in the grey city of East Berlin for an afternoon.

When Hausser got off the train at Ostbahnhof Allee, the rain was still coming down in sheets. And just before eight o'clock, he found himself in front of a large factory warehouse on Lange Strasse. He searched the throng of young people who were milling about outside, looking for Strauss without success. When the gates opened, he moved along with the crowd. A rudimentary poster nailed to the wall caught his eye as he entered: The Anemones were performing *Salomé* tonight. He felt a hand on his shoulder and spun on his heel.

"Good evening, Hausser," Strauss said with a smile. "Shall we go inside?"

"Are you taking the piss?"

"Not at all, comrade," Strauss said. "As representatives of the Ministry of State Security, it is imperative that we are seen *everywhere*," he chuckled. "I personally assigned myself to the job."

Strauss ushered Hausser through the doors and into the hall where the other spectators were finding their seats on folding chairs. A makeshift stage was erected at the far end of the hall; powerful spotlights in the ceiling and a large sheet of pink material served as a backdrop.

"We need to talk," said Hausser. They took their seats in two free chairs in the back row.

A young man with a mohawk handed them one of the spirit-duplicated pamphlets he was distributing in the hall. "Remember the demo on Thursday," he said. "It's important we stand together and resist the power of the State."

Strauss laid the pamphlet on the empty chair next to him and leaned over to Hausser. "The Midas Operation has attracted positive attention in Haus Number One; many words of praise for our division have been spoken—not least of all praise for your good self."

"What does this mean for us?"

"It means that the people at the top are following developments in this case with interest. In the current political climate, they are eager to display a head in the pillory for the public. Management is delighted that the case also implicates officials in the French embassy. They can hardly wait to nab the deserters in diplomatic vehicles at the border!" Strauss said. He took out a packet of brandy liqueur chocolates and ripped it open. "You said on the phone you had news of a development? What does Christoph Schumann have to say?"

"He . . . about Schumann . . ." Hausser trailed off. He couldn't bring himself to say that they would never catch the bastard red-handed. That if the morons in this hall would have their way, Midas would be the victorious one.

Electronic music boomed out of the loudspeakers, and the dancers came out on stage, wearing nothing but tiny G-strings. In their hands, each of them held a transparent veil, which they twirled around their naked bodies.

Strauss turned his full attention to the dancers. "Helga did the choreography. Look how beautiful she is," he said, pointing her out. Despite her small, rotund figure, Hausser had to admit that she was surprisingly graceful. The electronic music droned in his head, and watching the dancers twirl made him feel dizzy. "I . . . I need to get going," he said.

"What was so important?" Strauss asked.

"It's nothing . . . I managed to sort it out."

"So everything is going to plan?"

"Things couldn't be better."

A naked woman with a bush of pubic hair stepped on stage. She was holding a silver platter with a lid. When she reached the edge of the stage and lifted it, the audience cheered and clapped; on the platter lay a pig's head wearing a pair of thick glasses that were identical to the ones that Erich Honecker always wore. Even Strauss couldn't help smiling. He turned towards Hausser to comment, but the seat was already empty.

Hausser walked through the rain, oblivious to the fact that he was soaked to the bone. Everything he had known, everything he had believed seemed to be washed away. It was here, walking in the rain, that he realised why Midas's words had hit him so hard. It was not just envy and hate, although he could not deny that he felt both. It was something more fundamental. For the first time, he became aware of his own fear that Midas's premonition would come true; the manifestation of the capitalist nightmare the Stasi had forewarned from their first communal potty training in the Service. If Midas was right, he, Colonel Erhardt Hausser, would be stripped of all his privileges and powers, not just his position in the Service. Not to mention the pride that only a soldier knew. In its stead, he risked a prison sentence. To save their own skin, his inferiors in Division Z would sell him out to the new judges on the bench. And when they finally let him out of prison, he would end up like one of the aliases he had adopted in the Service: a supervisor, a newspaper salesman, a rubbish man, perhaps even jobless—like the lazy sons of bitches in the West.

Because, without the Stasi, without DZ and his rank as colonel, he was nothing. His work was all he knew how to do; his métier. When Hausser stopped walking, he realised that he was in the middle of Alexanderplatz. The iconic Television Tower stared at him, as if the eagle eye of the State, and he stared back with reverence.

It was time to step up to the plate; he was a son of the nation; he could not let down his country now. As he walked over the square, a plan started to take form in his mind. A bizarre plan. Desperate and absurd. But there was no other way. Irrespective of where the rest of the nation was headed.

27

Ravn was waiting for Louise on a sofa in the restaurant section of the Café Oven Vandet. She was late, and he had taking advantage of the waiting time to polish off the bread and drink half a jug of water in an attempt to sober up. He'd gone all out in celebrating his full ownership of *Bianca*, and he'd drunk more than he'd intended.

He saw Louise come through the door. She was wearing a large, expensive-looking scarf that fluttered around her face in the wind. Ravn waved her over, and she made her way through the restaurant the moment she saw him.

She arrived at his table with a hint of perfume and fresh air. Ravn offered her a seat on the sofa, but she merely greeted him briefly and sat down in the chair opposite him. "I'm glad you could make it on such short notice," he said.

"I'm sorry to have kept you waiting, but I had to wrap up some things before I could leave."

"You work late, then," he said.

Louise nodded. "I have a lecture to prepare, and I'm not quite done with it yet."

A waiter arrived to take their order.

"I can highly recommend the lamb," said Ravn.

Louise shook her head. "I already ate," she said. "So I think I'll just have a soda water, but feel free to order whatever—"

"Not even a glass of wine?" Ravn said, looking at her in surprise.

She politely declined. Ravn ordered a Ramlösa for Louise, a beer for himself, and returned the menu to the waiter.

"I'm eager to hear what news you have of my brother's case," said Louise.

"It's not much," Ravn said, leaning back in the sofa. "I have spoken to a former colleague who had read the police report. All evidence indicates it was your brother who planned and executed the theft of his employer."

"Yes, I know. But I thought there was something new," she said.

"They are doing their best, but—"

The waiter arrived and put their drinks on the table. Ravn poured the Ramlösa for Louise, who simply stared at the bubbles rising to the surface. "So they still don't know anything?"

"I'm afraid that's how it goes in cases like these. You have to be patient."

"Well, thank you for trying." She smiled and nodded farewell as she pushed to her feet.

"Wait a moment, please," said Ravn.

She sat down again. "What is it?"

"It is my opinion that your brother is someplace in Europe, starting over."

"But he doesn't have any money, and it's been months since he disappeared . . ."

"I think he took quite a bit more money than was reported missing to the police. In fact, it might have been a substantial amount of money."

Louise sipped her soda water deep in thought. "Can you explain that in more detail, please?"

Ravn gave her an outline of what he had heard at The Sea Otter, albeit without mentioning the location, who he had been with, or the number of drinks he'd consumed to arrive at his conclusions. Instead, he told her he'd received confirmation from a reliable source that the firm possibly made use of black-market labour, and that after Mogens's disappearance, Lauritzen Enterprises was in financial difficulty. "All of which indicates that Mogens must have stolen a large sum of money."

Louise stared down at the table. "But how can I know this for sure?"

Ravn picked up his glass and took a sip of his beer. "You can't. Unless you contact the firm and speak to the director. That's what I would do."

"You would?" Louise's face lit up in a smile. "That would be a great relief."

"You misunderstand me. I mean: If I were in your situation, I would contact the firm directly."

"Oh, I see," she said, wringing a white serviette from the table in her hands. "But I would die of embarrassment if I had to face someone who Mogens had stolen from."

"I know. I didn't say it would be pleasant."

"But why would the director talk to me? If you are right, I'm sure he wouldn't want it made public that it was black-market money that had been stolen."

"Yes. Unless he saw a chance of getting some of the money back," Ravn said with a smile. "You are just interested in finding out what happened to your brother, and he could get the money back . . . you could tell him so."

"But how can I promise him that?"

"You can't. But that's not the point. The point is to get him to believe that you would try to get the money back, so that he would admit how much money was actually stolen. In that way, you could at least find out if Mogens has enough money to get by." Ravn could see on her face that he had managed to surprise her in a positive way after all.

"It seems you've given this a lot of thought," she said with a tentative smile. "I don't know if I dare to follow your plan, but I should probably call up the firm tomorrow and make an appointment."

"No, I wouldn't do that. It's best to arrive unannounced; never underestimate the element of surprise."

She let go of the serviette. "Would you go with me?"

"It's not my case, Louise."

"It would mean the world to me." She reached out and put her hand over his on the table.

Her gesture surprised him. Not in a bad way. "You're hard to say no to," he said.

"Really, you mean it?"

He liked her smile. And the fact that she smiled because she already knew that he would say yes. It was a smile that reminded him of good times, and a smile that another woman had given him in what felt like ages ago.

"Sorry?" he said when he felt her squeeze his hand, realising that she had asked him a question.

"I asked if you'd like to share a dessert. They make a fantastic crème brulée here."

"Oh, you know it," he said, returning her smile.

28

Prenzlauer Berg, East Berlin
2 October 1989

Hausser stubbed out his cigarette in the kitchen sink and blew out the smoke. He took a swig from the half-full bottle of vodka on the table, gargled it, and then swallowed, letting the spirits burn all the way down to his stomach, waking up his body. He took a medium-sized knife out of the drawer and spat on the blade. Then he slowly started to whet the knife against the edge of the steel sink. The sound cut to the marrow, but Hausser was oblivious, his mind fixed on the task ahead of him.

Hausser ascended the stairwell soundlessly. When he reached the Schumanns' flat on the top floor, he listened by the door for a moment. Then he proceeded to pick the lock. Moments later, he was standing in their entrance, inhaling the smell of Lena's perfume. He took the knife out of the pocket of his blue overalls and continued calmly into the living room. He looked around. It was always strange being in the rooms he'd had under surveillance on monitors for an extended period of time, as if he were on a film set. He walked through the living room and continued to the bedroom. The door was closed. He gave it a shove, and the door opened slowly with a creak on its hinges. The empty bed was unmade. On the floor, Lena's nightdress and panties. For a moment, he imagined he could hear the shower running in the bathroom on the other side of the corridor, and that Lena was standing naked under the running water.

Hausser turned round and focussed his attention on the socket that was placed on the doorframe. He pried the front cover off with the knife.

With two fingers, he carefully pulled on the wire attached to the microphone and brought it out of the wall.

A few minutes later, he returned to the caretaker's flat and returned the knife to the drawer. The first part of his plan had been executed. He stuck his hand into his pocket, pulled out Lena's panties, and buried his face in the silky-soft material.

Christoph let himself into the Schumanns' flat at exactly 3:45 p.m. On Wednesdays, he was the first one in the family to get home; Lena worked late at Madeleine, and the daughter was at gymnastics practice as usual. Hausser was at his post in front of the monitors. He watched Christoph put down his attaché and loosen his tie in the entrance.

Hausser knew from countless hours of surveillance that Schumann would now head straight for the living room, fix himself a whiskey at the bar, and take the glass into the bedroom. He would sit down on the end of the bed and down the glass in one gulp. Then he would flop over backwards and doze until his wife woke him one and a half hours later, when she came home from work.

True to form, Hausser watched Schumann sit down heavily on the bed and down his whiskey. He was staring straight ahead of him idly, but then he noticed the open socket. The wiring, and the small microphone dangling. He frowned in confusion. Put down the glass on the mattress, stood up, and went to take a closer look at the socket. He pulled the wiring carefully, then yanked it out of the doorframe. There was a screech of static on Hausser's loudspeakers, then silence. Schumann's hand flew to his mouth. He looked round the bedroom with an expression of fear and horror. Hausser leaned back in his chair in satisfaction, enjoying the muted recording. He smiled. This was like watching Buster Keaton on cocaine.

Exactly one and a half hours later, Hausser watched Lena enter the flat with her shopping. As if turned to stone, she dropped her net shopping bag and stared at the scene of destruction before her in the entrance: the doorframes to the bedroom, kitchen, and living room were splintered and broken, the wallpaper next to the door was torn and large strips of it were strewn on the floor. "Christoph!!" she screamed, and ran into the living room.

* * *

Hausser followed her movements on the next screen. In the living room, the destruction was even worse: the bar was shattered and split into a pile of tinder in the corner; the bookshelves were toppled over, their books and records all over the floor; the doorframes were hacked apart, the sockets and wires exposed. In the midst of the chaos, she saw Christoph himself, sweating profusely with a crowbar in his right hand.

"What the . . . have you lost your mind?" Lena said.

Christoph put a finger to his lips, signalling that she should be quiet. But Lena ignored the gesture. "You . . . you have destroyed our home?! Why?"

Christoph threw down the crowbar and took hold of her arm. Then he frogmarched her out of the living room and made for the back stairwell. Hausser could not follow their movements anymore because Christoph had found and destroyed the cameras in the bedroom, the kitchen, and study.

Hausser was impressed by his diligence and determination, and he was pretty sure that Schumann would find the remaining cameras and microphones he'd had his men plant in the flat—other than the ones set up in the rear stairwell. He knew from years of experience that for some reason folks felt safe there, as if the back entrance were a sacred refuge on neutral ground. Nothing could be further from the truth. Hausser shook his head and smiled, listening to Schumann and Lena via the camera equipment and bugs that were installed right above their heads.

"We're being watched," Schumann said in a hoarse whisper, holding a pair of the microphones he had found up to Lena's face.

Lena stared at the bugs in horror. "What are you saying? Watched? By whom?"

"Who do you think? By the Stasi, of course!"

Lena's jaw dropped as realisation dawned. A look of utter defeat came over her face. "What . . . what are we going to do?"

"We're going to find each and every bug and camera in our home and get rid of them."

"Cameras? Do you think they have filmed us?" Lena started to cry.

Schumann took her by the shoulders. "Not now, Lena my girl. I need you to be strong. This is serious. Things could get really bad for us if we don't hold it together."

"But . . . what's going to happen now? Will they come for us? Do they know about . . . about the escape?"

Schumann hushed her. Leaned over the railing and spied down the stairwell to make sure they were alone. "That's a good question. We have no idea how long we've been under their surveillance."

"But maybe they heard us talking to Braun. That we've decided not to run after all. Could that be our saving grace?"

"No. On the contrary. We could be tried for treason on the grounds of that conversation alone."

"But who could have betrayed us? You said Schröder was our safeguard."

"That's what I thought too, *Liebling*."

Lena dried her eyes carefully so her mascara would not smudge. "Do you think Schröder has betrayed us? He's a member of the Stasi, after all."

Schumann shook his head. "No, Schröder is the one who has the most to lose. Braun and I are financing him; he'd have nothing if it weren't for us. Besides, we have leverage over him. Schröder likes to whip Pankow boys in his free time. I've seen the pictures."

Lena started to cry again. "Oh . . . that's . . . disgusting," she said. "I can't believe that strangers have been spying on us. Watching us whilst we, we . . . and our *daughter* . . ."

Apparently, Lena could not bring herself to finish her sentence, but then she got angry. "Why did you invite them into our home, Christoph?" she yelled, and started beating his chest so hard he stumbled backwards.

"What do you mean?"

"You could have held your meetings somewhere else. Why here? In *my* home?!"

"But . . . how could I know that they—"

"So make a plan! *Do* something!"

"I'm trying, Lena. I'm doing the best I can."

Lena took her eyes off her husband and leaned against the wall behind her. "Bloody . . . Do you think it could have been Klara who reported us to the Stasi? I think she's stealing from us. And I know she wears my clothing when we're not home; I always find my stuff on the wrong hangers when she's been in to clean."

"I'm pretty sure it wasn't Klara. But someone here in the building is watching us, that much is clear. The wires lead out onto the landing. To the common electrical lines in the apartment block."

"Do you think they will come and arrest us?"

"I don't know, Lena. But I don't think so. There have been other investigations into my affairs before, but I always had managed to stop them. I know people. Important people in positions of power. People who are dependent on me and my contacts in the State Bank. My guess is that, considering all the other resistance movements that are gathering force, the Stasi has more than enough to do at the moment. I think we have a reasonable chance to ride out the storm. Either we turn on the others, inform on them, or we buy our way out."

"What about Braun? Should we tell him about this?"

Schumann shook his head. "There's no reason for him to know."

Hausser was sweeping the yard, and the sound of the broom's stiff bristles reverberated in the dark. There was a bug behind the radiator in the Schumanns' kitchen, and after he had heard Lena tell Midas to throw the damn surveillance equipment in the rubbish downstairs, Hausser had hurried out into the yard with his broom. Before that, Hausser had listened to the conversation around the dinner table. Lena and Christoph lied to their daughter. They said her father had heard a rat in the wall. That this was why he'd torn up the place. But luckily, he'd found the rat and killed it. The story didn't seem to bother the daughter, who was more interested in talking about her gymnastics practice and the upcoming tournament.

Schumann came into the yard. "You're out sweeping late," he said to Hausser. "Can you even see what you're doing?" He threw his rubbish bags in the container in the far corner. Stuffed them down among the others.

"It's fine," said Hausser with a smile. "As long as you watch out for the rats, right?"

Schumann stared at him but made no reply.

"Yeah, I think there aren't any left. But you can never know for sure, right?"

No more than five minutes later, Hausser was back in front of his monitors in the caretaker's flat, sipping at the glass of absinthe in his hand. Midas and his pretty young wife were on the rear stairwell landing.

"It's the caretaker!" whispered Schumann. "I think he's the one who is watching us."

"That awful man? Does he even have the brains to do something like that?"

Midas shrugged in reply.

29

On Greifenhagener Strasse, people were hurrying off to work. Hausser took refuge from the biting cold in the doorway to e Number 9 and lit up a cigarette. Gusts of wind whipped up the leaves and other debris he had just swept together in neat piles. He was waiting for the Schumanns to emerge from the yard, just as he had been doing every morning since Midas had discovered the surveillance equipment in his flat. They had not confronted Hausser since the day he had heard Schumann voice his suspicions about the caretaker; Midas had wondered whether the caretaker was an agent for the Stasi, or just another fucking rat informant. It was as if Midas and Lena were afraid to have their worst fears confirmed.

The door to the yard opened and Hausser saw the Schumanns making their way over.

"Good morning," said Hausser, flicking his cigarette stub onto the pavement.

Lena flat out ignored him and kept walking towards the car on the other side of the road, but Christoph nodded briefly in his direction as he passed.

"Herr Schumann!" Hausser called after him.

Schumann stopped and looked over his shoulder.

"Is the drain working like it should?"

Schumann looked at him in confusion for a moment, then he nodded. "Yes . . . I think so."

"I'd be happy to come up and check on it," said Hausser.

"That won't be necessary, thank you."

"Yes, I mean, your daughter and lovely wife need to be able to have a bath."

Lena stopped in her tracks and turned round slowly. The expression on her face was furious. It seemed she was about to say something, but Schumann put a hand on her arm. He fished the keys to the car out of his pocket. "You can go and wait for me in the car, Lena."

Keeping her dagger-eyes on Hausser, Lena snatched the car keys from her husband's hand, spun on her heel again, and crossed the road with her daughter.

"Did I say something wrong?" asked Hausser, leaning against the wall with a sinister little grin on his face.

Schumann sauntered up to him. "You seem like the kind of guy who knows how to keep an eye on things, Erhardt. May I call you, Erhardt?"

"You can call me anything you like, Herr Schumann, sir."

"Thank you. And you can call me Christoph. There's no need to be so formal. We are neighbours, after all. Am I right in understanding that you keep an eye on things around the apartment block?"

"I'm not sure I know what you mean, Herr Schumann—Christoph. But I am the caretaker, so yes, I guess I do keep an eye on things."

"Where do you come from, exactly, Erhardt?"

"Me? I come from Graupa, a small town just outside Dresden. I'm sure you've never heard of it."

"And how long have you lived in Berlin?"

"Long enough to know that there is a parade on Karl-Marx-Allee in three days," Hausser said with a grin. "Are you going to join the jubilee celebrations? It's wonderful that our Republic has survived for forty years, isn't it?"

Schumann ignored his question. "Where did you work before?"

Hausser rolled his eyes. "Well . . . quite a lot of places, actually. I go where I am needed."

"And how long have you been working as a caretaker?"

"Quite a while."

"Who hired you?"

"The Administration," Hausser said, rubbing his chin. "I get the sense there is something you're not happy with, sir? Have I done something that is not to your satisfaction, Herr Schumann?"

"I know everyone on the Administration Board. Who appointed you as supervisor for our building?"

Hausser laughed. "Ah, so that's how you managed to get the flat on the top floor! You are a clever man with all the right contacts, isn't that so?"

"Are you going to give me the name of the person who hired you, or do I have to investigate the matter myself—without your help?"

"You should do whatever you think is right. But may I just say what a stunning home you have. Very impressive indeed," said Hausser. He took out his cigarettes again and politely offered one to Schumann, who shook his head.

"Not your brand? I'll bet you smoke an overseas brand, am I right? You look like a man who smokes . . . Marlboro. A Marlboro Man. A Yankee, maybe?" he said with a wink.

A chilly smile came to Schumann's lips.

Hausser followed Midas with his eyes as he crossed the road to his shiny car, where his equally shiny wife and daughter kept their eyes averted demonstratively, as if the sight of Hausser alone would dirty their perfect world. The moment Midas started the car, Hausser closed his eyes and enjoyed the sound of the BMW's engine; a potent hum that appealed to all his senses, a roar of precision technology that was a quantum leap from the stuttering motor of the East German Trabant's two-stroke engine. Despite all the technological wonder of his champagne-coloured BMW, Midas was going straight to hell; and despite the demonstrations in Leipzig, their soldiers would march down Karl-Marx-Allee for the Republic's fourty-year Jubilee in three days' time.

30

LAURITZEN was written in Irish-green letters on the yellow gable wall of the three-storey factory building in front of them. It was an intimidating building, despite its turret on the roof and lack of any kind of ornamentation. Louise and Ravn peered through the entrance gates into the front courtyard, where a group of seven or eight men in overalls were busy unloading two vans. Judging from the lively activity in the courtyard and the workshop beyond, the rumours about Lauritzen Enterprises' financial difficulties appeared to be greatly exaggerated.

They walked into the courtyard casually and made for the main entrance. As they took the stairs up to Reception on the second floor, Ravn gave Louise a sidelong glance. "Are you okay?" he asked.

"Yes, thank you, but . . . I'm really happy that you agreed to come along," she said.

A girl who looked to be in her midtwenties with red hair and a huge bust was sitting behind the counter at Reception, talking into her headset. When her conversation was over, she gave them both a cool stare.

Ravn introduced them both and asked if they could see Director Axel Pondus Lauritzen.

"Do you have an appointment?" asked the receptionist.

"No."

"Then I am very sorry, but Director Lauritzen is in a meeting. It would be best if you call and make an appointment."

"We need to talk to the director today. It's about a former employee, Mogens Slotsholm, so do you mind if we wait here?" Ravn smiled and pointed at the leather sofa that was placed opposite the reception desk.

"Just a moment," said the receptionist, nodding at the sofa. She took off her headset and put it down on her desk.

Louise and Ravn took a seat on the sofa and watched the receptionist squeeze round the end of the desk and disappear down the corridor.

Director Axel Pondus Lauritzen was leaning back in his office chair. His enormous body blotted the entire windowsill behind him. Louise and Ravn had taken seats in the chesterfield chairs on the opposite side of the director's desk. Louise's business card disappeared in Pondus Lauritzen's huge paw and he studied it thoughtfully, all the while smacking his chops.

Ravn was thinking the director reminded him very much of Møffe. Not just on account of the sheer size of the man and the slobbering of his chops, but his impressive underbite, large jaw, and lopsided ears with tufts of hair growing out of them; the resemblance was striking.

"So, apart from being Mogens's sister, you are an architect as well?" Lauritzen grumbled.

"That is correct. I lecture at the school over on Holmen."

Lauritzen put the card down. "It's folks like you we live on. You're the butter on our bread."

"I'm glad to hear it."

"If you lot didn't do such a slovenly job all the time, there'd be nothing for us to fix and renovate. But at least you look like someone who has a positive influence on her pupils . . ." His eyes slithered over her body until Louise dropped her gaze and studied the tip of her boot.

Lauritzen shifted his attention to Ravn, clearly not enamoured with what he saw. "And you? You don't look like an architect. What branch are *you* in?"

"I'm kind of between jobs at the moment," Ravn said with a shrug. "So I'm just here to offer Louise moral support."

"Unemployed, huh?" Pondus stared at each of them in turn, as if he was trying to figure out if their relationship was more than platonic. "And why have you come to me? So many months after the . . . fraud?"

"We . . . I have come to apologise on behalf of my brother."

"Uh-huh. Have you heard from him?"

"No. Unfortunately there is no word from him." Louise shook her head. "I can't understand how he could have done something like this—"

"But he did, believe me," Pondus said, interrupting her. "Your brother fleeced me and my firm out of a fortune," he added, pointing at the large safe standing in the corner. "Abused everyone's trust—most of all mine!" he said, thumping a fist against his chest.

"That's . . . I'm really sorry . . . something must have made him—"

"Did Mogens have the code for the safe?" Ravn interjected.

Pondus Lauritzen stared at Ravn. "Of course not. Only my secretary and I knew the code. He must have stolen it somehow. Just as he found a way to break into my office. The door was locked, but he still managed to get in, which proves how conniving he was. Obviously he'd planned everything carefully—"

"And yet he didn't manage to get away with more."

Lauritzen's eyebrows gathered like two thunder strokes. "Fifty thousand kroner is a lot of money!"

"Forty-five thousand three hundred, to be precise. That's the sum that was reported missing, right?" said Thomas. "Who reported it? I mean: Who found out the money was missing?"

"My secretary. Why do you ask?"

Ravn paused. Something about the look on Lauritzen's face told him that the report to the police had not been made with the director's blessing. Perhaps the secretary acted in his absence. If, as Ravn suspected, the money came from black market profits, Pondus would have wanted to handle the problem himself—sent an army of his Slavic workers after Mogens to collect the dough that was his—rather than involve the police. "I'm just trying to understand what happened, exactly, so we can find out where Mogens might have gone," Ravn said.

"As far as I'm concerned, he can go straight to hell," Pondus said.

"I understand your anger," Ravn said, leaning forward in his chair with an earnest expression on his face. "There's just one thing I can't quite wrap my head around, Mr. Lauritzen: With all the meticulous planning that went into his actions that day, I'm surprised that Mogens did not manage to steal more than forty-five thousand kroner—even though this definitely is a great deal of money that he took from you."

"It isn't the sum of money that makes you a thief, it's the fact you took it."

"So true, but Mogens must have known that he would be on the run for the rest of his life after the fact, and for this, the sum simply is not enough."

"Perhaps he didn't think that far ahead," said Lauritzen. "Or perhaps he thought there was more money in the safe," he added, shaking his head like a befuddled boxer in a ring. "Do you mean to tell me that *I'm* the one who has to explain why a thief robs me blind?"

"So you keep large sums of cash in your safe from time to time?"

"What business is that of yours?"

Ravn ignored the question. "Because if Mogens thought there might be more cash in the safe, it would explain a lot—did he have a *reason* to believe there was more money in the safe?"

"Who are you anyway? I could swear I know you from someplace."

"We are practically neighbours," said Ravn with a genuine smile. "I live a little further down the canal. As I said, I'm just here to offer Louise some moral support. I'm sorry if I said something to offend you, sir."

Holding Ravn's gaze, Lauritzen smacked his chops again. *Yup, Møffe, just before dinnertime,* thought Ravn. "So what if he believed there was more in the safe?" said Lauritzen.

"It would explain why Mogens went to so much trouble," said Ravn. "As things stand, there is no explanation how he could have disappeared for such a long time, because forty-five thousand kroner would be used up by now."

"What are you insinuating? That we reported less than went missing? That's ludicrous!"

Ravn shrugged. "There are many kinds of money."

"I think our meeting is over," Lauritzen said, showing them the door with his paw.

Louise stood up and gave him her hand. "I apologise again for my brother," she said.

Lauritzen took her hand and gave it a gentle squeeze. "Despite everything, I hope you find him, so you don't have to look so sad. I'm sure you're a lot prettier when you smile."

Louise withdrew her hand and turned to leave.

Ravn pushed to his feet and regarded the big man behind the desk. "The sooner we find Mogens, the greater our chances to return what was stolen to its rightful owner," he said in parting, and followed Louise to the door.

"Wait," said Pondus, waving them back.

"Am I to understand that you are looking for a reward? Some kind of finder's fee?"

"No, not at all," said Ravn. "We are only interested in finding out what happened to Mogens. Get him back on the right track, if you will. We have no interest in the money."

Lauritzen threaded his fat fingers. "Mogens stole more than my dimwit secretary reported. This matter should never have come to light."

"How much more?"

"Eight hundred seventy thousand in cash."

"Eight hundred seventy K . . ." blurted Louise in shock.

"Not just that," Pondus admitted. "He also took an accounts ledger. The kind I don't want anyone to see. And I would very much like to have it back. As soon as possible. Including whatever remains of the money. If that happens, I'm willing to let bygones be bygones and withdraw the charges. I can explain to the authorities that this was all a big mistake."

Ravn and Louise walked along the canal in silence. Her Fiat 500 was parked in the lot outside the War Museum. Just before they reached her car, she turned to face Ravn. He was surprised to see that she was on the verge of tears. "You were really good up there," she said.

"It was nothing. But at least we found out how much money your brother actually has."

"I mean it. I'm impressed."

Ravn shrugged awkwardly. Nodded briefly. He didn't know what to do with compliments. "After meeting Pondus Lauritzen in person, one can almost understand why your brother stole from him," he said with a tentative smile.

The tears started to run down her cheeks. "I'm sorry," she said. "I didn't mean to . . . it's not your fault, it's just that I . . . I thought I would feel better if I knew that he had enough money to survive, but . . . but it's so much money, and it just makes me worry about him more because obviously something is very wrong . . . someone must have persuaded him to do this, and he must be in a lot of trouble—" She turned to unlock her car door. "I'm sorry," she said simply, and got in the car.

"Louise?" Ravn wanted to open the door again, but she started the engine and drove off immediately.

Ravn took a deep breath. He felt as if an elephant were sitting on his chest. Before the meeting with Lauritzen, he'd thought that everything would end here. But now he wasn't so sure.

He took his phone out of his pocket to see if Mikkel had left him a message, but he wasn't that lucky. All at once, he was very thirsty. He set off again, with a beeline for The Sea Otter.

31

Prenzlauer Berg
Berlin 7 October 1989

The crowd waved a sea of red flags on the TV screen. An armada of Russian tankers in parade formation, missile carriers, and soldiers marched in goose step to the booming rhythm of a massive military orchestra. Guests of honour and the top dogs in the Socialist Unity Party, SED, gathered round their leader, Erich Honecker, and clapped their hands on the rostrum. Heads of state from all over the world had come to celebrate the 40-Year Jubilee of the German Democratic Republic, including representatives from North Korea, Cuba, and Romania—even leaders of communist parties in the West stood side by side with leaders like Kim Il-Sung, Nicolae Ceaușescu, and Yasser Arafat. In the back rows of the rostrum, the highest officials from the German ministries as well as the leaders of the Ministry of State Security had taken their seats; Hausser had already spotted Strauss in the crowd. If he had played his cards differently and been more politically minded, he could have been sitting beside Strauss right now, rather than in front of a TV screen in this shithole, he thought. But he wasn't political. He didn't believe in politics, he believed in the apparatus beneath it. He believed in a strong Stasi without political restrictions. In truth, there was only one politician who Hausser respected, and that was the old man, Honecker. Not so much because of his status as the "father of the nation," but because he was a stubborn old bastard.

The doorbell chimed. Hausser had no idea who it could be. He glanced over at the monitor. Lena was wringing her hands on the sofa in the Schumanns' living room. The doorbell chimed again and Hausser went to the door to see who it was.

He found Herr Schumann standing on his doormat. He was trying to smile, but Hausser could see he was nervous. "Herr Schumann. What a surprise. I thought you would have joined in the celebrations today."

"May I come in?"

"Actually, I was just on my way out. So if there's something I can help you with, it ought to be quick. Are you having trouble with your sink again?"

"There's no need for the act. I know you're not a super," said Schumann.

"Well, I have the apron and belt that goes with the job," said Hausser.

"I've contacted the building's administration office. No one there knows what happened to our former superintendent. They're worried about him and wanted to call the police."

"Really? What stopped them from doing so?"

"I did. So what happened to him? Where is he?"

"Not that it's anyone's business, but I think he got into trouble." Hausser shrugged. "Problems relating to security. But how can I help you, Herr Schumann?"

Midas was breathing heavily. "I found this behind the radiator in the kitchen," he said, taking a microphone attached to a length of wiring out of his pocket. "It's not the only microphone I found in my flat." Hausser reached for the equipment, but Schumann kept it out of his reach. "As well as several hidden cameras."

"It must be very unpleasant to be spied on like that," said Hausser. "Especially for your beautiful wife and your lovely daughter. But why are you telling me this?"

"Because I am relatively sure that you are the one who is watching us," said Schumann. "I think you are working for the Stasi," he added, pointing into the flat behind Hausser.

Hausser laughed. "That sounds a little paranoid."

"And yet, you don't deny it."

"Why would the Stasi put you under surveillance? Have you done something wrong?"

"Stop being such a smart-arse. I don't know what division you work for, or what rank you hold. But just so you know it, *I* am not a Nobody in this town. I have power and influence in the Party, and the same Service that you work for—at a significantly higher level than *yours*. At times like these, no one can be sure how the wind will blow. And it is in times like these that you have to choose your allies with care," Schumann said, staring Hausser down.

Hausser deliberately dropped his gaze to his feet. "Was there something you wanted to ask me, or are we done?"

"How does this work, exactly? I haven't seen anyone else go into your flat. So I'm guessing that you are the only one who knows the contents of the recordings?" Schumann narrowed his eyes. "I think it might be interesting, at first, to spy on some arsehole, spy on women in the bath, folks having sex. It must be very entertaining. But then routine kicks in, and you realise it is the same little lives that people live. The same shit, day in and day out. In the end, you don't even feel like looking at the recordings you've made. It's just exchanging one tape for another, and delivering what you've recorded, but you're not the one who's responsible for laying charges; that's a decision taken by folks a lot higher up in the system than you are. I think that, as time passes, you become aware of your own life. Begin to ask yourself what the purpose of all this is? The isolation is all that remains. Quite literally, you see your life pass you by. Am I close?"

Hausser shrugged. "You should have been a writer with that fantasy of yours."

"I get by just fine with my job at the State Bank, thank you. Do you have a wife? A family waiting for you somewhere? Does your job for the Service even allow for that?" Schumann tried to muster an empathetic smile, which died on his lips. "Do you see my point?"

"And what if I did?"

"What would happen if you chose not to deliver your recordings? What if they for some or other reason were damaged, or destroyed by mistake? 'Tape salad,' I believe it is called."

"I'm not sure I understand," said Hausser with a cryptic smile.

"I think we might be able to agree on a suitable arrangement, you and I. If there were particular tapes that you thought might interest me—not that anything illegal has occurred in my flat, but there might be things that could be misunderstood. The company of some guests, who we would prefer others not to know anything about, episodes from our private life, which we would prefer strangers not to be privy to. You know, that kind of thing."

"'Tape salad' is a good phrase," said Hausser.

"I'm happy to hear you think so," said Schumann. "In return, I could make your life more interesting. Access to the Intershop could be arranged. Payment in dollars for your trouble. I'm sure we could come to a very reasonable arrangement."

Hausser scratched his head. "You know, that almost sounds like a bribe."

"More like a reward to a superintendent who has executed a good piece of work. Whether it be a blocked drain, or 'tape salad' . . ." Schumann put out his hand, as if to seal the deal. "You will soon find out that I am a generous friend to have."

Hausser looked at his outstretched hand without taking it. The little smile that had been playing at the corners of his mouth disappeared. He gave Schumann a chilly stare instead. "I have always marvelled at how powerful people like yourself tend to believe that they can control everything, just because they are successful in a single area. You mentioned that you weren't sure what division I worked for, and that you have contacts in the Service as well." He added a smile, this time decidedly mocking. "I suggest you give your good friend Braun a call in the morning. Ask him how he is doing, and you will get the answers to your questions. A good day to you, Herr Schumann. And send my regards to your beautiful wife and talented daughter."

Hausser closed the door in Schumann's face and went back into his living room. He dumped himself into his easy chair and reached for his glass of beer, which was flat. He also hated Midas for this. After he had watched the parade on TV for a few more minutes, he felt for some coins in his pocket. It was time to give Müller a call.

32

At the rear entrance to the building, the naked bulbs flickered all the way down to the deep hole of the stairwell. Midas and Lena came out onto the top landing. He was still wearing his coat. Hausser had been looking forward to this moment with great anticipation. The desperate look on the man's face on the monitor did not disappoint him.

"Something terrible has happened, Lena."

"What is it, Christoph? Tell me now . . . you're scaring me."

Schumann took two or three gulps of air. Then swallowed repeatedly, in obvious distress. "It's Braun . . ."

"What about him?"

"There's been an . . . an accident."

"But . . . how?"

"I have just spoken to Vera—she is beside herself. Braun went to walk their dog, Laika, yesterday. He's usually only gone for twenty minutes, so when he hadn't returned an hour and a half later, she got worried. She went to look for him. When she got to the Spree, she met a young couple who had found Laika, alone and whining pitifully on the riverbank. After looking for Braun for two hours without any luck, they called the police. Then it was all Vera could do to go home and wait."

Lena's hand flew to her mouth. "Is he still missing?"

Schumann shook his head. "The police reported that they found Braun's body further up the river, washed up on land. There will be an autopsy in a few days, but they say there are no signs of violence, so they assume he must have fallen into the water and drowned."

"That's horrible," said Lena. She threw her arms round his neck and held him tight. "Do you think it could have been suicide?"

"I don't know, but I doubt it."

Lena pulled back and looked at her husband fearfully. "What, then? You are hiding something from me . . . I can see it in your face."

"When I spoke to Hausser yesterday—"

"Yes? What did he say?"

"He ended our conversation by suggesting I call Braun. He said this would give me the answers I wanted regarding the power he had in the Stasi . . . I think this is his . . . answer."

Lena freed herself from Christoph's embrace. "But you said the two of you had come to an arrangement. That he just wanted money like everyone else."

"I didn't want to worry you."

"So you lied to me instead?"

"No! I was trying to protect you. So you wouldn't be unnecessarily afraid. Perhaps it's just a coincidence after all."

"Surely you don't believe that. So what do we do now?"

"We don't panic. Even if what I want to do most is just leave, get as far away from here as possible."

"But we can't. Our plans for escape have already been discovered. And it's not what you want anyway."

"No, I know, I know. I'm just thinking aloud. But there are other ways to get away. Even though it would be a catastrophe for life as we know it."

Hausser smiled. Despite the chaotic situation in the land, Operation Midas was moving in the right direction.

He listened to the Schumanns trying to reassure each other. But neither of them believed the other. Midas spoke of "hoping for the best" and that "the tide would soon turn." If that was his "master plan"—the very best he could come up with—then he was easier prey than Hausser had imagined.

It was time to launch the next phase.

33

"No, I don't know when he'll be back in the office," said the Criminal Division assistant on the other end of the line. "But you are welcome to leave a message. What did you say your name was again?"

"I'll try again later," Ravn muttered into the receiver, and ended the call. There was a time when everyone at Station City knew his name. Now it seemed as if the entire Criminal Division had been replaced by Boy Scouts. And Mikkel wasn't returning his calls. He'd simply vanished, and Ravn suspected he'd gotten cold feet about tracking down the guy who'd been texting Eva on her work phone. Mikkel had always been a paragon of virtue, but he had always been a loyal friend as well, in professional and personal matters. Although they had kept the personal to the minimum; as if neither of them wished to tarnish their personal lives—what they cherished most—with the dirty business of their work. If Mikkel, rather than that moron Brask, was in charge, he could almost consider returning to the fold. Almost, but not quite. He dumped his phone into his pocket moodily and went up on deck.

"Got any coffee on board?"

Louise was standing on the quay, smiling down at him.

"Always," Ravn said. "If you can stomach a cup of Nescafé."

Louise stepped down onto the deck. It warmed his heart that she didn't look nearly as sad as the last time he saw her.

Ravn cleared the clothing and newspapers off the sofa, and they took a seat next to each other. They sipped their steaming coffees. A few minutes passed with neither of them talking; the only sound was the companiable lapping of the waves against the hull, the creaking of *Bianca*'s rigging above. "I've never known anyone who owns a boat," Louise observed dreamily. "I have to say she's a very fine ship." She smiled and put her mug aside to cool.

Ravn wasn't sure if Louise was making fun of him or not. "She still needs renovating," he said cautiously. "But I'll get there."

"She's really peaceful. You're very lucky to have her."

Again, Ravn studied her face, wondering if she was being serious. He didn't know much about her, but Ravn had the distinct impression that Louise was used to something more luxurious than the cabin on an old trawler. But looking at her now, she genuinely seemed to enjoy being on board.

"I'm sorry I just left you standing on the quay the other day."

"Don't worry. It's fine—we were done anyway."

"I was upset. It wasn't just finding out how much money was involved. It was being in the place where Mogens used to work, for all those years— with that awful man!"

Ravn couldn't help but smile. "Yes, Lauritzen is a strange fish," he said. "But at least we got what we wanted from him, and you never have to see him again."

Louise nodded. "It makes me so sad that Mogens never told me how horrible it must have been to work there, and I never thought to ask. I feel guilty about that."

"Well, you shouldn't. It was your brother's choice to work there. Just as it was his choice to get away from it all."

Louise picked up her mug to warm her hands. "Even though he was my big brother, I was the one who took care of him when we were children. I protected him from the other kids at school, made sure the bullies left him in peace."

"I'm guessing he was a loner back then as well?"

"Oh, definitely. Mogens was a first-class nerd. Top of his class, the boy with glasses that nobody ever invited to birthday parties."

"What about you?"

"Oh, I had good grades too. But I wasn't short of invitations either."

"Yup, I figured as much," Ravn said with a smile, but Louise didn't return it.

"I charmed the bullies when they were after Mogens. Protected him, regardless of the price."

"He's lucky to have a sister like you. But what about later, when you grew up?"

"It seems Mogens never really grew up."

"And you did?"

Louise surprised him with a lopsided grin. "Sure, I did. I found a husband—a professor and architect—we had a son, Theo, who grew up much too fast and is now in college," she added, shaking her head as if she couldn't believe it. "But for some or other reason, Mogens didn't become a part of our family."

"You said you hadn't seen him since your mother's funeral."

"Yes, we . . . my husband—my ex-husband—and Mogens didn't get along. They didn't argue, exactly, neither one of them would dream of behaving in an uncivilised manner, but whenever we met there were a lot of prolonged silences in our conversation. Fathomless oceans of silence."

"Hmm. Sounds like your average family to my ears," said Ravn.

Louise laughed. "Thanks. I'm relieved to hear you say that."

Ravn drained the last of his Nescafé and looked her in the eye. "If you want a good word of advice, I think it's best to let it go."

"I know," she said, looking down into her cup. "That's what every-one says. But I can't stop worrying about him. The hefty sum of money he took just makes matters worse. I think someone made him take the money. Threatened him in some way."

"But the police have interviewed his colleagues, and there is no indi-cation of collaboration."

Louise returned his gaze. "Can I ask you one last favour?"

Ravn leaned back in the sofa. "What favour is that?"

"Would you come up to Mogens's flat with me? It's right over there," she said, pointing in the direction of Applebye Square on the other side of the canal. "It would take half an hour of your time."

Ravn sighed. "Why?"

"Because if there is something in his flat that could give me a clue as to what has happened to him, then I am sure you are the one who can find it."

"But the police have already been there. Haven't you been up there yourself?"

She nodded. "But you can do something that no one else can . . ."

"I . . . er . . . thank you for the compliment, but you don't know me, Louise. And the last thing I need right now is to get involved in this case."

"Twenty minutes of your time, that's all. Then we'll be back here. And I will never bother you again. You will never see me again."

"I didn't mean it like that."

Louise looked at him with that vulnerable look in her eyes, which she'd probably used on other men for her brother's sake many times before.

He had to admit that it worked on him as well.

34

Prenzlauer Berg, East Berlin
13 October 1989

Tear gas hung in the air and Greifenhagener Strasse was deserted. People who had come home from work in the late afternoon had hurried into their homes, and kept their doors and windows closed. Only Hausser remained on the street outside. In the distance, you could hear the demonstrators' yells on Schönhauser Allee, which ran parallel to Greifenhagener. The metallic sting of the tear gas always reminded him of wet cobblestones after rain in his hometown, Graupa, which gave off a similar acrid smell. He was leaning up against a tree, waiting for Christoph to come home from the State Bank.

Schumann had changed his routine and managed to avoid him the last two days; he used the rear entrance, got up much earlier before Hausser was out of bed, and slipped away unnoticed to work in the mornings. Hausser felt some satisfaction that Schumann was obviously rattled by Braun's sudden demise, but it was about time he had a little chat with him. The clock was ticking, and if his plans for Midas were to succeed, the process had to keep moving forward.

Further down the road, Schumann's hard-to-miss, champagne-coloured BMW turned into Greifenhagener and crawled towards Hausser's vantage point. Moments later, Schumann pulled to the kerb and parked in front of Number 9. He collected his attaché case from the passenger seat, got out of the car, and locked the door behind him.

Hausser pushed off the tree and made his way across the road. Schumann was distracted by the commotion coming from Schönhauser Allee and didn't see Hausser until the agent was standing right in front of him, his hands buried deep into his pockets.

"What . . . you scared me, Hausser," said Schumann, trying to regain his composure.

"Really? Why's that, then?" said Hausser.

Schumann shrugged and tried to slip past Hausser, but he wasn't that lucky.

"Did you get a hold of your friend Braun?"

Schumann stopped in his tracks. "What do you want, Hausser?"

"Hmm. That's a relatively broad question. Let me see . . . world peace, for one. A new pair of shoes. And a trip in your Beamer."

Schumann tried to smile and failed. "No, I'm serious," he said.

"So am I," said Hausser. "Get in the car. I'm taking you for a drive."

"Where . . . to?" said Schumann.

Hausser made no reply. Instead, he took one hand out of his pocket and snapped his fingers. "The car keys. Now."

With Hausser at the wheel and Christoph in the passenger seat, the big, fat BMW glided down Greifenhagener Strasse. Hausser put his foot on the accelerator and changed gear gently; he loved the fluid shift into third gear and nodded with approval. "What an exquisite car you have, Christoph. If I had the dough, I would buy myself one just like it. What does a beauty like this cost, anyway? Twenty, thirty, forty thousand?"

"I . . . I'm borrowing it from a friend. Or rather: His company has loaned it to me."

"Wow. I'd love to have a friend like that. He lives on the other side of the Wall, I take it?

"The car is legally registered. All the papers are in order. I can assure you—"

"Fuck the paperwork. I don't give a shit how you came by this car, Christoph."

"I think my . . . my wife is expecting me, so . . . perhaps we should turn round . . . if that's okay with you?"

"You don't look like the kind of man who lets his wife dictate his actions—no matter how beautiful she is. Now lean back, relax, and enjoy the ride. Switch on the radio. Let me hear what you listen to on your way home from work."

Schumann hesitated.

Hausser flicked his wrist in an impatient gesture, and Christoph reluctantly put on the radio—"Aruba, Jamaica, ooh I wanna take ya . . ." The Beach Boys crooned their way through "Kokomo."

"I'm pretty sure this is not GDR-1 Radio we are listening to!" barked Hausser.

"I'm sorry . . . I . . . I don't know . . . the channel must have jumped over automatically . . ." Schumann leaned forward to change it.

Hausser burst out laughing. "No worries. I'm just taking the piss. It sounds good. Must be the Hit Parade. I listen to it myself. Can I bum one of those cigarettes from you?" he said, pointing at the pack of Marlboro that lay on the dashboard. Christoph reached for the pack and offered Hausser a cigarette.

Hausser pressed the cigarette lighter in the mid-console and took a cigarette from Christoph. "I knew you were a Marlboro Person."

"I think it's called Marlboro Man," mumbled Schumann. "But it doesn't matter."

Hausser lit up, drew the smoke deep into his lungs, and exhaled with satisfaction. "You live a comfortable life, Christoph, I've gotta hand it to you."

Schumann kept his eyes on his shoes.

Hausser took a right and continued down to Schönhauser Allee. When he got to the intersection, he pulled over and parked the car. The tear gas formed a veil over the road and enveloped the viaduct, where a train emerged from the mist. Accompanied by the Beach Boys, Hausser and Schumann watched the demonstrators retreat. "'Down in Kokomo'" . . . Hausser repeated in English with a strong German accent.

The demonstrators were making a run for it past their car. Many of them were wounded and bloody, their banners hitched onto their shoulders, as if the demonstration were a crusade from the Middle Ages. WIR SIND DAS VOLK was written on most the signs. Hausser pointed them out.

"Do you identify with them? Do you feel as if you are a part of the German 'Volk'?"

"I . . . I don't know what to say."

"Because you do not sympathise with them, or . . .?"

"Because I have a feeling that no matter what I say, it won't be what you want to hear."

"It's very simple: I am interested in hearing the truth and nothing else," said Hausser, stubbing out his cigarette in the ashtray. "Right now would be a very good time to tell me everything that happened in your flat."

"I . . . how much do you know about the plans we have discussed? I mean, how long have you had us under surveillance?"

"Christoph, this is not the way you want to start your confession."

"I'm sorry . . . I just . . . didn't want to repeat something that you already know."

"Whether you bore me or not ought to be your last concern right now."

Christoph sighed in resignation. Then he began explaining how his consortium planned to take advantage of opportunities arising as the countries in the Eastern Bloc disintegrated, and a secret faction in the GDR developed, which gave rise to their plans to flee the country.

Hausser listened without expression. He had heard most of this narrative before, but it felt good to hear Midas admit his sins with tears in his eyes. He concluded by saying that it had never been his intention to flee, that he had been swept along on the basis of false loyalty to the consortium, which he regretted bitterly. This was why he and Braun had agreed not to take part in the escape. Hausser noted with interest that Midas defended his actions, even though he must realise that Hausser knew his actual motivation for remaining behind in the GDR. But he made no comment, just let Midas pour his heart out; it was all part of his plan.

On Schönhauser Allee, the police vehicles came past with water cannons on their roof. Two officers with batons in their hands charged over to the BMW. Hausser unzipped his jacket and slapped his ID card against the pane of the driver's seat window. The officers checked the ID, studied Hausser's face, and made a smart salute before leaving them in peace.

"What happens now?" asked Schumann. "Am I arrested?"

Hausser fished a fresh cigarette from the Marlboro pack, and Schumann hastened to whip out his gold Dunhill lighter.

"When do they plan to attempt their escape?" asked Hausser, blowing out a cloud of smoke.

"There is no fixed date yet. But it will be soon. Schröder has had some difficulty with the necessary papers. But everything else should be ready by now."

"So, in the next couple of weeks?" said Hausser.

Schumann nodded.

"Need I point out that your own neck depends entirely on whether we trap the deserters in the act?"

"I will help you. You have my word."

"From now on, you are working for me. Your code name is 'Midas.'"

Schumann nodded. "I understand. 'Midas,' as in the mythological king who transformed everything he touched into gold?"

"No. 'Midas,' as in 'the man who will rot in a hole if he does not do as he is told.'"

"I'm sorry. I'm really sorry. I should have informed the authorities as soon as I heard about all this."

Hausser couldn't bear to listen to Schumann for another second and he got the hell out of the car. He stood watching the uniformed police with their German shepherd dogs on a leash. The dogs were barking viciously, as if eager to finish the job with the demonstrators. Hausser admired these bloodthirsty animals; the deep-seated instincts that were excited on a day that must give meaning to their existence. Even a dog must be alive to this sensation. He waved at Schumann behind the windshield, indicating that he should piss off.

35

From the chamber of the silver brouilleur the ice gradually melted, slowly diluting the strong absinthe in the glass below. Hausser was careful not to disturb the glass as he paged through the files on Christoph. On the monitor in front of him, Christoph and Lena were sitting on the rear entrance landing outside their kitchen with a bottle of beer each. They looked like old friends, drinking directly from the bottle and sharing a cigarette.

Christoph had just told Lena about his terrible meeting with Hausser that day, admitting that he'd thought his hour had come when Hausser asked for the car keys and drove off with him.

"But you handled the situation well," said Lena. "Hausser is a bloody swine."

Christoph nodded. "The Stasi are merciless, but also dumb and predictable; as long as you play the underdog, act all submissive, you've got them eating out of your hand. I figured that out immediately. That's why I survived."

Hausser scoffed. Christoph had clearly found his balls—with impressive speed, considering the fact that only two hours ago he was about to shit himself with fear.

"But it's horrible that you have to be an informant for him now. What would happen if someone were to find out? What would folks think?"

"I can't imagine that any of this would ever come to light, Lena," Christoph said, and took a sip from his beer. "In fact, we're in a relatively good position now."

"What do you mean? I don't think it could get much worse."

"At least we have a measure of protection now."

"But what about the others?"

"We can't do anything about their situation. It's not as if we ratted on them to begin with. They would have been caught anyway. Besides, if things develop as we hope, and there is a regime change in the country, their period of incarceration will be short."

"But shouldn't we warn them? Surely, we owe them that much . . ."

"Don't be naïve, Lena. That kind of attitude could get us killed. Instead, we should regard their attempt to flee as a positive for us; something that will place us in a favourable negotiating position with the Stasi, including Hausser. What we need to figure out is how to use Braun's contacts, despite his regrettable passing. I think we should try to get Vera on board. As a straw man, perhaps.

Lena kissed her husband on the lips. "You are the smartest man I know," she said. "Always three moves ahead of everyone else." She stood up and made for the kitchen door.

"Did I tell you that I was a chess master at school?"

"Only about a hundred times," she said with a smile, and disappeared into the kitchen.

Christoph remained on the step and finished smoking their cigarette. The light on the landing went out and only the glow of the cigarette remained on Hausser's monitor, as if a defective pixel. "Chess master," he mumbled to himself.

Hausser found what he was looking for at last: a yellow manila envelope. He smiled, lifted the empty brouilleur off his glass, and had a sip of absinthe. Then he opened the envelope and took out the black-and-white photographs; about ten pictures of Christoph, naked with two prostitutes in a double bed. The pictures were taken at a conference in Leipzig, as an insurance policy for blackmail, before Christoph Schumann was put under surveillance. Hausser was the one to initiate the case; the Stasi had thousands of such secret "sleeping cases" on folks in the Party and administration of the government. Including one on Honecker; nothing serious, just a little extra-marital activity, which few would hold against him considering the looks of his wife, Margot, thought Hausser.

Hausser returned the pictures to the envelope. Tomorrow he would ensure Lena received them at work; it would be harder for her to handle in public, at the Intershop, than the comfort of her own home. Her steel character and pride would prevent her from making a scene in front of her colleagues, but the other women would know something was terribly wrong when they saw the shock on her face. *Lena would be terrified of what the other women would think*, Hausser thought, smiling to himself. The golden girl, the GDR's "top model," who had married so well. The shame, the loss of the others' respect and envy would hurt Lena much more than her husband's sexual infidelities with prostitutes; Hausser was counting on it; Midas would be isolated, as if he already was locked in the Chamber in Hohenschönhausen.

36

Louise had to push against the pile of junk mail that had gathered in the entrance to Mogens's flat in the months that had passed after his disappearance. The power had long since been cut, and his flat was as dark, cold, and musty as a mausoleum. It reminded Ravn of his own apartment not too long ago.

"So how come you have a key to the apartment?" he asked.

"Mogens gave me one when he moved in," Louise said. "It's an old tradition of ours to exchange spare keys—we've done it since college."

"So he has one for your flat as well?"

"Well, no . . . I . . ." Louise looked down. "I never got round to giving him a set . . . Andreas—my ex-husband—didn't think it was a good idea. And Mogens never asked for one, so . . ."

"Shall we take a look round?" Without waiting for her reply, Ravn went into the living room.

A fine layer of dust covered the sparse furnishings in the flat. Ravn searched the bookcase and started opening drawers. "Have you been through everything yourself?"

Louise nodded. "You'll only find old documents in the top drawer; the others are empty.

Ravn skimmed the contents of the top drawer; Louise appeared to be right. He went over to the sofa and lifted all the pillows to see if anything was hidden underneath. "What about the flat? Will it be sold?"

"Yes. Bankruptcy auction."

He bent down and felt under the sofa to check if anything had been wedged under the springs but found nothing.

They continued into the bedroom. Mogens's futon bed was neatly made. "With his sense of order, one could take your brother for a military man," observed Ravn.

"No, not Mogens. He was rejected by the force." Louise sat down on the edge of the bed carefully, as if she did not want to crease the covers. "I'm sorry I dragged you up here for no reason."

"Well, we're not done yet."

"But we've looked through everything without finding the tiniest clue of his whereabouts," she said sadly.

"Sometimes it helps to check for things that aren't there."

"I'm not sure I understand . . ."

Ravn stepped onto the bed and took a Maglite out of his pocket. "I mean the things that he appears to have taken with him in flight that could point to his destination," he said, shining the beam of the flashlight over the top of Mogens's wardrobe.

"What are you looking for?"

"Chances are that Mogens is no different from most, who ninety-five per cent of the time either store their suitcase under the bed or on top of their wardrobe. Mogens's futon is too low, so he probably used the space on top of his cupboard," Ravn explained. "Yup, you can clearly see a difference in the layer of dust up there."

Louise craned her neck but remained seated where she was.

"I reckon he's travelling with a medium-large suitcase with space for sixty to seventy litres," Ravn said.

He hopped off the bed and opened the cupboard doors wide. Ran a hand along the hangers. Cheap-looking suits next to blue polyester shirts. A few empty hangers. "Apart from the suit he was wearing on the day he disappeared, I think he's taken one spare suit along. Perhaps one or two shirts." Ravn studied the half-empty shelves. "A middle-aged man has an average of six pairs of underwear, an equal number of pairs of socks, and a few orphans on the side," he said, showing Louise a single white sock with a smile. "Judging from the lack of underwear on the shelves, I think it's reasonable to assume that Mogens took most with him."

Ravn bent down to search the bottom shelves. A few T-shirts, a sweater, and two creased flannel trousers were left. "It looks like Mogens is travelling practical and light."

"And what does this tell us?" Louise asked.

"That his travel plans were just as carefully planned as the theft of Lauritzen Enterprises. His duffel coat is still hanging on the hook in the entrance. His winter boots are still here. So perhaps he's gone somewhere warm."

"Hmm. Mogens hated heat more than anything else."

Ravn shrugged. "Okay. Does he have a driving licence?"

Louise shook her head.

Ravn sat down on the bed beside her. He scratched his beard thoughtfully. "We know that he took his passport with him, but he didn't apply for a visa. This could mean that he's still in Europe somewhere; this would be easy enough as there aren't major border controls in the Schengen countries, for instance."

Louise nodded. "And with Lauritzen's cash he wouldn't have had to use his credit card, which would reveal his location."

"Maybe he took a bus or train out of the country?"

"Mogens gets carsick easily; he wouldn't survive a long bus trip without puking over the other passengers in a bus."

"Okay, so let us assume that Mogens has skipped the country by train and headed for somewhere else in Europe, directly from work with just shy of nine hundred thousand kroner in his pocket. If he's smart, he would have chosen a big city where it is easy to hide."

"Which means that he could be anywhere from Amsterdam, Paris, Hamburg—or hundreds of other cities for that matter," said Louise.

Ravn nodded. "Does he speak any language apart from Danish?"

"No, he took the math route at school, so languages are not his thing."

"You said he likes Wagner, right?"

"Yes, but not enough for him to skip the country and move to Germany." Louise stood up, went over to the wardrobe, and turned to face Ravn. "We're not getting any closer to finding him, are we?"

Ravn shrugged.

Louise sighed and headed for the door. Ravn followed her into the entrance.

"Did you check the pockets?" he said, nodding at the coat on the hook.

"Yes, they're empty."

Ravn needed to take a leak. *Bloody Nescafé*, he thought. "Is it okay if I use the bathroom?"

Louise nodded, and Ravn walked to the other end of the corridor to use the toilet.

He fumbled for the switch just inside the door, till he remembered that the power had been cut. He fished out his penlight and rested it on the sink. When he was done, he washed his hands and glanced at himself in the mirror above the sink. Something behind his head caught his attention. He turned round and inspected the utility box just below the ceiling; the paint on one screw was chipped, indicating that it had been opened recently. He fished his Leatherman out of his pocket and used the screwdriver to take off the cover.

"Is everything okay?" Louise called from the entrance.

"I'll be with you in just a second," Ravn called back.

He wedged his screwdriver into the gap and pried open the box cover. A breeze from the hollow in the wall behind cooled his face. He used his penlight to search the hollow. In between the web of cables and orange fibreglass insulation he caught sight of a shoe box. He stuck his arm in the hole and drew it out. Very carefully, he lifted the lid and looked inside. "Louise, I think I've found something . . . important."

37

Prenzlauer Berg, East Berlin
19 October 1989

Kollwitzplatz was shrouded in darkness. The monotone rush of the wind resounded in the naked trees surrounding the little park in the centre. Christoph swayed on his feet as he took a leak against the park fence. Once he was done, he zipped up his pants and dried his fingers on the hem of his coat. Then he stumbled over the square towards Husemannstrasse.

Hausser was following him at a safe distance. He knew that Christoph was on his way to the same pub he had retreated to each night after Lena received the pictures of him with the prostitutes in bed. The Schumann residence had been a madhouse for days, as the other tenants of the building on Greifenhagener Strasse 9 could testify; their arguments rang all the way down the stairwell. Lena had screamed and yelled at her husband, now throwing things at him in a fit of rage, now sobbing her heart out. Christoph had been driven from his smashed living room bar to the pubs in the neighbourhood. Contrary to Lena, he was silent with shame. Throughout the week, Lena had demanded a divorce on a daily basis, and Christoph had begged her to stay. Hausser thought the timing of their split was ironic; everyone in Germany was talking about the possible reunification of the country. Christoph on the other hand was rejected by his wife and thrown out on his ear, just like Honecker was forced out of the SED. The latter upset Hausser; good ol' Honecker had stood his ground, while the world around him wobbled. In return for his loyalty, Honecker was replaced by the lap dog Egon Krentz, who had made his fame as the leader of the Young Pioneers movement. Hausser scoffed—*What the country needed now was not a Boy Scout with a paedophile past! Now was the time for a soldier–an iron fist!*

Standing on the opposite side of the road, Hausser saw Christoph stumble through the doors of the pub Budike 15. There was no rush, so Hausser lit up a cigarette and leaned against the wall behind him. He liked this neighbourhood. The old Weimar houses that miraculously survived the Allies' air strikes during the war. This part of the city was not as beautiful as the quarter around Karl-Marx-Allee, but it had a certain dignity and pride about it. His cigarette done, Hausser crossed the road and entered the pub that Christoph had disappeared into.

The room was only half full, and he spotted Christoph sitting at a table at the back, staring into a bottle of Urquell. Hausser ordered an Echt Berliner from the bartender and sauntered over to the table with his beer. Christoph looked up when Hausser took a seat opposite him. *"You . . ."*

"Cheers, Midas," said Hausser, raising his beer in a toast.

Christoph did not return it. "Why did you send those pictures to Lena? I told you I would help you."

"Is this the part where I say 'What pictures?'"

Christoph shook his head. "Was it to punish me?"

"Do you feel the need to be punished, Midas?"

Christoph ignored the question. "Is that it? Tell me. Why?" he banged his fist onto the table so hard his beer almost toppled over.

Hausser sighed. "Maybe I just don't like you," he said. "Maybe I chose you, just like a predator chooses its prey. No one would ask a wolf that has already eaten why he killed a lamb. It's his nature to kill. Or perhaps he cannot stand weakness? Perhaps he sees the lamb's vulnerability as his worst enemy?" Hausser said thoughtfully, and smiled. "Then again, I am not a wolf. And I didn't send those pictures," he lied. "Why would I do that? You work for me now, and that would just ruin our relationship, is that not so?"

Christoph didn't reply and took a sip of his beer instead.

"I know what is really bothering you: You are terrified of losing control. That is your greatest weakness—alongside your all-consuming arrogance."

"You sound like a fucking priest, Hausser."

"I'm sorry you think so. Try to think of me as the . . . ugly instrument of truth instead."

"So what is the truth, then?"

"That the State will abide. That it is stronger than the individual. And you, my friend, are part of the machine now. For the first time in your miserable, insignificant life, you are doing something useful; you are acting for the benefit of the State rather than your own well-being. It must feel good for a change."

Christoph stared stonily at the table in front of him. "I don't have any news about the escape plans," he said in a hushed voice. "To be honest, I think they might have changed their minds."

"Why? They're almost at the finish line."

"There's too much upheaval in Berlin at the moment. The level of security restrictions is too high."

"Is that so? I see you've developed a taste for Czech beer," Hausser remarked, nodding at the Urquell. "So what are *your* plans in the current climate?"

"You have me under surveillance twenty-four seven, so you know that better than I. But I have no plans to go to Czechoslovakia if that's what you're insinuating."

Hausser scratched his chin and regarded Christoph intently. "If it were up to me, I would let the plebs flee; all those who are demonstrating, everyone who is complaining about the State. This country doesn't need reform, it needs loyalty. What the State needs is idealists. For a strong society that fights for their country, isn't that right?"

Christoph muttered incoherently into his beer.

Hausser fished a folded piece of paper out of his inside jacket pocket and laid it in front of Christoph.

"What is this?"

"A list of bank accounts that I want to investigate. I need a report on the money transactions funnelled through these accounts. Content. Size. Timing."

Christoph picked up the paper and scanned the column of numbers. "Who do they belong to?"

"That is secondary. Just get me the details I need."

Christoph threw the piece of paper onto the table. "I can't do that; it's not my department. And besides, that kind of unauthorised access will be discovered very easily."

Hausser chuckled in his seat. "My dear Midas, you have already been discovered. That's why you are sitting here with me. This is the essence of our relationship: I ask you for information, and you provide it. Period."

"But I could be fired for this."

"You've never had a problem with taking that risk in order to grease your own palms. Now you will be doing it as a matter of state security. Consider it an act of heroism for your country."

"Bloody hell," muttered Christoph, getting to his feet. "This is never going to end, is it?"

Hausser smiled and took a sip of his beer.

Hausser was lying on his bed, listening to Christoph once more begging Lena not to leave him. A plea fit for an altar and the immaculate Virgin. But Lena was an iron virgin with a will of steel.

"But it was more than ten years ago, Lena. I was not myself that night," Christoph cried. "The Stasi poisoned me; they pumped me full of drugs and set the whole thing up. That's their job, Lena; they poison us. Pitch us against each other."

Listening to Christoph's pathetic excuses, Hausser couldn't help laughing. But then Lena's voice wiped the smile off his face. "It's not allowed to happen ever again. Do you understand? I won't tolerate that kind of weakness from you. It's disgusting and primitive."

Hausser sat up abruptly and went into his living room. On the monitor of his remaining camera in the living room, he could see them sitting on the sofa, holding hands. He realised that Lena had not removed her wedding band. *Perhaps he had relied too heavily on her demands for a divorce?*

"If you give me another chance, I'll make sure that you never regret it," Christoph was saying.

"Promise me that we will have the kind of life we have always planned to have. Away from all this," she said, casting a forlorn look around the living room.

"I promise, Lena. In fact, I'm wondering whether we shouldn't leave after all."

"Do you mean to say that we shouldn't flee with Schröder and the others?"

"No. I don't think that's going to happen for them anyway. I'm saying that maybe we should try to get to Warsaw, and move on from there . . ."

Hausser smiled and punched the air in victory; the final push on Midas had proven successful as expected.

"I'm sure we can make a good life for ourselves, as long as we get away from here—"

Lena let go of his hand. "And end up like all the other refugees, with nothing but the clothes on their backs?"

"I still have my contacts in the West. We can start over *there*."

"You mean start at the bottom again? You said yourself it was here the new opportunities would arise if the State failed. Was that not the whole reason why you wanted to stay? Wait for a regime change that must come? Wait for the redevelopment and investment in a unified Germany? So that we will become rich?"

"Yes, that's what I said, Lena. But things have just become a little more complicated."

"So make them uncomplicated, Christoph. If you and I are going to give our marriage another chance, you have to forget everything about escaping and ensure that we have a future *here*." She stood up and walked out the door, leaving Christoph alone in the living room.

Hausser slammed his fist on the desk in front of him. *It almost worked. He was so damn close to making it work!*

38

Louise stared at the contents of the mouldy shoe box that she had opened on the kitchen table in *Bianca*. It had started to rain, and there was a light pitter-patter on the cabin roof.

"It seems I knew even less about my brother than I thought," she said.

"We all have our secrets," said Ravn. He was standing just behind her, looking over her shoulder, and now he started searching the kitchen cabinets for something other than Nescafé to offer her. The only thing he could find was a tot of Gammel Dansk bitters, which Louise politely declined.

"I don't understand why he would keep these," she said.

"Maybe the box is his trophy, and he simply didn't have the heart to throw it away, even if he knew he was never coming back. It obviously meant a lot to him. So he decided to bury his treasure in a place he knew no one would ever find it."

"No one except you," said Louise, sitting down heavily on the sofa.

Ravn turned round to face her. "I think I know where I can find some wine, if you'd still like some?"

"More than ever before," she said.

Ravn nodded and went up onto the deck. A few minutes later, he returned with a sopping-wet bottle of white wine without a label.

"That was quick," said Louise in surprise.

Ravn made no reply. He found a bottle opener in a drawer and popped the cork. He was sure the wine would be more than drinkable because he knew Eduardo's taste in wine was generally good; he also knew Eduardo would give him an earful when his friend realised the bottle he'd been cooling over the railing had been snatched. Ravn shrugged, picked two clean glasses from the cupboard, and took a seat on the sofa next to Louise.

"Mogens seems to be very organised," said Ravn, pouring them each a glass.

The shoe box was filled with dozens of letters and printed-out emails from women. It appeared that he had been corresponding with these women for a period of years; the letters were organised alphabetically—Mogens had printed his replies and attached them to the letters with paper clips.

"I don't like the idea of rifling through his private life," said Louise, sipping her wine. "It feels wrong to spy on him."

Ravn couldn't help thinking of his own snooping into Eva's private life, but hastily pushed the thought to the back of his mind. "I get that. But on the other hand, the letters might reveal who he was in contact with just before he left Denmark."

Louise shrugged and started leafing through the stack of letters. Some of the women had included photographs of themselves in various stages of undress. She picked up a random letter dated a few years previously and started to read. "Vivi, from Brande, describes herself as 'an erotic Aries and mother to four cats,'" she said, shaking her head. Then she read Mogens's response: "He replies that he is a pilot for Scandinavian Airlines. He tells her about some of the many destinations he flies to, and how much money he earns."

Louise put down the stack of correspondence with Vivi and picked up another stack. "In this one, Mogens appears to have risen in the ranks; he says he's a chief surgeon—and his salary has also increased."

"Impressive," said Ravn ironically. "Is it okay if I help you read?" he asked, pointing at the stacks of letters.

"Please," said Louise, and they began going through the letters together, more systematically.

It soon became clear that Mogens had no lack of imagination. And all the correspondence followed the same formula, wherein Mogens had created long and colourful stories about his wealth and achievements. Taken as a whole, the letters testified to several doctorates, military and civilian titles, as well as a formidable fortune earned in a lengthy list of financial ventures; he was an IT millionaire, trader on the stock exchange, property magnate, and entrepreneur in various fields. "It's amazing to see how many women played the game," said Louise. "As if they wanted to believe the illusion."

"Until he blew them off," said Ravn. "I haven't found a single email indicating that he actually met any of these women, have you?"

Louise shook her head. It seemed as if Mogens dropped the women as soon as the question of the inevitable first meeting came up. There were also several bitter letters from women who had called him all sorts of names.

"I hate it that he made a fool of these women," said Louise. "Nobody deserves that."

"Well, at least he didn't try to con them out of any money. Unlike these people," he said, tapping a pile that he had just gone through. "These are typical 'Nigerian prince letters.'"

"What are 'Nigerian prince letters'?" asked Louise.

"They're letters from con men who try to get their victims to send money, usually for a young woman who needs financial help for an airplane ticket or a sick family member. They can also be from a businessman with a brilliant idea, or a frozen bank account whose millions can be shared after payment of a modest fee. These letters are dubbed 'Nigerian prince letters' because most of them often originate in Nigeria."

"Do you think Mogens would fall for something like that?"

Ravn shrugged. "Well, he answered these letters by email. So let us try to find out which one of these women he wrote to last."

Louise nodded and they jumped to the most recent pile of letters and emails in the shoe box.

Most of the correspondence was from foreign women who Mogens had come into contact with through international dating platforms.

"This looks like an email from a woman sent not long before Mogens disappeared," said Louise. "She calls herself 'The Berliner'—like Marlene Dietrich."

"And what does Mogens call himself this time? 'Frank Sinatra'?" Ravn said with a smile.

Louise shook her head. "This time he seems to tell the truth, perhaps because she asks him to. The Berliner says she's tired of everyone's lies," she said, glancing up at Ravn, before she began translating the email, which was written in English: "'I don't want to meet people who lie about their age, or pretend to have more money than they do. We are all people made of flesh and blood, irrespective of age, shape, or size. We are all driven by the hope of a better future, the belief that tomorrow will be better than today, and that our happiness is just round the corner, waiting for us. Is my happiness waiting for me with you? Is your happiness waiting for you with me?'"

"What does Mogens write in reply?"

Louise smiled. "The truth. He says he lives here in Christianshavn. That he has a boring job, but he loves to walk along the canal on his way to work every morning."

Ravn sat up on the sofa. "Does he mention anything about a meeting?"

Louise flipped through to the end. "No, it doesn't look like it. Their correspondence seems to end quite abruptly with an email about a month before Mogens disappeared," she said, pointing to the date at the top. "She writes that Berlin is lovely at this time of year and tells him about a concert that she attended. Mogens either didn't reply, or he didn't print out the email."

"Does she give him her real name or some kind of address?" Ravn asked.

Louise skimmed the letters. "It doesn't seem like it, but there is an email address: Schumann48@yahoo.com."

Ravn downed his glass of wine. "What about Mogens's address?"

"Just a Yahoo! address as well. He must have created it specially because it's not the email address I have for him."

"You could write to him at this address. Chances are he probably still checks it."

"Yes, of course. I could do that," she said, pausing to take sip of her wine. "But I have no idea what I should write, to be honest."

"Tell him that you miss him, and that you would like to help. Tell him that if he returns with the money and Lauritzen's accounts ledger, they will drop the charges against him. Even if the police insist on charging him, it won't be more than a minimum sentence. Tell him that things aren't nearly as bad as he might think."

Louise nodded thoughtfully and laid the emails back in the shoe box.

Ravn accompanied Louise to her car, which was parked on the other side of the road by the canal. He deposited the shoe box on the passenger seat.

"Thanks so much for your help, Thomas," she said. "I have no idea what I would have done without you."

Ravn put his hands in the front pockets of his jeans and shrugged. "Don't mention it, Louise. I hope you get hold of him, and maybe talk some sense into your brother's head."

Louise stood on her toes and planted a kiss on Ravn's mouth.

The kiss surprised him, and he kept his hands in his pockets as he returned the kiss.

She smiled at him briefly, then got into her car and drove away.

Ravn felt as if he were rooted to the cobblestones. He stared after her Fiat as it headed slowly in the direction of Christianshavn Square and disappeared round the corner.

"Who the hell has stolen my wine?!" Eduardo's voice resounded over the dark quay behind him.

39

Seven months earlier
Berlin
19 September 2013

The cold brought Mogens back to consciousness. He opened his eyes, but it was impossible to see anything in the darkness. The water covering his body was so cold it cut to the bone, and his body went into spasms. He tried to get out of the water, but his ankles, wrists, and neck were chained to the bath, his head restrained so that only his mouth lay above the water's surface. Yanking at the chains, he started to panic because the more he struggled, the grip of the chains tightened, and he screamed for help. His screams echoed in the dark, the water sloshed over the sides, and the dog chain around his neck was about to strangle him. He tried to calm down as best he could. Overcome by fear, cold, and exhaustion at last, Mogens began to weep. He had no idea how he had ended up in the cold-water bath, nor where he was. His mind grappled to remember . . . Lauritzen . . . skipping the country . . . waiting . . . emails . . . Schumann48 . . . The Berliner . . . Teufel Berg . . . the whispering wind . . . dark . . . utter darkness.

The sound of footsteps. A scraping against stone. *A chair dragged across a cement floor?* he wondered. "Help!" yelled Mogens. "Help me!"

Silence descended in the dark once more.

A sweet smell of perfume filtered through the stench of dirty water and the dank air around him. Again, he called for help. No answer.

Then a squeaking sound, as if a tap being turned. The next moment, ice-cold water poured over his head. Mogens screamed in terror and gasped for breath. He tried to avoid the stream, but the dog chain held his head fast. The bathwater rose till it covered his jaw and mouth, and he dared not scream lest he drown, and concentrated on trying to breathe through his nose. When the water rose over his head completely, he held his breath for as long as he could. His heart was hammering in his chest. He felt himself sink to the bottom of the bath, and then all his senses disappeared.

When Mogens came to, everything was dark. He was still chained to the bath, naked. He was no longer submerged in water, but the tap above his head was dripping as an evil reminder that, at any moment, the water could gush out and drown him, as if he were a rat in a barrel.

Again, he caught a faint scent of sweet perfume in the air.

40

Lichtenberg, East Berlin
19 October 1989

Strauss's fat fingers burrowed into the little glass bowl of brandy liqueur chocolates beside him on his desk. He grabbed a handful and popped them into his mouth, which was already full. The chomping sounds resounded in his cramped, dark office, where the blinds were drawn. Hausser was slouched in the chair opposite Strauss's desk, chewing on his nails. The dark rings under his eyes and his unshaven face reflected his lack of sleep and miserable state of mind.

"Do you think I could put in a request for one of those spotlights the guys from border patrol use?" asked Hausser.

"What do you need a spotlight for?" asked Strauss.

"To deprive Midas of his beauty sleep," said Hausser. "We could set it up in the convent garden next door to his place. Erect some scaffolding and leave out some paintbrushes, as if it's part of a major renovation of their residential block."

"It looks like you're the one who doesn't get any beauty sleep. And I'm sure the army needs all the spotlights they have for their own work."

"Hmm. Perhaps you're right," said Hausser, spitting out a piece of nail. "How about food poisoning, then? We could gain access to his flat and arrange for a daily dose of strychnine in their food. We could break down Midas's reserves like that instead."

"Have you lost your mind?" Strauss said, staring at him in horror.

"Are you suggesting we poison an entire family? They have a child, don't they?"

"Yes, a daughter, Renate, nine years old." Hausser shrugged. "It's no different than what they are doing in Hohenschönhausen every day; the boys over there are experimenting with radiation, I believe. Many inmates suffer from cancer now. Leukaemia, I believe. Personally, I think this kind of process is much too slow to be effective."

Strauss stopped chewing and frowned at Hausser. "We do not operate in Hohenschönhausen. We are conducting an investigation of a normal family in the heart of Berlin Mitte. They are citizens of the German Democratic Republic, Hausser."

"Which is precisely why this case is so unique!"

"Oh yeah? What's so unique about it?"

Hausser sat up in his chair. "What are the founding pillars of each and every incarceration and interrogation of enemies of the State?" He went on without bothering to wait for Strauss's reply. "First: Ensure the enemy's loss of identity. Second: Disorientate the enemy. And, most importantly, third: Undermine the enemy's authority. Every junior officer of the Stasi knows this. But, in Midas's case, I have proved that we don't *need* to incarcerate the enemy in order to achieve these objectives, because we can attain the same results within the confines of the enemy's home."

Strauss folded his arms over his chest. "I'm worried about you, Hausser. This case has . . . gotten the better of you."

"But I've almost broken him, Strauss. I'm so close."

"Müller tells me there is no longer an indication Christoph Schumann or his collaborators intend to flee. Also, the implicated French attaché at the embassy has been recalled to France."

"Müller doesn't know squat," said Hausser. "Midas still has plans to escape—so do the others. It's bound to happen any day now!"

Strauss extracted another packet of brandy liqueur chocolates from his drawer and emptied the contents into his bowl. "I'm just telling you what has been reported. By the way, what's the story behind the bank accounts that Schumann is investigating? Division Seventeen is up in arms about that. They were just about to arrest him, when they were told he is one of our informants."

"The accounts themselves are not important," said Hausser. "I ordered him to collect that information merely to put pressure on him, undermine his authority with the bank—the third rule. Get it?"

"Bloody hell, Hausser. You go too far. I have to close the case. There's no point in pursuing it."

"What are you talking about? This man has committed acts against the State for years. Not to mention the fact that he's now planning to desert the Republic!"

"Hausser, in the current climate, every single citizen of the Republic wants to flee the country! The streets are overflowing with 'enemies of the State'! The first free trade union has just been established. We have hundreds of other cases to take care of at the moment . . ."

"A trade union?! In the GDR?!"

"Yes, for fuck's sake! 'Reform,' they call it. I need you, Hausser. Close the file on Operation Midas, get some sleep, sober up—if it helps—or take some pills. I don't care what you have to do to return to reality—just *do* it!"

Hausser rubbed his tired eyes. "You're right," he said. "Perhaps it's a waste of time . . ."

"Brandy chocolate?" Strauss said, offering him one.

"No, thanks."

Strauss shrugged and popped a few more into his own mouth. "There's a rumour that Krentz intends to grant amnesty to all demonstrators and citizens who have fled over the border. What do you think about that?"

"I think that's what happens when you put a Boy Scout in charge of the entire nation."

"They should have appointed Margot as the direct successor to her husband," said Strauss.

"You would have Margot Honecker elected as the leader of the nation?"

"Why not? During her tenure as education minister, she wished to introduce compulsory weapons training in high schools. *That* is the kind of strength and sharp vision we need in this country," said Strauss.

"You know what, you're right!" said Hausser, jumping to his feet with a manic expression in his eyes. "Of course!"

"What now?" said Strauss with a sigh.

"There's nothing wrong with the process, Strauss. The three pillars are still valid," said Hausser. "But the subject is all wrong."

"What the hell are you talking about, Hausser?"

Hausser didn't reply, dashing for the door instead.

"Where are you going? We're not done here!" yelled Strauss. To no avail, for Hausser was already out the door.

Hausser hurried down the corridor. Halfway through the DZ he noticed a hissing sound coming from the shredding room at the end of the hall; two employees were feeding documents into the machine with the same speed and agility as Strauss popping brandy liqueur chocolates. It was not a pretty sight. It was undignified; the picture of retreat. But no matter how critical the situation for the Republic was, he, Colonel Erhardt Hausser, would not let Operation Midas die—especially now that Straus had given him the scent of a solution. *Yes, Strauss had a point,* thought Hausser. It had been a mistake only to go after Midas and not his wife; just like Margot, Lena was the stronger of the two in the relationship. And therefore *she* was the one Hausser had to break in order to make them run—directly for the death strip in front of the Wall. *The politicians might be wavering, but the soldiers at the border still had their rifles poised,* Hausser thought with satisfaction as he crossed the parking lot, where the dark buildings of the Stasi HQ bowed like dutiful towers to the heavens. The sight gave him a sense of calm, and he forgave himself for his stupidity for not pursuing Lena before. He knew it was the power of money that motivated Lena; *the promise of material wealth* was her weak point.

41

Copenhagen
April 2014

Ravn stood on the corner of Viktoriagade and Halmtorvet, leaning against the wall. Møffe lay at his feet, apparently pissed off by the long waiting time. On the benches dotted around the square, parents with their prams and local bums alike were sitting in the sun, enjoying the first hint of spring in the air. Ravn was keeping an eye on the parking bays in front of Station City, which were designated for civilian police vehicles. He had tried to reach Mikkel on the phone that morning, but to no avail. A subsequent call to Crime Ops confirmed that Mikkel was out on patrol and would only be back in the late afternoon. Ravn decided to wait— stake out Station City till Mikkel pitched up—as if the station were one of the zillions of biker gang HQs they used to stake out together.

More than once, Ravn's thoughts wandered to Louise. He hadn't heard from her since the day they parted in the parking lot after going through Mogens's letters. He had felt like calling her, but hadn't known how to handle the situation. He had no idea what to make of the kiss they'd exchanged—*was it merely an expression of gratitude from her side, or was there more to it?* Either way, he couldn't help feeling guilty, as if he'd betrayed Eva—which was absurd—not least because he was waiting here to find out with whom *she* had betrayed *him.*

A dark blue Golf pulled up into the parking bays directly in front of him, interrupting his thoughts. Ravn immediately recognised Mikkel behind the wheel. He crossed the road with Møffe at his heels just as

Mikkel and Dennis Melby got out of the car. "Mikkel!" Ravn called out as he approached.

The two officers turned to face him. "Is that ol' mutt of yours still alive?" Dennis laughed, looking at Møffe.

Ravn ignored him and looked at Mikkel. "I have tried to reach you on the phone. Millions of times."

Mikkel locked the car. "You know how it is," he said with a shrug. "We've been run off our feet after the new reform and—"

"Have you got anything for me?" Ravn said, cutting Mikkel off mid-sentence.

Mikkel turned to Dennis. "You go on ahead; I'll be there in five minutes."

"Stay chipper, Ravn," said Dennis. "You're starting to look like your dog," he added, pointing at Møffe, who sat at Ravn's feet with his tongue hanging out of his mouth.

Again, Ravn refused to take the bait and merely stared after Melby, who walked over to the main entrance of the station, all arms and bulging legs like a gorilla. He had never been able to stand that arsehole, who apparently hadn't stopped popping anabolic steroids since he last saw him.

"So, did you find out who was texting Eva or not?" Ravn said, training his gaze on Mikkel once more.

"Not yet."

"Okay. Any particular reason why not—apart from being so busy implementing new reform measures?"

"I thought I was doing you a favour."

"How so?"

"By giving you some time to think things over. So you could consider whether it was such a clever idea to track this guy down."

"Thank you for your concern. But I have spent more than enough time thinking things over, which is why I came to you, because I thought you would help me."

"Can't you see what a stupid move this is? What a shit parade this is going to cause?"

"There isn't going to be a shit parade."

"No?" Mikkel looked at him sceptically. "So tell me what's going to happen if I find this guy's name for you?" he said, not waiting for an answer and leaning against the car instead. "Ten minutes later, you'll pitch up at somebody's door—and headbutt the guy first and ask questions later. Then the guy slaps you with charges of assault, the whole thing boomerangs back to me when the prosecution finds out who gave you his name, and there goes my career down the drain."

"Don't be ridiculous. I'm not going to headbutt anyone. I'm crap at headbutting folks, you know that. I always end up hurting myself instead," Ravn said with a smile.

Mikkel didn't return his smile. "I know you, Ravn. You can't let things go. Melby is right; you're just like your dog."

"Nah, we've both mellowed with age. Besides, I've met someone."

"Seriously?" Mikkel pushed of the car. "Who?"

"No one you know," Ravn said, looking at his feet. He hated lying to Mikkel. "It's . . . still new, and she's the reason I want to get to the bottom of this as soon as possible."

"Are you home tonight?"

"Yeah, or at The Sea Otter."

"I'll figure something out," Mikkel said, banging on the roof of the Golf. Then he turned and made for the station entrance.

Ravn felt like a jerk. He promised himself he would keep Mikkel out of this mess with Eva.

"Move your arse, Møffe," he said, pulling on the leash, but Møffe refused to budge.

It was a crock of shit, Ravn thought. *Neither he nor Møffe had mellowed with age. On the contrary.*

42

Hausser banged on the front door so hard it resounded up the stairwell. He had trimmed his moustache, and the single vodka he'd had with his morning coffee had given some colour to his cheeks. All in all, he felt almost presentable.

After some shuffling of feet inside, the door opened, and Klara's head appeared round the side. She looked at Hausser with tired eyes. "Good . . . morning, Herr Hausser. What can I do for you?"

Hausser gave her a cold, hard stare. "I know that you do some chores for the Schumanns," he said. "You clean their flat, wash their clothing, and babysit their daughter from time to time."

Klara opened the door a little wider, which revealed that she was wearing a stained morning robe and a scruffy pair of slippers. "Yes . . . and?"

"As of today you will no longer do this work for them."

"Wh-why?" said Klara.

Hausser ignored her question. "How much do they pay you?"

"That . . . that is a personal matter between myself and Frau Schumann. It is no business of the caretaker," she said, arching her neck with a show of pride.

"We know that you have taken foreign money for your work. The Schumanns obtained this money by illegal means, and by accepting this money, you are implicated in their crimes."

Klara gaped at Hausser. She was about to reply, but Hausser whipped out his Stasi badge and held it in front of her face. "We have been watching you, Klara," Hausser said, shifting his gaze to her heavy breasts, which bulged just below the surface of her dirty flannel robe. "We appreciate that you have always been loyal to the Party, Klara. We have not forgotten your dutiful assistance back in the days at the furniture factory in Leipzig, when you pointed out co-workers who were hostile to the State."

Klara dropped her eyes and stared at the ground.

"For this reason, I am willing to assume that your transgression with the Schumanns is merely a misunderstanding, am I right?" With a single index finger Hausser raised her chin and forced her to look at him. "Am I right, I said."

"Yes, I . . . I'm very sorry."

"So? How much do they pay you?"

"It varies. But, as a rule, I get one mark an hour. D-mark, that is. I can fetch the money for you; I've been saving it. I don't want that money . . ."

"You've accepted the money, Klara, so you should keep it." Hausser could see that the woman was on the verge of tears. Her lips were trembling, and her eyes were shiny. Hausser thought she looked like a cow being led to slaughter. *A fair assumption*, he mused.

"I . . . I promise that I will never go near those people again," she said.

"Excellent, Klara, I'll make a note of that. Anything else would have disappointed me."

Hausser patted her on the cheek. Gently, at first. But then the pats became smart, staccato slaps, and Klara accepted her punishment without a word. He kept an eye on the tears brimming in her eyes, while her cheek turned red, then scarlet. When at last the tears fell, he stopped.

"That should do," said Hausser. "Go inside now and dry your tears, Klara."

43

Berlin Mitte
21 October 1989

Just after midday, Hausser walked up Unter den Linden. Folks had their noses pushed up against the windows of the Intershop, which only accepted currencies from the West, meaning only a select few of his fellow citizens of the GDR would have the possibility to buy anything inside. Despite the Deutschmarks that she had earned from the Schumanns, Hausser doubted that Klara could afford much more than a pair of pantyhose.

Hausser crossed the road. The traffic was heavy, mostly Trabants and more mundane cars with number plates from the West. He continued down the boulevard till he arrived in front of the fashionable clothing store Madeleine on the corner of Friedrichstrasse and Unter den Linden. There was a long queue in front of the store, but when he showed his Stasi badge to the young man at the door, he was immediately shown inside.

Inside, the walls were painted in pastel colours, the lighting was dim, and the scent of perfume wafted in the air; all in all, the boutique exuded exclusivity and luxury. The clientele appeared to be middle-aged women and their grown-up daughters who generally had a self-satisfied expression on their faces, as if they belonged to a chosen race—which was not far from the truth in the GDR.

Hausser began looking through a display of dresses on hangers. When he glanced at the price tags, he immediately thought there must be some mistake, but no, it was true: Every single dress cost several hundred D-marks each; one dress in particular cost over a thousand D-marks!

"Can I help you?" a familiar voice said behind him.

Hausser turned round and smiled at Lena.

"You . . . ?" she said in utter surprise. It was also obvious that his presence made her nervous.

"I've always wondered what one of these boutiques looked like on the inside," he said. "It is very . . . charming."

"Are you looking to buy anything in particular, Herr Hausser?"

"Please, call me Erhardt, Lena. We are neighbours, after all. And no, I'm not here to shop. The items here are out of my price range anyway."

"So this is an official visit?"

"Not at all, Lena. You seem nervous," he said, resting a hand on her forearm, and she froze immediately. "There is no need to be afraid. You are all in very good hands," he said, laughing. "I must say I'm impressed. I have no doubt that Madeleine could hold its own with any of its kind on Kurfürstendamm in the West."

"I wouldn't know. But here we do our best to serve the State," said Lena. "If there isn't anything else I can do for you, Herr Hausser, I must attend to our other customers now."

"But of course," said Hausser. "Nor would I want to detain you longer than is absolutely necessary." He unzipped his jacket and took out a large manila envelope. "I came to give you this." He extended it to her, but she made no attempt to take it from him.

"What . . . what is it?" Lena stammered.

With the memory of a similar envelope containing pictures of her husband fresh in her mind, the manila envelope had obviously upset her. Hausser suppressed a smile. "Pictures. Photographs that I have requested."

"What kind of photographs?"

"Hmm. I think one calls them 'portraits'? Art? Fashion, I imagine, but I'm hardly an expert on the subject," he laughed. "Open them. Now."

Lena reluctantly took the envelope from him. "Thank you, but I think I will wait until later, when I have a break. I really have to go now."

"Oh, but I insist, Lena."

She took a sharp intake of breath and looked over her shoulder before opening the envelope. Then she carefully extracted them halfway. "How did you find these?"

Hausser shrugged. "I have my ways."

Lena turned the envelope upside down and took out the pictures. She couldn't help smiling when she looked at them. "It was such a long time ago . . ."

"Nineteen seventy-eight, to be exact," Hausser said. "Your first shoot for an agency. There are also a few posed pictures taken on Alexanderplatz. Apparently, one can look good in clothing from the GDR, rather than from the West—if you have the figure for it, that is," he added with a smile.

"These pictures were taken for *Sibylle* magazine," she said.

"You are by far the prettiest of the lot," Hausser said. "You appeared on nineteen covers, I'm told. From *Sibylle* to household names like *Modische Maschen* . . ."

"Yes. I appeared on more covers than any other model in the country," said Lena. She leafed through the stack, which contained pictures from her entire career.

"You are more beautiful than any actress I have ever seen."

"I don't know what to say," Lena said, returning the pictures to the envelope. "But why are you showing me these?"

"I came across them by coincidence, and just thought that you might find them interesting," Hausser said, stroking his moustache. "Funny that you should end up here."

"I have nothing to complain about."

"Really? Perhaps it's just me, but I thought you were more ambitious."

"I don't understand where you are going with this, Herr Hausser."

"Hmm. I'm not sure either." He gave her his hand in parting. Lena took it and tried to leave but he held onto her hand. "Oh, now I know what I wanted to say. I have realised that in your business, beauty and youth are exclusive commodities with a short sell-by date, which means that you need to sell yourself as quickly and expensively as possible if you are interested in a life of material means. And then all you can do is cross your fingers and hope you have made the right choice—that you are living with the right person who can deliver an eternally sun-kissed existence. So, now you know what I came here to say: Have a good day, Lena."

Dusk was already falling as Hausser gently strolled back down Unten den Linden, heading for the town square. As soon as he found a telephone box, he would call the Intershop office and make sure this was the last day Lena would know the perfumed, dreamworld work of Madeleine.

44

Christianshavn
April 2014

The high-pitched laughter of Eduardo's redhead rang in the air, drawing disgruntled looks from The Sea Otter's patrons who were trying to mind their own business with their beers in a corner. The noisy couple were holding hands at the bar, and Eduardo half-heartedly hushed his date as he poured beer into her glass with a fat grin on his face.

Ravn came up to the bar and ordered a round from Johnson. Victoria had just humiliated him in a game of pool, and she was already taking on the next contender by the billiard table. Ravn took a sip of his Hof and glanced at the redhead, who appeared to be a new acquaintance because he hadn't seen her with Eduardo before.

Mikkel came through the front door. He looked round in the dim light until he spotted Ravn and came over to the bar. "I'm sorry I'm late," he said.

"What are you having?"

"The same as you," Mikkel said, pointing at the Hof, and Ravn introduced him to Johnson.

"Ah, so you're Mikkel," Johnson said, putting a beer in front of him. "Since this old codger stopped working for the force, we don't see many cops around here."

Mikkel shrugged in reply. "Shall we find a quiet place to sit?" he said to Ravn.

They left the bar area and took seats by the window with a view of the canal. Mikkel unzipped his windbreaker, took out Eva's work phone, and put it on the table between them. "I thought you might like to have this back," he said.

Ravn looked at the phone without making a move to pick it up. "What have you found out?"

"I could tell you that I wasn't able to find him. That the telephone company no longer has his details, and that the investigation ends here . . ."

"But?"

"But I don't want to lie to you."

"Did you find him or not, Mikkel?"

Mikkel was distracted by another screech of laughter from Eduardo's date in the background. She clapped one hand over her mouth and waved apologetically to the room with the other. Eduardo simply pulled her close and grinned like a cat.

Mikkel returned his attention to Ravn. "You won't like what I have to say—"

"So, it's someone I know?"

Mikkel ignored the question. "—and quite frankly, it doesn't do anyone any good because regardless of what you might think, Eva loved you . . ."

"Is it someone I know?" Ravn said, a little louder this time.

"Yes."

"Who?"

Mikkel looked down at the table. "Those text messages are taken out of context."

"What do you mean?"

"It's not what you think . . ."

Ravn shook his head. "How can you possibly know what—" He stopped short and looked at Mikkel, whose shoulders drooped, his eyes nailed to the table. "*You* . . . ?" his voice broke.

"Nothing happened between us . . . nothing serious."

"*You* . . . and Eva?!" Ravn had stopped breathing.

"I wanted to tell you thousands of times . . . apologise for—"

"*You* . . . and Eva?!" Ravn repeated, stupefied.

"Just so you know: There was never anything physical between us."

"You . . . you were the one who wrote all that soppy bullshit to her?"

"I'm so sorry, Ravn, I didn't . . . it was the last thing I wanted . . . I felt awful about it . . . especially after her death."

"Yes," Ravn hissed, clenching his fists on the table. "That must have been really hard for you."

"Believe me, I feel like the biggest shit on earth . . ."

Ravn could hear the words coming out of Mikkel's mouth, but his brain kept telling him that it couldn't possibly be true, that any minute he would wake up on *Bianca* and try to shake off this nightmare. "How . . . ?" he said.

"Are you really sure you want to hear this?"

"How did this start?" Ravn said.

Mikkel swallowed the spit that had gathered in his mouth. "About five years ago, my mother became seriously ill. She had dementia, and her condition deteriorated rapidly. We—my brother and I—had her admitted to hospital, but things only got worse, and in the end, she couldn't even recognise us—"

"Jump ahead to the part where you and Eva started meeting each other."

"Anders, my brother, had a different view on who should be her guardian. I didn't want to share my mother's illness or personal family matters with a stranger, so I called the only lawyer I knew . . . and that's how it started."

"I didn't even fucking know you had a brother."

"I . . . we never spoke about personal stuff, Ravn."

"No, you used my girlfriend for that," Ravn spat out. "And what about your wife? Does she know about this?"

"No, nobody knows anything. It never went beyond what is on that phone . . . those ridiculous text messages I wrote."

Ravn could feel the rage rising inside. "Do not lie to me; you guys obviously met, it's clear from the messages . . ."

"Twice. We met twice, for a glass a wine, while Eva spoke of nothing but *you*. *I* was the one who lost my shit. *I* was the one who behaved unforgivably, *I* was the one who was in love with her, not the other way around."

"I think you should go now."

"I'm really sorry, Ravn. I don't know what else I can say . . . I'm sorry." Mikkel stood up and carefully pushed his chair back under the table. He lingered for a moment, as if he was hoping that Ravn would say something, but Ravn was dead silent, his fists clenched, staring at the table in front of him.

"Call, if . . ." Mikkel gave up, thinking better of it. He turned and made for the door instead.

Ravn emptied his beer and rested the bottle on the table. Swivelled the bottle so the label was facing him. Stared at the Hof insignia, tried to focus on that, but it was no good. Tunnel vision on Mikkel's back. Adrenaline pumping in his veins. His heart pounding in his ears. Instinct manifested in a glowing red rage. And the next thing he knew, Ravn was on his feet, and the chair toppled over backwards and crashed to the floor.

Mikkel half-turned in time to see Ravn throw himself towards him. They toppled over and landed on a table that broke under their weight, then crashed onto the floor hard with Ravn on top of Mikkel. The first punch landed on Mikkel's jaw, followed up by a blow to his nose, which immediately sprayed blood from both nostrils. Ravn meant to headbutt the bastard for good measure, but Mikkel managed to move in time, and his head slammed into the tabletop beneath them instead. Then everything went black. He felt a blow to the right side of his head, then Mikkel tried to squirm his way out from under him. Ravn lashed out in thin air. Shouts erupted above him. Then someone grabbed him by the collar and pulled him off Mikkel. "All right, the party's over—for both of you!" bellowed Johnson, who was holding him in an iron grip.

The tunnel vision faded, and The Sea Otter came into view on the other end. Ravn saw Mikkel get to his feet slowly. Bloody and beaten. "I suggest you get out of here while I hold onto this one," Johnson said. Mikkel got the point and made for the door. Ravn tried to shake off Johnson, but nobody got out of this man's grip.

"*Madre mia*, Ravn, what was that?" Eduardo asked by his side.

"I'm okay now, Johnson," Ravn said. "You can let go."

Johnson let him go reluctantly. "What the hell was that all about? I thought you guys were friends?"

"Yeah, well, sometimes you're mistaken."

45

On the square in front of the red-brick Town Hall, a thousand-strong crowd had gathered. The chief of police stood next to the mayor on the stairs leading up to the hall, making a speech before the demonstrators and flashing news cameras. On behalf of the police, the chief apologised for the rough-handed behaviour of his men during recent demonstrations. Then the mayor and high-ranking SED politicians spoke about reform and human rights. *Blah, blah, blah*, thought Hausser, who was watching the performance on television. The big shots on the steps clapped in unison, reminding him of a flock of penguins. To his mind, the men giving speeches from the podium were greater traitors than the people who had come to hear them speak. The only thing that surprised him was that the demonstrators didn't seem to realise that the politicians would say anything to survive and save face. Hausser turned off the TV in disgust and went out.

It was two thirty in the afternoon. Just over an hour before he had seen Lena leave the Schumanns' apartment with her daughter and two large laundry bags. After their little chat, Klara obviously didn't do the Schumanns' washing anymore, and Hausser saw a modicum of justice in the fact that Lena now had to do all the family's washing in the common laundry room in the cellar because they hadn't deigned to buy their own machine—as they had preferred to pay someone else to do their dirty laundry.

Hausser made his way through the labyrinthine dark cellar, wrinkling his nose at the stringent combination of mould and synthetic Fewa laundry detergent in his nostrils. A rumble of washing machines came from the door at the far end of the corridor. He stopped on the threshold and leaned against the doorframe. Four washing machines were spinning in the front room, and washing lines ran like telegraph lines just under the low ceiling of the drying room beyond. Lena was busy hanging up laundry on the first line. Dark sweat patches were visible under her armpits. Her daughter and a red plastic laundry basket on wheels stood beside her. Lena asked her daughter to pass her more washing pegs.

"Working hard, I see," said Hausser. He pushed off the doorframe and walked into the drying room.

Lena started in fright.

"Forgive me if I scared you," said Hausser with a smile. "Please, don't let me interrupt."

Lena accepted another peg from her daughter and continued hanging up the clothing in silence.

"I don't think I've seen either of you in here before. I think Klara is the one who usually does your washing, is that not so?"

"Klara is ill," said the girl.

"Renate!" Lena said in a curt voice, gesturing with her hand that she needed another peg.

Hausser stroked the girl's hair. "Ah, I see. Fortunately, you and your mother can wash the clothing yourselves. Besides, it's much better to do it yourself. It feels good to lend a helping hand, doesn't it?"

The girl nodded. "Yes, it works perfectly."

"Spoken like a true Young Pioneer," said Hausser. "How old are you?"

"Nine."

"That's a good age. Do you keep up with your homework?"

The girl nodded.

"And practice for gymnastics? I know you've won lots of medals, haven't you?"

"Yeah," the girl said, wide-eyed, clearly surprised that he would know that.

"Renate, be a good girl and go up to the flat for more pegs, please," said Lena.

The girl looked at the pegs in her hand and then at her mother. "But we have plenty—"

"Be a good girl and run along now!"

Renate put down the pegs in the red washing basket and sprinted out of the room.

Lena picked up the next item of clothing and hung it up.

"Good heavens, you're working up a sweat, Lena."

She was clearly trying to avoid Hausser's eyes.

"Not quite the same as working at Madeleine, is it now? Not quite the same as posing for the cameras on Alexanderplatz, is it?"

"I know what you're trying to do, Hausser," Lena said. She shook her head and hung up the next item of clothing. "But I'm just fine without my work at the boutique."

Hausser looked down at the washing basket. Ran his hand over the wet clothing. "Even your washing is decadent," he said, clicking his tongue. "Look at all these foreign brands."

"Are you going to inspect our washing now? Go ahead," she said, giving the basket a nudge, and it rolled over to Hausser.

"No, that won't be necessary. But you can know for a fact that whatever you do, I will know about it. For your own good sake, of course. Because you and your husband don't know how to behave properly." He handed her a pair of panties, which she snatched out of his hand.

Hausser watched her work. "You know, I don't believe you will ever become a part of our community. You would have been so much happier in the West. I almost wish you had escaped." He handed her another piece of clothing. "I think the two of you should have stuck to the original plan, instead of trying to double-cross the others. I mean, look how well things have turned out for the other traitors. They have just been awarded amnesty. Just imagine that while you are standing here, hanging up your own washing, they are shopping till they drop on Kurfürstendamm," Hausser said with a sinister little smile. "I can only imagine how much that has got to hurt. How unjust this must all seem to you."

"Do you really think that's all I'm made of?" Lena shook her head in disgust.

"Ooh, Lena seems to have forgotten that I know a great deal about her. Every single little detail about her," he said, looking her body up and down.

"What exactly is it you want, Hausser?"

"I want to ensure that you understand your predicament."

"*My* predicament?" she stopped her work and looked at Hausser. Behind them, a washing machine was spinning ever faster with a high-pitched whine. "What about *yours?*" Lena said. "Are you really so blind that you cannot see what is about to happen to this country? You keep talking about the West. Don't you understand that soon there will be neither a 'West' nor an 'East' Germany?"

"I know that this is the pathetic opinion that you share with your husband. Based on your hopes for a capitalist buffet for traitors and tricksters. But you will be sorely mistaken. Just like those morons who challenge the power of the State."

"Do you mean the three hundred thousand people who demonstrated in Leipzig yesterday?"

"Are you suddenly showing solidarity with the masses?" Hausser smiled sarcastically.

"No matter what happens, soon we will be able to travel wherever we want. All of us who do not have to take responsibility for the evils that have been committed in the name of the State. Where does that leave *you*, Herr Stasiman?"

Hausser was no longer smiling.

"What hole do you think you can hide in?"

"I think you should stop now, Lena"

"Why? Your time will soon be over. Little people like you with no life, people who are nothing without their Stasi badges." She put her hands on her hips. "Let me guess where you live—in one those concrete silos with all the other, equally pathetic and lonely Stasi men. I feel sorry for you. Do you understand?"

He took a step towards her and kicked aside the washing basket between them. "I wish I could respect your courage, but it's based on nothing but ignorance. Like all the other people who have betrayed their fellow men, who we blinded by their own arrogance; also *they* believed that the world they lived in with their families, neighbours, and colleagues was the only reality that existed. Even their utopian dreams of a life in the West were anchored in a tangible world. They don't have the fantasy to imagine the abyss that lies just beneath the surface. They never understood how close they were to the dark abyss, till they dropped into *my* world of darkness, Lena."

Lena arched her neck, but Hausser could see that his words had scared her, so he went on: "Because you never see us, you have no conception of what can hit you before it's too late. And we are deaf to your cries of remorse when you finally realise that everything is lost. *We* are the ones who feed the machine, the people who remove the grit in the cogwheels." Hausser smiled and removed the stray tuft of sweaty hair that was plastered to her forehead.

Her lips trembled, but her gaze was firm.

"No matter what you believe, you will never win. You are finished. All of you are finished."

The spinning machine behind them finally ceased and Lena's ragged breathing was the only sound in the cellar. Hausser was standing so close to her that he could feel her breasts against his chest. He could smell her body odour combined with the wet laundry—a stink that was far removed from the sweet perfume smell that he had always associated with her; *a Klara stink*, Hausser thought with a revulsion so strong he was sorely tempted to strangle her with the washing line and string her up between her shirts and underwear.

"Mother . . ."

Renate was standing next to the washing machine with a fresh pack of pegs in her hand.

Lena scraped past Hausser and took her daughter's hand. Together they hurried out of the laundry room.

Hausser took a step backwards and felt the wet laundry like a damp hand against the back of his neck. He turned round and in a fit of rage began tearing it down and trampling it into the dirt on the floor.

A few minutes later, he stopped and leaned against the washing machine, gasping for breath. The worst fucking part of it all was that she was right. Even for an unintelligent bird like Lena, the state of the nation was blatantly clear; the Republic was perched on the edge of a precipice. But for now, he still had the power. And before it was too late, he would let her feel the full force of his power and savour her fear; allow himself the pleasure of drowning in her terror.

46

Naked trees surrounded the playground on Helmholtzplatz, and the children were squealing in delight as they played on the swings and whooshed down the slide. Renate and her friends were oblivious to the misty rain as they balanced on the wooden poles that framed the playground. She performed a perfect pirouette and cast a glance over her shoulder with pride written all over her young face. "Mother, look at me!" she yelled at Lena, who was talking to another mother with a pram a little way off.

Lena turned round and nodded briefly. "Renate, Mother is going to fetch some matches," she said, waving at her daughter with her pack of cigarettes in her hand.

Renate was too absorbed in her game to reply.

Lena said goodbye to the other mother and headed down the gravel footpath that led to Raumerstrasse. When she reached the pavement, the side door of a white delivery van parked by the kerb opened, and Hausser and Müller got out. Lena stopped short in surprise, and before she could react the men grabbed an arm each and shoved Lena inside the van. "Help! Help!" she yelled, somewhat belatedly.

The woman with the pram turned round and saw the side door of the white van slide shut. Müller caught her eye, and the look on his face was enough to make her hurry away as fast as she could.

Inside the delivery van, there was a strong smell of urine that stung Lena's eyes. Dark blotches of blood were smeared on the floor.

Hausser shoved Lena onto a low seat along the far side and clasped her wrists in handcuffs that were fastened to a chain attached to a railing along the ceiling. She struggled in vain to free herself. "This is . . . you have no right to . . ." Lena stared at Hausser, terrified out of her wits. He was sitting on the bench opposite her. He looked down at his watch and took a Dictaphone out of his pocket. "The time is 1:34 p.m. on the thirtieth of October, 1989. We have arrested Lena Schumann, born in Fürstenwalde on the second of July, 1957. Are you Lena Schumann?" he said, and thrust the Dictaphone close to her mouth.

"My . . . daughter . . . she is out there alone . . ." Lena said, twisting her head towards the small, barred window behind her head. She could just catch a glimpse of the playground outside.

"Answer the question! Are you Lena Schumann?!"

"You know that I am . . . let me go . . . please—"

"The arrestee has identified herself," Hausser said. He banged his fist on the side of the van, and it immediately began to move.

Panic shone in Lena's eyes. "My daughter . . . she . . . she, please, I'm begging you to stop. She's alone!"

Hausser looked at her with cold, indifferent eyes. "Don't you think you should have thought of that before?"

"I'm begging you, please, let me go to her."

Hausser banged on the inside of the van once more, and this time the driver slammed on the brakes. Lena was flung sideways, and her head collided with the steel partition to the driver's cab. Bleeding from the wound on her head, Lena manoeuvred herself back onto the seat and desperately tried to see out the window. "I'll make a statement . . . do whatever it is you want . . . but I have to make sure that . . . my daughter gets home safely."

"Why didn't you start worrying about your child a long time ago? *Before* you and your husband began your illegal activities. *Before* you started falsifying documents and stealing inter-cheques."

"I apologise for and admit what I have done. But please let me go to my daughter."

Hausser shook his head. "It's too late, Lena. You only have yourself to blame for that. The only reason you are sitting here now is because you filled your home with material things, succumbed to an ugly greed rather than take care of your daughter."

"I'm begging you," she sobbed.

"You're *begging* me? What did I say to you in the laundry room the other day? I told you that we are indifferent to your screams for mercy. And what was your answer? You said that you did not fear me. That my time was over. Is that how you feel right now, Lena? Give me an honest answer."

Lena shook her head.

"Look out the window, Lena," Hausser said. He grabbed the chain and pulled her right up to the window. "What do you see out there, Lena? The surface. Exactly as I explained it to you; your daughter on the playground, mothers with their children, even folks on their way to yet another demonstration against the State." He pointed to a group of young men with homemade signs who were crossing the road. "Go on, take a look at the surface." Hausser let go of the chain. Lena hunched over by the window and sobbed even more.

"Tell me what I have to do . . . anything . . ."

"You're pathetic," Hausser said, pointing at the dark stains on her inner thighs. "You're already pissing yourself, and you haven't even seen the inside of one of our cells. Perhaps I should put you in one of our rubber cells so you cannot do injury to yourself, while you are tied up in perpetual darkness."

"I'm begging you to set me free, for Renate's sake."

Hausser shook his head. "Fortunately for Renate, the State has homes for children who have been let down by their criminal parents; fortunately we have a merciful government that takes care of such forlorn children."

"Please don't send her away—"

"I was brought up in one of these homes myself, and look how well I turned out," Hausser said. "That kind of experience makes you strong— you have to be, if you're going to survive—because children can be so mean to one another."

"Please don't let her suffer for what I have done."

"*You* are the one who has sealed her fate, Lena." Hausser leaned forward and looked out the window. In the distance he could just see Renate hopping from one pole to the next. "Luckily, she's so young, so there's a chance that she will forget her parents—her irresponsible mother."

Lena started to vomit, and small lumps of semi-digested food dribbled from her chin onto her pale linen suit.

"Just look at you. How weak you are." Hausser leaned over and unlocked her handcuffs.

Lena slid down onto the floor, into her own vomit and puddle of piss.

"I will do anything you say." Reaching up her arms towards him, she put a hand on his thigh.

Hausser looked down at the hand. He did not touch her, but let the hand rest where it was. "Will you testify for the State against your husband, Christoph Schumann?"

"Yes."

"Will you help us gather information that can be used against him in a court of law?"

"Yes."

"Will you testify against the conspirators who in conjunction with your husband planned crimes against the State?"

"Yes."

"But how can I know that you are telling the truth, Lena? Look at me. How can I know that you're just saying 'yes' so you can get out of here and flee with your daughter?"

"I promise I will help you, I swear—I swear on her life and my own."

"How can I be absolutely certain of your . . . loyalty?" He looked down, very briefly, at her hand, but it was long enough for her to start caressing his inner thigh.

"I am . . . loyal," she said.

"I recall that you called me pathetic and lonely."

"I'm sorry . . . I didn't mean it . . . I was angry and afraid."

"What if I said that you were right with regard to my loneliness? Who should take my loneliness away? Who will reward me for my generosity in this awkward situation that you find yourself in?"

Lena dried the vomit from her mouth and crept a little closer to him. "I will . . . I will reward you."

"Will you be my sweetheart? Call me daddy while you ride me?"

"Yes, I will . . . daddy," she nodded, then unzipped his pants and slipped her hand inside.

Hausser let her feel how hard he was before he removed her hand. Then he opened the door, letting in some fresh air and the sounds from the road and the playground. "We'll see each other again. Real soon, Lena."

Lena crept past him and got out of the van.

Hausser watched her run awkwardly up the rise to the playground and disappear behind the naked trees.

The rain hammered onto the roof, and the white headlights of cars on Schönhauser Allee penetrated the misty panes of the telephone box. Hausser fished a couple of coins out of his pockets, put them into the slot, and dialled the number. He was a little drunk, but no more than he could handle.

Keeping pace with Lena, who stayed in the living room with a bottle of vermouth till Christoph got home, Hausser had spent the entire afternoon and evening watching Lena and Renate Schumann on the last hidden camera with his bottle of absinthe. When Christoph got home, Lena kept up the façade and never mentioned a word about her ordeal; her husband hadn't noticed anything out of the ordinary—which says more about his lack of awareness than Lena's acting talents.

"Schumann," Christoph's voice came on the other end of the line.

Hausser put the Dictaphone up to the receiver and pressed "play."

"*Hallo…?*" Christoph said impatiently.

"*Will you be my sweetheart? Call me daddy while you ride me? . . . Yes, I will . . . daddy . . .*"

Christoph listened in silence as the recording from that afternoon resounded in the dark telephone box.

47

Christianshavn
April 2014

Ravn was in the captain's seat on the flybridge with Eva's telephone resting in his hands. It was long after midnight, and Christianshavn Canal was deserted. He looked down at the phone's green display, and the little battery icon blinked at him insistently.

The fact that Mikkel of all people was the one who had sent her those text messages rubbed salt in his wounds—not to mention the bitter irony that many of the messages must have been written while they were on duty together. Rage simmered below the surface of his mind. He gritted his teeth and brought a hand to his temple. His eye hurt like hell. Even though Johnson had given him a pack of ice to cool it immediately after the fight, it was still swollen. His only comfort was the hope that Mikkel's face was hurting half as bad.

He heard footsteps on the deck behind him, but Møffe was down there, and he didn't object, so it must be a friendly visitor on his way up.

"So this is where you're hiding."

Ravn turned his head and saw Eduardo come up onto the flybridge. "To what do I owe the pleasure? Do you need to borrow something?"

"Nah, just checking in on an old friend," said Eduardo. "Are you okay—ouch, that's gotta hurt!" he said when he noticed Ravn's black eye.

"Only when I blink."

Eduardo took a seat on the bench behind Ravn. "Well, you got in a few punches yourself. I've never seen you go so . . . ballistic before," he said, taking a handful of pistachio nuts out of his pocket and offering Ravn some.

Ravn declined with a wave of his hand. "I know. Don't think I've ever been that mad before."

"Your cop instincts coming back to life?"

Ravn shook his head. "On the contrary. When I was a cop, it was imperative to keep a cool head. If you pull a stunt like I did today, you're a dead man."

Eduardo cracked a nut between his teeth. "Hmm. But I understand you, *amigo*, one hundred per cent. I'm a pacifist, you know, but I don't think Johnson should have stopped you."

"Then I would have killed him."

Eduardo shrugged. "Point taken. That would've given rise to all sorts of problems as well." He leaned forward discreetly. "So, do you know how long Mikkel and Eva were together?"

"You don't need to whisper, Eduardo, it's the middle of the fucking night, and besides, I think half of Christianshavn already knows. And no, I have no idea how long—five minutes would have been too long."

"Even a second would have been unforgivable, *amigo*," Eduardo agreed. He spat out the nutshell and cracked another in his jaws. "I'm just having a hard time believing that Eva would do such a thing."

Ravn shrugged. "Mikkel did say that he was the one who made moves on her. Could *you* do something like that?"

"What do you take me for?!" Eduardo was genuinely hurt by the suggestion.

"I know, I just meant that . . . I mean . . . with all the women you've been with over the years, some of them might have been married, right?"

"Loads of them!" Eduardo sad. "But I don't know their husbands. It's their problem. You know, Danish men don't want to . . ."

"Have sex?"

"No, no, it's not that . . ." Eduardo shook his head energetically. "They don't want to . . . *listen*. That's very important. *Always* listen to women. If you want to get hold of Louise, you have to listen until you think your ears are gonna fall off."

Ravn smiled. "Well, I don't want to 'get hold of her,' so I expect I will keep my ears."

"Okay." Eduardo nodded and took another handful of nuts out of his pocket. "What about *el porco*, Mikkel?"

"What about him?"

"Well, I'm just thinking aloud here . . . could he have had something to do with Eva's death?"

"What do you mean?"

"What if it wasn't a thief who killed her? What if it was Mikkel, in a jealous rage? Maybe he thought Eva would leave you, they got into a fight, and she . . . died? Have you thought about this possibility?"

"I have, actually," said Ravn. "But Mikkel doesn't have anything to do with Eva's death."

"How can you be so sure?"

"Because Mikkel was on a sting with me when it happened," Ravn said firmly. He leaned back and glanced over at Eduardo's ketch, but no lights were on. "What happened to your date? Isn't she getting cold in bed by herself?"

"Simone had to go home. Or rather: I sent her home. So I could be there for my *amigo*," Eduardo said with a shrug.

"Touching. But your *amigo* is tired, and before you go, kindly remove the nutshells from my deck," Ravn said, pointing out the little pile at Eduardo's feet.

Eduardo laughed heartily. "Aha, that's what I needed to hear—my *amigo*'s going to be just fine." Then he leaned forward, gathered up the shells, and tossed them over the railing.

Ravn remained seated on the flybridge on his own for a while. The black velvet water of the canal stretched out before him. Then he fished Eva's phone out of his pocket and gave it one last look before flinging it over the railing.

Amazing how many hops an old Nokia like that can make, he thought as it disappeared under the water and sunk to the bottom of the canal for good.

48

Just after ten o'clock in the morning, Christoph discovered Hausser's last hidden camera in the living room. He ripped it out of the ceiling in a rage, and the last monitor downstairs in the caretaker's flat went black. Luckily, Christoph was so angry he failed to notice the microphone stuck to the light socket just below, and Hausser could hear Christoph damn him to hell.

The day after Hausser rang up Christoph and played the Dictaphone recording, the Schumanns barely said a word to each other. On the second day, Christoph called in sick at work and barricaded himself in the study, while Lena lay on the sofa in the living room, crying most of the time. It was only when Renate was home that Lena and Christoph tried to maintain some semblance of normality; the result was a false tone between them, which made Renate flee to her room the second she had the chance.

On the third day, after Renate had been tucked into bed, Christoph and Lena went out onto the landing of the back stairwell. In the dim glow of the naked bulb, under the one and only hidden camera still at Hausser's disposal, the Schumanns sat on the landing outside their kitchen door, sharing a beer and a cigarette. At first, neither one of them spoke, and when they did it was so quietly that Hausser had to turn the volume on full blast to hear what they were saying.

Lena broke the silence. "Everything I told that man was said only to save Renate."

"But would you have gone through with everything that you promised him?"

Lena was staring at her feet. "He threatened to take Renate away from us, Christoph. He said he would send her to some or other State children's home."

"And you believed him. How convenient," Christoph said sarcastically, and took a large gulp of beer.

"I was handcuffed and locked in a van while Renate was alone on the playground."

"I'm sorry . . . it's just . . . that swine . . . that fucking swine, Hausser . . . I could kill him for what he has done to us."

Lena shook her head. "We need to think rationally now. We have to get away from here."

"And let him win?"

"Don't you understand? We've already lost. We are lucky he hasn't already arrested us and thrown away the key."

Christoph took her hand in his. "I spoke to Schröder yesterday. He says that the walls are coming down around them, and the Stasi has started shredding all their files; they know the end is nigh. Several high-ranking officials have already fled the country. They're not pursuing new cases, nor are they making any more arrests. There are rumours that they've even started releasing political prisoners . . ."

"But then . . . why is this still happening to us?"

"It's Hausser. All of this is *his* work."

"That only makes our situation all the more terrifying. What if he goes after Renate?"

"I'll figure something out, Lena," Christoph said. He stubbed out the cigarette and crushed it under the sole of his shoe.

"What will you do?"

"Something."

"I can't stay here anymore."

"I know."

49

Hausser sat in front of the blank monitors wearing his headphones, trying to reconstruct what was happening in the Schumanns' flat. He had turned up the volume of the remaining bug in the living room to the max, but he could only partially follow their movements. It was clear, however, that there was a great deal of activity; furniture was being moved around, drawers and doors opened and closed, all of which was conducted under a confidential whisper. Hausser bitterly regretted that Christoph had found the cameras.

Just after midday, Christoph left the flat with his attaché case tucked under his arm.

Hausser wondered whether he should use the opportunity to confront Lena and find out what the Schumanns were planning. On the other hand, he was reluctant to interrupt, if they were now indeed planning to go ahead with their escape. With this in mind, he decided to follow Christoph instead.

Midas was headed down Greifenhagener Strasse. When he reached Stargarder Strasse, he ducked into a telephone box. Hausser knew the fact that he chose not to use the telephone at home was a clear indication Midas was up to something. He stayed in the box for almost fifteen minutes before he left and headed for the flower shop on Stargarder. He bought a bouquet of orange gerbera daisies and then headed back down Greifenhagener.

That night, after the Schumanns had eaten their dinner and Renate was put to bed, Hausser was surprised to see Christoph emerge onto the landing, dressed in his coat with an orange gerbera daisy tucked in his top buttonhole. He kissed Lena goodbye and went down the rear stairwell.

"Take care of yourself," Lena said in parting.

Hausser pulled on his coat and rushed into his kitchen in time to hear Christoph open the door to the backyard. Hausser waited a moment before slipping out. When he came into the yard, he heard the rear gate to Pappelallee slam shut.

Hausser sprinted through the yard and out onto the road, nearly getting himself run over by a Trabant coming past that exact moment. He peered down Pappelallee in time to see Midas reach the intersection with Stargarder Strasse and disappear round the corner. Hausser set off at a run after him and just caught a glimpse of Christoph crossing the road and heading for Gethsemane Church, where a large group of demonstrators had gathered. Midas walked past the crowd and went inside.

The church was full of people, and even though Hausser knew that it was used as a meeting point for new democratic movements in East Berlin, he was surprised to see just how many people were gathered there so late at night. A man was standing in front of the altar, talking about the demonstration the next day, which he believed would be a historic turning point in the fight for freedom. Hausser had seen him somewhere before, but he couldn't quite place him. He reckoned he was a writer, an actor, or a singer perhaps—some or other decadent! Christoph sat silently staring before him with crossed arms in the first pew, close to the baptismal font. He sat there for almost twenty minutes before getting to his feet and making for the rear door.

Hausser hurried after him. He stepped into the little garden behind the church and followed the gravel path that led to the road. About fifty metres ahead of him, Christoph crossed the square that lay before a large residential building. By the time Hausser reached the square, Christoph had disappeared. There was a narrow passage directly ahead of him, and he followed it past the residential gates on his right until he came to a dead end. He cursed himself for letting Christoph slip away, and it was all he could do to head back the way he came.

Hausser noticed two men coming towards him. Both of them held batons by their sides. He stopped short and cast a look over his shoulder, only to see two more men emerge from the shadows in the passage behind him, one of whom was swinging a motorcycle chain over his head; the other had a nail-studded wooden bat in his right hand.

The four men—obviously goons hired by Christoph—surrounded him. Judging from their weapons, they must have been cheap hooligans, but no less dangerous for it. "You boys really don't want to pick a fight with me," Hausser said.

"Oh yeah, you sure?" one of the goons behind him said. The man swung the chain at Hausser's head, but he managed to duck.

Hausser flipped out his ID card, mostly to gain time. "State Security Police! Stand back!"

"Your Stasi badge isn't going to help you here."

"Last chance. Piss off, or you're all under arrest."

Hausser heard a whoosh behind him, then a sharp pain in his leg as a nail from the wooden bat cut into his thigh. He stumbled but managed to stay on his feet. The chain swung towards his head. He ducked in time, but it wrapped around and trapped his forearm. The third man struck his kidneys with the rubber baton. Hausser saw the second guy charge with his baton raised over his head. He stopped him with a fist to the throat. The man squealed and dropped his weapon. Hausser was vaguely aware of the blows to his body as he picked up the baton. He struck the man with the chain on the jaw, which broke with a crushing sound. The man let go of the chain and Hausser pulled it towards him. He had the upper hand now. *Two men down—it was half a victory!* Hausser thought. Adrenaline pumped in his veins, dulling the pain, and he swung the chain at the man behind him. The guy ducked, and Hausser was about to take another swing when he felt a blow to the back of his head. He wobbled on his feet and the man in front went for him.

Hausser felt another nail cut into his arm, and he lost his grip on the chain. The next blow to the face blinded him, and the next second he was lying on the asphalt. The four men were standing over him. He could hear their breathing. They damned him to hell, spat on him, and then they began pounding his body in turn, as if foresters chopping firewood in collaboration.

From his vantage point, Christoph watched the men working on Hausser. He bit his fist, trying to suppress the urge to throw up.

At last the men stopped their pummelling of the motionless body on the ground. Hausser's face was beaten, and his clothing was bloody, his arms and legs out to the sides, giving him the horrible appearance of a frog that had been hit with a hammer. Satisfied, the men nodded and came over to Christoph.

"The money. Do you have the rest with you?" said the goon with the baton.

Christoph hastily produced a roll of twenty-dollar bills.

The goon counted the money with his bloodied fingers, clearly not in the least concerned about staining them. When he was finished counting, he stuck the roll in his pocket.

Christoph swallowed hard. "Is he . . . dead?"

The man glanced over his shoulder. "If he looks dead, he probably is."

"I just want to be sure."

"You're welcome to check yourself," the goon said, passing the baton to Christoph. Then he indicated to the others that they should split, and soon after the men were gone.

Christoph approached Hausser cautiously. He stared at the battered body at his feet. He poked it with the baton; it didn't move.

The baton slipped out of his hand and Christoph set off down the alley as fast as his legs could carry him.

50

Prenzlauer Berg, East Berlin
4 November 1989

Hausser was in a daze. Somewhere in the distance, he heard sirens. Then somebody was trying to strangle him. He tried to fight him off, but the person told him to lie still, and he didn't have the strength to resist.

The ambulance man tightened the neck brace. Another tended to Hausser's arm and put it in a sling. An ampoule of morphine helped him to sink into the darkness again, and Hausser fell into a turbulent dream.

A sharp light penetrated his eye, and Hausser woke up. His throat was dry. He tried to move, but his body would not obey him. He looked round, and slowly realisation dawned that he was in a hospital bed. By the window he saw a man dressed in a white coat, raising the blinds.

Hausser tried to sit up, but again the pain kept him down. He became aware of the neck brace, the bandages around his chest, his left thigh, his right arm, his head; he felt like a mummy. "Where am I?" he said.

The man in the white coat turned to face him. He was a doctor. His unshaven face and tired eyes told Hausser that the doctor must be at the end of the night shift. "You're awake. Impressive, considering how much morphine we've pumped into you."

"What time is it?"

The doctor looked at his watch. "It's twelve thirty p.m."

"Help me get up."

The doctor came over to the bed. "Take it easy now. You have a split cranium and a serious oedema as a result. We have been draining fluid from your cranium for the better part of the morning. I have seen people hit by a train who have fewer injuries than you have; it's a miracle that you are still alive."

"And it will be a miracle if you're still allowed to work here if you don't help me up right now. Do you have any idea who I am?"

"Colonel Erhardt Hausser, State Security Police. Yes, I've seen your badge." The doctor leaned a little closer and lowered his voice. "And if it weren't for the Hippocratic Oath, I would have been sorely tempted to let the pressure in your cranium grow until your brain was crushed, turning you into a vegetable. Get well soon," the doctor said, turned on his heel, and walked out the door.

Hausser closed his eyes in frustration. He had to get hold of Müller. Get him to arrest Midas—and send the bastard directly to the Chamber. He needed a telephone. *Right now.* He needed to focus. One step at a time: Once he was out of bed, he could get dressed; once he was dressed, he could get to Reception and get hold of a phone.

It took Hausser one and a half hours to get dressed. He kept his hospital gown on. Despite the high concentration of morphine in his blood, his body was in shock, and he was shaking uncontrollably, as if he had a fever.

When she saw the state of him, the young nurse at Reception looked at him with big eyes.

Hausser pushed his badge and a slip of paper with Müller's number over the counter. "Call . . . this number . . . Stasi."

The young nurse swallowed hard when she saw the badge, grabbed the phone, and called the number. "There . . . there's no one there."

"You . . . are calling the State Security Police . . . of course there is . . . someone there. Try again!"

The nurse tried again. To no avail. "The whole city has been turned upside down because of the demonstrations. Maybe that's why . . . shall I help you back to your room, sir?"

"Call me . . . a taxi."

Under serious protest from the doctors in the Trauma Division, Hausser finally succeeded in getting himself discharged from hospital and wheeled to the dilapidated Wolga-24 taxi that was waiting in front of the main hospital entrance. On the way into Berlin Mitte, the driver kept glancing in the rearview mirror, as if to confirm that his client was still alive. When they arrived in the area around Alexanderplatz, the traffic ground to a halt. Hausser looked out the window; all around them, people were walking between the cars on the road. "What's going on?" Hausser mumbled.

"It's the demonstration, sir. Everyone wants to go to Alexanderplatz. It's an absolute nightmare. Folks say there are about a million people taking part, and they just keep coming. All the Party leaders are going to be there—they're gonna try to ride out the storm, I reckon."

"Let them try," Hausser muttered. His headache was getting worse, and Lou Reed chanting "Perfect Day" to an untuned piano wasn't helping; he wasn't sure if the music was coming from the radio or somewhere deep inside his battered head.

Dusk had fallen by the time the taxi finally pulled up in front of Stasi headquarters. The main gates were closed, and four guards wielding machine pistols blocked their way.

The taxi driver helped Hausser out of the car and supported him up to the gate. Hausser identified himself with his badge and the guards let him through. Taking over from the taxi driver, the guards drove him to Haus 7 and helped him up to Division Z on the first floor.

The moment he stepped into their division, Hausser heard the rasping sound of the shredders at work. Further down the corridor, he saw a group of his colleagues feeding the machine. Hausser stared in horror at the huge mounds of confetti round them, *as if Judgement Day had come to DZ*, Hausser thought. He limped to the end of the corridor, knocked on Strauss's door, and entered without waiting for a reply.

Inside, Müller was standing in the far corner, emptying the file cabinet onto a trolley. Strauss was not there.

"Whoa, what happened to you?" said Müller. "Are you okay, Hausser?"

"Do I *look* okay?" Hausser snapped. "What are you doing in Strauss's office?"

"Cleaning up. We've got to make ourselves invisible. Orders from Haus One."

"Just because a few demonstrators have gathered in the middle of the city?"

"The demonstrators are not important. But all our leaders are going to be there. Even Wolf. I saw him on TV, talking about free speech and constitutional rights," Müller said, unable to suppress a smile.

Hausser leaned against the wall. "Markus Wolf? *Our* Wolf? The *Beast* himself?"

Müller nodded.

Hausser dropped onto the sofa by the wall. "Is Strauss there as well?"

"Strauss is on holiday. Indefinitely."

"Arrested?"

Müller laughed. "No. He fled to Hungary, and beyond from there, I'm guessing. Incidentally, accompanied by Schröder and a troupe of dancers. Apparently, the old goat decided to leave his wife and children behind. Brandy liqueur chocolate?" Müller said, picking up the bowl on the desk and offering it to Hausser.

Hausser shook his head and immediately regretted the motion; his head hurt like hell. "We have to arrest Midas. He was the one who made the escape possible. He incriminated himself."

"I thought you wanted him to flee."

"I did, but it looks as if our time is running out. Right now, I can't wait to get Midas sent to Hohenschönhausen."

"I'm afraid I can't do that. No more arrests. Direct orders from Haus One," said Müller.

"What the hell do you mean?! I want that bastard in the Chamber by tonight!"

Müller's gaze dropped to the floor.

"Müller, did you hear what I said?"

"But . . . it's not possible. The blacksmith and I have been to the prison and it's been broken it apart."

"What?!"

"The blacksmith cut out the doors and took them to the junkyard."

"You ordered the blacksmith to destroy my Chamber?" Hausser said through gritted teeth.

"Yes. He's good at that kind of thing. And we can't leave evidence of our work behind, Hausser, least of all *that* kind of work. It's only a matter of days before we're shut down," he said, pointing at the window. "And when that happens, I don't want to be here, boss." He smiled at Hausser tentatively, but the colonel appeared too lost in his own morbid thoughts. "I know where you keep your absinthe. Shall I bring you the bottle?"

"Yes, thank you, Müller." The piano music and Lou Reed sounded in his head once more.

Not long after, Hausser found himself alone in Strauss's office with his faithful absinthe. He brought the liquid to his lips. Blood seeped from the corner of his mouth and formed a murky purple cloud in the clear liquid at the bottom of his glass. *Someone was going to pay for this*, he vowed.

51

"Are you awake?"

Ravn opened his eyes. An indistinct face hovered over him. He wasn't sure if he was really awake or just dreaming. A hand came into view under the face, and it banged on the dirty pane of the hatch window over his bed, and then he realised that it was Louise, trying to get his attention.

"Good morning," she said. "I come with coffee." The bottom of two Styrofoam cups and a brown paper bag from the bakery appeared on the pane above.

Ravn sat up. "Give me two minutes; I'll come on up to you."

He got out of bed and stumbled into his tiny bathroom, where he did a sixty-second morning groom that included brushing his teeth, splashing water on his face and unruly hair, and donning a clean T-shirt; she'd have to bear with the sight of the crumpled jogging pants he picked up off the floor on his way out.

He found her sitting on one of his white plastic chairs on the rear deck, feeding Møffe a butter croissant from the bakery; apparently, she was already his new best friend. "Good morning," she greeted him with a smile.

"It's still the middle of the night, isn't it?" he said, taking a seat on the chair beside her.

"It's eight thirty in the morning," she said, handing him a cup of coffee.

"What brings you here so early?"

"I was on my way to work, but I thought I'd pop in with coffee as thanks for the other day," she said.

"I thought you'd already thanked me for that."

They exchanged a little smile.

Ravn helped himself to one of the croissants from the bag, removed the lid of the cup, and dipped his croissant into the warm latte.

"What happened to your face?" Louise said with concern.

"I hit a table."

"A table . . . how so?"

"It's a long and boring story," he said, and took a bite of the croissant. "Did you write to your brother?"

Louise nodded and looked down into her cup. "Several times. But he hasn't replied."

"He might just want to be left in peace with her . . . The Berliner."

"Yes, which is why I wrote to her."

"Really?" Ravn looked at her, genuinely impressed. "Did she reply?"

"No."

"Perhaps you should try again."

"I've written to her four times," Louise said with a sigh. "I asked her when she'd last written to Mogens; I even asked if she'd seen him. In the final email, I asked her if she could ask Mogens to write to me, if he's with her, but that email wasn't delivered."

"Why not?"

"Apparently the account was closed."

"Okay. But there could be any number of reasons for that."

"I know, but I have a feeling she's deliberately trying to erase her connection to Mogens. If he went to Berlin to see her, then she might be the last person who's had any contact with him."

Ravn finished his croissant before he replied. "Why don't you go to the police with this, Louise? Even though it's not exactly a high-profile case, the Copenhagen police might be willing to reach out to the German police, or trace the email address for you."

Louise scrunched her empty coffee cup. "I don't want to involve the police in this. I just want to find out if Mogens is okay. I also searched online for the woman, and it turns out there are only four people in the entire city of Berlin with her name.

"What name? The Berliner?" Ravn said with a smile tugging at his mouth.

"No. The email address she used is 'Schumann' followed by a number. And in her second email to Mogens, she says her name is 'Renate.' Mogens is the one who gave her the nickname 'The Berliner,' and after that she signs off her mails to him accordingly."

"Renate Schumann," said Ravn. "So you think Mogens is with her?"

"It's a possibility, so I've decided to take a few days off to go to Berlin. I intend to pay the four women I've found a visit."

Ravn nearly fell off his chair in surprise. "Do . . . do you really think that's a good idea?"

Louise shrugged. "I need to find out what has happened to Mogens."

"Why don't you just write or call these women?"

"*You* were the one who told me to use the element of surprise."

"Yeah, sure, but there could be a criminal background to Mogens's disappearance. You have no idea what you could be walking into there. It could be just about anybody hiding behind that woman's name."

"I know. Which is why I'm here to ask if you'd like to come with me."

Ravn fixed his eyes on the coffee cup in his hands. "Louise, I—"

"I'll pay for the ticket, of course, any and all expenses . . ."

"I'm really sorry, Louise," Ravn said, and he meant it. "It's just not possible."

"Okay," she said in a small, barely audible voice. "Other wooden tables you need to bash your head into?" she added with a melancholy smile on her lips.

He looked at her. "Something like that, yes."

Louise took the empty cup out of his hand and put it in the now-empty brown paper bag with her own. She patted Møffe on the head and stood up.

"Louise, I strongly recommend that you don't go to Berlin on your own. Call or write to them instead."

She nodded briefly and made her way up onto the quay. "Sometimes you have to act, even though your brain is telling you it's a bad idea—you know what I mean?"

52

In the modest gymnastics hall, the last light of day slanted through the windows in the ceiling. On the gym teacher's command, a smart line of little girls in leotards ran towards the springboard and summersaulted over the vault. In the back of the hall, Renate was practising her routine on the beam; she did a handstand followed by two perfectly executed backward saltos, but landed askew on the concluding flick flack and fell. She stayed down, tears welling in her eyes, but didn't say a word. The gym teacher, Frau Hertz, clapped her hands, telling Renate to get up at once and start over. Renate stood up gingerly and climbed back on the beam.

Hausser watched the girls through the porthole in the door. It amused him that the porthole reminded him of the Chamber's, but what he saw through it was entirely different to what he'd experienced at the prison. He appreciated the precision with which the girls performed their exercises; he respected their strength of will and the grace of their movements. Indeed, anyone who would hurt these girls was a devil. But this world is merciless and unforgiving.

An hour later, the girls had changed, done for the day and heading for the exit. Renate brought up the rear, limping along at her friends' heels.

"Renate!" Hausser called.

Renate stopped in her tracks at the sound of her name. She could see a tall man standing between the gym apparatus on the far side of the hall. "Come here for a moment, I have a message for you," he said.

Renate hesitated briefly, but curiosity got the better of her, and she did as he asked.

Hausser was leaning against the beam, resting his injured leg. He was no longer bandaged like a mummy, but his face was still battered and blue, and he looked like a boxer who had lost the fight in the last round.

Renate stared, and it was obvious that the sight of him frightened her.

"It looks worse than it is," said Hausser.

"A message from whom?"

"Not a message, as such," said Hausser. "But I need to talk to you."

"My mother is waiting for me outside."

Despite her diminutive size, she seemed fearless, and Hausser smiled, impressed by her courage. "I know. It will only take a moment. Do you know who I am?"

"Our caretaker," she said, casting her eyes down. "What do you want to tell me?"

"Sit down for a moment," said Hausser, pointing to the stack of gym mats to her left.

Renate shook her head. "I have to go now."

"There's no need to be afraid, Renate. Please, sit down."

Renate reluctantly perched on the edge of the stack.

"You probably know that I'm not *just* your caretaker, right? I'm pretty sure your mother and father have said something different. Something about me."

Renate stared at her feet.

"It's okay, just tell me what they've said."

"They haven't said anything. I really have to go now."

She made to get up and go, but Hausser produced his ID and extended it towards her.

Renate looked at it and started in surprise. "You work for the State . . . the Stasi?"

"Yes. I'm a colonel. See, it's written right here," Hausser said, pointing to the title before his name on the badge.

"But my dad said you were a spy."

Hausser shook his head. "That's not entirely true. Yes, I've been keeping an eye on you, but that was only to protect your family. To protect you."

Renate narrowed her eyes and regarded him suspiciously. "That's not what my dad said. I think you're lying."

"Ouch, that hurt, but at least it's honest," Hausser said. He returned his ID to his pocket. "But tell me, Renate, is your father *always* right?"

She nodded energetically.

"I see. So, when he says that gymnastics is just a game, and that you spend too much on such rubbish, is he right?"

Renate made no reply.

"And when he says that you won't be able to compete in tournaments anymore, unless your grades improve, is he right about that too? Is that fair?"

"How do you know what father has said to me?"

"Because I know everything. What does your dad say is important?"

"He says I must get an education, so I can get a good job and earn money."

"But that's not your dream, is it, Renate?" Hausser tried to catch her eye. "It's all right, you can tell me what your dream is; in fact, I already know. It has something to do with gymnastics, isn't that true?"

She nodded.

"Tell me your dream, Renate."

"I want to win Olympic gold in gymnastics for the GDR."

"Precisely. And do you know what? No matter what your father says, it's a beautiful dream."

"It's a stupid dream. I can't even stay on the beam," Renate said sadly, and gingerly touched her bruised shin. "Frau Hertz says I'm a klutz."

Hausser leaned towards her. "That's not true. You're the bravest nine-year-old girl I know. And that's why I want to show you something special."

"Actually, I'm nine-and-a-half," she said. "What do you want to show me?"

"You'll need to follow me if you want to see it."

"My mother is waiting . . . and she doesn't want me to talk—"

"Talk to strangers. I know. You mother is right. You should never talk to strangers. But you and I know each other, we're neighbours. Besides, I'm a colonel, and therefore your superior officer," he said with a smile, gently tugging on the red Young Pioneer neckerchief at her throat. "It will only take a moment, Renate. And it's something very special."

Taking refuge from the wind under the eaves at the front entrance to the school, Lena smoked a cigarette while she waited for Renate to come out. Most of the other girls had already come past, and she was starting to wonder where her daughter could be.

Frau Hertz came out of the building, and when she locked the door after her, Lena hurried over to her.

"Frau Hertz?"

The stout woman turned to Lena and gave her a curt greeting.

"Have you seen Renate?"

"She came out with the other girls long ago."

"No, she hasn't come out yet."

"She must have, because all the girls have gone."

"Please open the door."

The woman frowned at Lena, clearly annoyed. "I checked before I left, of course."

"Open up, my daughter is in there!"

Frau Hertz started at Lena's vehement outburst. She took out her keys and unlocked the door.

Lena pushed past the teacher and rushed into the school. Her heels echoed in the dark corridors as she ran towards the sports hall. "Renate!" she yelled as she flung open the door and fumbled for the light switch on the wall. The neon rods in the ceiling flickered, then lit up in turn. "Renate!" Lena yelled again. She ran into the changing rooms. There was no sign of her daughter.

Hausser helped Renate up the last few rungs of the fire escape onto the flat roof of the school building. The wind seemed stronger four storeys up. "Oh boy, this is quite a challenge for two wounded warriors like our-selves," Hausser joked, smiling at Renate.

"What do you want to show me?"

"Patience, my friend," said Hausser. "This way." Hausser led her past the skylights in the roof and the large ventilator. "Tell me, have you ever heard the story about the Pied Piper of Hamelin?"

"I don't think so. What is it about?"

"It's about a village that had a terrible rat infestation. Then one day a ratcatcher came by, and the villagers begged him to make the rats go away. They offered to pay him all the money they had. The ratcatcher, who was a good socialist, said he only wanted money enough so he wouldn't have to go to bed hungry. And do you know what he did then?"

"No. Because I said I don't know the story."

"Well, he brought out a flute and started playing a melody. Soon, all the rats came out of hiding to listen to him play, and they followed the music as the ratcatcher led them out of town."

"Where did he take them?"

"Well, he crossed a stream, and the rats followed him; the water was not very deep, but it was deep enough to drown all the rats."

"So . . . he helped the villagers?"

"Exactly. But when he returned to the village, no one wanted to pay. They said he had just been lucky, that anyone could have done what he did."

"That wasn't very nice."

"No, it wasn't, was it. But that's just the way capitalists are; greedy and deceitful. So the ratcatcher made sure they would never forget their betrayal of him: He began to play again—"

"But why? There weren't any rats left."

"True. But this time, the village children followed him."

Renate's eyes opened wide. "Did he drown them as well?!"

"No, of course not," Hausser laughed. "What a macabre imagina-tion you have! But the ratcatcher took the children to a beautiful social-ist state, where all their dreams could come true. A place where no one cheated on anyone else." Hausser patted her on the head. "Now, can you see those towers over there?" Hausser pointed to the large light towers silhouetted against the night sky.

"Yes, it's the spotlights on Friedrich-Ludwig-Jahn Stadium."

"Precisely." Hausser looked at his watch. "Now, watch carefully," he said. The next instant, the spotlights on the four towers switched on. Together, they formed a brilliant ring that descended over the city. "Aren't they glorious?"

Renate nodded.

"A shining symbol of the greatness of our nation. Named after Jahn, father of our proud German gymnastics movement."

"*Frisch, fromm, fröhlich, frei,*" said Renate. "It's our motto. It comes from him, Frau Hertz said."

"You impress me with your knowledge, Renate. In that stadium I have seen great deeds achieved by our national heroes. Once, I saw Uwe Hohn break the world record in javelin; he was the first athlete to cast a javelin further than a hundred metres."

Renate's eyes shone and smiled at Hausser.

"Renate! Renate!"

Lena's voice reached them up on the roof. Hausser and Renate stepped over to the edge and looked down into the schoolyard. Lena and Frau Hertz were desperate, looking for Renate everywhere.

"You'd better let your mother know where you are," said Hausser over Renate's shoulder.

"Mother . . . mother! I'm up here!" Renate yelled as loudly as she could.

Lena spun round and Renate called out to her again. "Up here!!"

Lena and Frau Hertz looked up and saw Renate and Hausser on the roof. Frau Hertz's hand flew to her mouth in fright. Lena stood as if turned to stone, staring up at her daughter; Hausser was merely a black shadow behind her, but Lena recognised him immediately.

Hausser stroked Renate's hair and kept his eyes on the stadium. *One little shove, and Renate's life would end at the feet of her traitorous mother*, Hausser thought. *A tragedy for Lena that no measure of future wealth could change.*

"Hausser, I'm begging you!"

Hausser looked down and smiled at Lena. "I am the one who removes the grit in the machine, Lena. Do you understand at last?" he called out.

Lena could not speak. She merely gaped at Hausser with desperation in her eyes, utterly powerless. Hausser looked lovingly down at her, then he turned to Renate.

"You'd better go to your mother now, Renate."

Renate turned away from the edge and ran back over the flat roof the way they had come.

"Renate!" Hausser yelled after her. "Tell me again what your dream is!"

"To win Olympic gold for the GDR—for all of us!" yelled Renate with a grin.

Hausser bowed slightly, then stood to attention and gave Renate a smart farewell salute.

53

Hausser watched Christoph pull Lena into his arms. They were sitting on the rear landing, and Christoph held her for a long time, but it did not help to calm her down.

"We have to get away from here," she sobbed.

"We can't, Lena, that would be suicide."

"It's suicide staying *here*," she said. "Why the hell didn't you just get him killed?"

"That was the plan. We thought he was dead; he looked dead."

"You should've made sure, Christoph."

"I know, *Liebchen,* I know." He kissed her hair and her forehead. "But we need to wait. They said on the TV news this evening that reforms are on the way. More freedom. I'm sure the tide is turning in our favour."

"But when?"

"Within a few weeks, maximum."

She freed herself from his embrace and stood up. "Weeks? It's no more than a matter of hours before that psychopath attacks us again. If you don't do something, I'll flee with Renate tomorrow. On my own."

"But, Lena—"

"I mean it, Christoph. And you will never see us again," she said.

Christoph stood up and took her in his arms again. "All right, *Liebchen,* we'll do it together. I'll figure something out."

"Promise?"

"Yes."

"Can you get hold of your . . . contacts?"

"What contacts? They've all left the country or gone in hiding . . ."

"What are we going to do, then?"

Christoph stared into thin air for a moment. "Braun once mentioned a last resort, a 'back door strategy,' he called it. It's not nearly as sophisticated as Schröder's plans with the diplomatic cars, but it's not impossible to execute."

Hausser leaned back in his chair. *At last*, he thought. After all these weeks and months of disappointments and pain, his plan was finally about to succeed.

54

Ravn put the old adapter next to Victoria, who was perched on the edge of the counter with her arms folded across her chest and a cigarette clenched in the corner of her mouth. It was just the two of them in the bookshop, and the chilly look she gave him through a blue cloud of smoke gave him the distinct message he was in the doghouse.

"What? I thought you'd be happy to have it back," he said.

Victoria held his gaze in stony silence.

Ravn looked away. "I've put this whole thing behind me now, Victoria. It's definitely over," he said, venturing a smile in her direction.

Nothing. Just that hard stare.

"Come off it, Victoria," Ravn said, unable to bear her silence any longer. "Why don't you make us a cup of coffee instead of just looking at me like that?"

"I don't feel like drinking a coffee," she said, stubbing out her cigarette in the ashtray.

Ravn shrugged. "Who pissed on your battery today?"

"You. And not just today. You've really disappointed me, Ravn."

"What have I done now?"

"When you were drinking yourself to death, I thought you couldn't sink any lower."

"Well, I'm sober now, most of the time."

"Yes, I noticed, and sobriety almost doesn't suit you." She took her pack of tobacco out of her vest pocket and began rolling herself a fresh cigarette.

"I honestly don't know what I've done to make you so mad at me."

Victoria shook her head. "You can't just beat the shit out of people because you're angry."

"Is that what all this is about?" Ravn said. "Considering what Mikkel had done, he got off lightly with a broken nose."

"Honestly?" said Victoria. "So violence is your solution to solving all the problems in the world?"

"I have never claimed that I could solve all the problems in the world—with or without violence. In fact, I'd rather you didn't involve me in world affairs; I've got more than enough to handle as it is," he said with a smile, trying to lighten the mood.

Victoria lit her cigarette and blew another cloud of smoke in his direction. "I told you it was a bad idea to start snooping around in Eva's life. But you couldn't let it go. Instead, you tried to move heaven and earth to find out who was behind those messages. And what good has it brought you?"

"The truth," Ravn said with a shrug.

"Congratulations. All I see is a man with a black eye and one friend less."

"That sounds like something you read in one of your self-help books. But I think you're forgetting that I'm not the one who was unfaithful. I'm not the one who lied and cheated."

"But you were the one who started dealing out punches. You've created a mountain of bad karma for yourself, you know that, don't you?" Victoria said, pointing at him with the end of her cigarette.

"You could use some good karma yourself, Victoria. Shall I make us some coffee or what?"

"Not today, thanks. Eduardo tells me you're seeing someone. So why all the fuss about Eva?"

Ravn crossed his arms. "Eduardo has a big mouth. I'm not seeing anyone."

"But he distinctly told me that—"

"I'm just helping someone to look for her brother, okay?"

Victoria's glasses had slid to the tip of her nose, and she pushed them back in place. Ravn got the impression she was softening up at last. "Hmm. Perhaps you've still got some sense in your head after all."

"Perhaps. But there's not a hell of a lot I can do for her."

"So . . . she's found him?"

"Her brother? No, it seems he's gone to Berlin. And . . . she invited me to come along to look for him—"

"And?"

"What do you mean 'and'? And nothing. I'm not going anywhere."

Victoria shook her head. "No, of course not," she said with a thick undertone of irony. "Berlin is made for people like you. It's a city of navel-gazers. You'd fit right in."

"Thank you. But I thought your favourite people to hate were the Swedes, the people from Stockholm in particular."

Victoria didn't reply. Instead, she walked over to the closest bookshelf, where she kept her travel literature. She ran her finger along the spines, picked out a book, and tossed it to Ravn. More by reflex than anything else, he caught the book in his lap. "What the . . . ?" he looked down; it was a guide book for Berlin, of course. "Victoria, I told you: I'm not going anywhere."

Victoria put her hands on her hips. "You're not sitting here all day either."

Ravn levelled his gaze on her. "You seriously think I should go?"

She nodded.

"But I barely know this woman. I don't even know where she lives or anything."

"Get a move on, Ravn. If not to Berlin, then at least out of my store."

"Are you throwing me out?"

"Yes, I can't bear the sight of you another minute."

He stared at her. "Just because I punched Mikkel in the face?"

"Yes. That and a list of other reasons. You have one week's quarantine."

"Quarantine? What the hell are you talking about?" he stared at her, flabbergasted. "As if you were running a pub."

"Whatever. But I'm the one who's in charge in here."

Møffe could barely keep up with Ravn as he walked back to *Bianca* along the canal. He was deep in thought. He couldn't understand why Victoria was making such a fuss. *Quarantine? Seriously?* Ravn shook his head in disbelief. She'd kicked him out the door as if he were a naughty boy in her class at Christianshavn Gymnasium. She'd taught for half a lifetime before changing lanes and buying the bookshop. If her behaviour was an expression of Victoria's concern for his moral welfare, she had a funny way of showing it.

He stuck his hands in his pockets and realised that he'd taken the Berlin guide with him by mistake. He was inclined to fling it into the canal—see if it could hop as many times as the old Nokia—but he pulled himself together and took a seat on a bench on the quay instead. He wished he still smoked, or at least had a beer to keep him company. Møffe leaned against his shins as if sensing his master's mood, and Ravn scratched the dog's ears fondly. Ravn's thoughts wandered to Louise. He had to admit that he enjoyed her company; more and more, every time they met. And then there was the disappearance of her brother, which had stirred his hunting instinct.

He had hated the rules and regulations and strict hierarchy of his old job, but he sorely missed the investigative work itself. He was a good investigator, and he was proud of that; he could find leads that even the forensics team missed, and he could get a confession from the toughest criminals on the street. He missed being the first man on the scene of a crime. He missed the weight of his bulletproof vest and the cold steel shaft of the Glock in his palm. He missed the metallic taste of adrenaline in his mouth and his tunnel vision that made him focussed as a bird of prey on its victim. He was a cop down to the marrow of his bones, with-out or without his badge.

He thought about The Berliner. It was a good name; somewhere in his mind he heard Marlene Dietrich singing "Lili Marleen" . . .

Perhaps his cards were dealt the moment he met Louise; he had to help her. He wanted to help her find Mogens and his mysterious contact in Berlin.

55

Prenzlauer Berg, Berlin
9 November 1989

The traffic was moving at a snail's pace on Danziger Strasse. Hausser was waiting on the pavement impatiently. A black Lada broke free from the queue and pulled up to the kerb in front of him. He opened the passenger door and got in, wincing in pain from the broken ribs, but he was happy to see Müller behind the wheel.

"You've shaved your moustache," his deputy said, returning Hausser's smile.

"Yup. Feels liberating."

"You're cheerful this morning," said Müller. "Haven't you seen the news?"

"Fuck the news. I make my own."

"There's been a change of guard at the Politburo."

"They can change guard as much as they want."

Müller raised his eyebrows, clearly surprised by Hausser's indifference. "But this changes the landscape for us completely."

"It doesn't alter the fact that I have found his Achilles heel; the key is his daughter—even traitors have parental instincts. We need to remember that, Müller: Regardless of how much we despise these vermin, they do have feelings for their offspring."

Müller nodded in reply but made no comment.

"Midas is going to flee!" Hausser said in genuine excitement, giving Müller a collegial clap on the shoulder. "I think it will happen tonight!

He's in the process of arranging everything, so we haven't a moment to lose," he added, waving his hand as a sign for Müller to drive.

Müller made no motion to pull away from the kerb.

"What are you waiting for, Müller?!"

The deputy took out his pack of cigarettes and lit up. "It's no longer of any consequence, whether he flees or not."

"Have you lost your mind? Of course it's significant."

"Not after the amnesty ruling; now the chances of us being able to prosecute them are minimal."

"My dear Müller, I have no intention of arresting Midas. Instead, I'm hoping for a legitimate reason to shoot him the moment he tries to cross the border."

Müller stared vacantly through the windshield. "I don't think that's going to happen. I understand that you want to nail him, but I'm afraid it's too late."

"Aren't you listening to a word I've just said?! They're going to flee *tonight!*"

Müller stubbed his unfinished cigarette in the ashtray in the console between them. "What if we arrange a car accident instead, or throw him in the Spree like we did with Braun and finally get a good night's sleep?"

"Hell no. I want the bastard shot at the border so that his death is official and his crimes against the State are made public; perfect justice must be served."

"I think you are the only one interested in that kind of justice, Hausser; we are in the process of closing down the Stasi and eliminating our tracks. The shredder is at work day and night. And you are vying for a public execution? That's pure madness."

"We are the ones who do the dirty work of the State. The guardians of truth," Hausser said ecstatically. "Our politicians may be on their knees, I see that Müller, but this means *we* have to stand even stronger. One thing is certain: The Wall is unforgiving!" he smiled at the significance of his own words—*one ought to write them in caps on the side of the Wall so it would be the last thing the traitors saw in their damned lives,* he thought.

"Apparently, you haven't heard the latest rumours," said Müller.

Hausser shrugged. "There are always rumours. Why should they interest me?"

"Because this one comes directly from the Party HQ—from Egon Krentz's very own office."

"I don't care about that shit-shoveller. They could hang him in public for all I care."

"They're not going to hang him. My source says they're preparing a speech to be delivered to the nation at a press conference tonight."

"What kind of speech? His swan song?"

"No. A speech informing the nation that all East Germans will be permitted to travel through checkpoints in the Wall."

"But they can't do that!"

Müller shrugged. "According to my source, Comrade Schabowski will announce it to the international press tonight."

Dumbfounded at last, Hausser stared ahead into thin air.

"Can you just imagine what will happen if Schabowski goes through with it? All the streets, every checkpoint will be stormed by the people; they will mow it down . . ."

"Mow down what?"

"The *Wall*, Hausser."

Hausser shook his head in disbelief.

"Forget Midas, forget all about the operation. After tonight, *we* are the ones who will be hunted; it's time to make a hasty retreat, Colonel."

"*Never*. Get out of the car, Müller," Hausser snarled.

"What?"

Müller didn't react fast enough for Hausser's liking, so he simply leaned over his deputy and opened the driver's side door. "I said get out!"

Müller did as he was told. Hausser manoeuvred into the driver's seat and started the car, stepping on the accelerator. Oblivious to much honking of horns and the screech of tyres behind him, Hausser swung the Lada into the opposite lane and headed for Greifenhagener Strasse.

56

Ravn knew that Copenhagen's Royal Danish Academy–Architecture, Design, Conservation was located on Holmen not far from Christianshavn. One of the navy's old warehouses had been converted into an auditorium, and when he entered, he was impressed to see that it was filled to capacity with students. Louise was standing behind the podium, wearing a headset as she delivered her lecture. The title of her lecture was projected against the wall behind her, and even though Ravn had no idea what "The Memory of the City" meant, he was fascinated by Louise's natural authority over her audience. There was something stoic about her calm voice and measured gestures. It reminded him of the time he'd seen Eva deliver an argument in court; he couldn't remember exactly what the case was about, but he had enjoyed watching her work, impressed by her strength and professionalism. He was so proud that everyone in the courtroom was spellbound by *his* girlfriend. He had never confessed this to her, he regretted that he never had—regardless of those stupid messages—and he hoped that she knew how proud he was of her. How much he had appreciated her.

Forty minutes later, Louise's lecture was over and the audience applauded. When she left the podium, a stream of pupils followed her out of the auditorium and it was impossible for Ravn to get close to her, so he simply enjoyed watching her from a distance till she slipped out the door to the canteen in the courtyard outside.

Ravn entered the canteen, which had a vaguely familiar smell of fried food and sandwiches. Seated at the long mess tables, the atmosphere among the students was boisterous. He spotted Louise standing not far off with her back turned. He tugged on Møffe's leash and walked over to her. "Louise," he said.

She turned at the sound of her name and the expression on her face was equal parts surprise and happiness at seeing him. "*Hej*, Thomas . . . how did you know I was—ah, of course, the business card I gave you."

Ravn nodded. "That was an interesting lecture you gave."

"You were there?" she smiled, took his arm, and led him away from the crowd of students who seemed to wonder what business this strange man in a leather jacket with a very fat dog on a leash could have with their elegant teacher.

"I didn't know you were interested in architecture."

"Sure I am—especially 'the memory of the city,' and stuff like that, is right up my alley," he said, making her smile again. "Any news on your brother?"

"No, he's still not replying to my emails. I have also tried writing to Renate Schumann again, even though I know her account is blocked."

"So you're still set on going to Berlin?"

"Yes, I leave in three days' time, just as soon as the symposium is over; why?"

Ravn yanked on the leash because Møffe had his nose inside the nearest trash bin. "Well, if you still want me to come along, I—"

She grabbed his arm and squeezed it impulsively. "Honestly, you mean it?"

He nodded.

She grinned and blushed pink with pleasure. "I'll be sure to book another plane ticket and a room for you at the hotel—we'll be staying in Alexanderplatz, which I think will be a good point of departure for—"

"Louise," Ravn said, interrupting her gush of excitement. "Before you say 'yes' to taking me along, there are a few things we need to clarify."

"Of course," she said, letting go of his arm immediately.

"I pay my own way—and that's not up for discussion."

"Okay. What else?"

Ravn sighed. "I know that it's only natural for you to care about your brother, but that doesn't change that he has committed a crime."

Louise's gaze dropped to the floor.

"So, if we find Mogens, and he does not give himself up, I will be obliged to inform the authorities where he is."

"I understand," she said, looking at him sadly. "Is there anything else?"

"Yes, regarding the money that might still remain: It belongs to neither Mogens nor Lauritzen; instead, it will revert to the public treasury. This could result in an increased sentence against Mogens, and a charge against Lauritzen for trying to avoid taxes, of course."

"Okay, if that's the way it has to be," she said. "I just want to make sure that Mogens is all right. And then let the chips fall as they may."

"Does this mean that you still want me to come along?"

"You'd better go pack your toothbrush," Louise said with a smile. Then she returned to her students, who had not shifted their curious stares from Louise and Ravn for a second.

57

Prenzlauer Berg, East Berlin
9 November 1989

Hausser sat in the black Lada on Greifenhagener Strasse, keeping an eye on Christoph's shiny BMW. He opened the glove compartment and took out the pistol that was inside; it was a 9-mm Makarov with room for eight cartridges in the chamber, a crap Russian pistol that required you to be very close to the target if you wanted to be sure you'd hit something. He loaded the pistol, which gave a characteristic smack against the chamber.

Hausser cursed himself for failing to ask Müller what time Schabowski was supposed to hold the press conference to announce a general permission to travel across the border. If Christoph heard the speech, he would naturally abandon his plans to flee. And in that case, Hausser would go directly up to their flat and put a bullet in Midas's brain—come what may. He fumbled in his jacket pocket for his pain medication, took three pills out of the vial, and crushed them between his teeth. The car radio was tuned to DDR-1, and he slid back against the seat in exhaustion. For now, they were playing Prokoviev—good ol' Sergei . . .

By the time dusk fell, the door to Number 9 opened. Hausser straightened up in his seat and caught sight of Christoph coming out to the road with two kitbags slung over his shoulders. Renate was close on his heels with her Young Pioneers rucksack. Lena and Klara followed a few paces behind, the latter dragging a large suitcase that the two women ultimately managed to get over the road. Christoph looked severely pissed off that

Lena had packed such a large suitcase, and they bickered with each other as he manoeuvred it into the boot.

Moments later, the BMW set off down the road and Klara waved, as if the family were going on holiday rather than fleeing the country. She crossed the road again and made her way to the gate. Hausser put the Lada in gear and drove towards her at high speed. He slammed on the brakes just behind her, and she spun around in fright.

"Where?" snarled Hausser through the open side window.

Klara gaped at him.

"Where the hell are they going, Klara?!"

"To Lena's family in Dresden—her mother has fallen ill . . ."

"I *forbade* you to have contact with that family, didn't I, Klara? I'm not finished with you!"

Klara stared at him.

Hausser stepped on the accelerator and sped after the BMW, which had just turned the corner at the bottom of Greifenhagener.

Dresden was a nicely fabricated cover story that Klara would certainly spread to the neighbours if anyone were to ask. Hausser still had no idea how they would try to cross the border, or where Braun's "back door" could be. Christoph might be in possession of expired travel documents or falsified visas that Braun had acquired before he died, but Hausser doubted that this would be his plan; the guards would see through it immediately.

Hausser caught up with the BMW on Schönhauser Allee and was now right behind them. Through the rear window, he had a glimpse of Renate's ramrod spine, her blood-red Young Pioneers neckerchief; a true party soldier she was. Truth be told, it pained Hausser that he had to put her through all this; it wasn't her fault that her parents were traitors. He was proud and impressed that Renate hadn't let herself be infected with their weakness, that her innocent mind was loyal to the socialist ideal. It was a tragedy that her fate was sealed; her dream of Olympic gold for the GDR was ruined in its infancy. Neither West nor East offered her a chance to thrive; her future was doomed, muddied and impure. But his thoughts were interrupted by the DDR-1 Radio newscast, and Günter Schabowski began to read the Central Committee's statement to the press. His voice shaking and hoarse, Schabowski proclaimed that all East Germans were permitted to travel to the West. A journalist asked if the proclamation was valid with immediate effect. After a moment's hesitation, Schabowski replied: "Yes."

Hausser banged his fist onto the steering wheel. His only hope was that the Schumanns were listening to the Hit Parade in their car, or were simply too nervous to listen to the radio. But even in the best-case scenario, it was only a matter of time before they reached one of the checkpoints. If Christoph was heading for one of the northern posts with less traffic, like the one at Bornholmer Strasse, for instance, they would be able to cross the border within minutes, and he had no idea how to stop this catastrophe from happening.

Ten minutes later, the BMW drove past Bornholmer Strasse and took the road out of Berlin city in the direction of Pankow. Hausser was confused; it appeared they were heading neither for one of the border crossings nor in the direction of Lena's parents in Dresden. The streets were all but deserted, apart from the occasional truck loaded with lignite coal in the open countryside. Here, the BMW picked up speed, and Hausser had difficulty keeping up in his subgrade vehicle. He glanced at the petrol gauge, but the damn thing was obviously not working, and he had no idea how much petrol he had left in the tank.

After half an hour's drive, they took the exit at Neuruppin and continued towards Wittstock. Their route started to make some sense to Hausser. It struck him that the "back door" that Braun had mentioned had nothing to do with Berlin. He remembered that Braun came from Salzwedel, a town that lay in the borderland between East and West Germany; a door that was as far as possible from Berlin and right on the doorstep of the West. Braun would have had intimate knowledge of this area, and this must be the information he passed on to Midas.

It was *here* the Schumann family would try to slip across the border; it was *here* they would fall.

58

For over two hours, Hausser followed the Schumanns along the dark country roads to the West. It was almost eleven o'clock at night by the time they reached the small town of Altmark, which appeared completely deserted. Salzwedel lay ahead, the borderland just beyond. Hausser was sure that Christoph was smart enough not to cross the border in the centrum, and choose to find an area where the security and patrols would be relatively low.

Once they passed through Altmark, Christoph sped up again. Hausser put his foot down flat on the accelerator, but this time he couldn't keep up with the BMW, whose tail lights became ever fainter in the distance, then disappeared altogether. A few kilometres further, there was a fork in the road, and Hausser chose the one that led away from Salzwedel.

He continued driving for another quarter of an hour without meeting any other cars on the road. Occasionally, he came past intersections with lesser roads that all led towards the forest and the border zone between East and West. There was no way of knowing whether Christoph had taken one of them, and Hausser decided to keep driving dead ahead until the road ended at a minor control post with a boom and two soldiers in a small wooden guardhouse. Here, the Restriction Zone began: a five-kilometre broad strip of land before the inner German border.

One of the soldiers came out of the guardhouse, leaving his SKS carabine behind. Hausser rolled down his window and presented his Stasi badge. The soldier, a young man of about twenty, saluted the colonel smartly.

"Has anyone passed through here recently," Hausser said.

"Only the change of guard at twenty-one hours, Colonel," the soldier said, pointing down the road to the border.

"No one else?"

"No, Colonel Hausser, sir."

Hausser nodded and made to roll up his window again.

"Have you heard the news, sir? They've opened the border, Colonel. It was on the radio earlier," the soldier said with a smile.

"Open the boom immediately!" Hausser snarled. The soldier saluted, spun on his heel, and hastily did as he was told.

Hausser slowly drove along the patrol road in the Restricted Zone. He reckoned that Christoph must have taken one of the lesser country roads and left his BMW in the forest—in all likelihood as close as possible to the border, so they wouldn't have to walk too far; he couldn't imagine that Lena was much of a hiker—Renate maybe, but not Lena.

He drove up to the gate and the next guard post by the first signal fence. Beyond the first fence was the "death strip," about one hundred metres wide; out here, it was a barren strip of land between the trees, and on the far side, Hausser had a glimpse of the outer fence just before the borderline to the West. Unlike the first checkpoint, this guardhouse was empty, and Hausser made his way directly to the command tower and parked his car there. The concrete command post towered six metres into the sky before him, and an observation compartment at the top provided an unhindered view of the borderland.

As he got out of the car, Hausser noted a web of communication wires and antennae were mounted on the roof. He could hear voices and the sound of a radio coming from inside the tower. When he opened the door, he saw four young soldiers round a table, drinking steaming cups of tea. The soldiers looked up at him with surprise written on their faces, and Hausser presented his identification.

The soldiers belonged to Border Patrol Unit Two, Hausser noted, and neither of them appeared to be impressed by his rank or the fact that he was a member of the Stasi; *local boys with provincial attitudes*, Hausser thought to himself.

"I have information that an escapee is in the area," he said.

"Well, he's very welcome," mumbled one of the soldiers.

"What did you say?" Hausser snapped.

The first soldier's comrade smiled. "The border has been opened, Colonel. Several hours ago. It's all over the radio. Folks in Berlin are ecstatic. Groups of East Germans have already arrived at the check-points. They say thousands of people are standing in queues to cross the border," he said with a grin on his face.

"What is so fucking amusing?" Hausser said.

The soldier shrugged, nonchalant.

"You're right, Colonel," said the heftiest soldier at the table. "I don't think this is funny at all. We're all going to be without jobs, which means I have to go home and look after my father's cows instead."

"Is there anyone upstairs?" Hausser said, pointing to the ceiling above them.

The soldiers shook their heads and resumed their jovial conversation.

Hausser brushed past the table and limped up the steep steps behind them. From the uppermost observation point, he had a view over the death strip. The next tower stood approximately five hundred metres further along the fence; it appeared to be a BT-9 observation tower, which was slightly narrower and a few metres higher than the control tower he was standing in. He picked up a pair of binoculars from the shelf and trained his gaze on the BT-9. It appeared to be empty, and he guessed that two of the soldiers downstairs were probably meant to be standing guard over there. For the sake of the nation, Hausser sincerely hoped that the other border patrol guards were taking their orders more seriously than this lot.

He was distracted by a yellow light blinking on the panel before him. The panel showed a diagram of the signal fence before the death strip, and the blinking light indicated that a tripwire on the fence had been activated at a point about two hundred and fifty metres away. Hausser trained the binoculars along the fence, but he couldn't see anything except darkness just yet.

Hausser considered whether he should alert the guards downstairs, but that would just complicate matters, he decided. And then he saw them: Christoph came running out of the darkness, holding Renate's hand and two kitbags slung over his shoulders. Lena was just behind them, empty-handed, so apparently, she had ditched her heavy suitcase. Hausser could see that Christoph was holding a bolt cutter in his other hand, and they were headed straight for the fence.

Hausser knew that at this distance, he didn't have the slightest chance of hitting Christoph with his hand pistol. *Midas is getting away*, he thought. In a cold sweat, he looked around the platform desperately for a solution, and saw that one of the soldiers had left his Kalashnikov on a low table. It was old and rusty, as if the rifle had been abandoned by the Red Army after the war. A "Kalash" was not the most precise automatic weapon available, but it was deadly, and as such would do just fine, thought Hausser as he grabbed it with both hands.

Midas was only a few metres from the fence now, and Hausser steadied the Kalash against his cheek, got him in his crosshairs, and squeezed the trigger.

The Kalashnikov made an infernal noise in the tower, and the soldiers downstairs started in fright. Hausser kept his finger on the trigger. His body shook under the force of the recoil, and a golden meteor rain of empty cartridge shells jetted into the dark night air. In that moment, Hausser felt as if he were a god of revenge, the true protector of the Republic, and he did not stop until the hammer made a dull thud against the empty chamber.

Hausser loosened his grip on the trigger. He lowered the smoking-hot barrel of the Kalash. He heard some anguished cries coming from the death strip, and could just about make out three figures by the fence; he could not make out who was dead and who was alive.

One of the soldiers had come up the stairs and looked over Hausser's shoulder.

"*Mein Gott*," he choked out.

59

Mogens strained to get his head above the surface, and the chains holding him down clanged against the sides of the bath. He coughed and took huge gulps of air. The water level sank slowly, and he was able to breathe at last. When the last water gurgled down the drain, he started to sob, shaking with cold in the darkness.

He had no idea how many times they had tried to drown him. He had screamed for mercy every time the ice-cold water rose up over his body. None of it made sense. There was no explanation why someone would want to torture him in this way. By now, all he wanted was to die.

Then he became aware of a sound other than his own crying and the clang of chains. It sounded like music. Not the kind he had heard at the festival. This sounded like marching music with drums and a whistle. Then a children's choir began to sing cheerfully; they were singing in German, and he tried to listen and understand the words. *"Wir tragen . . . wir tragen . . . die blaue Fahne . . ."* *What is the blue flag?* Mogens wondered in confusion. He guessed that it was an old German scout song, perhaps a choir from the Young Pioneers. *But why were they playing music for him?*

He screamed for help. The volume of the music grew louder and louder until it drowned out his voice. Mogens fell silent, utterly forlorn and anguished by the joyful children's voices, but soon after, the music stopped playing and everything was still in the dark once more. He waited, terrified, anticipating the moment when the water would gush out of the tap above his head. But the moment did not come. Instead, a raspy voice came over the loudspeakers. The acoustics in the room seemed to bounce the words off the walls: "WHERE . . . IS . . . THE MONEY? YOU . . . SAID . . . YOU . . . HAD . . . MONEY!"

"Renate? Renate? Is that you? Are you here?" he said in broken German.

After a long pause the voice spoke again. "YES . . . I . . . AM . . . RIGHT HERE . . . YOU PROMISED . . . ME . . . MONEY."

"Why are you doing this to me?" Mogens started to cry again. "Why?"

"YOU . . . CANNOT . . . BE TRUSTED . . . WHERE . . . IS THE MONEY?"

"Let me go, Renate. I'm begging you!"

"WHERE . . . IS THE MONEY?"

"You won't get a cent!" Mogens yelled. "Not until you let me go!" His voice broke. "Please let me go, Renate!"

"YOU . . . ARE . . . A FOOL . . . WEAK . . ."

Then he heard the dreaded squeak of the tap above, and the water poured over his head once more. As the water level rose, Mogens screamed for mercy.

Again the Young Pioneers began to sing, and they kept singing cheerfully, till the water covered his head and transformed their voices into a manic howl above the surface.

60

After they had checked into the Park Inn hotel, Ravn and Louise decided to go for a bite to eat at Spagos . The bar behind them was pumping with a lively atmosphere. There appeared to be a large delegation of businessmen in town. Most had taken off their suit jackets and ties, singing along to the German pop music that blared from the loudspeakers.

It was just after eleven o'clock at night, so Louise and Ravn had to make do with the limited selection from the hotel bar menu. Louise had not touched her salad Niçoise. Instead, she flipped through the file she had brought with her, occasionally taking a sip from the bottle of soda water in front of her. Ravn was eating his burger, watching her. He had noticed that the file contained travel documents and copies of the emails exchanged between Mogens and Renate. She had also included a city map on which she had circled the locations of the four women named "Renate Schumann," to whom they would pay a visit the next day.

"You're very organised," Ravn remarked.

Louise nodded. "I have arranged to have the chauffeur meet us here tomorrow morning at eight thirty. I think that should give us enough time. It is a Sunday, after all."

Ravn nearly choked on his burger and washed down his food with a huge gulp of beer. "A driver?" he said once he'd recovered from his coughing fit sufficiently to talk.

"Yes. I thought it would be convenient if we had our own driver for the day."

"Investigation in first-class style," Ravn said with a smile. "Sounds good. Then we don't have to bother with public transport."

Louise closed her file. "I just hope that one of these women knows where I can find Mogens."

"I'm sure he'll turn up. Mogens is probably having a quiet evening with Renate Schumann right now, drinking coffee with her homemade apple strudel."

Louise rubbed her hands and avoided his gaze. "Mogens doesn't drink coffee . . . we have three days to find him . . . if we don't, I don't have a clue what to do next . . ."

Ravn caught her gaze. "Let's just take it one day at a time, Louise. Tomorrow, we will visit the four ladies on your list. And take it from there."

She put the file back into her handbag. "I wish I could be as calm as you are."

"Are you sure you don't want to eat something?" he pointed at her untouched plate of food.

Louise shook her head and stood up. "I'm exhausted. I think I'll go to my room and email Mogens that we've arrived in Berlin. Perhaps that will motivate him to contact me."

Ravn shrugged.

"Do you think that's a bad idea?"

"No, no, not at all. I was just thinking that if he hasn't contacted you yet, he's unlikely to do so now."

Louise sighed in frustration. "See you tomorrow morning. Shall we say eight o'clock. for breakfast before we go?"

Ravn nodded. "Goodnight, Louise."

Louise didn't reply, and Ravn watched her walk through the dark restaurant and disappear into the lobby. He dabbed the corners of his mouth and tossed his serviette on the table. He wasn't exactly sure what he'd expected from this trip. He understood that Louise was anxious about what she might find, but he was struggling to understand why she had barely spoken to him since they left Copenhagen. When he had managed to start a conversation of sorts with her, she merely gave him a monosyllabic reply. As if she were deliberately trying to distance herself from him. He couldn't figure out why. And was it merely a coincidence that the two single rooms she had booked at the hotel were separated by twelve floors?

Behind him in the bar, the businessmen kept singing.

Ravn downed the dregs in his glass. The thin beer and the horrible song made him miss The Sea Otter. *Right, time for some fresh air and a decent beer*, he thought.

Victoria's travel guide led Ravn over Alexanderplatz, through Berlin Mitte, on to Hackescher Markt and further along Oranienburger Strasse. It was a warm evening, and many folks were out on the streets, most of them tourists, but also students drinking out of half-litre bottles of beers while they flirted with one another.

Ravn was looking for a bar and finally found it on the corner of Auguststrasse and Oranienburger Strasse. It looked relatively decent, which to his mind meant dim lighting, a laid-back clientele, and a sufficient choice of beers and bourbon. He found a seat at the long mahogany bar and got what he came for. While he enjoyed his dark beer, he fancied that Mogens might even have been there. Then again, what little he knew of the man told him that this probably wasn't Mogens's scene. The big city life of Berlin would not be Mogens's cup of tea; it was worlds apart from the quiet ambience of Christianshavn that he was used to. At least he had Renate to cling to.

Through the panorama window at the end of the bar, Ravn watched a young girl leaning up against a lamppost outside. Knee-high red boots and a tight mini-dress patently signalled her profession. Ravn thought about the "Nigerian prince letters" that he had found amongst Mogens's correspondence, which he wisely had not responded to. But the risk that Mogens had been lured to Berlin by someone who was more sophisticated in their fraud was still present. If this had happened, he could only hope that Mogens hadn't run out of money yet. Because in cases like this, money was usually the only thing that kept folks alive . . . thereafter . . . Ravn emptied his glass and decided not to pursue this thought to its logical conclusion. There was no reason to poke the devil.

A few hours and double as many drinks later, Ravn left the bar and made his way back to the hotel. Unfortunately, he got lost in the streets around Rosa-Luxemburg-Platz and landed in front of a jazz club called B-flat. The sound of a piano and a saxophone drew him inside.

He found an empty table at the back of the club and collapsed in a chair. A waitress appeared almost instantly with an Old Fashioned for him. He was too drunk to remember whether he'd actually ordered a cocktail, but it suited his mood perfectly. He listened to the music and drank; drank and listened to the music. He wished that Louise hadn't gone up to her room but come out with him instead, because he was sure she would have appreciated B-flat and this magical moment that he was caught up in.

He ordered another drink just as a different ensemble came onstage. He was loving the understated atmosphere, but all at once he felt an unease in his reptile brain, that part where alarm bells rang, and while he sipped his bourbon, he scanned the room. All the people around him seemed like friendly folk, but his brain knew for a fact that someone was watching him. Someone with ill intentions. But apparently, whoever it had been had disappeared again, his reptile brain told him, along with the fact that the trumpeter on the scene was playing an excellent rendition of "Summertime."

61

The darkness thundered around Ravn. Eva's and Louise's voices emerged from the noise; Mikkel was there as well, and Møffe was barking at all of them. The noise got louder, and he thought it must be *Bianca*'s hull ramming into the embankment. His body felt drained, but he knew he had to get out of bed and save his ship before she sank.

The moment he opened his eyes, he looked directly into a large metallic eye staring back at him; then his brain kicked in sufficiently to tell him that it was the dome of the TV Tower, which was right in front of his hotel window, and that the thunder was actually someone banging on his door.

"One moment . . . *bitte*," he rasped.

He wrapped the thin duvet around his waist and dragged himself to the door. The moment he opened it, his hangover hit him with maximum force.

Louise was standing on the corridor. The look on her face expressed exactly what she thought of the sight of him. "Good morning," she said. "I have called you several times. We agreed to meet in the restaurant at eight o'clock."

"I know," he said, and cleared his voice. "What's the time?"

"Quarter past nine."

"Give me five minutes. Do you want to come in?"

Again, she gave him a look that said more than words. "I'll wait for you in the lobby."

Ten minutes later, Ravn was in the lift on his way down to the lobby from the twenty-fourth floor of the Park Inn. Ten minutes were enough time for him to swallow four headache pills and drink half a litre of water but, most importantly, he'd been able to ransack his kitbag for his Ray-Bans, which would protect him from the merciless daylight and Louise's looks of disapproval. This was the second time in their short acquaintance that she had woken him up, and he'd been made to get himself presentable in record time. He hoped she wasn't going to make a habit of it, because he loved his long, lazy mornings.

The moment the doors slid open and Ravn stepped into the lobby, Louise stood up from the sofa opposite the lift. She pointed to the exit, he caught up with her at the sliding doors, and they went out into the parking lot together.

Louise made a beeline for the black Mercedes S-Class and a chauffeur in a dark suit who opened the door for her.

"*This* is the car and driver you've rented?" Ravn rasped.

Louise didn't reply, other than getting into the back seat of the car, which was just as long as a police van's. Ravn went round to the other side and got in beside her. Moments later, the driver climbed into his seat and asked in German, "Where to?"

Louise paged through her file and found the address of the first Renate Schuman. "Dieffenbachstrasse, *bitte*."

The driver turned in his seat and looked at her with a blank look on his face. Louise repeated herself, slowly this time and more articulated, but it didn't help. Ravn took the file from her and paged to the map where Louise had circled the addresses. He pointed out the first one to the driver.

"Ah, Dieffenbachstrasse!" he said. Without another moment's delay, the chauffeur put the big car in gear, drove out of the parking lot, and took a right onto Karl-Marx-Allee.

Ravn leaned back in the seat and helped himself to one of the small bottles of water that were strategically placed inside the door. They continued their drive in silence, heading over the bridge towards Kreuzberg.

The black Mercedes stopped under the high elm trees that flanked

Dieffenbachstrasse. Louise and Ravn got out of the car and, apart from a few birds singing in the trees, the street was quiet.

Number 34 was a large red-brick residential complex. Louise scanned the intercom outside for "Renate Schumann"; she hesitated a moment and turned to Ravn.

"I have no idea what to say to her . . ."

"How about the truth? As a rule, that's always easiest: Say that you're looking for your brother, and the rest will come to you naturally."

Louise was about to ring the bell when the main door to the complex opened and two boys burst out, each swinging a plastic sword over his head. Louise stumbled back a few steps, and Ravn grabbed the door before it closed. "You coming?" he cast over his shoulder as he entered the stairwell.

"It's on the second floor," Louise replied.

Shortly after, they knocked on Renate Schumann's door.

A young woman of about twenty years opened the door. The sound of loud music and a child crying came from the hall behind her, and she looked as if she'd just woken up. It was hard to miss the huge round belly that stretched her T-shirt and jogging pants to the max; she probably had no more than a month to go.

The pregnant woman looked at them in surprise. "Can I help you?" she said in German.

"Are you Renate Schumann?" Louise asked politely.

"*Ja*," she said. "What is this about?"

Louise introduced them both and explained as best she could in her high school German that she was looking for her brother, Mogens Slotsholm, who had disappeared about six months ago, and that the only trace she had was a woman named Renate Schumann, who lived in Berlin.

"I'm afraid I don't know anyone by that name," said the woman.

Louise took out her iPhone and showed her a picture of Mogens. "And you've never seen this man?"

A young guy in a T-shirt carrying a little boy in the crook of his arm appeared in the doorway behind his wife. "What's this about?" he asked with a friendly smile.

"They're looking for this lady's brother," said Renate. "But I've never seen this man before. Have you?" she said, turning to her husband. He looked at the picture and shook his head.

"I'm sorry," said Renate. "But we can't help you. Good luck. I hope you find him."

When Louise and Ravn came down onto the street again, the driver was ready with the door open, and they got into the back seat.

Louise turned to Ravn thoughtfully. "They were telling the truth, right?"

"Yes, I think you can safely cross the first Renate off your list," he said, and pointed out the next address to the driver. Moments later, they were making their way back through Kreuzberg and Berlin Mitte, heading for Charlottenburg, where Renate Schumann number two reportedly lived.

Ravn looked out the window. The city centre seemed to be waking up reluctantly so early on a Sunday morning; even Kurfürstendamm, with its parade of designer boutiques, was quiet and almost devoid of traffic, so the old champagne-coloured BMW had no trouble at all following the black Mercedes, just as it had done since they'd pulled out of the parking lot in front of the Park Inn on Karl-Marx-Allee.

62

Charlottenburg was a wealthy neighbourhood dating back to Prussian times. Palatial houses on large grounds with immaculate lawns mowed with immaculate precision stood back from the roads. The black Mercedes S fitted in perfectly. Neither the police patrolling the streets on foot nor the guard dogs behind the gates took any notice of them as they passed. When they reached the corner of Bismarckallee and Delbrückstrasse, the driver pulled over to the kerb. He pointed to a low building that was partially obscured behind a massive oak tree.

"This is it: Delbrückstrasse number four," the driver said.

Ravn checked out the building. Some kind of institution, he reckoned. "Hmm, looks unusual," he remarked to Louise. He leaned forward to the driver. "Do you know what this place is?" he asked in German.

The driver nodded. "*Was sagt man* . . . place for old *Mensch* before dead."

"What's he saying?" Louise asked, looking at Ravn.

"I think he means it's a retirement home."

The driver pointed to a sign that stood on the lawn nearby: HERTHASEE SENIORENZENTRUM was written in curling letters above an image of a setting sun.

"I think we can probably cross off Renate number two," said Ravn.

Louise squinted up to the main entrance, where a caregiver in a white coat had just exited with an elderly man in a wheel chair. "Well, now that we're here it can't hurt to ask." She said as she opened the door and got out.

Ravn sighed. "Do they even have access to the internet here?" he mumbled as he clambered out of the back seat.

When Ravn and Louise entered Herthasee's sunny reception area, they were greeted by the smell of coffee, homemade bread, and synthetic cleaning agent. The latter was due to the fact that the shiny floor tiles had just been washed, but this didn't temper Ravn's dislike of the home's distinct institutional flavour. They walked over to the reception desk, where three women were chatting over their morning coffees. The eldest of the three was wearing a white coat, the other two, who were probably assistant caregivers, were in matching red shirts.

"Bitte?" said the white-coated woman.

Louise gave a brief explanation for their visit in German, and asked if they could talk to Renate Schumann about Mogens's disappearance.

The white coat replied with a tight-lipped smile. "Are you Renate Schumann's kin?"

"No, my brother is the one whom Renate may know."

"I'm terribly sorry, but if you're not part of the family or here on official business, then we cannot under any circumstances allow you visit one of our residents."

The woman's scraped-back hair and grey teeth reminded Ravn of Nurse Ratched in *One Flew Over the Cuckoo's Nest*. "Are you sure there is absolutely nothing you can do to make an exception, considering the fact that we have come such a long way?" Ravn asked the nurse, with a big smile.

"If you had travelled all the way from the moon, sir, there is nothing I could do," the nurse replied primly.

The girls in red shirts behind her suppressed their giggles.

"We owe it to our residents, and not least their kin, to stick to the rules," the nurse clarified. Her phone rang, interrupting her speech. "Good day," she said, dismissing any further discussion, before she took the call.

Ravn and Louise exited the main entrance and stood outside the door together for a moment. "What an idiot," Louise muttered.

"Yes, she was," said Ravn, looking about the grounds. "But maybe we could ask one of the residents if they know Renate, if you think it would be useful."

Louise shrugged.

One of the red shirts came out of Reception, took a seat on the railing on the edge of a flowerbed nearby, and lit up a cigarette. She blew out a cloud of smoke and smiled at Ravn. "She's a bit of a battle axe, your boss," Ravn remarked.

The young woman flicked her ash into the flower bed. "She's all right, as long as you do as she says," she said. "But you guys wouldn't have had much joy in talking to Renate Schumann anyway."

"Are you sure?" Ravn said, returning her smile and walking over to her.

The red shirt smiled again. "Dead sure. Renate is ninety-eight years old and lives in her own world. Dementia, you know, but she's very sweet. Loves sitting in the garden with a blanket over her knees. And a glass of apple juice," the young woman said, flicking her cigarette again, as if it were a nervous habit.

"What about family, someone who visits her regularly?"

The girl laughed. "No one here gets visitors. That's why the residents are in this place; so their family doesn't have worry about them." She narrowed her eyes and gave him a flirtatious smile. "Are you some kind of private detective?"

"Well," he said, a little flattered by the attention. "Something like that, I guess—"

"Shall we get going?" said Louise. Without waiting for his reply, she made for the car.

Ravn nodded goodbye to the girl and followed Louise across the lawn to the waiting Mercedes.

The third Renate lived in Adlershof. They found her in her front garden, and she struck up a conversation with them immediately.

She'd been living in Adlershof for almost twenty-five years. She looked to be about sixty years old with a hard-working life behind her, not that this had dampened her sunny disposition. She voluntarily offered the information that she was a widow now, that she liked to babysit her two grandchildren, who were skipping around the garden as they spoke. Her daughter was a doctor and her son-in-law an engineer, she said. They were out looking at a house north of Pankow, so she'd offered to look after the kids, she explained with pride. When Ravn and Louise finally managed to turn the conversation to Mogens, Renate said no, unfortunately she did not know him.

"I know how you feel, my dear," she said to Louise.

"In the old Berlin, before that bloody wall was pulled down, young men often disappeared from one day to another—sometimes entire families were never seen again. The State had secret prisons all over the country. Those were dangerous times," she said without further explanation, but it seemed as if she was speaking from personal experience.

"Thank you for your time," said Louise.

Renate number three gave her a hug of encouragement before she left. "I hope nothing bad has happened to him, and that you find him soon, my dear; family is the most important thing a person has."

It was just past midday when they drove in the direction of Neukölln, where Renate number four lived. Ravn's hangover had abated and was now replaced by a raging appetite. "Hungry?" he said.

Louise shook her head and stared vacantly out the window. He could see that she knew that this was their last chance if they were to find any trace of Mogens in Berlin. Ravn had already considered a few alternatives should their tour today prove to be in vain, but none of them were particularly promising; they all involved the German police, and he was sure that Louise would prefer to not go down that route if they could avoid it.

The old residential block where the last Renate lived was right opposite Treptower Park. There was something foreboding about the building with its deep cracks in the walls and peeling façade that had clearly seen better days. Ravn and Louise checked out the list of names at the main entrance, but Renate's name could not be gleaned through the graffiti that was sprayed over the intercom and front doorway.

"Who are you folks looking for?" a slurred voice asked in German from the first-floor balcony to their left.

Ravn and Louise took a step back and looked up. In the semidarkness, under a frayed awning, they spotted a podgy middle-aged woman in a green T-shirt. She swirled the ice in the glass she was holding and regarded them curiously.

"We're looking for a Renate Schumann who lives here," said Ravn "Do you know her?"

"Is that your car?" said the women, nodding at the Mercedes. "It looks pretty snazzy. Are you estate agents? Lawyers?"

"No, we've got nothing to do with the property," Ravn said with a sigh. "But does Renate Schumann live here?"

"I should think so," she said. "I'm Renate Schumann. Are you lawyers? *She* is, but *you're* not, are you?" she said, pointing at Ravn with her glass.

Ravn shrugged. "Yup, you got me right," Ravn said. "Could you let us in, please?"

Soon after, they were standing in Renate Schumann's living room, which was stuffed to capacity with clothing on a washing line, an easel, paintbrushes, tubes, and canvasses in all shapes and sizes. On his way in, Ravn had surreptitiously scanned the entrance and stuck his head in the bathroom to see if there was anything indicating the presence of a man, but it appeared as if the woman lived alone.

"Have I inherited or am I being charged with a crime?" said Renate, taking a sip from her drink.

"Neither nor," said Ravn. "We're looking for this man." He showed her a picture of Mogens on Louise's iPhone.

Renate leaned in and squinted at the picture. "Never seen him," she said, swaying on her feet. "But he seems nice-looking enough."

"His name is Mogens. Have you been writing to him?" Ravn asked.

"Writing? I'm dyslexic. Can't even spell my own name," said Renate.

"Honestly? So you don't even have a computer?" Ravn looked around the living room.

"What would I need a computer for?" she said, downing the dregs in her glass. "Sure you don't want to buy a painting? I have a few nice things." She pointed with her empty glass at the stack on the sofa. "I'm sure there's something that would do nicely for a lawyer's office."

Louise slumped in her seat in the back of the Mercedes. Ravn was about to join her when he got that eerie feeling again that he was being watched.

Exactly like he had at B-flat Bar the night before. He cast a look over the roof of the Mercedes. A little way down the road he noticed an old champagne-coloured BMW parked between two delivery vans. He could see a figure behind the wheel, but the branches of trees next to the road obscured his view.

"Are you coming?" Louise said.

Ravn climbed into the back seat next to her and slammed the door closed.

They drove back to Alexanderplatz in silence. The sun had gone down and was replaced by rain on the toned glass in the roof. Ravn stole a glance at Louise. She was staring at her feet despondently, and he could hear from her breathing that she was fighting back tears. He reached out for her hand and stroked it gently. "It was against the odds that we would find her today. But you ought to be proud that you tried your best," he said.

Louise removed her hand from under his. "I feel like such an idiot. I don't know what I was thinking. I should never have come to Berlin . . ."

63

The black Mercedes pulled into the parking lot in front of the Park Inn. The rain had picked up, and the wipers fought a losing battle against the cascade that hit the windshield. The driver apologised that he hadn't brought umbrellas along, but the weather had been so fine in the morning he didn't anticipate it would be necessary. He drove them right up to the entrance of the hotel while Louise was checking her emails.

Ravn turned to her. "Anything from Mogens?"

She shook her head.

"He could still reply," Ravn said.

"It's over, Thomas. Don't you get it?" Her voice was all but drowned by the thundering rain on the roof. The next moment, she jumped out of the car and made a dash for the entrance.

Ravn grabbed the file that she had left behind on the seat, thanked the driver, and followed in Louise's footsteps. "Please, wait a moment," he said as soon as he caught up with her in the lobby. "There's no need to give up just yet."

"I don't know what else we can do."

"We could contact the German police and ask them to initiate a search for him."

"I'm not going to lay a charge against my own brother, if that's what you're suggesting."

"Fair enough. So let's start by looking at the hostels."

"Hostels?" She shook her head. "How would that help?"

"It's just a thought: If he's been tricked out of his money, he could've gone to a hostel as a last resort."

"Mogens has not been tricked. And also, he's much too proud to go somewhere like that. This is my brother we're talking about . . ."

"Louise, I'm just trying to help."

"Honestly? Like when you get drunk as a skunk and pitch up with a hangover, or flirt with the nurses instead of . . . of . . ." She turned on her heel and fled into the lift.

"Louise, please wait." He went after her, but the lift doors closed in his face. He considered whether he should take the next one up to her room, but reckoned she probably needed a little space to calm down.

Ravn sat alone at the end of the hotel bar with a club sandwich and a Weissbier. He was enjoying neither. The rain was whipping down onto Alexanderplatz outside, making the square look more desolate than usual. Recalling Renate number three's words, he pondered what this area must have been like before the Wall came down. Whole families disappeared overnight, she'd said. He took a sip of his beer, which was already a little flat. He understood Louise's frustration, and he regretted pitching up with a hangover that morning. The beer in front of him was going to be his last on this trip, he decided. He paged through Louise's file and started reading through the emails again.

The relationship between Renate and Mogens seemed to be real. They'd shared their thoughts, their common interests in history and classical music; they'd given each other compliments, and their hopes for a future together seemed genuine. Ravn could understand how a life with Renate could have been attractive to Mogens. And he could see how Mogens tried ever harder to match her language skills, whether he was writing in English or using the few German expressions he knew. But the emails gave no conclusive indication whether his hopes for a future with Renate had motivated his crime and his wish to escape from it all. There was, however, something completely different that caught his attention; some leads began to appear in the fragments. He asked the bartender for a pen and started systematically underlining certain passages in Renate's emails.

A little while later, he ordered another beer, even though he had promised himself not to; the simple truth was that his brain worked better with some hops in his blood—and he needed his full brain capacity right now.

Louise lay flat on her back on her bed. Darkness had fallen over Alexanderplatz, and the dome of the iconic TV Tower stared out over the square.

There was a knock at the door, and she sat up. "Who is it?" she called.

"Room service," said a familiar voice.

Louise opened the door.

Ravn was standing in the corridor, holding a tray; he had gone into the kitchen and arranged a thermos of tea, some fruit, a few sandwiches, and a bottle of Perrier. "I thought you might be hungry," he said.

"Thank you, that's very sweet of you."

He came into her room and put the tray down on the little table by the window with the view. "That thing makes me a little paranoid," he said, jerking a thumb at the tower.

She smiled. "I'm sorry I took my frustration out on you this afternoon; that really wasn't fair. Can you accept my apology?"

"Forget it," he said. "I understand how you feel." He poured her some tea and took a seat at the table. Louise joined him.

"Actually, I think I've found something that might help us track down Mogens."

"Really?"

"Have you read through all their emails," he asked, taking the file out of his pocket.

"Yes, or course. They're very personal."

"Exactly," Ravn said, pulling out the file. "Especially Renate's emails, which are written in quite elaborate language. It appears she's a great romantic at heart."

"Okay. But how is this going to help us find Mogens?"

"Well, I've tried to focus on the factual details and filtered out the romantic prose," said Ravn. He turned the file at an angle so Louise could read along with him. "For example, here she writes: 'looking out over the convent garden from the kitchen window. The trees and shrubs have closed for the winter.' This sentence gives a description of where she lives," he said.

"But there must be countless churches in Berlin."

"Yes, but here she writes about Monastery Garden. And I've found more clues," he said, paging to the next email: "'drinking morning coffee on Helmholtzplatz in the rays of the sun . . . think I might have to make a habit of this, my morning ritual.'" Ravn levelled his gaze on Louise. "I think this could indicate that she lives near Helmholtzplatz, which is in a neighbourhood called Prenzlauer Berg." He had circled the area on the map with a red felt pen and showed it to Louise.

"Hmm. But it's still quite a large area to look for someone whose address we could not locate."

Ravn nodded. "True, but I think we can limit our search to a single road." He paged to the next mail. "In this one Renate writes that she has been out to buy gardenias at her favourite flower shop, which is on the road where she lives. So I checked Interflora's webpage, and according to that there are only three flower shops in all of Prenzlauer Berg. The one that is closest to Helmholtzplatz is on Greifenhagener Strasse. I wasn't able to find out if there is a convent on that road, but there is definitely a church."

Louise looked at the map. "It surprises me that she never gave Mogens her address."

"Perhaps she did so at a later point, in emails that Mogens chose not to keep, or maybe they spoke on the phone and exchanged addresses."

"So you think that Mogens might be in Prenzlauer Berg?"

"That's probably hoping for too much, but I think that a Renate Schumann lives there—the Renate we're looking for."

"But why didn't her name and address come up in my search?"

Ravn shrugged. "Some people don't want to be found; they stay below the public radar."

"Not your radar," she said with a smile. "So, what's our next move?"

"I say we go to Prenzlauer Berg and search the area. And we keep searching until we find either Renate or your brother." He was about to get up from his chair, but she leaned forward and rested her hand on his thigh. "Are you leaving?"

"I don't want to disturb you any longer."

"You're not disturbing me. Or rather: maybe a little, but in a good way." She got up from her chair and sat on his lap, straddling him on his chair. She leaned into him, letting him feel the heat of her body. Then she lowered her head and kissed him. He put his arms around her and pulled her close. They kissed deeply, for a long time, till his head began to spin and he stood up from his chair and carried her over to the bed.

They undressed each other and climbed in under the duvet. Ravn could feel his desire for her, held her gaze as he thrust inside her. He held her arms over her head and felt her teeth bite into the side of his neck, his shoulder. The gasps that escaped her throat only excited him more, and he abandoned himself to her.

64

Eight months earlier
Berlin
23 September 2013

Mogens woke up in complete darkness. The bath was empty, and he could feel the chains cutting into his ankles, his wrists, and his throat. He didn't know how long he'd been unconscious, but the last memory he had was being swallowed by the water again, the distorted chime of the Young Pioneers' march above, and Renate's eerie voice demanding the money.

He tried to swallow, but his mouth was dry. It was ironic, he thought, that he could be so thirsty while fearing his death by drowning. He braced his feet against the end of the bath, trying to see if he could shift a little higher and reach the tap that he knew was just above his head, but the chains held him fast. He collapsed in the bottom, sobbing quietly, till he hammered a hand against the side in frustration. When his wrist made contact with the side, a loose object scraped the enamel. Mogens repeated the blow and felt it swing again. *Perhaps a bolt securing the handcuffs around his wrist?* He lifted his arm as high as he could and immediately felt the chain tighten around his neck. This time, instead of giving way to panic, he relaxed his arms, and he felt the pressure on his neck diminish as he did so. It was so dark that he couldn't see how he was chained down, but it seemed as if she had used one long chain to wrap around his limbs and fasten him to the bath, rather than individual lashings; clever, because every time he moved, the chains tightened. But now he realised the weakness to this system: the chain was secured by a single lock. If he could break it, he was free.

Mogens raised his arms, straining against the chains as much as he could, then he hammered his wrist against the side once more. The crashing sound scared the hell out of him. He lay completely still for a moment, trying to glean if Renate had been alerted, but the dark was still. Once he'd regained his breath, he smashed his wrist into the side again. He repeated the process again and again, and every time the chain cut deep into his throat. Finally, his strength was sapped, and he gave the chain on his wrist one last, half-hearted clang against the side. His hand was swollen, and he was afraid he might have broken it. Then he heard a scraping sound, and something clunked against the bottom. He lifted his arms and this time the chain around his wrists loosened. Yanking on the chain now, it suddenly gave and his legs and ankles were free. He kept pulling until his left wrist and neck were free as well.

Gripping the sides of the bath, he pushed himself up. His legs could barely carry his weight as he tumbled out of the bath, coming down hard on the cold cement floor. He lay there for a moment, trying to recover. Getting out of the bath was a victory on its own, but he knew that it was only a matter of time before Renate returned. He had to move. *Now.*

Mogens stretched his arms out and fumbled forwards in the dark. If he could reach one of the walls he could feel his way towards a door, he reckoned. His foot came against something hard; he tripped and almost fell as something crashed to the floor; the music started to play and the cheerful voices of the Young Pioneers filled the stagnant air once more. Mogens stumbled forwards in panic and finally his palms came up against the cold, damp wall. He felt along the surface as quickly as he could, desperately hoping to find a door, but then he heard a scuttling of bolts behind him and turned round.

A door opened opposite him, letting in a shaft of light that revealed a glimpse of a tall person with long hair in the doorway, before it slammed shut.

The darkness closed around him again. "Renate . . . I'm begging you . . . I can't take any more . . . I've told you everything . . . please let me go . . ."

The music stopped. He could hear his own gasping breath. Inching along the wall, he could feel the cold cement against his back and buttocks. "I promise I won't tell anyone . . . spare me, Renate, please . . ."

No one answered.

Mogens stopped and listened. He could smell her sweet perfume; she must be close. In his weakened state, he probably would not be able to defend himself, but he resolved to throw himself at her. Strangle her. He clenched his right fist and took a few swings in the air. He heard a sound behind him, turned, and felt something cold against his neck. The blue spark of the stun gun gave him a glimpse of her long, blonde hair and blood-red lips before a heavy object hit his temple, and everything turned black.

The ice-cold water ran over Mogens's face and woke him up. He tasted the drops and drank a little of the rusty water. The water pressure increased, and he tried to move his head in vain. Then the water began to rise in the bath.

"THE MONEY . . . YOU TRAITOR . . . WHERE IS IT? YOU . . . HAVE . . . BETRAYED ME . . . DO YOU UNDERSTAND?"

65

Ravn and Louise walked down Raumerstrasse, which ran along the park on Helmholtzplatz. The weather was warm, and they could hear the children squealing in delight on the playground in the middle of the park.

They had both risen early and had breakfast together in the hotel restaurant. It didn't seem as if Louise had regretted her night with him; but she hadn't given him any signal that it could be the beginning of something between them, nor for that matter, whether she wanted to spend another night with him. Most of all, Ravn was relieved that he hadn't woken up to a bad conscience or any kind of moral dilemma with regard to Eva's memory.

The sunshine had drawn people to the outdoor tables of the cafés they passed on the pavement, and Louise couldn't help looking for Mogens's face among the guests. "That probably would have been too much to hope for," she muttered, and Ravn nodded in agreement.

Fifteen minutes later, they finally came upon Greifenhagener Strasse, which was almost deserted under the shade of the elm trees on either side. They continued down the idyllic road towards Gethsemane Church, involuntarily scanning the area as if Mogens could appear at any moment.

Soon they arrived at the square by the church, which lay in a small park with low trees and dense shrubbery. In one of the front flower beds, an elderly man in overalls was weeding the soil with a rake.

"Could this be the garden that Renate mentions in her letters?" Louise said, voicing her thoughts to Ravn.

He shook his head. "I don't think this garden matches what she described."

The sharp light reflected on the windowpanes of the building opposite, and Ravn couldn't tell if anyone was standing up there, watching him, but he had that same paranoid feeling he'd had before.

"Is something wrong?" asked Louise.

Ravn shook his head and went over to the elderly man in the flower bed. "Lovely garden," he said to the man in German.

The man nodded without interrupting the flow of his work.

"We're looking for a convent that should be nearby," Ravn said.

"A convent?" the man muttered without looking up.

"Yes, or rather: a convent garden."

"A convent garden?" The man shook his head. "No idea."

Ravn wished the man a good day and turned to Louise. "Hmm. Maybe this really is the garden that Renate referred to."

Louise shrugged, not at all convinced.

"Saint Joseph's!" the old man burst out, as if uttering a curse.

Ravn and Louise spun round.

"Saint Joseph's Home. It's run by the sisters," the old man said. "It's over on Pappelallee. But the garden runs all the way along Greifenhagener. You folks would've passed its red-brick surrounding wall on your way over here." He shook his head and muttered to himself as he continued his weeding. "Of course, good old Saint Joseph's."

Ravn and Louise hurried back down Greifenhagener Strasse and soon spotted the red-brick wall, which was sprayed with graffiti. "Come over here," said Ravn, kneeling down by the wall and threading his fingers together.

Louise looked at him in surprise. "What are you doing?"

"I'm giving you a leg up so you can see over the wall. Come on, then," he said.

Louise hesitated for a moment but relented and came over. She put her boot in his interlocked hands and he gave her a lift.

Louise pulled herself up and could just see over the wall.

"And?" Ravn puffed. "Can you see anything?"

"Yes," she said through gritted teeth.

"Are you sure? What can you see?"

"Nuns. Put me down again."

Ravn let Louise slide down onto the ground again and stood up.

Louise rubbed her hands together. "The garden looks like the one Renate described. There's a little pond in the middle, pretty flower beds around it."

Ravn stepped out onto the road and searched the façade of the closest buildings; only the property to his right had a direct view of the garden. "This way," he said, pointing at the gate to Number 9.

The gate was locked. A sizable intercom pad was located on a wall right beside it with a plate of about forty buzzers and the names of the residents in the front and back buildings.

"Can *you* see Renate's name anywhere?" Ravn asked after they had scanned the plate together.

Louise shook her head.

Just then, the gate opened and a young woman in an elegant coat and a knitted hat came through with a pram. Ravn was quick to hold the gate open for her, and the woman thanked him as she manoeuvred the pram through the opening.

"Excuse me, but maybe you could help us?" Ravn said in English and gave her a smile. "We're looking for a Renate Schumann. Do you know if she lives here?"

"I'm afraid I've just moved in, so I don't know many of the others living here," she said.

Louise held up a picture of Mogens before the woman. "Do you know this man? He's my brother. He's been missing for over six months."

The woman shook her head. "I'm sorry, no, I've never seen him."

A young man in a velvet suit and a full beard came up to the gate on his bicycle. He dismounted and greeted the woman. "Maybe you can help these people?" she said to the man. "Do you know if a Renate . . . Schumann lives here?"

"Hmm, the name doesn't ring a bell," the man said, scratching his beard. "Folks move in and out before one gets a chance to greet them," he said. "And those of us who stay are quite happy in our own worlds—we are the superficial generation," he added with a nervous laugh as he went through the gate. Then, as he entered the yard, he looked back. "But why don't you ask Frau Graf on the first floor?" he said. "She's been here for a lifetime, and she knows everyone."

Louise and Ravn stepped into the yard. "What did you say her name was again?" asked Ravn.

"Frau Graf . . . Frau Klara Graf."

66

Ravn rang the doorbell, and moments later Klara Graf poked her head into the narrow gap between the door and the frame. She stared at them through a thick pair of glasses. The wig cut in a bob was askew, as if she had donned it in a hurry. Ravn apologised for the intrusion and introduced himself and Louise. He explained that a friendly neighbour had referred them to her because she was the only one who knew everyone in the complex. It was meant as a compliment, but the latter comment brought a suspicious look on Klara's face. "A friendly neighbour, you say?" She spoke a German dialect that made her raspy voice seem rough and deep. "Who was he, if I may ask?"

"I didn't catch his name," said Ravn. "He has a large beard and is probably in his late thirties."

"I don't know anyone fitting that description," Klara said. She started closing the door, but Louise stepped forward.

"Frau Graf, we have come all the way from Denmark to look for my brother, who disappeared here in Berlin."

Klara opened the door a little wider. "Your brother? Disappeared? Are you both from . . . Denmark?"

Louise nodded and showed Klara a picture of Mogens on her iPhone.

Klara seemed confused, looking down at the picture. "He looks overweight. Never seen him. Are we done?"

"Do you know a Renate Schumann?" Ravn asked.

"Renate?" Klara said in obvious surprise. "Yes, of course I do. Why do you ask about that?"

Louise smiled. "We really need to talk to her."

"But . . . but that's impossible."

Ravn sighed. "Does she still live in the complex?"

"Renate? No."

"Do you know where she moved to?"

"Renate has been dead for almost twenty-five years."

They were invited into the small apartment that had a bitter smell of burnt cabbage in the air. Entering Klara's living room was like stepping into a time capsule from the former GDR; the yellow paisley–patterned wallpaper, vinyl-covered dining chairs, and the veneered plywood bookcase at the far end. Souvenirs, memorabilia, and old photographs of former Soviet states were packed on the shelves and surfaces. Even a beer mug bearing a portrait of Leonid Brezhnev.

"Renate lived with her parents on the fifth floor in the rear building," Klara said. She stood by the window, pointing up to the top floor on the other side of the yard.

Through the tall bushes, Ravn caught a glimpse of the convent garden on the neighbouring property; from the fifth floor of the rear building, you would have had a fine view of the garden, exactly the way Renate described it in her letters to Mogens. "Who lives up there now?" asked Ravn.

"Gabby and Wolfgang and their little baby. Gabby always wears the prettiest little knitted caps. I think she makes them herself."

Ravn reckoned her description matched the young woman with the pram they had spoken to earlier. "How long has the convent garden been next door?"

"The convent was here before I arrived. That's almost forty years ago."

"And how long had Renate lived here before she disappeared?"

"I think she was nine, maybe ten, I don't remember exactly. The poor child," said Klara, shaking her head. She closed the curtains, as if she was afraid people would spy on her. "She was a sweet girl. I looked after her when her parents had company or went out on the town." Klara rolled her r's in disapproval.

"You didn't like Renate's parents?"

"No. 'Class traitors,' that's what they were. I know the expression has no meaning in modern times, now that it's every man for himself, and the old and frail are left to their own devices. But back then . . ." she shook her head again. "That was a different time."

"Better times, I hope." Ravn smiled. "But what made you think her parents were traitors?"

"They advanced themselves, thought they were better than all the rest of us. The father worked in the State Bank, a very important man, and she, Lena, was a former model. They threw money around—foreign money, of course," Klara said, rubbing her thumb and forefinger together. "They raked in piles of money! No surprise that it ended badly."

"What happened?" said Ravn.

"The Stasi is what happened. The entire complex was under surveillance. Even I, a loyal Party member, was interrogated. Not that I could tell them anything; I'm not one to interfere.

"No, they fled, but they didn't get very far. Some say they were shot by the border patrol guards, others say it was a land mine, but either way they all died. Poor little Renate." Klara had tears in her eyes.

"Are you sure about all this? Sure that Renate is dead?"

"That's what I heard," said Klara. "And I never saw any of them ever again. A month after the reunification, their flat was emptied. All their expensive furniture and fine things were put in a container out on the street. I'm not sure if it was the new authorities or the estate administrator who organised this. But, of course, people pounced at the opportunity and the container was ransacked before the day was out." She looked down and smoothed the orange tablecloth. "Even I took a single item, but it was mainly to have a memento of Renate. *Moment, bitte*," she said, and went out into the other room. Soon after, she returned with a faded photograph in a cheap frame and a plastic medal painted gold. "This picture of Renate was taken at a gymnastics tournament in Leipzig. She was so good at gymnastics. She had so many dreams."

Ravn and Louise looked at the faded photograph of three girls in leotards with medals slung around their necks.

Klara pointed at the little girl in the middle. "Her greatest dream was to win Olympic gold for the GDR." She looked up at Louise. "I'm sorry that you can't find your brother, but his disappearance cannot possibly have anything to do with Renate."

"Is there anyone other than yourself here in the complex who knew Renate Schumann?" asked Ravn.

Klara shook her head. "I'm the only one left from back then. Now it's only young people. Folks with bags of money and no social conscience. People without an inkling of their own history." Klara's wig slipped further to one side as she shook her head in a gesture of defeat.

67

Ravn and Louise were sitting at a table outside Café Blume on Koll-witzplatz. Louise pushed her untouched ham sandwich away. She had taken an age to decide what she wanted, and now she seemed to regret her choice. Ravn had almost finished his own, including a Berliner Pil-sner, and it was clear to him that she was still upset about Klara's story. He dabbed his mouth with a serviette and regarded Louise thoughtfully. "This changes the situation, Louise."

"I know," she said.

"Whoever wrote those letters and emails to Mogens had a hidden agenda."

She looked out over the square. "Who the hell would steal the profile of a dead girl and write to Mogens as if the girl were still alive?"

"Either someone who is very ill, or—"

"Or what?"

"Or Renate is still alive. We only have Klara's testimony regarding Renate's supposed death, which Klara has on hearsay."

"But if it really is Renate who wrote to Mogens, why did she make it sound as if she were writing from her childhood home? Why not write about the place where she actually lives?"

"Perhaps because the life she lives now is not worth writing about?" he said, taking a sip of beer with a loud slurp. "Regardless of who is behind those letters and emails, Mogens has been lured to Berlin under false pretences."

"Do you think he was also lured into stealing from Lauritzen?"

"Perhaps. If so, it would have to be by a person who has a great deal of power over him. I think the most important question is: What happened when they finally met?"

"You're scaring me."

"As things stand, it might be wise to be a little scared at this point. My suggestion is that we contact the German police with this."

"How will that help?"

He was reluctant to explain exactly what he had in mind, because part of his plan involved a visit to the morgue to see if Mogens turned up in a drawer among the unidentified cadavers. "We could simply knock on their door," he said instead. "For starters, I'm sure no one has initiated an investigation into his disappearance just yet; their only knowledge of Mogens at this time would be a missing person's report on Europol's homepage."

"Don't the police automatically start looking for people registered as missing?"

"Only if they've had their arms twisted. The police are lazy by nature," he said, pointing both thumbs at himself and downing his beer.

Louise took out her phone. "I'll try emailing Mogens one last time before we contact the police. Maybe he will respond if I tell him that I know about Renate, and that he needn't be embarrassed if someone has tricked him."

"You could add that if he doesn't respond, you'll be obliged to contact the German authorities."

Louise looked up from her phone and nodded.

The sun had disappeared behind a massive cloud once more and it started to drip from the heavens. The next minute, the rain came down in sheets, and Ravn and Louise ran across the square to the taxi rank. They threw themselves into the back seat of the first available car and asked the driver to take them back to the hotel.

The streaks of lightning in the night sky gave the impression that Berlin was under bombardment like in the war. It was as if the tall Park Inn hotel swayed in the storm and the wind whistled eerily through the long, empty corridors. In Room 3429, Ravn and Louise were naked, their arms wrapped around each other in an intimate embrace against the panorama window facing Alexanderplatz. Ravn pressed her up against the cold glass and took her in deep, rhythmical thrusts.

"Promise me that we will find him," Louise whispered in his ear.

"I promise," Ravn said.

It was just before one thirty in the morning, and still the storm raged over the city. Despite the lateness of the hour, the internet café Rosenthaler Platz was jam-packed. The air in the dark café had the sour smell of AeroPress coffee, cheese pops, and wet coats. Most of the customers were international students who were either on Facebook or YouTube or Skyping with their friends and family. No one paid any attention to the person sitting at the PC right at the back, wearing a large raincoat and a hat pulled low over the face.

The person logged in to the email account MOGENSDK69. The next moment, the inbox popped up and Louise's email from that afternoon was marked "unread" at the top of the list. With a single click, the email was opened, and a low, melodic hum sounded from under the hat.

68

Berlin
7 May 2014

The sharp morning sunlight cut through the large hotel window. Louise turned onto her side and slipped out of Ravn's embrace. She stretched lazily and felt Ravn stir behind her. He stroked her cheek with the back of his hand, which gave her goose bumps. "Good morning," she said. He kissed the back of her neck in reply and pulled her back into his arms. He felt her buttocks against his crotch and wanted her again.

The alarm on Louise's iPhone went off and she reached for it on the bedside table. She fumbled to switch the damn thing off and noticed on her display that a new email had come in overnight. Louise sat up and opened her inbox.

"Something the matter?" asked Ravn.

"It . . . it's Mogens . . . he's sent a reply."

Ravn sat up against the headboard. "What does he say?"

Louise didn't reply, just sat staring at the display. Then the tears started to run down her cheeks.

"He . . . it says he's fine . . . started a new life and I shouldn't look for him . . ."

"Well, at least he's broken the silence and reached out to you at last; that's good, isn't it?"

The telephone slipped out of her hand and landed on the bed between them. "Yes . . . but . . ." she looked at Ravn with fear written on her face. "Only if Mogens is the one who wrote this."

Ravn picked up the phone and read the email on the display; it was short, written in a staccato style.

Hi, sister. Thank you letter. Do not look for, am fine. Do not mix Police in, thanks. Not want to be found. Thank you for care.

Farewell.

Your brother, Mogens.

"Okay," said Ravn. "I think the most likely scenario is that the person who wrote this email made use of a translation program to write this in Danish. Under pressure to respond quickly, it is obviously written in response to the email that you wrote yesterday." He laid the phone down beside him on the mattress.

"Do you think Mogens is dead?" Louise said in a small voice.

"I don't know, Louise, but I think we have no choice but to contact the police now."

She nodded and got out of bed.

"What did you write in your previous emails to Mogens? How much does this person know about our plans?"

"I only wrote that I was worried about him, and that I have come to Berlin to look for him. I didn't write anything about you, because I thought it might scare him away if he knew that someone else was involved. But I wrote everything in Danish, of course; perhaps the person didn't understand everything I wrote."

"I think it's safe to assume that the person would make use of an online translation program to read the emails you wrote. Irrespective of the quality of the translation, I'm quite certain that he or she would have been able to understand the content. Did you say in which hotel you were staying? Your room number?"

Louise nodded anxiously. "Both."

"Let's move your things over to my room before we speak to the police. Okay?"

While Louise packed her things, Ravn called Reception and asked them to provide him with the number and address of the nearest police station.

Half an hour later, they were sitting in a taxi on their way to Keithstrasse 30, where the Fourth Division of the German criminal police was located.

69

In the large waiting area of the police station, Ravn and Louise were shown to a bench at the foot of a massive stone stairway that led up to the Fourth Division of the Crime Department. The high domes and the pillars of granite lent the station the atmosphere of a kitsch medieval castle. They had been waiting for almost ninety minutes, and as they were the only ones in the waiting room, it was hard to imagine why it was taking so long.

"*Hallo . . . kommen Sie bitte mit,*" a voice above them said.

Ravn stood up and looked at the thin man in shirtsleeves who was standing on the stairway. He had a file under one arm and waved them over with his free hand.

Louise and Ravn walked over and introduced themselves. The man didn't return their greeting but merely asked them to follow him.

When they reached the second floor, the man showed them into a small office at the end of the corridor; there was just enough space for a desk and two free chairs in front of it. The window faced out onto a yard and a brick wall beyond. "So, you would like to report a missing person, am I right?" said the deputy in his shrill German voice.

Ravn said yes.

"And you are both from Denmark?" said the deputy, taking his seat behind the desk.

"That is correct," Ravn said, holding out the chair for Louise before he sat down himself.

The deputy glanced down at the form they had filled out in Reception upon their arrival.

"How long has your brother been missing?" the deputy asked. "More than twenty-four hours? Because if it's less, we can't do anything," he said, crossing his arms over his chest.

"Louise's brother has been missing for more than six months," said Ravn patiently. He had met officers like this guy before; an arrogant arse devoid of both empathy and smarts. It was pricks like this guy who were usually promoted up the ranks and eventually ended up in the Chief Commissioner's Office.

The deputy leaned back in his chair. "I'm not sure I understand: Did he disappear here in Berlin or in Denmark?"

Louise briefly explained the circumstances surrounding the theft, Mogens's subsequent disappearance, and the reason they believed he was in Berlin. That she feared for his life. She had to speak very slowly because the deputy had trouble understanding her German.

The deputy looked at Louise and Ravn in turn. "Excuse me, but are you saying that your brother is on the run from the Danish authorities?"

Louise nodded.

"You can check his details on Europol's homepage," said Ravn.

The deputy stretched out his arms, so his fingers just reached the mouse and the keyboard of his computer. He brought up the homepage, and after a few clicks, he arrived on the page listing Danish citizens who were missing. A picture of Mogens that was taken at a company party came up alongside people who were wanted in connection with tax evasion as well as a few tough-looking drug smugglers. The deputy looked up from the screen and gave them a hard stare. "Could I see your passports please?"

Louise immediately started rummaging in her bag for hers and gave it to the deputy, but Ravn just looked at the guy. "You do realise we are here to report a missing person, right? A man whose life we believe is in danger?"

"Passports, please."

Ravn unzipped his sweatshirt, took his passport out of his breast pocket, and tossed it over the desk to the deputy.

The deputy caught the passport reflexively and stared at Ravn. He studied both passports. Then he got to his feet, taking their passports with him. "I ask you to remain here while I investigate this," he said.

"What would you like to investigate?" said Ravn. "We have come here to report a missing person."

"This man must not be found, he must be investigated," said the deputy. "That is two completely different things. The latter is a serious affair."

"But what does this have to do with us? Why are you taking our passports?"

"I know nothing about your role in this case; for all I know, you could be involved." He lifted his eyebrows, apparently in an attempt to appear authoritarian, which had a parodic effect.

Ravn was on his feet. "For heaven's sake. I've been an investigator for the Copenhagen police, and your approach is the dumbest I've ever seen, on both sides of the border."

"Sit down, sir," said the deputy.

Louise looked at Ravn. "It's okay, Thomas. You'd better do as he says."

Ravn shrugged and returned to his seat. The deputy nodded and walked out of the office with their passports.

Ravn sighed. "I'm sorry, Louise, my mistake. We should never have involved the police."

"We don't have any other choice, Thomas."

After waiting for another thirty minutes, Ravn and Louise heard voices out in the corridor. The door opened and the deputy came in with a stout little man. He was about forty years old, sporting a well-worn leather jacket and a Hertha Berlin scarf round his neck. "I'm sorry you had to wait so long," he said in English with a thick German accent as he extended Louise his hand. "My name is Detective Arnold Kurtz."

Kurtz shook Ravn's hand and took a seat on the edge of the deputy's desk. "Matheus caught me just as I was leaving," he said, nodding at the deputy who remained standing at the door. "It's a big day, today," he added, waving his scarf. "We made it to the final."

The deputy gave Kurtz the details he had printed from their system. The detective thanked him, moistened his finger on the tip of his tongue, and started paging through the report rapidly. "Thomas Ravnsholt. We're colleagues, I see," he said, glancing up at Ravn.

"Well, I'm retired," Ravn replied in English.

"Okay. But before that you were in a . . . how does one say . . . *Einsatzgruppe*? Special Crime Ops? So you were one of the tough-knuckle guys, I assume?"

Ravn shook his head. "I kept quietly in the background."

Detective Kurz laughed heartily. "I'm sure that's an understatement. For my part, I prefer to stay safely behind my desk." His gaze shifted to Louise. "I understand that your brother has fled from Denmark after a case of theft, and you think he is in Berlin?"

"Yes, we have good reason to believe he came to Berlin, but we haven't been able to find him yet."

"This must be very difficult for you," Kurtz said with a sympathetic smile.

Louise nodded.

"But we can certainly write up a report and alert the uniformed police; we have many highly skilled and trained law enforcement officers on our streets." He smiled at Louise again. "I am sure they will find your brother for you."

Kurtz stood up from the edge of the desk and returned their passports from among the papers that the deputy had given him. "Again, please forgive the wait," he said, giving them each his hand in turn. "Well, I've gotta go," he said, flipping his scarf around his neck. "My boy's waiting back home; he's just as big a football fan as his father. Matheus will take care of the details," he said in parting, and opened the door.

"Detective Kurtz?" said Ravn.

Kurtz looked over his shoulder.

"Regardless of how well-trained your law enforcement officers are, I don't think they'll have any luck finding Mogens at one of Berlin's tourist attractions. Louise's brother is the victim of a crime."

Kurtz hesitated in the doorway. "It was my understanding that Miss Slotsholm's brother was the one who committed a crime and is on the run from the law."

"Yes, but we believe he could have had a collaborator, someone who he has confided in, here; there are clear indications that he was lured to Berlin."

"Okay . . . I'll bite. So how much money did he take with him on the run?"

"Converted to euros, approximately one hundred and fifty thousand in cash."

"Wow, that's a lot of money," Kurtz said with raised eyebrows. "And do you have any idea who his collaborator could be?"

"All we know is that my brother replied to a personal ad from a woman with a fake profile," said Louise.

"The profile of a woman who has reportedly been dead for years, but the swindler has intimate knowledge of the dead woman's life," Ravn added.

The boyish smile on Kurtz's face had disappeared, and he closed the door again.

"A personal ad?"

"Yes. But the relevant email account has been deactivated in the interim," Ravn replied. "And last night, this person gained access to Mogens's email account and pretended to be him; he or she asked us *not* to contact the police."

"What else do you know?"

Louise told Detective Kurtz about how they had tracked Mogens to Berlin. She took out her file and showed him the correspondence between Mogens and the mystery person. Kurtz went through the file while he listened. When Louise came to the part about Klara Graf and the apartment on Greifenhagener Strasse, Kurtz looked up.

"Tell me more about this . . . Klara Graf woman. How well did she know Renate Schumann when she was alive?"

"Klara looked after Renate Schumann when she was a child. She said that Renate fled with her parents and was reportedly killed at the border."

"Did this person send any pictures to your brother—a portrait, anything?"

"No. Or rather, we didn't find anything amongst his things in Denmark or the emails that he printed out. But Klara . . . Frau Graf . . . she had a picture of Renate from when she was little."

Kurtz untangled the scarf from his neck, took a seat in front of the deputy's computer, and started tapping away furiously. They couldn't see what he was doing, and he didn't offer an explanation, but moments later he pushed to his feet. "Right, I need to ask you to come with me."

"I take it we're not going to a football match?" said Ravn.

"No, unfortunately not. I've just checked Charité Hospital's database."

"Has Mogens been admitted to hospital?" Louise burst out.

"No. Our Forensic Institute is at Charité. They've had an unidentified man in the morgue since January. I suggest we go down there and see if you can identify him. Are you up for that?" he said, looking at Louise gravely.

Louise swallowed hard. "Does the man's description match Mogens's?"

Kurtz shook his head slowly and sighed. "We just don't know."

70

Forty-five minutes later, a young pathologist accompanied the three of them down the long, chilly corridor of Charité Hospital's Forensic Institute on Turmstrasse. Ravn thought that the institute must use the same synthetic cleaning agent on the floors as the retirement home in Charlottenburg, but it could've just been his imagination. Louise seemed tense, clearly feeling the strain under the circumstances, so he put his arm around her as they entered the morgue.

"Do we know how the man died?" asked Ravn.

The pathologist glanced at Kurtz as if to ascertain whether she may speak freely. Kurtz nodded for her to go ahead.

"All evidence indicates that he drowned," she said.

"Any sign of violence?" Ravn asked.

"He has marks on his wrists, ankles, and neck that could indicate he was restrained."

The pathologist opened the drawer in front of her. A pair of waxy-looking feet stuck out from underneath the sheet the corpse was covered in. A yellow tag was attached to its right big toe. The pathologist pulled the drawer out all the way.

"How long have you had him here?" Ravn asked.

The pathologist checked the yellow tag. "Since 12 January . . . so he's been here for five months."

Kurtz looked at Louise. "Are you ready for this, Louise?"

She nodded and, without delay, the pathologist pulled off the plastic sheet, which made a loud crackling sound in the bare room.

The corpse had skin like parchment that varied from yellow to pale purple. A large Y-shaped incision from the autopsy stretched down its torso, roughly held together by only the essential, large black stitching. The deceased was missing an ear and part of its nose, which the fishes in the Spree must have nibbled at, Ravn observed.

"Do you know this man?" Kurtz asked Louise.

She turned her head and buried her face in Ravn's shirt, and he pulled her close to his chest in a protective embrace.

"Is this man your brother?" Kurtz asked again.

Louise looked up and dried the tears off her right cheek. "No. It's not Mogens," she said with obvious relief. "I don't know this man."

Kurtz buried his hands in the front pockets of his jeans and nodded to the pathologist to signal that she could pack away the corpse again.

"We'll see each other again soon enough, Kurtz," the pathologist said, and covered the corpse again.

The detective nodded in parting to the pathologist and Ravn and Louise followed him out of the morgue and along the chilly corridors of Charité.

"I'm happy for you that it wasn't your brother, Louise, so there's still hope," said Kurtz as they made their way to Reception.

Ravn was watching the detective out of the corner of his eye. Despite his cheerful demeanour, Kurtz seemed somehow disappointed.

"So what will the police do now?" asked Louise.

"We will look for him. Perhaps take a closer look at the IP addresses that the person who contacted your brother used in the correspondence."

"I don't think that will get you any closer," said Ravn. "It will merely send you on a wild goose chase in various internet cafés, libraries, and public offices or similar where there is free access to computers."

"I didn't say it was going to be easy, but with small steps, we might be able to trace your brother, Louise, and find out what happened to him."

Kurtz rested his hand on the swinging doors into the large reception area of the hospital, but Ravn reached out his arm and obstructed his path. "What aren't you telling us, Kurtz?"

Kurtz let his hand fall back to his side.

"Come on, Kurtz," Ravn said with a confidential smile. "I know you're hiding something."

"Not at all. Shall we get going?" Kurtz said, resting his hand on the door again.

"There have been other cases, haven't there? Other people who have disappeared?"

Kurtz blinked his eyes rapidly. Then he pushed through the door, and they all went out into the light and airy reception area of the institute. Many people were milling about, and Kurtz soon blended in with the crowd. "At least tell us how much danger we're in—you owe us that much!" Ravn called after him.

Kurtz came to a halt and turned to them. "No, I don't think you're in danger. There haven't been any prior cases." He looked away. "At least not officially."

"But you think otherwise?"

"What I *think* is irrelevant," said Kurtz.

"Not to us," said Louise.

Kurtz shifted his gaze to her. "If you want a good piece of advice, I think you should go back to Denmark and let us look for your brother. As soon as we find him, I will call you personally. I promise."

"That's not good enough, Kurtz. We came here to find Mogens alive, not amongst those people in there. What aren't you telling us? What kind of case are you working on?"

Kurtz rubbed a hand over his chin. "Obviously nothing I can discuss with you."

Ravn shrugged. "Then we'll just have to go back to the police station and find someone else to tell us what's going on."

Kurtz gazed at him in silence, and Ravn stared back at him with a Møffe-look that, above all else, signalled that he wasn't going to budge an inch, come hell or high water.

Kurtz sighed deeply. Looked around as if he feared the walls had ears. "Not in here. Come with me," he said.

71

Ravn and Louise crossed Turmstrasse together with Kurtz and went into the Kleiner Tiergarten, which lay opposite the buildings of Charité Hospital. They walked along the broad boulevard, past the table-tennis courts, and on into the park.

"It's not so much a case as a hunch or an instinct, which you have to treat with care in my profession."

"How so?" said Ravn.

Kurtz regarded him intently. "I don't know what the protocol is in the Danish police, but here in Germany if you don't follow your superior's orders to stop following your *hunch*, you get fired. I've already had fair warning, and I won't get another."

"Yup, things work in a similar way in Denmark," said Ravn with a sigh. "So what's your hunch?"

"I think that over the last five years, perhaps even longer, someone has been killing people in Berlin; if I'm right, the body count is up to ten victims so far."

Louise gaped at Kurtz. "And . . . and you think that Mogens might be his latest victim?"

Kurtz shook his head. "After our trip to the morgue today, I once again have my doubts that this perpetrator exists at all."

"Because it wasn't Mogens in there?" asked Ravn.

"That's not the only reason. Many little things don't add up. And I can't explain them."

"Okay, assuming there is a perpetrator, what's his modus operandi?" said Ravn.

"Even that is difficult to pinpoint. All I know for certain is that in the last five years, an unusually high number of men with a similar profile have turned up dead in the Spree River."

"A similar profile?"

"Yes. White, middle-aged men foreign to Germany who come to town for the first time and simply disappear without explanation. With the exception of one guy who had just been fired, all of these men abandoned steady, well-paid jobs. All of them had little or no contact with their families, generally were described as loners by their colleagues and neighbours. That might explain why they were able to leave and come here with little to no warning, but it doesn't explain what they intended to do when they got here. All I know about their stay in Berlin is that they booked themselves into relatively cheap accommodations, either two- or three-star hotels, or with private landlords, despite huge withdrawals from their bank accounts while they were here."

"How huge?"

"Twenty, thirty, sometimes up to two hundred fifty thousand euros. One of the men, a British citizen, sold his house and withdrew all the money from his bank the day the sale went through; the money vanished without a trace."

"It must have taken you a long time to investigate all of this," said Ravn.

Kurtz rolled his eyes. "You have no idea how long. Especially because all the men were found naked, and none of them had any priors or were under investigation or otherwise known to the police. It took months just to find out who they were."

"To this extent, Mogens is different because he appears on Europol's list of missing persons."

"Yes. Let's hope that's a good sign."

"You don't seem convinced."

"I'm not convinced about anything. In Mogens's case, what worries me most is the significant amount of money he had with him, and the length of time he has been missing."

"Are there any common points regarding the murder method?"

"Yes. Apart from the fact that it cannot be proved with certainty that they were murdered."

"Why not?"

"As I said before, all the men were found naked, and drowned in the Spree. But we haven't been able to prove conclusively that drowning was the cause of death, or if they were dead before they landed in the river."

"Lesions on the bodies?"

"Sure, plenty of damage: Most of the bodies had been in the water for months before they were found; some showed signs that fish, birds, and rats had nibbled on them; others were caught in the turbines of the tour boats and suffered missing limbs."

Louise swallowed; she was pale to begin with.

Ravn looked at her with concern. "Are you okay, Louise?"

She nodded. "It's just a lot to take in, especially because Mogens is still missing."

Ravn led her to a bench nearby and they sat down. Louise took out the bottle of water that she had brought along from their mini bar in the hotel. In the distance, they could hear the table-tennis balls being smacked against concrete tables. Otherwise, the park was still.

"Do you know if there are any similar cases in any police districts other than Berlin?"

"No, but I've had my hands full investigating the cases I have, so I can't rule that out."

"Again, what about the modus operandi? You said it was difficult to determine, but you must have found something useful."

"Yes and no," said Kurtz, leaning forward and folding his hands thoughtfully. "At first, I had a theory that the murderer found his victims in the city, amongst arbitrary tourists. That he killed and threw them in the river after he had coaxed money out of them. But this theory has too many loose ends. Which is why I was so interested in Mogens's case; what stands out most is the possibility that the victims knew the murderer before they arrived in the city, and that they might have been lured to Berlin under false pretences—a personal ad, perhaps, like you say—which is consistent with the fact that all the victims were single men."

"But have you found emails or letters on any of the others that might indicate a connection like that?"

Kurtz shook his head. "All the deaths were regarded as accidents, which is why I was unable to glean much information from the other police stations. All it got me were complaints to my boss for my obstinance and sticking my nose in where it didn't belong." He clapped himself on the thigh and stood up from the bench. "Well, at least I have found a possible motive."

"Which is?"

"Money, of course."

Ravn shook his head. "I'm sorry to say so, Kurtz, but I don't think that's the whole story."

"But what else could it be?"

"I'm not sure, but after hearing everything you said, the motive cannot possibly be greed and money alone," Ravn said, and stood up.

"I'm not sure I understand," said Kurtz.

"Well, if you are correct in assuming that all the deaths were caused by a single perpetrator, you have to immerse yourself in his mindset: The first time he kills and throws the body in the river, it's the culmination of a careful plan; the second time, it's because it works and he wants to do it again; the third time he succeeds, his ego comes to the fore, he feels powerful, perhaps invulnerable because he thinks he can get away with anything; the fourth time he consolidates and reinforces all the assumptions he has made about his power. But your perpetrator kills up to ten times," Ravn held up the fingers of both hands in front of Kurtz. "Forget money, forget megalomaniacal ego, there's something completely different driving this one. . ."

"Like?" Kurtz said, somewhat flabbergasted.

"My hunch tells me this perp is drawn to water, to strangulation, to the power he has over the victim in the act; the method is entirely significant to him. If it were just a matter of an uncomplicated way to get rid of the body, there are other, much more effective ways to do it. This guy wants his victims to be found in the river. Drowned. The way he lures his victims has a similar character; not just because it's practical or he enjoys it, but because it means something to him; it's one long ritual."

"Like using a fake profile of a girl who has been dead for twenty-five years?" muttered Kurtz.

"Perhaps. But right now, we have no idea if Mogens's disappearance has anything to do with your cases, or whether there is more than one perpetrator, just as we have no idea what really happened to Renate Schumann. It's all pure speculation."

"But quite a refined one, I must say," Kurtz said, impressed. "It surprises me that you weren't working for the murder squad, Ravn."

Ravn shrugged. "I've always preferred being on the street."

"Why is your boss not happy with the way you have run the investigation?" asked Louise.

Kurtz turned to face her. "Because my superiors and management hate the phrase 'serial killer' just as much as the press loves it. And there is no one at city hall who wants to start a rumour that a psychopath is killing tourists in Berlin, least of all when we're celebrating a jubilee."

"What jubilee?"

"It's twenty-five years since the Peaceful Revolution and the Wall came down."

"What? Already?" said Ravn.

Kurtz nodded. "Yes, even if it feels like yesterday that The Hoff was singing 'looking for freedom' while the rest of us were hacking chunks out of the Wall."

Ravn smiled. "Good ol' Hasselhoff."

"What is your impression of Klara Graf?"

"She seemed clear enough in the head," said Ravn. "Even though she lives in her own world."

"Klara knows both Renate and her family, and the neighbours," Louise added.

Kurtz looked out over the park. "I think I'll pay Frau Graf a visit tomorrow. I might be able to get some more information out of her. Perhaps she even knows who wrote to your brother—without being aware of it."

72

She had undone his chains and Mogens lay curled in the foetal position in the bottom of the bath. His skin was gnarled and almost transparent after so many weeks under water. His muscles were slack from inactivity and lack of food. As he lay there dying, he felt as if he were reduced to an awkward chunk of dead meat that refused to go down the drain.

"YOU . . . ALWAYS . . . LIE . . . TO ME. WHY?" Renate's metallic voice rang in the dark.

"I'm not lying," Mogens mumbled. "I've told you everything."

"I looked where you said . . . but there was no money."

"Then . . . I don't know . . . where it is . . . someone must have taken it."

"YOU . . . HAVE . . . BETRAYED . . . ME . . . ON PURPOSE."

"I have told you . . . everything . . . if it isn't in the third room . . . to the left . . . in front of the entrance . . . to the fort . . . then someone . . . has taken it."

"LIAR!"

"I've searched Teufel Berg, Mogens. The money isn't there, which means you're a liar that deserves to die."

"YES . . . DIE . . . DREAM . . . AND DIE . . ."

Mogens closed his eyes. Not that it made any difference whether they were open or closed in this bloody darkness. He thought he'd heard someone other than Renate's metallic voice—a soft yet deep voice—but it must have been his imagination, the dark hollow playing tricks on his mind.

The music started to play: the Young Pioneers once again. He heard retreating footsteps. He knew that he would die soon. Because he had been weak. Gave her everything. Details and PIN codes. Internet codes. Even the location of the money. He had nothing more to give.

He missed his sister. Louise had always taken care of him. The thought warmed his heart. She was the only person in the world who had ever loved him. She never judged him. Always smiling and encouraging. This is the thought he wanted to hold onto before he left this world. Louise. The two of them, walking hand in hand in an eternal summer without darkness. He missed her so much. Loved her tenderly. She had always been the woman in his life.

73

The Vietnamese restaurant Monsieur Vuong was filled to capacity. The walls were painted scarlet, and loud electro-pop accompanied the guests eating exotic food and colourful cocktails. Near the back wall, Ravn and Louise were crammed into a small two-person table, every inch of it covered in little bowls of steaming food that exuded the smell of fresh herbs. Had it not been for Mogens's disappearance, this could have been the beginning of a wonderful evening. But both of them were picking at their food in silence.

"I'm sorry," said Ravn. "We should have gone to a quieter place."

"No, this is fine," said Louise, trying in vain to clasp a dumpling between her chopsticks.

"You were very brave at the morgue today," he said.

"Thanks," she mumbled. "I just hope we find out what has happened to Mogens soon."

"We'll find him," Ravn said, but he could hear how hollow his words sounded, and he picked up his beer and took a big gulp.

"I no longer believe we have any chance of finding him alive." Louise looked at him sadly. "I can feel it . . . do you really think he could be the victim of a . . . serial killer?"

"No," he said, and almost meant it. "There is no way of knowing whether there is any substance to Kurtz's theory. And even if there were, we don't know if it has anything to do with Mogens's disappearance.

But hopefully the detective's conversation with Klara will provide some information to help us move forward."

"And if it doesn't? Then we go home tomorrow without knowing what happened?"

"I'm quite happy to stay in Berlin a little longer, but whatever happens, you need to prepare yourself that the investigation will take time."

Louise was still trying to clasp her dumpling, in vain. She gave up with a sigh and sipped her soda water instead. "Why don't we try emailing the person who is pretending to be Mogens."

"How would that help?"

"Maybe we could write that we know it's not Mogens writing, but that he can keep the money, as long as he tells us where Mogens is? And say we'll go to the police if he doesn't?"

"We're not in a position to make threats," Ravn said, and put down his chopsticks. "And we have no idea how much this person knows either about the money or Mogens's whereabouts. At this point, we only risk making matters much worse if we contact the swindler."

"What if we write back and pretend we think it *is* Mogens, and try to get some information out of him that way?"

Ravn shook his head. "I think it's best we remain silent, so we don't scare the person away. He or she hasn't closed the email account yet. That's one thing in our favour that might come in handy later."

"I'm sorry, I guess I'm just not as patient as you are." She gave the dumpling one more try, but failed again, and dropped her chopsticks in frustration.

"Hey, how about we search the hostels? I'm still up for that. We could also try looking at flats to let to tourists. Perhaps we'll find someone who had rented a room to Mogens."

"That will take more time."

Ravn nodded. "Yes, it would. But just think about it: Before you came to me, Mogens had been missing for six months, and look how far we have come in just a few days," he said, trying to cheer her up.

"You're right. I'm sorry I'm being so 'doom and gloom,'" she said, trying to smile.

"You're not. Shall I show you how to handle dumplings that don't wanna be eaten?" Without waiting for a reply, he picked up one of her chopsticks, deftly impaled her dumpling, and handed the chopstick to her.

She snatched it out of his hand playfully. "Do you have a solution for everything?"

"Most times," he said with the hint of a smile.

74

Klara sat on her sofa, watching the late-night news, enjoying a cigarette and the last dregs of coffee in her thermos. She wasn't sure the coffee was such a good idea, because she knew she would have problems sleeping, but she didn't like anything to go to waste. She leaned forward and ran a finger over her coffee table. Tomorrow she would dust and perhaps vacuum a little. If she had the energy, she would do some laundry as well. There was a knock at the door and Klara started in fright.

She had no idea who would call on her so late and decided not to open the door. But the person knocked again. Harder this time. She stubbed out her cigarette in the ashtray and snuck into the hallway. She remained standing a safe distance from the front door, wishing she had one of those peepholes so she could see who was there. The person knocked again. Harder and more insistent. Driven by curiosity and a sense of duty, she went to the door and opened it.

Klara looked at the stranger standing in front of her. "Yes, what can I do for you?"

The stranger didn't reply, just stood tall and dead-still before her. Klara adjusted her glasses on her nose and squinted. There was something familiar about this person. "Have we met before?"

"Ah, yes, indeed we have, Klara."

After all these years, she recognised the voice. "Is it really you? But I thought you were dead. This is what I'd heard."

"An exaggeration, Klara. I'm alive, even though we've all seen better times, am I right?"

Klara nodded. "Why don't you come inside; at the very least I could offer you some coffee."

"If it's not too much trouble and you could also do with a cup, I won't say no."

Klara smiled briefly and waved her guest inside.

"Please forgive the mess," Klara said as she came back into the living room. Her guest was standing with his back to her, taking in all the knick-knacks and memorabilia on the bookshelf. She had put on the kettle in the kitchen and now she invited him to take a seat on the sofa. Quickly coving the hole on the armrest with her knitting, she took a seat in the armchair opposite him. "It's a great surprise and honour to get a visit from you after all these years, Herr Hausser."

Hausser smiled. Even though he was in his early sixties with thinning hair and deep lines on his face, his body was still fit and strong. His coal-black eyes were set even deeper under the hood of his brow, and on guard as always.

"You look well, still strong and healthy."

"Thank you, Klara . . . so do you," Hausser replied politely, for his hostess looked like a haggard old woman slumped in her chair.

"What have you done with yourself all these years, if I may ask?"

"Oh, this and that. I've done my best to survive in the new Germany—even if it's been twenty-five years since the damn reunification I still say 'new'; I will never get used to it."

"Indeed. The reunification hasn't brought much good to our Republic. The politicians promised so much, and look what we got: unemployment, violence, and crime. I don't dare go out after dark anymore," she said, moistening her lips. "I . . . daresay the revolution must have been particularly hard for someone like you, a patriotic man from the Service. No one really appreciated what you did for the country."

Hausser shook his head. "I believe one calls it 'victor's justice.' We—members of the Stasi—have been prosecuted more thoroughly than the Nazis after the war. *We* have been branded as the traitors. It's impossible to get a decent job; we have to take what we can get for next to no money.

And now the foreigners have come over our borders and taken whatever jobs were left; we have to live off state support now.

"It's not fair."

"No. This is the consequence of capitalism. We have to take matters into our own hands, Klara. With calm patience, like water incrementally forming stones in a stream," Hausser said quietly. "The Republic belonged to different times. And at least we kept law and order. That's the problem nowadays. People don't have any respect. No sense of community."

Klara nodded. "Today everyone thinks only of himself."

"Capitalism has beaten us. The victor takes all; it has taken our souls," Hausser said, staring at the floor gravely.

"Not *your* soul, Herr Hausser," Klara said, trying to catch his eye. "No one can undo *your* loyalty to the State. You are our last protector."

"You are too kind, Klara."

"I have often thought of you all these years. Did you ever marry?"

"No, that was not in the cards for me."

The kettle whistled in the kitchen and Klara stood up. She gave Hausser a big smile, flashing her grey teeth. "I think I may have a few biscuits left."

Hausser got to his feet as well.

"Please, stay seated, you are my guest, Herr Hausser."

"Thank you. Let me help you in the kitchen."

Klara carefully poured the boiling water over the ground coffee beans while Hausser leaned against the doorframe watching her, and the delicious smell of coffee filled his nostrils as the water bubbled through the filter that Klara had placed directly on her thermos. Reaching into the cupboard, she brought out a transparent Tupperware with homemade biscuits.

"You are a good hostess who spoils her guests, Klara."

"Thank you," she said. "I seldom have guests these days."

"But you had visitors recently, didn't you, Klara."

She turned round in surprise. "No, I—"

"Yes, you did, Klara. You received foreigners in your home, a couple from Denmark."

Klara blinked rapidly in confusion. "Oh . . . yes, those two. How did you know?"

"What did they want to know from you, Klara?"

She put down the kettle. "The woman's brother has disappeared . . . they believed he had met . . . Renate. Do you remember her?" Klara asked, but she knew very well that he did.

"And what did you tell them?"

"I told them that was impossible because Renate died years ago."

"And what did the foreigners have to say about that?"

"Not much."

"Don't forget the coffee," Hausser said, pointing to the empty filter.

Klara poured more water over the ground coffee.

"Did you say anything about me?"

"No, of course not. Not at all. I told them that the Schumanns had been under surveillance because they were criminals, and that is why they fled."

"Did you say anything else?"

Klara swallowed hard. "Only that the Schumanns never came back. And that the rumour was that they were killed by the border police. That's all I knew about it. And it happened so long ago."

"Yes, of course," said Hausser. "May I use the sink to wash my hands?" he said, coming into the kitchen without waiting for her reply. He went round Klara, turned on the tap, put the plug in the sink, and picked up the soap beside the tap on the counter.

"Do you know what happened to them, Herr Hausser?" Klara asked.

"How would I know what happened?" he said, turning to glance at her as he lathered the soap between his fingers.

"Well, I remember that it was your investigation. It was a feather in your cap that Schumann was arrested," she said with a smile.

"I remember that you asked me where the family was going the day they fled. And you drove after them. Was that the day it happened—the day they were . . . shot?"

"Klara remembers well," he said, submerging his hands deep into the sink of ice-cold water. "I think your drain is blocked."

"What? No, I don't think so?"

"No, really, take a look." He stepped aside so she could come closer.

Klara bent down and stared into the soapy water.

Hausser grabbed her neck from behind and pushed her head under the water. Klara sprawled her arms and tried to free herself, but Hausser brought the full weight of his body to bear and kept her head down. With his free hand, he turned on the tap again to compensate for all the damn water she was splashing everywhere. "Easy now, little Klara, it will all be over soon," he said.

Klara tried to kick out with her legs and bubbles rose from her mouth. Soon after, her body cramped, and he hushed her. "It's all right, you can let go now."

When Klara's body went limp, and her arms fell to her sides, Hausser turned off the tap. For a moment he was distracted by her wig, which had slipped off her scalp and lay on the surface of the water like a torn piece of kelp. *There was something so peaceful about the drowned*, he thought. As if the water in their lungs had cleansed their souls. This is how it always made him feel, ever since the good old days with his Chamber in Hohenschönhausen.

Hausser carried Klara's corpse to the bathroom and undressed the body. Her dress, ugly underwear, and brown stockings lay on the floor next to the bathtub. He regarded the naked, fat corpse in the bath. Dear Klara, she had never been blessed with good looks, neither dead nor alive. Nature had created her for hard work and reproduction, and she had served her country well.

Hausser turned on both taps and let the water gush over the body. He suddenly remembered he had forgotten her wig and went back to the kitchen to fetch it. After he had cleared up a little, he let himself out. He walked through the familiar dark courtyard and exited onto Greifenhagener Strasse, which was deserted. Satisfied that no one was watching, he crossed the road and climbed into the old champagne-coloured BMW.

He had always loved this car, envied its owner, but now it was his. He started the engine and savoured the vibrations in the steering wheel for a moment. Then he pulled away from the kerb and drove into the night.

75

Louise was dressed and putting on her make-up in the bathroom, which was separated from the rest of the room by a glass panel. Ravn was sitting in the bed, watching her while he ate his croissant. There was something so peaceful and harmonious about this hour, and he could feel how much he had missed it. Making love on lazy mornings that ran on to coffee and croissants in bed at noon. He could get used to this with Louise.

Everything indicated that they would fly home empty-handed that evening, but at least they had done everything they could to find Mogens, and now they had put Kurtz on his trail. He feared for Mogens's fate, and he knew that the chances of finding him alive had shrunk significantly. If Mogens had been murdered, he hoped that the police would at least find the killer so Louise would not have to go through the same anguish of uncertainty that he had experienced with Eva's unsolved murder.

Ravn looked out the window and wondered how many murderers who had avoided justice were lurking about out there. The weather had been perfect all morning, but now the clouds were gathering. There was a knock at the door and Ravn tossed his half-eaten croissant onto the plate next to him.

"Didn't you put the do not disturb sign on the door?" Louise said, giving him a look.

"Of course I did." He got out of bed and put on his jocks as the person kept knocking. "*Ja, ja,* I'm coming," yelled Ravn.

"You're not seriously thinking of opening the door," said Louise, jabbing the end of her mascara at him as if it were a lance.

"Yup, that's the plan," he said, traipsing over to the door and opening it.

"But what if it's—"

"Good morning," said Ravn.

Detective Kurtz was standing in the corridor outside. "Good morning," he said. "I'm sorry to disturb you."

Ravn invited the detective inside. He seemed a little tired, wearing the same battered leather jacket but without the Hertha Berlin scarf, which Ravn took as a sign that he was definitely here on official business. He found his T-shirt on a chair and pulled it over his head. "I'm afraid we can't offer you any coffee," he said, nodding at the empty thermos.

Kurtz greeted Louise briefly as she came out of the bathroom. "I have bad news," he said.

"Is it Mogens? Have you found him?" Louise said anxiously.

Kurtz shook his head. "No, not yet. It's about Klara Graf," he said. "Early this morning, the resident living below her flat called the caretaker because water was leaking through the ceiling. Klara wasn't responding to calls, so the caretaker used his master key to get inside and found her dead in her bathtub. He called an ambulance and contacted the police. I was only notified once she was taken to Charité."

"What was the cause of death?" Ravn asked.

"The initial report assumes that she fainted in the bath and drowned; there was no sign of violence. But I have requested an autopsy."

"What about her flat? Has it been searched for clues?"

"The officers on the scene found no indications of a break-in or a struggle in the flat," Kurtz said. "It appears that Klara simply drowned. An unfortunate accident?" he added sceptically.

"Did anyone other than the three of us know that you intended to question Klara Graf?"

"No. As I said: I have to tread carefully with this case. This is my day off. Why do you ask?"

"Because someone must have tipped off the perpetrator," Ravn replied.

"Explain?"

"From the moment we set foot in Berlin, we have been watched."

Both Kurtz and Louise stared at him in surprise. "Are you sure?" asked Kurtz.

"Positive. If Klara was murdered by the same perp who killed your tourists and is responsible for Mogens's disappearance, then he or she took a massive risk to track down Klara and kill her; we have forced him out of hiding."

"How do you suggest we proceed?"

"I think we need to inspect Klara's flat. Is that possible?"

An hour later, Ravn, Louise, and Kurtz walked through the gate and entered the residential complex at Greifenhagener Strasse 9. The thick black hose that had been used to pump water out of the flooded flats on the first and ground floors still lay in the entrance hall of the front house. The door to the ground-floor flat was open, and a young man wearing gumboots was standing in the hallway, tossing sodden and ruined books into a large rubbish bag. Kurtz went over and showed the man his police badge. "Looks like quite a lot of water damage you have there," Kurtz said.

"My entire study and the kids' rooms are flooded," the man said bitterly.

"Are you the one who reported the damage?"

The man nodded. "I woke up to water gushing down like a waterfall."

"What time was that?"

"About four or four thirty in the morning. Terrible thing about Frau Graf."

"Did you know her?"

The man shrugged. "Not really. We greeted each other on the odd occasions I bumped into her. Frau Graf liked to keep to herself."

"And last night? Did you see or hear anyone come to her flat?"

"No, why?" The man looked at Kurtz curiously.

"Just routine," said Kurtz. "So you didn't see or hear whether she had a visitor?"

The man shook his head. "Nope, not a soul. I've actually never seen anyone come and visit her. As I said: Frau Graf was reserved and didn't like to chat."

Kurtz thanked the man for his time, and Ravn and Louise followed the detective up the stairs to the first floor. The door to Klara's flat was ajar, and the pump was jammed in the gap that led into the entrance. Kurtz pushed open the door with two fingers.

"I don't think we need worry about prints; all traces will be contaminated by the team who responded to the alarm," said Ravn. For starters, he sat on his haunches and inspected the doorframe and the area around the lock. "No immediate signs of a forced entry," he said. "Which means that either the perp had a key, or Klara opened the door and invited him in."

They went inside and followed the pump on the floor to the bathroom at the back of the flat. Here there was still a lot of water on the floor and the toilet seat, which was down; Klara's wet clothing lay in a heap with the wig on top.

"I wonder how the killer was able to lure her into the bathtub," said Ravn.

"It's a good question," said Kurtz.

"Maybe they had an intimate relationship?" said Louise. "Perhaps they were in the bath together?"

"I doubt that. According to her neighbour, Klara kept to herself and had no regular visitors," said Ravn. He turned to Kurtz. "Could he have strangled her first and then dragged her over to the bathroom?"

"No. There weren't any signs of violence."

They backed out of the bathroom and went into the living room. It looked the same as it did when Ravn and Louise were there, except for the knitting on the armrest of the easy chair and the single coffee cup that sat next to a full ashtray.

Ravn stared into thin air, his brain working at full throttle. "So, the killer surprises her in the middle of her evening coffee," he mumbled to himself. "Klara invites him in, perhaps he asks if he can use the bathroom, calls her over, and drowns her. He leaves the coffee cup on the table, so it looks as if she was alone the whole time. Does that sound right?"

"Hmm. Too complicated," Kurtz replied. "Why would she be lured over to the bathroom?"

"You're right. Too complicated, much too intimate. So, what's the alternative?"

"If he drowned her, then that just leaves the kitchen sink," Louise said in a quiet voice.

They all went into Klara's dark little kitchen. Ravn went over to the sink, opened the cupboard below, and sank onto his haunches. Louise handed him her iPhone and he lit up the area below.

There was a puddle of water on the shelf and the wallpaper was sodden. "Yup, either Klara had done a huge pile of dishes before she died, or it was here that she was drowned. My guess is the latter."

Ravn checked the contents of the dustbin and briefly inspected the lid. Two used coffee filters lay on top; below was a transparent Tupperware containing a few biscuits. "Maybe she knew her killer so well that she invited him in for coffee? An old friend from her past who pops in unannounced?"

"So you're saying that the killer saw you visiting Klara, then came back to eliminate the only person who could identify him?" asked Kurtz.

"That could be part of the explanation. But what connects Klara, the killer, and our visit?"

"Mogens," said Louise. "The fact that we're looking for my brother."

"Yes, but that's only part of it; Klara did not know Mogens. Or at least that's what she said."

"But all of them could have known Renate Schumann," Kurtz replied.

"Exactly," said Ravn. "Klara must have known something about Renate that would incriminate the killer."

"But what could that be?" asked Kurtz. "If Klara knew something about Renate that would incriminate him, why did he use a fake profile of her to lure Mogens—perhaps also the dead tourists—to Berlin?"

Ravn shook his head. "I have no idea. But using Renate is important to him; just as the method of drowning his victims is important to him. Perhaps it is founded on desire, jealousy, or revenge. Who knows?"

"Regardless of his motive, we are dealing with a rather disturbed mind," remarked Kurtz.

76

As they exited the gate onto Greifenhagener Strasse, Kurtz's telephone rang. He answered the call and made a brief reply before turning to Ravn and Louise with the news. "That was our IT department. They have tracked down the IP address of the last email that was sent from Mogens's account."

"And?" said Louise.

"It was sent from an internet café, so that's not particularly useful. But we were able to open your brother's inbox."

"So I can read his emails?" asked Louise with a glimmer of hope.

"No, unfortunately, the email from the café was the only one that hadn't been deleted."

They continued down Greifenhagener in silence till Louise suddenly stopped in her tracks and hauled her iPhone out of her handbag. She opened her emails, found Mogens's address, and started typing furiously.

Ravn realised what she was doing and looked over her shoulder. "It's not a good idea to write to him, Louise, least of all in that kind of language."

"I don't give a shit!" she said. "That pig has killed my brother!"

"We don't know that, Louise."

She looked at him with tears in her eyes. "How can you be so blind? He deleted Renate's account, he killed Klara, and now he's deleted Mogens's emails!"

"Louise, please don't send that message; it will destroy what little hope we still have of finding your brother."

"We can't let him get away with this!"

"We all agree on this point, Louise; none of us wants him to get away with this."

Ravn looked at Kurtz, who didn't understand anything they'd exchanged in Danish, but he clearly understood Louise's anger. "Is there some kind of register listing tourist accommodations in Berlin?" he asked Kurtz.

"Do you think Mogens arranged a private accommodation for himself when he arrived in the city?"

"Perhaps. A hotel would have required his ID immediately, so he would have avoided that."

"Okay. The only problem is that there must be at least three thousand registered lessors in the area, and at least double that number who aren't registered; cheating the taxman has become a national sport."

"Exactly; it's hopeless, Thomas. We're never going to find Mogens," said Louise, adding another litany of swear words to her message.

"It really isn't helpful to write to him, Louise," said Kurtz.

"Then who can we write to? Everyone is either dead or missing!" Louise said in frustration.

Kurtz shrugged. "Well, at least we're in Berlin, a city where even the dead inform on others."

"How so?" said Ravn.

"I have an old school friend who works in the national archives. We could contact him," said Kurtz.

"Which part of the archives?"

"The Stasi archives."

"And how will that help us?"

"If Renate's parents were under surveillance by the Stasi, I'm certain that the reports will also describe the daughter's activities; who Renate spent time with—friends, neighbours, and teachers."

"The Stasi spied on *children*?"

"Yes, of course; the Stasi knew that children were the weakest link in the chain that could be used to blackmail parents, or even report them.

It worked the other way round too; sometimes parents used their children as couriers to transmit information to people who intended to flee. So the Stasi always watched *all* members of the family. If the connection among Klara, Mogens, the dead tourists, and the killer is Renate, then there might be useful information in the surveillance reports that indicate who the killer might be," Kurtz explained.

"It's worth a try," said Ravn. He looked at Louise. She nodded reluctantly and put away her phone.

On the way to Helmholtzplatz, Kurtz called his friend at the Stasi archives. When he finally got through, the sound of Rammstein's hard rock music on the other end was so loud he jerked the phone away from his ear.

"Alex!" Kurtz yelled into the phone.

"Jo, Kurtz! Wie geht's!" a voice answered just above the music.

Kurtz briefly explained to his friend what he needed, an unofficial enquiry, in exchange for a couple of Hertha tickets. Apparently, this did the trick, because the next moment, Kurtz relayed to Alex the only information they had on the Schumanns—their names and address as well as the fact that they might have been under surveillance just before the Wall came down—and asked him to see what he could find.

"Do you realise how long this is going to take me?"

"Alex, if there's someone who can solve this problem, you're the guy. When do you think I can pop in?" They could hear more complaints from the other end. "Yes, today, Alex!" Kurtz said, and soon after he ended the call and looked at Ravn and Louise in turn. "Right, Alex is on board. We can go to the archives tonight after closing time. Hopefully he'll have found something for us by then."

"But our plane for Denmark leaves tonight," said Ravn.

"To hell with that plane," said Louise. "I'm not going anywhere until we've found the bastard—even if I have to emigrate to Germany and move into the Park Inn!"

77

The dark, monolithic buildings were silhouetted against the orange sunset sky. Kurtz had taken the front seat in the taxi, and as they approached, he turned to Louise and Ravn in the back and pointed out Haus 1 of the old East German Ministry of State Security with its grandiose pillars at the entrance. "Here it is: the infamous HQ of head honcho Erich Mielke and his communist bandits."

The middle-aged taxi driver with a walrus moustache gave Kurtz a dirty look, which could have been either in response to his remark, or the overpowering pong of the steaming Styrofoam takeaway packs of currywurst that Alex had given him strict instructions to pick up at Curry 36 on the way over. Apparently, they made the best *Currywurst mit Pommes rot-weiss* in the city, and Alex refused to eat anything else. Alex's request had reminded Ravn of Victoria's incarnate passion for Lagkagehuset's cinnamon rolls, which were tantamount to tradable currency in her bookstore. Despite their recent argument, he missed her.

"The Stasi had nine thousand permanent employees on the payroll," said Kurtz. "And two hundred and seventy thousand informants who reported to them on the activities of GDR citizens who were considered more or less hostile to the Republic; it is estimated that there was one agent for every sixth citizen of the country. That's even more agents than Stalin had—or Hitler, for that matter."

"Where did you live when you were growing up?" asked Louise.

"In the silos in Pankow," replied Kurtz. "I'm still out there, but now I live in a semi-detached house with my wife and son; once an *ossie*, always an *ossie*," he said with a grin.

The taxi came to a stop outside the entrance to the archives in Haus 7, and Kurtz paid the driver. Alex was waiting for them in the doorway, wearing a black T-shirt that had a Rammstein logo printed on it. He had a blond beard and curly hair that was cut short in front and left long at the neck, which made him look like a young version of Rudi Völler. "Who the hell is this? I thought you said you were coming alone," Alex said in a grumpy tone.

Kurtz smiled and gave him a friendly pat on the shoulder. "Good friends, Alex. Ravn is a colleague from Denmark, and Louise is a sworn witness," he lied. "Her brother has disappeared, and that's why we are here."

"Kurtz, you know the archives are not a tourist attraction. The museum is over there." Alex pointed his toothpick arm at Haus 1. "And she won't find her brother in the archives—there isn't a soul down there. Luckily, because they'll fucking fire me if they find out I'd let unauthorised folks into there." He puffed out his chest and crossed his arms in the doorway, as if he was some kind of bouncer, but the effect was more like a pair of laces tied in a bow.

"Alex, take it easy with the cussing, will you? I've brought currywurst from Thirty-Six for you, as requested. And besides, I'm keen to take a look at whatever you've found for us. Come on, stop being such a hard arse; I know you want to show us."

Alex accepted the currywurst boxes eagerly and looked at Kurtz. "Hey, what about the Hertha tickets, my friend?"

"Don't worry, I'll get them for you. Are you going to let us in now, or what?" said Kurtz.

"*Klar*," Alex said, and pushed open the door with his butt.

They followed Alex through the dark hallway to the stairs that led down into the cellar where they could hear loud music playing.

"I know it might be hard to believe, but Alex is one of the leading historians on the Cold War in the country," said Kurtz, "even though he compensates for his insecurities by swearing like a trooper."

"*The* leading historian in the country," yelled Alex, who had obviously

heard him. "And I don't compensate for shit because I know I'm King."
They came into the front room of the archive, where glass cases containing the index card system were on display. "And this is my kingdom,"
Alex added, stretching out his arms to the side with a currywurst meal-
deal in each hand. "Fifty shelf kilometres and eighteen million index
cards to keep track of it all."

They stayed on Alex's heels as he led them into an enormous archive
room where the shelves were lined from floor to ceiling, filled with boxes
and faded case files. Rammstein's "America" blared from the loudspeakers above their heads.

"This is the memory centre of the old GDR's brain. And even though
the bloody Stasi tried to destroy everything, we are getting things back
into working order; we are fucking brain surgeons," Alex said, rocking to
the heavy rhythm and looking for all the world like a teenager who was
spending his first night home alone. He started singing along: "We're
all living in America . . . *wunderbar* . . . Coca-Cola, sometimes WAR . . .
We're all living in America . . ."

They came to an alcove with a long table and chairs on either side.
Alex spun on his heels and tried to animate them to sing along with the
chorus, but Kurtz went over to the music system in the corner and turned
it off. All at once it was dead quiet in the cellar.

"Fascist," muttered Alex.

"So, I assume you have something to show us," said Kurtz.

Alex dumped the meal-deals unceremoniously on the table in front of
him. "But of course; what do you take me for?"

"Was it difficult to find?" asked Kurtz.

"Yes, but only because you gave me the names; you could have just
said it was about Operation Midas," Alex said. He went off to the side
between two rows of shelves and brought out a trolley laden with boxes,
files, and video cassettes.

"Are all these files about Renate?" asked Ravn.

"No, about her father: Christoph Schumann alias 'Midas,'" said Alex.
"But Renate is obviously mentioned in some reports, and there are video
recordings from her bedroom." He held up the top one on the pile. "The
fucking Stasi rigged their entire flat with cameras and bugs."

Ravn looked at the voluminous stack of materials on the trolley. "It sounds as if you've heard about this case before."

"Everyone with a little bit of background has," replied Alex. "But for the plebs, it's been lost to the annals of history—just like everything else that doesn't scream for sensation; the Schumann family were the last victims of the partition of Germany into East and West; they died the night the Wall came down, but because they were killed in a remote forest and not at the Brandenburg Gate, nobody remembers them anymore."

"We have quite a lot to get through," said Kurtz, tapping the top file, as if he had read Ravn's thoughts.

"This is nothing," said Alex. "Unfortunately, most materials regarding Operation Midas were shredded—just like all other Division Z cases."

"What is Division Z?" asked Ravn.

"It's the secret division of the Secret Service," scoffed Alex. "Only the tip of the Stasi hierarchy knew of its existence. DZ investigated high-profile cases within the Party, Stasi, or financial sector—the latter included Schumann's position at the State Bank. As a rule, DZ cases had a fatal end for the persons investigated, usually in Hohenschönhausen Prison," he added, drawing his index finger across his throat to demonstrate.

Ravn picked up the first pile and put it on the table in front of him. "We'll need to divide the materials among us and find those files on her father that involve Renate; that will focus our search."

Kurtz and Louise nodded, grabbed a pile each, and joined Ravn at the table.

"After that's done we can find out who she had contact with and to what extent. Alex, if you could check whether any of these people were also under surveillance, and perhaps are even still alive, then—"

"I only concentrate on the past, *Herr Dänemark*, so unless they died after the fall of the Wall, the good Detective K is the one you need to ask."

"Just take a seat and eat your wurst, Alex," said Kurtz patiently. "After that, it would be great if you could connect the TV, so we can watch these old video cassettes."

"*Jawohl, mein Führer*," said Alex.

78

They sorted through the case files and put aside the ones that involved
Renate, and as their search progressed, a sinister portrait of the investigation into the Schumann family began to form. Christoph Schumann's
numerous acts of fraud became clear immediately, but even so, the inva-
sion of the family's privacy was grotesque.

Alex rigged up the TV at the head of the table, and Ravn and the
others glanced up occasionally, which made the files they were scanning
seem like film scripts of the narrative that unfolded on screen. One of
them recorded a meeting between Christoph and some men with whom
he planned to flee. Another showed Christoph abandoning this plan in a
meeting with a man named Braun.

"She was beautiful, Renate's mother," said Louise when the recordings of Lena came on the screen.

"Yes," said Kurtz. "A former catalogue model who worked at Madeleine, an Intershop, till she was fired for 'matters of state security,'" he
quoted from the file he was reading.

"Firing people in a society where there is work for everyone was one
of the Stasi's twisted methods to put pressure on people they were investigating," remarked Alex.

By midnight, they had sorted through most of the case files. The pile
in the middle of the table concerned Renate in one way or another. A
recording taken in the girl's bedroom was playing on the screen; it showed

Renate changing out of her Young Pioneer uniform and putting on her pyjamas. They watched with a sick feeling in their stomachs, and not even Alex made a smart remark. Once Renate had climbed in under her duvet, her father came into the room and sat on the edge of her bed. She seemed so tiny beside Christoph's hulking size. Alex turned up the volume to the max, and they could just hear the conversation through the static; Christoph told his daughter that they were going on a long holiday in the West, but if anyone asked, she should say they were going to visit Granny:

"But you're not supposed to lie," said Renate.

"We have to make an exception in this case."

"When will we leave?" asked Renate.

"Tomorrow night."

"But, Daddy, I have a tournament coming up."

"I'm afraid you won't be able to go."

Renate looked forlorn, and Christoph tried to comfort her without success. The girl became visibly upset, her frustration mounting, and in the end she and her father were yelling at each other; then the screen went black.

Everyone at the table sat in silence for a while. It felt wretched to know that Renate and her father would be dead less than twenty-four hours after that recording was made.

Ravn, Louise, and Kurtz studied the selected reports and made a list of all the people who knew Renate: friends of her parents; some neighbours, including Klara, who had babysat her regularly; classmates; her gym teacher.

After a search of the people on the lists, Alex could confirm that Braun died in a drowning accident just weeks before the Schumanns' planned escape, and Klara and the gym teacher, Irene Hertz, were registered informants for the Stasi.

Ravn stood up, stretched his legs, and yawned. A glance at his watch told him it was quarter past three in the morning. Kurtz seemed to be half-asleep in his chair, but Louise still seemed wide awake, paging through the last of the reports.

"Renate could have done great things," Louise observed. "Everyone praises her talents; even the head of the surveillance team wrote reports on her."

Kurtz stretched and twisted in his chair. "Apart from Klara, who is dead, the gym teacher, Frau Hertz, had the closest contact with Renate. Perhaps we should check her out? See if she's still alive?"

"I doubt she has anything to do with it," Ravn said, staring into thin air. "Who shot her? Who shot Renate?"

They all looked at Alex, who yawned audibly. "No one," he said.

"What do you mean 'no one'? There was a court case involving the border patrol guards, wasn't there?" said Kurtz.

"Of course there was a court case, but no one was sentenced." Alex sat down in front of his computer. "Incidentally, very few border guards are ever sentenced because in this country we have a sterling record of saying we were just 'following orders' and then asking for the world's forgiveness *ex post facto*, which is what my next book will be about."

"That book has been brewing for ages," muttered Kurtz.

Alex ignored the remark and concentrated on his monitor. "But in the Midas case, the circumstances were somewhat different." He scrolled through the cases and clicked on a file identified by five § symbols, opened two sub-files, and finally found the ones that included the relevant court record of the case, which was heard more than twenty years previously. "According to the five border sentries who were present—or rather, four guards and an officer—the Schumanns were killed by two SM-70's."

"What is an SM-70?" asked Ravn.

"A death machine. On their side of the border, the East German regime had planted landmines that were connected to a hidden tripwire; if anyone tried to climb over the fence, the mine was activated and hundreds of steel bullets were fired; the Schumanns were killed on the spot," Alex explained.

"Was there an autopsy?"

Alex skimmed his notes on the monitor. "The corpses were incinerated by the minor forest fire that resulted after the detonation of an SM-70."

"But are we sure that all three of them were killed?" asked Ravn.

"According to the five witnesses and the court record, yes," said Alex. "Why?"

Ravn scratched his bard. "If one of the Schumanns survived, the motive could be revenge; revenge against a society, or men in general."

"Are you thinking of Renate, the young girl?" asked Kurtz sceptically.

"Why not? She would be in her midthirties now. She would have been very capable of writing those emails to Mogens. Who knows for sure what happened in that forest twenty-five years ago? How reliable are those witnesses?" Ravn said. "Their arses were on the line."

Alex gave him a lopsided smile. "Well, I'm usually game for a good conspiracy theory, but I don't see why the guards would lie."

"Maybe they coordinated their testimony so no one would be sentenced. Maybe they actually *believed* the family was killed. Or something else entirely. There could be any number of motives," Ravn pointed out. "But you said a Stasi officer was present, isn't that unusual?"

"The Stasi had folks planted everywhere in the system, including among the border sentries; the regime trusted no one."

"But an officer? What was his rank?"

Alex looked at the monitor. "He was a colonel. Colonel Erhardt Hausser."

Ravn looked at the archive shelves. "Can we find out what other cases he was on?"

"Sure, unless the files have been shredded." Alex wrote down Hausser's reference number and made for the index system in the glass cases they came past earlier.

"Do you really think that Renate could still be alive?" Kurtz asked in a tired voice.

"We can't afford to exclude any possibilities," Ravn said, taking a seat next to Louise.

They stared at the frozen black-and-white image of her on the TV screen; a portrait of a frustrated little girl in pyjamas.

"Either way, I feel sorry for her," said Louise.

Neither of them could know for sure how much time passed before they heard Alex come running back into the archive, but suddenly he appeared before them, flustered and excited, and threw four files down on the long table where they sat. "Hausser is from fucking Dee-Zee! He was also the agent who led the surveillance on Operation Midas."

"So he followed them all the way to their deaths in the forest?" said Ravn.

Alex nodded.

Ravn took the first file and paged through it. "What is this?"

"I found some of his previous cases. That one took place just before Operation Midas. It concerns a network of human traffickers that Hausser infiltrated. The leader was a man by the name of Leo Danzig; I've come across this name before in other cases, a colourful personality who ended his days in Hohenschönhausen."

"Cause of death?"

"Officially 'bronchitis,' which many inmates died of back then; most were incarcerated in a damp cellar cell until they became ill and died in the infirmary. But there are rumours that the agents used some kind of waterboarding in their interrogations in Hohenschönhausen—a seriously creepy place."

"Colonel Hausser used water torture?" Ravn said, sitting up straight in his chair.

Alex shrugged. "As I said, it's just rumours, and we don't know if Hausser was directly implicated."

Kurtz met Ravn's gaze over the table. "Ten male tourists who drowned, Klara Graf in a sink, Christoph's co-conspirator in the Spree, and now information that Colonel Hausser's detainees might also have had their heads under. Am I the only one here who's seeing this connection?"

"I think we should find out if Erhardt Hausser is still alive and, if so, where he lives," said Kurtz, getting to his feet.

79

Flanked by high residential blocks and old warehouses, Gensler Strasse basked quietly in the morning sun as Kurtz's dark Audi led a convoy—two police patrol cars and a special ops van—into the suburbs. The detective was gripping the steering wheel so tight his knuckles were white. Ravn was sitting in the passenger seat beside him and turned round to check on Louise in the back seat. "Are you okay?" he said. Her mouth was set in a thin line, but she nodded in reply and seemed more focussed than ever; none of them had slept yet, and only the adrenaline in their veins was pushing them forward at full throttle.

"Welcome to Stasi-land," muttered Kurtz, casting a glance out his window. "This entire neighbourhood used to belong to the Stasi. Until the Wall came down, this area wasn't registered on any map."

"Seems like an appropriate place for a former colonel to settle down," Ravn observed.

Kurtz nodded. In the early hours of their archive-search expedition, he had been able to secure a warrant and mobilise a police squad. Instead of voicing his suspicions that Erhardt Hausser had committed the serial murders of ten men in the city, Kurtz had explained to his boss that he had reason to believe Hausser was a war criminal connected to a series of unexplained deaths, as well as the disappearance of a Danish citizen. He did not mention that Ravn and Louise would participate in the action; officially, they were merely "international observers."

When the convoy reached Schleizer Strasse, they turned up a deserted road and continued up a hill until they reached a small grey house. A champagne-coloured BMW was parked in the driveway. Kurtz pulled over on the opposite side of the road, and all three of them got out of the car. Over the rooftops, they could see the watchtowers of Hohenschönhausen Prison that lay just a block away, now the site of a GDR museum.

"Hausser must have enjoyed the view," Kurtz remarked drily. He signalled to the squad leader to start the operation. Moments later, officers in full combat gear entered the grounds with their firearms raised. A unit of five men with a battering ram took up positions by the front door while the rest went round the back of the house. Once they had it surrounded, the leader gave the signal for the first unit to break down the door. They rammed it open, and the team was about to enter, but a cloud of white smoke made them stop in their tracks.

"Pull back! Pull back!" yelled the leader, and his men ran back down the front stairs and dived for cover.

Ravn grabbed Louise's arm and they ducked behind the safety of the nearest patrol car. He spied over the bonnet. The volume of smoke increased, and one of the officers in the patrol car ran up to the house with a fire extinguisher and put out the flames that had ignited in the entrance. The next moment, the squad entered the house.

"Let's go," said Kurtz with his service pistol raised. Ravn and Louise followed him across the road, and they waited in the driveway until the squad leader appeared in the doorway and signalled to Kurtz that everything was okay. They followed the detective into the hallway with the stench of petroleum in their nostrils. Ravn noticed two jerrycans up against the wall.

"The house has been secured and found empty," the squad leader said. "We cut off the electrical supply to minimise the risk of explosion."

"Why the smoke?" asked Kurtz.

"Both doors were armed with an improvised explosive device, sir," the squad leader said. "But fortunately for us, the detonator of the first was defunct, and we were able to defuse the second."

"What kind of explosives?" Kurtz asked.

"There wouldn't have been anything left of the house if they'd gone off. Luckily, they were only old Russian devices, and the first one failed."

"So Hausser knew that it only was a matter of time before we found him and tried to eliminate his tracks," said Ravn.

"Yes, including us," replied Kurtz.

They continued into the living room, which was nothing out of the ordinary; it looked like any other home in the suburbs with its leather sofa arrangement, two comfortable easy chairs in front of the television, and a half-empty bookcase against the far wall. Porcelain figurines of children and a man with a white beard playing the flute had pride of place on the shelves, but there were also a few books.

They went into the bedroom, where a large double bed with bedside tables on either side was made up neatly, but the floor was strewn with clothing and the cupboard doors were open, as if someone had packed in a hurry. Ravn walked over to the wardrobe and looked inside. "Was anyone other than Erhardt Hausser registered to this address?"

"No, why?" said Kurtz.

Ravn stepped aside so Kurtz and Louise could see the contents of the wardrobe: dresses, jackets, skirts, and silk blouses; on the bottom shelf, high-heeled shoes. "It seems the colonel didn't live alone," he said.

"You're thinking maybe Renate survived? That she's been in hiding all this time?"

Ravn nodded. "Whether she's still a victim or something else, time will soon tell."

"Do you think they could've planned all of this together?" Kurtz asked.

Before Ravn could answer, the squad leader called to them from the entrance and they hurried back to hear what he'd found.

"I think you should take a look down there for yourself, sir," the squad leader said to Kurtz, pointing to the cellar stairs.

With their torches switched on, two officers in the cellar provided some light in the low-ceilinged space. Also here there was a strong smell of petrol. A row of high archive cabinets stood along one wall. Ravn walked up to them and took a yellow faded file from the first one. "Looks as if Hausser stole a chunk of Stasi files from the archives before he left HQ."

Kurtz inspected a few files as well. It appeared the files all came from DZ and implicated Hausser in their clandestine activities. It was not clear what his motive could have been, whether it may be to hide his crimes or merely was an expression of nostalgia for old GDR times. Either way, Alex would be thrilled to have them back in the national archive coffers.

A long table stood in the middle of the room with piles of documents, video cassettes, and photographs spread out on its surface. Kurtz shone his torch over the table. The photographs featured middle-aged men who clearly were unaware of being photographed.

"Do you recognise any of them?" asked Ravn.

"Yes, two of my drowned tourists," replied Kurtz. He pointed to the first pile and held one of them up. "The men weren't the only ones he photographed." It was a picture taken of Ravn and Louise on their way through the gate to Klara Graf at Greifenhagener Strasse 9.

Louise snatched a torch from the table and shone the beam towards the back of the cellar: Along the wall, suitcases were lined up neatly in a row. She walked purposefully up to one of them, pulled it out of line, and searched for a name tag; she found Mogens's name and address next to the handle. Laying the suitcase on its side, she flipped it open. Inside were his clothing, shoes, and a toiletry bag. The tears slowly ran down her cheeks as she gently laid a hand on his clothing.

Ravn sat on his haunches beside her. "I'm so sorry, Louise."

She rested her head against his chest. "Why did he keep Mogens's things? Why has he kept all their suitcases?"

"I don't know. Maybe to cover his tracks, maybe as . . ." He was going to say "as a trophy," but there was no need to go into details.

"I think you will both want to see this," said Kurtz.

Ravn helped Louise to her feet, and they joined Kurtz as he went through one of the files; printouts of Mogens's emails, including the ones that Renate had replied to, and a pack of black-and-white photos of Mogens. All the photos were taken during his stay in Berlin; his arrival at Hauptbahnhof, wandering through Friedrichshain, and a series of shots taken in a wooded area.

Ravn picked up the photos and sifted through them. "Any idea where this could be?" he asked.

It was a picture of Mogens looking disorientated, standing between a flock of young people dancing in front of a stage. Kurtz studied the photo carefully; in the unfocussed background behind the stage was the outline of a large radar dome.

"It could have been taken on Teufel Berg," he said.

"Which is?"

"An abandoned American radar and communication complex from the Cold War era. Music festivals are regularly held up there; the Teufel party, for instance. It's over in the Grunewald Forest. Our guys from Narc raided the place a couple of years ago."

"And apart from festivals? Is the communications station still active?"

"No. Most the time it's deserted."

"Right. If Mogens was lured all the way out there, I don't think they intended him to come back," Ravn said. "Maybe Hausser and Renate are hiding out there."

Kurtz put the photo down on the table and turned to the squad leader. "Get your men together and call for a Search and Rescue Unit, Lieutenant."

80

Clouds had gathered over Teufel Berg. The old military fort and radar towers loomed over the dark woods. The thunderclouds rumbled, bringing in the rain that fell in sheets over the police.

Police units had surrounded the mountain. Ravn and Louise accompanied Kurtz with the first unit that headed up the road to the main entrance while smaller units searched the paths through dense shrubbery on the slopes.

When they reached the main entrance, the SAR unit leader divided his men into small groups with SAR dogs; two groups searched the ruins they had passed on the way up while the rest of the force made its way up to the main building. Littered with broken bottles, the remains of an interim music stage was mounted just in front of it.

Ravn and Louise followed Kurtz up the stairs, and they began to search the floors systematically from the bottom up. On the roof, the tattered and frayed tarpaulins covering the metal skeleton of three radar domes made an infernal noise in the wind. Together with Kurtz, Ravn and Louise took refuge from the rain behind the largest tower. From there, they had a view over the entire complex. Below them, the various units followed the trail of the SAR dogs.

Forty minutes later, the unit leader came to Kurtz with a report. "We've been through the entire complex, sir, without finding anything."

Kurtz nodded to the leader and turned to Ravn. "Well, it was worth a shot," he said.

Ravn looked down over the complex and the SAR Unit before the stage below. The dogs were barking frantically, and their handlers were struggling to control them. "Why are the dogs still barking as if they've caught a scent?" he asked the unit leader.

"I've no idea," said the leader. "Perhaps they've got the scent of a dead animal in the woods nearby."

"Yeah, or something down below," said a middle-aged man in a much too large camouflage coat.

"What do you mean, exactly?" said Kurtz.

The man in the oversized coat stamped his feet. "After the Second World War, when Berlin had been flattened by the Allies' bombs and the clean-up operation began, approximately seventy-five million cubic metres of slag was transported out here by Nazi war criminals sentenced to punitive labour—"

"Spare us the history lesson and get to the point," said Kurtz.

"The point is that we are standing on top of the largest bunker in Berlin's war history. The radar station is merely the tip of the berg—literally speaking," he said, laughing at his own remark.

"How do we get down there?"

"Can't be done," said the man. "When Uncle Sam cleared out this place, he poured cement down all the shafts and sealed the entrances. It would take months to break through the cap."

"Hausser seemed like a patient man," Ravn said to Kurtz.

Kurtz looked at the unit leader. "Check all the entrances again," he said.

Down below, a commotion broke out amongst the SAR Unit and a high-pitched whistle cut through the air from the rear entrance of the main building. The unit leader tried to contact his team via walkie-talkie, but no one answered.

When Ravn and the others exited the rear entrance, they immediately saw the group of officers standing around a narrow gap in the wall. Beside them stood a dog handler restraining his excited Alsatian, which was straining against the leash while the other policemen pried open a steel gate.

"What have you found?" yelled Kurtz.

"He's picked up a scent by this gate," said the dog handler, pointing into the darkness beyond.

The heavy steel gate was forced open. Behind it, they found a one-and-a-half-metre-high gap hacked into the grey concrete. Kurtz switched on his torch and worked his body through the narrow passage. The beam of his torch ran along the one wall, revealing the length of the shaft. A strong stench of rotting rose up towards them, making the dogs howl and bark frantically.

"Perhaps it's best if you two stay up here," Kurtz said to Ravn and Louise.

"That's not going to happen," said Louise, giving him a hard stare.

"Okay, as you wish," Kurtz replied. He motioned for them to follow, and the beams of light from the policemen's torches danced along the walls towards a steep steel staircase at the end of the tunnel.

The stairs led fifty metres down into the old bunker and brought them to a narrow corridor at the bottom. The stench made it difficult to breathe in the claustrophobic confines below. The SAR dogs barked loudly and pulled on their leashes to move forwards as quickly as their handlers allowed. The unit leader gave a signal to his men to search two doors, and they quickly secured the first two rooms.

The team continued to the next few doors at the end of the corridor. Ravn lit up the closest room; apart from two inverted officer chairs and a whiteboard on the wall, the location was empty. Together with Louise, they forged ahead to the next location, which was also empty. Louise coughed in the stale air.

"Are you sure you don't want to go back up?" Ravn said.

Louise shook her head firmly and regained control of her breathing.

All of a sudden, march music erupted in the bunker, and they turned back down the corridor.

The unit leader was standing in the doorway of the next room, and he waved Kurtz over. "I think we've found him!" he yelled, but the moment he caught sight of Louise he said: "Not her . . . keep her away from here!"

"Louise!" Ravn called as she threw herself forwards and pushed past him and Kurtz.

The unit leader tried to bar her entrance to the room. "Let me through!" she screamed at him before he could lay a finger on her.

The stench in the room was tangible, as if walking into a wall, and Louise stopped in her tracks. The beam of torches revealed the contours of a rusty tub at the far end of the room. A large water tank was mounted above, and a pump was screwed fast to the wall. Two rubber hoses were attached to the pump; one hose had a tap over the edge of the tub, the other was mounted to the drain underneath; the closed system ensured that water could continuously be pumped in and out of the tub. In front of the tub stood a small folding table. On the table was a tape recorder, slowly turning on the final energy from a 12-volt battery on the ground below, drawing out the Young Pioneers' choir song into a slurred moan.

"Shut down that racket!" yelled the unit leader, but no one was paying any attention to him because everyone had their eyes trained on what lay inside the tub.

Ravn pushed his way into the room and caught up with Louise. Together, they walked over to the tub, which gradually revealed its contents: Curled up in the bottom was a discoloured and rotting corpse, a gelatinous clump of flesh covered in a purple web of fungi. Despite the advanced stage of decomposition, Louise recognised Mogens's features. She stumbled back a few paces and almost fell, but Ravn grabbed her in time. "Come, Louise, we need to get you away from here," he said firmly.

A moaning voice replaced the Young Pioneers chorus behind them. "YOU ARE LYING . . . WHERE IS THE MONEY. . ."

81

Two uniformed police officers yelled at the journalists and photographers, trying to keep them away from the station's entrance. Whenever the door was opened and someone came out, it was as if a wave went through the crowd that again would press against the entrance, insistent to see who was there.

Immediately after the news about Erhardt Hausser and the murders he'd committed broke, the media went into a frenzy. Kurtz gave instructions to cordon off Hausser's house and Teufel Berg to keep curious onlookers at bay. Newscasters vied for attention and supremacy in the race to find the most macabre details about the ex-Stasi colonel and his victims, the charges the police had brought against him, and his sinister past at Division Z of the Ministry for State Security.

The moment Louise and Ravn stepped out of the taxi, they were surrounded by the press. The flash of cameras hailed over the heads with the same merciless intensity as the lightning of the storm over Teufel Berg had done the day before. Journalists yelled questions at them from all sides in German, English, and Danish. Ravn kept his arm around Louise, and they managed to force their way through the wall of media up the front steps of the police station. The two policemen guarding the door helped to push the most rabid press away so they could open the door and slip inside.

Contrary to their previous visit, there was no waiting time. A deputy met them in Reception and escorted them up to Chief Detective Kurtz's office immediately.

"Are you okay?" Ravn asked Louise. She nodded and he put his arm around her again. They were both exhausted; neither one of them had been able to get a wink of sleep. Louise had cried most of the night. Not even the two sleeping pills Ravn had managed to arrange could calm her down, and finally she simply lay with her head on his lap while he stroked her hair till the sun came up. Later in the morning, they'd turned on the TV and put on the news, which reported the ordeal that they had experienced firsthand less than twenty-four hours before. The only consolation was that the German police had initiated the greatest criminal chase in history, not just in Germany but all over Europe; it was hard to imagine that Hausser would be able to hide for long. They'd watched Kurtz appear on TV alongside the German Chief Commissioner of Police to brief the press, which indicated that he was in from the cold with his boss. There was no visible frown on the latter's face, not even when Kurtz referred to Hausser as a "serial killer." The commissioner's satisfaction was probably due to the fact that the unexplained deaths of the tourists were no longer a thorn in his side, but a shining example of the efficiency and power of the German police.

"I apologise for all the fuss," said Kurtz in greeting. "I should have instructed my men to sneak you guys in through the rear entrance."

His office was not much bigger than the deputy's whom they had met with the last time they were there, but Kurtz's view was better with a window facing the road, and he invited them to take a seat opposite his own at the desk. He had dark rings under his eyes, and it seemed he hadn't slept either, relying on adrenaline and the coffee thermos at his elbow. He offered them a cup, but they both declined.

"I am really sorry for your loss, Louise. I wish we had found your brother in time," Kurtz said as he slumped into his chair.

"I'm sure you did everything you could," Louise said with her eyes cast down.

"We have initiated an international search for Hausser," said Kurtz.

"Yes, we heard that on the news," said Ravn. "Hopefully, you will catch him soon."

"Hopefully, yes."

"You seem unsure about your chances," Ravn said.

Kurtz crossed his arms over his chest. "No, we will catch him eventually, but he's had a long time to get ahead of us, and he probably has the resources to hide. We are relatively sure that Hausser is in possession of your brother's bounty, Louise. As well as the money he in all likelihood stole from his other victims."

Louise raised her eyes. "How can you be so sure he has the money Mogens stole?"

Kurtz gritted his teeth. "There isn't an easy way to tell you this."

"Just tell me the truth. I need to know what happened to my brother."

"Okay." The chief detective stepped in, shifting to the front of his seat and leaning his elbows on his desk. "Hausser installed a system whereby he could alternately fill and empty the water in the tub that Mogens was chained to."

"Waterboarding?" asked Ravn.

"Something like that, yes. The tapes we found in the room reveal that Hausser interrogated Mogens and his other victims. Most of the tapes were ruined by damp, but on one of the recordings, Mogens tells Hausser that he hid the money in the third room in the fort."

"And your team is sure that Hausser found the money?"

"We have searched every corner of Teufel Berg—including that part of the underground bunker that Hausser had access to—without finding it. So we are assuming Hausser is on the run with the money and is hiding somewhere, possibly beyond German borders."

"What about Renate? Was it her voice we heard on the tapes?"

Kurtz nodded.

"Are you looking for her?" Ravn asked.

"We are relatively certain that Renate Schumann died at the forest checkpoint with her parents twenty-five years ago. We are on the trail of the border sentries initially charged in the case. We will question them again and get to the bottom of what really happened that night."

Ravn shook his head. "I'm not sure I understand. If Renate was killed at the border that night, how do you explain the recordings of her voice and all the women's clothing we found at Hausser's place?"

"Well, we've found several tape recordings of Renate's voice in Hausser's cellar; all these tapes originate from his surveillance of the family in 1989. It appears that he edited the tapes in such a way that he was able to interrogate Mogens and pose the relevant questions to locate the money."

"That man is a sick bastard," said Louise. "But why?"

"Your guess is as good as mine," said Kurtz. "But we believe with relative certainty that it was important for Hausser to keep the illusion of Renate alive. Not only to bait his victims; we found numerous videocassettes of her at his home, as well as a leotard and a Young Pioneer uniform that belonged to Renate when she was a child."

"So you're saying it was Hausser who wrote the emails to my brother?"

"In all likelihood, yes."

"He seems obsessed by her memory," muttered Ravn.

Kurtz nodded.

"When will you release Mogens's body so I can take him home?" asked Louise.

"As soon as the autopsy is complete, so it won't be more than a few days from now. When are you guys planning to return to Denmark?"

"I'd like to bring Mogens home personally," said Louise.

"Yes, I'm staying as well," Ravn added.

"Excellent. I'll try to hurry things along," said Kurtz. He picked up a plastic bag standing beside his chair and put it on his desk. "Forensics need to inspect Mogens's clothing and suitcase, which we will naturally return to you as soon as they're done, but I have a few personal items here that you can take with you now, Louise."

Louise thanked him and took the bag.

Kurtz showed them to the door personally. He once more uttered his regret that they had been unable to save Mogens in time. Then he turned to Ravn, smiled, and shook his hand.

"I must say, you are one of the best investigators I have ever had the pleasure to meet."

"Thank you, but I'm no longer in service. And Louise made an equal contribution to putting the pieces of the puzzle together," Ravn replied.

"It's a shame you're no longer a detective. You shouldn't let your talents go to waste. I'm sure the Danish police need your help."

"Well, the question is whether I still need to be a detective for the Danish police," Ravn observed. "I hope you'll find time to take your son to watch football soon," he added, nodding to the Hertha Berlin scarf that was slung over the architect lamp on the chief detective's desk.

"*Gott sei Dank*," said Kurtz. "The team stinks at the moment," he added, clapping Ravn on the shoulder in parting.

82

The civilian police car dropped Louise and Ravn at Gendarmenmarkt, where they sat down under the green marquee in front of Lutter & Wegner among regular breakfast patrons, tourists, businessmen, and media personalities. When their drinks arrived, Louise sipped her white wine despondently. The line of starched, white tablecloths reminded her of corpse sheets in the morgue, she remarked, ensconced behind her dark sunglasses.

"Let me know if you'd prefer to go back to the hotel," Ravn replied.

"No, it's comforting to be surrounded by people after everything that happened yesterday."

"Perhaps we should've left the SAR operation and Teufel Berg to Kurtz."

"Perhaps. On the other hand, it feels important that I was able to see where Mogens was killed," Louise said. She took out the bag of personal items that Kurtz had given her and emptied it onto the table. Apart from his worn black wallet was a set of keys, a small Mayland calendar, a city map of Berlin, and a few 1-euro coins. She flipped through the calendar and noticed that he had circled her birthday.

"May I?" Ravn asked, pointing to the city map. Louise nodded, and he unfolded the map to see if Mogens had marked anything. Nothing caught his eye, so he refolded the map and returned it to the table.

Louise opened the wallet. Mogens's Danish medical card was still inside. In the notes sheath, she found a few receipts from a store at

Hauptbahnhof and one from a bakery in Friedrichshain. A local train ticket for the U-Bahn and a harbour tour in Copenhagen. "We took this harbour tour together when we were kids," Louise said, holding it up to show Ravn. "Mogens always got seasick, but he loved going on those trips anyway." She put the slips back into his wallet and noticed a small photo. It was a faded portrait of herself and Mogens, twenty years younger. "This was taken in one of those old photo booths at Copenhagen Central Station. I'd just graduated from high school. I can't believe he kept it all these years."

"He must have loved you very much, Louise."

She nodded and choked back the tears. "Things could have been so different if only . . ." she shook her head and wiped away the tears that had started to run down her cheeks. "If only I'd been there for him, visited him or called him more often."

"You can't blame yourself for that now."

"Mogens deserved better. Deserved a better sister than I was."

"I think you were the best thing he had in his life."

"If that's the truth . . . it's too sad for words . . ."

Ravn reached over the table and took her hand. "I think I know how you feel."

She withdrew her hand and shook her head quietly.

"Louise, it's not your fault that Mogens is dead."

"So why does it feel like it is?"

Ravn took a sip of his beer. "When Eva died, and I couldn't find her killer, I fell into a black hole. I hated myself for not being home and taking care of her, I hated myself for not being able to find her murderer, hated myself for everything I never told her, everything I didn't get round to doing for her, everything we ought to have done together. In the end, I even started hating everyone around me—friends, neighbours, and colleagues. The mountain of hate became so huge I didn't want to live anymore, and I tried to drink myself into oblivion."

"What made you stop?"

"I don't really know. Time. Friends who pulled me back from the edge. Or maybe I just realised it was taking too long to drink myself to death, so I simply gave up. But at least I was able to free myself from all the hate and bitterness I felt. Until recently. I found out that Eva was seeing someone else . . . then it started all over again; all the bitterness came back with full force."

"So, you're saying it never ends?"

"No. I think that maybe it's about focusing on all the good things we had together, everything that we *did* manage to do in the time we were given. And put all your self-recriminations, all your regrets behind you," Ravn said with a shrug. "I don't have all the answers. The only thing I do know for sure is that if you're not careful, it will eat you up for the rest of your life."

Louise nodded and dried her cheeks where her mascara had run. She excused herself and went into the restaurant to look for the toilets.

Ravn watched her go and emptied his glass. He felt sorry for her, and he doubted that anything he had said would make a difference; personally, he hated it when other people—especially Johnson—burdened him with some or other words of wisdom.

83

Louise entered the ladies' toilets, which had six cubicles along one wall and an equal number of washbasins on the other. A mirror was mounted above the basins and it reflected the entire room. She went down to the last basin, took a paper towel from the dispenser, and carefully began dabbing the mascara off her cheeks.

The door opened, and out of the corner of her eye, she saw a woman enter. Louise didn't like titivating in front of other people, so once she'd gotten rid of the mascara, she did her best to freshen up her make-up as quickly as possible. The woman at the other end apparently didn't have the same qualms as she painted her lips with a dark-red lipstick.

Louise returned her cosmetics bag to her handbag and looked at her reflection in the mirror. Satisfied with her patch-up job, she made for the door, but the woman with the long blonde hair suddenly turned and blocked her path. The woman's features were coarse, her make-up vulgar and hastily applied. Her hair appeared to be a cheap blonde wig that was slightly askew. She stared at Louise with deep-set black eyes. "Not so fast, Louise," a man's voice said. "We have a lot to talk about."

"C-Colonel . . . Hausser . . ." Louise stammered.

"You can call me Renate," he said with a sarcastic laugh.

As if a claw, Hausser's rough hand with painted nails closed around her neck. He lifted her off the ground and shoved her towards the first cubicle. Louise tried to scream for help, but the iron grip on her throat choked all sound. He closed the door of the cubicle behind them and pressed himself against her. The sickly sweet smell of his perfume and sour body odour filled her nostrils.

He looked down at her and stroked her hair with his free hand. "You're so beautiful, *Liebchen.* Majestically beautiful. It's hard to imagine that weakling was your brother. You have no idea how much trouble he caused me," Hausser said, rolling his eyes. "Every time I poured water over his head, he squealed like a pig. Was he afraid of water as a child as well?"

"You . . . fucking . . . swine . . ."

"Hush, Louise. Such ugly words from your sweet little mouth." Hausser cocked his head and looked at her intently. "You know, you remind me of Renate. Perhaps she would've grown up to be just as beautiful and pure as you. Not like this pathetic parody of a woman," he said, pointing to himself. "But with all the pictures of me in the media, I had to bring poor little Renate back to life again."

"You . . . are sick."

"Not at all. Okay, perhaps a little desperate. But I admit that my disguise is more suited for the dark of Teufel Berg than daylight. It's amazing what a man who is about to drown will tell a sweet woman," Hausser said, clicking his tongue. Then he tightened his grip on her throat. "And now you are going to tell me where your brother's money is. I know you came to Berlin to find it."

"You're out of your mind," said Louise. "I came here to look for my brother. *You* took the money. You tortured it out of him!"

"I'm asking you one last time, Louise. Where is the money?"

"I don't know, but I'm glad you don't have it. They're going to catch you and put you away for—"

Hausser tightened his grip even more, and Louise gasped for breath. "Tell me right now, or—"

"Or what? You'll kill me? Like you did with all the others . . . like you did with Renate?"

"I didn't kill Renate! What do you take me for? Those men were greedy pigs who thought they could buy love. They abused their positions to buy a pure heart. They were pathetic, your brother most of all!" Hausser snapped in her face, and she felt the spittle on her cheeks.

"You're no better, you fucking psychopath."

Hausser stared at her, as if her resistance surprised him. "That's . . . that's not true . . . I merely tried to adapt to modern times."

Louise shoved Hausser hard in the chest and he took a step back, far enough for her to ram her knee into his crotch. He screamed and doubled over. Louise yanked the door open. Hausser tried to grab her, but she slid out of the cubicle, ran out of the toilets, and into the restaurant, calling for help. The waiter came over immediately and looked at her in surprise without knowing what else to do. The next moment, Ravn came running in from outside.

"What's wrong, Louise? Are you all right?" he said.

"Hausser . . . he attacked me . . . dressed like a woman . . . in the ladies' toilets," she said, trying to catch her breath.

Ravn brushed past her and ran into the toilets. On the floor lay an abandoned pair of red high heels. He checked the cubicles but found them empty. He returned to Louise, who had alerted the head waiter and asked him to call the police. The head waiter was a pompous elderly gentleman and he hesitated to call the cops until Louise told him that the most-wanted criminal in the country had just been in his restaurant.

Ravn ran outside and peered down the road but saw no sign of Hausser. Moments later, Louise came to his side. "They're calling the police now, but maybe we should call Kurtz directly?"

Ravn was still searching the road and surrounding area, but he stuck his hand in his pocket and gave Kurtz's business card to Louise.

A car honked behind them, and Ravn spun on his heel. At the end of Charlottenstrasse the traffic had stopped, and a man was waving his arms in the air. Ravn stepped into the road to get a better look at what the holdup was about. He caught sight of Hausser, who had lost his wig in the tussle and was trying to pull a woman out of her car. Another man had intervened and was pulling on the arm of Hausser's dress.

"Wait here," Ravn said to Louise, and immediately started running down the road.

Hausser headbutted the man to the ground and tried to get into the car. The woman fought back tooth-and-nail, beating Hausser about the head with her handbag. Ravn was so close now that Hausser saw him coming towards him, and he gave up the fight with the woman, got out of the car, and started running down the road. A crowd had gathered, trying to help the woman and the man, who lay bleeding on the ground. Ravn elbowed his way through and set after Hausser.

Hausser had a good lead on Ravn, but his gawdy dress made him stick out on the street. Ravn tried to pick up speed, but he felt as if he were wading in cement. It had been years since he'd chased after someone, and he'd spent the interim guzzling beers, which didn't make his chase any easier. And yet, he managed to close the gap on Hausser. It seemed as though the old Stasi man was feeling some strain himself, and the tight dress he was wearing wasn't helping either.

"Stop . . . that man!" Ravn yelled, almost completely out of breath, but no one on the pavement reacted to his call for help.

Hausser ran over the crossing at Mauerstrasse.

Ravn was about ten metres behind him, so close that he could hear Hausser's laboured breathing and smell his sweat perfume like a slipstream behind him. It was only a matter of seconds now till he caught up, and Ravn was already looking forward to smashing Hausser to the ground. He heard a screech of tyres, and the next moment his legs disappeared from under him. For a millisecond, he flew through the air and then hit a windshield, which shattered under his weight. Ravn slid down the bonnet, and when he hit the asphalt, he stayed down.

The air had been knocked out of him and he struggled to breathe as he slowly got to his feet. His head was spinning, and he had to lean against the bonnet of the car that had torpedoed him, a Porsche Boxster. His body only partially responded to commands, still in shock after the massive blow, and he knew he had to keep moving, force himself to make use of the adrenaline before the pain took over. An elderly gentleman in a pink polo shirt got out of the Porsche to inspect the damage to his car. He started to yell at Ravn, who was already on his way.

About fifty metres further, there was a lineup of tourist buses on either side of the road. Ravn caught a glimpse of Hausser among the tourists before he disappeared behind the first bus. When Ravn reached the bus, he forged his way through the tourists and around the buses. He took a moment to look out over the enormous Holocaust memorial on the square in front of him. Several thousand concrete pillars of varying height formed a dense and complex labyrinth. Tourists milled in between the pillars, taking pictures. Ravn scanned the crowd for Hausser, but there was no sight of him. He felt the pain begin to pound in his side. He had to make a move, *right now*, or he would lose him. If Hausser was in the labyrinth of the memorial, he would try to get out of it as soon as possible, Ravn figured, but he needed to know whether Hausser would make a run for the Tiergarten park on the opposite side of the road, or whether he would emerge on Unter den Linden and try to blend in with the tourists on that end.

Ravn spotted an old camper parked a little further along the way. At the back of the camper was a narrow ladder that led up to the roof railing. Ignoring the pain, he ran over to the camper and climbed the ladder onto the roof. From here, he had a clear view over the entire square and the labyrinth of pillars and, in the farthest corner, he spotted Hausser heading for the Brandenburg Gate and Unter den Linden. Back down the ladder, he ran along Cora-Berliner-Strasse, which flanked the left side of the memorial. His body was aching, the pain in his right ankle slowing him down the most.

About ten metres ahead of Ravn, Hausser emerged from among the pillars. He bent over to catch his breath and wiped the sweat off his face, smearing the make-up into a grotesque mask. When he looked up, he saw Ravn and stared at him in surprise. Then he set off and made a run for Unter den Linden.

It was rush hour on the boulevard and the cars whizzed past in all four lanes. Hausser stepped into the traffic, and the drivers honked their horns as they did all they could not to hit him. Fifteen or twenty metres behind him, Ravn was running towards him with the cars rushing past mercilessly, almost making him lose his balance.

Hausser leapt onto the centre kerb and dashed over the next two lanes. Ravn was right behind him now, but he had to wait in the centre to let cars pass. When the traffic lights on the next intersection turned red, the cars slowed down and Ravn took the gap to cross over and continue along Wilhelmstrasse. He could see Hausser, who had paused on a bridge over the Spree River. He was holding his arms out to his sides and threw back his head, as if gasping air into his lungs. Then he turned his head and stared at Ravn bearing down, albeit limping, battered and obviously in pain. In a split-second decision, Hausser climbed over the bridge railing. He stood on a ledge for a moment, looking out over the river. Then he jumped.

Ravn stumbled to the middle of the bridge and peered over the edge in time to see a tour boat pass underneath. On the top deck, surrounded by a group of flabbergasted Chinese tourists in matching orange windbreakers, Hausser stood bent over, clinging to the railing.

With his back to the bridge wall, Ravn sank onto the ground and pulled out his phone. All he could do was call the police and report where he had last seen Hausser, even if the bastard would be long gone before they could dispatch a unit.

84

Twenty minutes later, Ravn pulled up in a taxi in front of Lutter & Wegner. The restaurant was surrounded by uniformed police, and he found Louise sitting at one of the tables with Detective Kurtz.

Ravn greeted them both briefly and dropped into a chair opposite them. "Any news?"

Louise stared at him in concern. "Are you hurt?"

"Got hit by a Porsche. Luckily, it was only a Boxster."

Louise's eyes opened wide. "You were hit by a car?! But . . . shouldn't we get you to a hospital?"

"I can manage," said Ravn, turning to Kurtz. "What about Hausser?"

"He got off the boat before the marine police came on the scene, even though they were there within ten minutes. Other units have been dispatched in the area where the boat docked."

"At least now we know that he's still in the city, on the run without Mogens's money."

"Yes, that's definitely in our favour," said Kurtz. "Disguised or not, Hausser cannot hide for long."

"But I thought Mogens told him where he'd hidden the money," said Louise.

Kurtz shrugged. "Perhaps someone else got there before him. Or maybe Mogens didn't tell him the truth. The fact remains that we've found no trace of the money, neither in Hausser's house, the flat Mogens rented in Friedrichshain, nor Teufel Berg."

"Mogens came here by train. What about the Left Luggage boxes at Hauptbahnhof?" asked Ravn.

"We've checked those too; none of them have been rented as far back as Mogens's disappearance. But he could have deposited the money elsewhere, or buried it, for that matter."

"So it remains a mystery," said Ravn.

"I think you've scared Hausser enough that he won't take the risk of approaching you again, but I've made sure that you're both under protection for as long as you're in Berlin."

"Thank you," said Louise. "But right now, all I want to do is go home."

"Same here," Ravn said, and bent down to check his swollen ankle. The pain had descended with a vengeance. He'd turned down a checkup from a doctor, but he could definitely use a bartender.

85

As a tribute to Mogens, the organs in the Church of Our Saviour were playing Wagner, a section from the Prelude to *Tristan und Isolde*. His mortal remains lay in the dark coffin in front of the main altar. Ravn was standing right at the back of the enormous church, watching Louise and her closest family, who were sitting in the first pew before the white marble angels. It was the first time Ravn had been in the church since Eva's funeral. That time, the organist played Kim Larsen's "Om lidt bli'r her stille," and the church had been packed with citizens who had heard about the tragedy of her death in the press and gathered to pay their last respects. For Eva, it seemed as though all of Christianshavn came to wish her adieu. Mogens was not paid the same respect, and the church was almost empty.

A week had passed since they had brought Mogens's body back to Denmark. The release of his corpse and the transport itself had been unproblematic. The funeral was delayed only because Louise had insisted it be held at the Church of Our Saviour.

Ravn kept his eyes trained on Louise, who was dressed in black. Even when she mourned, she was incredibly beautiful. It was the first time he had seen her since they got back. They had spent the night on *Bianca*, had made love before falling into a deep sleep together, but when he woke up the next morning, she was gone. In the days that followed, he had called and sent messages without getting any replies. Worried about her, he eventually rang the school to hear if she was back at work and received confirmation that she was. He left a message with the receptionist, but again, Louise had not returned his call.

Ravn figured that the reason for her silence could probably be found in the people who were sitting with her in the first pew. Next to her sat her ex-husband—if that is what he was—with his arm around her shoulder. He must have been ten or fifteen years older than she was, dressed elegantly, and with a suntan and a full head of steel-grey hair. On her other side sat Louise's grown son. He had long blond hair and was wearing a creased suit jacket. The young man must have been called home from college so he could attend his uncle's funeral. It looked as if the period of mourning had brought the family together again, as if creating a new bond among them. Ravn didn't see any reason to hang around till the end of the ceremony, so he limped to the door and left the church.

Ravn filled Møffe's bowls with food and water and carried them up onto the deck. Møffe gave him the evil eye without making any sign of moving till hell freezes over. The hunger strike was one of many ways the dog had expressed his dissatisfaction at having been deserted while his master had gone off to Berlin; five of his T-shirts had been chewed to shreds, and now Ravn had discovered that Møffe had taken a shit in a pair of his trainers. "Aw, come off it, Møffe! Eduardo took excellent care of you while I was gone, so don't give me that look."

Møffe slobbered and smacked his chops in reply.

"*Seriously?* This is not the way to show someone that you've missed them. It's time you started behaving yourself properly," said Ravn, stomping up the stairs to the flybridge.

Ravn dropped into the seat at the helm and swung his legs onto the bench opposite. Even though the wind was cool, the sun warmed his face, and he took his newspaper out of his jacket pocket and unfolded it. There was an article on the case in Berlin, including a foreboding picture of Teufel Berg and a portrait of Hausser. Ravn read that the ex-Stasi officer was still on the run, and that this was putting Kurtz under pressure with his superiors, not least because the number of possible victims had risen to nineteen. The press had also learned that a hefty sum of money had disappeared and was possibly hidden at Teufel

Berg, which had prompted a flurry of treasure hunters to ransack the mountain.

Ravn looked up from the newspaper and stared over the canal to Applebye Square and the large residential complex where Mogens used to live. It was strange to imagine that, for years, Mogens must have walked past *Bianca* on his way to work. Some days, full of expectation and hope when he'd received a letter from "Renate." It was here, in Christianshavn, that he had plotted his coup against Lauritzen, here he'd made his master plan for the future. His morbid thoughts were interrupted by slobbering sounds coming from the other end of the flybridge.

"Are we friends again?"

Møffe finished chewing and looked up at him with his ever-sorrowful eyes. Then the dog sneezed and grunted, which Ravn interpreted as a sign that he was coming round.

That night, Ravn dreamt of having sex with Louise. Harder, wilder than what they had shared. In his dream it was more of a bestial act; as if snarling animals snapping at each other, then he put his hands around her neck, but felt as if he were the one being strangled, until he noticed that they were underwater, and it was impossible to come up to the surface; they fucked and drowned at the same time.

Ravn started and sat up straight in the bed, banging his head against the low ceiling of the cabin. He looked into the kitchen, which was flooded with the glow of the moon. Møffe was in the doorway, barking at the aft deck. Ravn couldn't see if anyone was out there, but moments later he heard footsteps retreating up on the quay. He called Møffe inside, and a short while later the dog came in and curled up on his blanket.

Ravn lay back in his bunk and listened to the water lapping against the hull. He closed his eyes and tried to fall asleep again. He should never have gotten involved with Louise and her search for her brother.

86

The next day, the sun bore down on the canal and gradually drove away the mist. It seemed as if spring had finally come to Christianshavn. As always at this time of year, the quay was alive with people enjoying pizzas, lattes, beers, and joints.

Ravn was taking the opportunity to sand the wood on the hatch above the foremost cabin. The meteorologists had promised sun for three days in a row, and his plan was to lacquer all the railings and wood on deck. He spotted Eduardo parking his bike on the quay before making his way over. Eduardo waved with his leather satchel and Ravn waved back.

"Busy day at work?" asked Ravn.

"Nah, it's the slow season," said Eduardo, stepping onto his ketch. "I'd love to hear more about your case in Berlin—I'll keep your name out of the story."

"There's not much more to tell," said Ravn. The truth is that Ravn hadn't told Eduardo anything, and merely referred him to Kurtz. And considering the lack of coverage the story had had in *Information*, Ravn was pretty sure that Eduardo had not yet taken the time to call Kurtz at all. Besides, serial murders were hardly the kind of story the editor-in-chief at Eduardo's paper was interested in publishing.

Eduardo put down his leather satchel and pulled his T-shirt over his head, revealing extraordinarily pale skin on his skinny chest. "All right. Then why don't you fill me in on what is happening between you and Louise; I'll refrain from having it published on the cover," he said jokingly.

"That's easily done: Nothing's happening."

"But I thought—"

"No, no, we're just good friends," Ravn said, concentrating on the hatch, which he gave a good going-over with sandpaper. "Hey, you don't happen to have an A4 envelope lying around, do you?"

Eduardo nodded and went to look for one. Not long after, he returned with a large manila envelope, which he gave to Ravn. "Will this do?"

Ravn nodded and thanked his friend. "By the way, did you hear anything last night?"

"What do you mean?"

"I woke up to Møffe barking, which he rarely does."

"Nope, I slept like a rock. Do you think someone wanted to break in?"

"It wouldn't be the first time," said Ravn. "But it could've just been a drunkard who had lost his way."

"Hmm. Perhaps I should also get a guard dog. But one that isn't such a sourpuss like yours in the mornings," Eduardo remarked, and lay back on his bench to enjoy the sun.

Later that afternoon, Ravn sat down at his table in the mid cabin. Mogens's personal belongings and the file Louise had made lay spread out before him; she'd left it behind the morning after they had returned from Berlin. It didn't look like she was coming back, so he had decided to send them to her instead. Unfortunately, he didn't know exactly where she lived, just that it was somewhere in Østerbro. He was going to put everything into the envelope and have a courier bike it over to the architect school, but he wasn't sure how to word the note he wanted to add; he didn't want to sound all wounded, because he wasn't, actually; her sudden silence surprised him more than anything else. And he understood her need to put this whole ordeal behind her—and that included him. After some deliberation, he simply wrote that he hoped she was well and that they could always grab a coffee sometime.

He studied the note for a moment. *The wording is okay, but the handwriting is goddamn awful*, he thought. He had never worried about his handwriting before.

Ravn popped Louise's file and the note into the manila envelope. Then he upended the plastic bag with Mogens's belongings onto the table. He put the worn leather wallet into the envelope, but considered throwing away the city map of Berlin and the tickets. Then again, he had no idea what objects might hold sentimental value for Louise; for two years he had held onto a hairpin that had belonged to Eva. With this in mind, he decided not to toss anything and let Louise decide what she wanted to keep.

He felt *Bianca* rock and knew that a harbour tour was gliding past on the canal, and he picked up Mogens's harbour ticket that lay before him. He was about to pop it into the envelope when he noticed the date and time stamp printed on the front; Mogens had boarded the harbour trip boat at 12:52 p.m. on the day he stole the money from Lauritzen. Ravn smoothed out the ticket before him and stared at the time: *12:52 p.m. was right after he stole the money on his lunch break.*

Irrespective of how much you love going on harbour tours, it was a very odd thing to do when you're on the run from the law. For one, it would cost him a lot of time to take the trip. For another, regardless of which tour he took, he would inevitably sail through Christianshavn canal and pass directly in front of the workplace he had just robbed. *Why would Mogens take such a risk?* Unless it was important for him to see the scene of the crime one last time, similar to a pyromaniac who likes to watch the fire burn right after he has set it alight? Ravn doubted that Mogens's case applied. He stood up and decided to go up on deck to think.

Everything Mogens had done had been planned in minute detail, so the harbour tour was unlikely to have been a spontaneous, last-minute joyride. So why didn't Mogens just take a taxi to the main station and leave the country at once? Ravn began pacing on the aft deck as he tried to figure out Mogens's plan: Either he'd stowed his suitcase at the main station in advance, or he'd returned to his flat after the theft. The former was more likely because then Mogens could leave immediately. Mogens must have come past *Bianca* on his way to work in the morning. He was probably shitting bricks, while at the same time feeling exhilarated by his plans. Perhaps for the first time, he'd felt as if he had a significant purpose to his life. He'd had managed to show up everyone at work; all those people who had excluded him, looked down on him for years. While his boss had been in a meeting right next door, Mogens had simply emptied the safe in cold blood. It must have been an incredible moment of victory for him. An unprecedented stroke of revenge! Ravn started to mutter to himself, oblivious to passersby who were giving him curious looks.

"Mogens feels like a god of revenge, a modern-day Vishnu who slips out of Lauritzen Enterprises with almost 1 million in hard cash, on his way to a new life with Renate at the other end, his reward . . . and takes a harbour trip?" Ravn shook his head. "*Why* the trip, Mogens? You've *already* won, you've *already* got your revenge, there's no need for you to go back, so why the hesitation to leave?" Ravn scratched his beard. *Is that the answer? Doubt?*

Mogens hesitated. He didn't just throw himself on board the next train that would take him to an exciting future with Renate. Ravn could sympathise; their relationship was based on emails, and he was yet to meet her. He'd not even seen a picture of her—unless Hausser had sent him a fake one, but Ravn doubted it. The intimate emails might have been enough to motivate his flight, but was it enough to win his trust? Perhaps he'd factored in the risk that things might not work out between them in Berlin. So the harbour had to be part of his detailed plan. Ravn was sure of it.

He leaned on the railing and looked out over the mirror-surface water. *Why had Hausser, Kurtz, and half of Berlin on a treasure hunt on Teufel Berg not been able to find Mogens's money?* Maybe for the simple reason that it wasn't there. Maybe he didn't take it with him. *What if he hid the money here, in Copenhagen, before he left?* The problem with that theory was that Mogens had told Hausser where he had hidden the money. And Ravn was certain that Mogens wasn't a person who could withstand torture for a long time. So he must have been telling the truth; the money was "in the third room of the *fort.*"

Ravn returned to the cabin and picked up the harbour tour ticket. As far as he knew, Canal Tours was the only tour operator that sailed to Trekroner. Perhaps the answer was obvious: They had all been looking in the wrong fort.

87

Louise's mobile phone deferred to her answerphone, so Ravn left her a message. He briefly explained that he might have an idea where Mogens had hidden the money, and that it was in all likelihood somewhere in Trekroner Fort, rather than a bunker on Teufel Berg. He asked her to call him back as soon as possible so they could discuss what to do next.

He put the phone on the table in front of him and stared at it, willing her to call him back immediately. He had to admit that his hunting instinct was fired into action; if *Bianca*'s engine had been working, he'd have turned the key and set course for Trekroner immediately. Of course, he could also have rung Station City and handed the police this case on a silver platter. But with his luck, the job would be assigned to Mikkel—and he wasn't letting that happen. He reckoned the incriminating accounts ledger that included the fake balance sheet from Lauritzen Enterprises would be hidden along with the money. Ravn liked the idea that the land of the living could offer Mogens some kind of justice for his former employer's exploitation and crime; a few months behind bars would do Pondus Lauritzen some good.

Ravn waited an hour—or forty-five minutes, to be exact—before his patience with Louise ran out. Ransacking his clothes cupboard, he found an old backpack and threw in a sweater, a water bottle, and a crowbar; he patted his jeans pocket to make sure he had his Leatherman multi-tool on him.

Møffe wagged his tail in anticipation when he came out onto the aft deck. "You stay here," said Ravn. Møffe sneezed in reply, and Ravn knew that their delicate truce was in jeopardy, but this was a risk he'd have to take.

Ravn went up on deck and called after Eduardo but got no reply. He hopped over onto the ketch and checked the cockpit and the cabin, but Eduardo was not at home, so he took out his phone and called him.

Moments later, Eduardo picked up. Ravn could hear noise in the background. "Hey, where are you?"

"I'm at Canal Restaurant drinking rosé with . . . with the sweetest *señorita*."

"You can't even remember her name, you sod, but I need to borrow your tender boat."

"Sure, no problem. Where you going?"

"Trekroner."

Eduardo laughed, as if he thought Ravn wasn't serious. "Each to their own."

Moments later, Ravn was untying the tethering of Eduardo's rubber dinghy. Without a moment's delay, he sat down on the bench and pumped the outboard motor's throttle.

88

In the dark shadows of a backyard on the other side of the canal, a figure was watching him. He'd taken shelter in a shed, where he waited patiently, keeping an eye on *Bianca* from a distance. Not eating, not drinking, barely sleeping for more than twenty-four hours. It was an art to make yourself invisible for such a long time, a skill that only supreme investigators could master; an art that age rewarded with patience, albeit at the cost of a nervous bladder.

The man from the shadows emptied his bladder while he watched Ravn in the rubber dinghy vanish under the bridge just before Christianshavn Square. When the figure had finished answering the call of nature, he hurried out of the yard.

After many days on the run, Hausser was haggard with exhaustion, but his black eyes still glowed like those of a hungry wolf. It had taken him thirty-six hours to get here from Berlin on various freight trains. He removed his white earbud and bundled the cord of the little receiver in his hand. It was an outdated piece of equipment and had its limitations, but it had still done the job, allowing him to listen to conversations on *Bianca*, thanks to the sender he had placed at the door of the cabin the night before. Had it not been for the bloody dog on board, he would have planted the bug in the cabin itself, so the sound would have been better. But he had heard the essentials; enough to hear the words *Mogens, money, Teufel Berg,* and *Trekroner*. He knew where Trekroner was—as any visitor who could read a tourist guide. They were proud of their history, the Danes. A legacy of repeated defeat in battle. But they were also a nation of people who didn't stick to the rules, a strange species of man that invented devious solutions—the raven-man was an incarnation of the kind.

Hausser had no idea how the Dane had sniffed out his trail, but he knew that *he* had been the one—not the German police—who had forced him to flee. The way he had hunted him down on the streets of Berlin proved this man would never give up. The two of them shared the same kind of killer instinct; the taste of blood on the tongue, even though the other tried to repress his bloodthirst. If anyone could find the money, *he* could: *der Ravn Mensch*.

Hausser knew that it had been a big risk to cross the border and come to Copenhagen, but it seemed as if it was about to pay off. If he could secure Mogens's bounty, he would have enough money to survive. He had no idea where he would go next. Maybe Cuba? Wasn't that what Strauss had once recommended? He smiled at the sheer absurdity of the thought. But perhaps it was possible to get on board a container ship headed for Havana and be welcomed as one of the last true heroes of socialism. For wasn't that exactly what he was?

89

Ravn held on tight to the rope that was fastened to the rubber dinghy's bow and leaned backwards to keep the nose of the little Zodiac above the waves. He sailed past the massive cruise liners at Langelinie Pier and set a course for the old maritime fort on Trekroner on the opposite end of the harbour. Due to the large mouth of the port and the fierce winds, the dock could just as well have been open sea. The high waves even made the much larger harbour tour boats that passed him pitch and roll in the water. The unstable outboard motor sputtered, and Ravn cast a look over his shoulder. In his eagerness to leave, he'd forgotten to check how much petrol Eduardo had left in the tank; if the motor died now, he would lose momentum and capsize. He eased his grip on the throttle, and the motor regained a regular rotation. After a few more minutes, he could see the entrance to the old fort buildings ahead. Ravn allowed the Zodiac to glide into the protected inlet, where the water was almost completely still. One of the harbour tour boats docked in front of the castle and the tourists went ashore. Ravn sailed to the fort's southern bastion and tethered his dinghy close to the former commander's residence, which now housed a café. He walked up the path to the café and stuck his head through the open door. A waiter was wiping tables inside. "We close in ten minutes," he said.

Ravn nodded. "When does the last harbour tour leave?"

"In twenty," said the waiter.

Ravn walked up the slope of the overgrown citadel; from the top he had a view over the entire island fortress; its massive cement walls and white lighthouse had always reminded him of Alcatraz. It was much larger than he remembered, and Ravn realised with a sinking feeling that there was a myriad good hiding places that could have struck Mogens's fancy; he hadn't really thought this through properly.

Another harbour tour boat arrived and docked by the pier. Most of the fortress was abandoned, but some of the buildings housed historical exhibitions that were open to the public, and he saw a group of about ten tourists heading that way. Ravn figured that Mogens would only have had a brief period of time on the island before he had to head back to the city to catch his train to Berlin. With this in mind, he must have gone directly to the hiding place he had chosen in advance, and then made haste to return to the boat. His greatest obstacle would have been the other tourists. Most would have gone straight to the castle, but some might have taken to wandering on the slopes between the armoury and the old cannon stations. Factoring this into the equation, Mogens would either head for the more remote northerly bastion of the fort, which lay furthest from the castle and the café, or chosen a hiding place in the castle itself. Laying his bets on the latter, Ravn trundled down the slope and walked over to the main castle entrance.

It reeked of damp on the first level, almost as bad as the smell in the bunker at Teufel Berg, apart from the sickly sweet stench of a corpse. He could hear the faint voices of tourists echo from the far side of the fortress. With its complex of storerooms and archways, the first level seemed like a labyrinth; all the rooms were connected with one another and most consisted of raw concrete walls without any obvious hiding places.

Ravn continued up to the next level. The voices of the tourists disappeared and were replaced by the screech of seagulls outside. This level was identical to the first, and none of the storerooms were sufficiently remote or suitable for hiding Mogens's bounty. When he reached the far end, Ravn took the stairs leading to a plateau on top of the building and the old cannon stations. The cannons themselves had been removed and only the niche and the firing platform remained. Ravn looked out over the dock, where the last tour of the day was about to board the harbour boat. The waiter from the café came charging down the path and along the pier to the boat; when this one left, Ravn would be alone on the island.

Ravn returned to the storerooms and continued down the stairs to the lowest level of the citadel. The corridors were dark, and he took out his torch. He could hear the waves breaking against the outer walls, and inside the cells that faced the water, the salt deposits looked like stalactites. This level was crumbling, and rocks obstructed the entranceways. Ravn shone his light through the gaps between the rocks and wrote these cells off as impenetrable, taking into consideration the relative bulk of Mogens's body.

Half an hour later, Ravn was back on the pier by the dock. He took a sip of water from his flask and made his way over to the northern bastion of the island and the armoury. He inspected the old warehouses that faced the dock, and the armoury itself was locked, but he could see through the window that the latter was used as a storeroom for the café. As he made his way along the water's edge out to the inlet, he was almost blown over by the force of the wind. He was not looking forward to the trip home in the rubber dinghy in the dark. Soon after, he had circled back to the main castle building, none the wiser about Mogens's hiding place, and he walked back through the corridors with slouched shoulders. Then he caught sight of a gap between two narrow doors that were ajar. He walked towards the doors, pushed them open, and followed the narrow passage that led into the armoury. He switched on his torch and walked past the three first rooms, which were completely empty. He came to a dead end of crumbling bricks. Ravn shone a beam of light over the pile. He took out his crowbar and tapped the bricks to gauge how hard and time-consuming it would be to bury something underneath. Sitting on his haunches, he took a break for a sip of water. Mogens had said that the money was hidden in the "third room"; if he was referring to the armoury, this would be the storeroom behind him. Ravn stood up and shone his torch into the armoury. He listened to the silence. In all the other storerooms, he had heard the waves and the seagulls, but in here it was dead quiet. He shone the beam of light up to the low ceiling and caught sight of a rusty ventilation hatch about twenty centimetres in diameter just below the ceiling.

Ravn stood underneath and reached his fingers through the grille; strangely, there was no draught. The vent could be blocked for any number of reasons, but he took out his multi-tool and unfolded the largest knife to take a closer look. The moment he stuck the blade into the slit between the wall and the hatch, it came loose and landed at his feet. He shone the light into the ventilation shaft. There appeared to be a black plastic object in the shaft. He stuck his arm inside and hauled on the plastic. A cylindrical plastic bag appeared in the opening. Ravn kept pulling, and banknotes began to sift out of the bag and slowly waft to the ground.

90

Ravn looked down at the little mountain of money. He had no intention of counting it, but he assumed the bulk of Mogens's bounty was right in front of him. Lauritzen's ledger was included in the bag and rolled together with an elastic band. Ravn stuffed everything into his backpack.

When he returned to the pier, it was already dark. He ran along the embankment with the backpack over one shoulder and his crowbar in his hand. The moment he reached the Zodiac on the southern bastion, he bent down to undo the tethering. When he stood up, the back of his head was dealt a blow that made him topple over. His ears were ringing and his body felt like jelly. Somebody pulled the backpack off his shoulder, and Ravn remembered the steel crowbar still clenched in his hand. In a sweeping motion, he hit out into thin air. A boot came down on his chest and forced him to the ground. The pressure made it hard to breathe. He let go of the crowbar and tried to shove away the boot with both hands.

"Perfect. You've done a formidable piece of detective work," a voice said in English with a thick German accent. Hausser looked down at him. He was holding a rubber baton, and judging from how outdated it looked, it must have been an old service weapon. "I like you. Your instinct, your bloodthirst. You are a true hunter, a predator, just like me."

"I like you better in woman's clothing," Ravn said. He felt as if his ribs would break at any moment under Hausser's boot. "But we are . . . not in the least bit . . . alike."

Hausser stepped down harder on Ravn's chest.

"Of course not. I am a winner, and *you* are about to take your last breath."

"Fuck you, Hausser."

"Don't be bitter. It's my job to weed out the weakest."

"Is that why you . . . killed Renate?"

Hausser clutched the baton so hard his knuckles went white. "I had nothing to do with her death."

"There's no reason to lie: You're a child murderer." Hausser leaned his weight on Ravn's chest.

"I blew off her father's head and killed her mother in a rain of bullets from my Kalashnikov; I assure you, those bullets made one hell of a mess. But I never touched Renate. God forbid. Only she was pure."

Ravn gave him a mocking smile through gritted teeth and pain. "You fucking liar. I can spot a child murderer from a mile away, and there's one standing right in front of me."

Hausser struck Ravn's temple with the baton, and it felt as if his head had exploded. "Shut up!" Hausser screamed. "I never touched her!"

Ravn laughed and spat blood. "You can hit me as much as you like . . . you are still a child murderer. I read the report. You set the forest on fire to cover your tracks . . . but that doesn't change a thing, you bastard."

Hausser leaned back, slightly reducing the pressure on Ravn's chest. "You're right; we set fire to the forest to hide the corpses, but before that . . . I tried to save Renate. That's the truth. I wouldn't dream of hurting a hair on that little angel's head." He looked out over the dock. It was almost completely swallowed in darkness now. "She could have been alive today . . . *should* have been alive . . . but she was afraid of me." He looked at Ravn. "I ran through the death strip to the fence. She was sitting on the ground between her parents; the white shirt of her Pioneer Uniform was drenched in their blood, as red as the neckerchief she always wore. Renate was Germany's future. She wanted to compete at the Olympics for the Republic. That was her dream."

"So why the hell did you kill her?" Ravn choked.

Hausser shook his head and almost looked human for a moment. "I didn't kill her. I told her everything was going to be all right, but she was afraid. I thought she could understand that I had no choice; I did what needed to be done. A traitor remains a traitor, family or not. When I was a child, I sacrificed my own parents for the greater good. I reported them for their corrupt behaviour, and I thought that Renate understood necessary sacrifices. But the bullets and the blood had scared her, so she ran . . . ran into the fence behind her."

Hausser shrugged. "I would have had mercy on her, but the tripwires did not, nor the mines." He dabbed his mouth. "She set off two of them at once. A terrible sight. Like seeing a child in a meat grinder. Her death is the only thing that still pains me. There was nothing I could do, other than cover the tracks. Now that Germany has lost its mind and reunified, no one will understand it."

"Understand what? That you slaughtered an entire family?"

"No will understand the necessity of my actions." Hausser released the pressure and swung the baton to deliver the final blow. With his last reserves of strength, Ravn twisted Hausser's foot, lifting it enough to roll out from underneath his boot. He grabbed the crowbar and stood up. Hausser attacked him immediately, swinging the baton, and Ravn fought him off with the crowbar. Blood ran into his eyes, blurring his vision. Hausser struck his ribs so hard his legs caved, and Ravn lunged forwards and headbutted Hausser, sending the older man reeling backwards.

Hausser scrambled for the backpack, made a run for the Zodiac, untied the lines, and jumped into the boat. In a desperate attempt to stop him, Ravn threw the crowbar at Hausser. It hit him in the back, but the next moment, the outboard motor squealed, and the Zodiac shot forwards. Hausser clung to the bench and managed to get the boat under control and steered for open water.

Ravn limped to the end of the pier and stared out over the water. When Hausser was about one hundred metres out, the motor started to sputter, then died with a bang. Hausser yanked on the start cable frantically. He was struggling to keep his balance at cross angles to the waves. Ravn saw the boat drift in the strong current. Without warning, a wave washed over the railing and filled it with water. It began to sink rapidly and Hausser jumped into the water. His arms flailed, trying to keep his body above water. Ravn couldn't understand why Hausser didn't try to swim to land, but then he realised that Hausser was pulled down by the backpack, which he tried to shrug off in vain. Finally, when he could tread water no longer, Hausser's pale and desperate face appeared above the dark waves—once, twice—and then he was gone.

91

Two days after Hausser drowned, his body washed up on Langelinie Pier, not far from the Little Mermaid. The body was found by two female joggers, but it was only later, when a rescue team pulled him out of the water, that the backpack was opened and the money was discovered.

A media frenzy erupted shortly afterwards; the news that a serial killer with a huge sum of money in a backpack had washed up a stone's throw from a national icon hit the headlines. The fraudulent accounts ledger attracted all sorts of unpleasant attention that brought Axel Pondus Lauritzen within the radar of the police. Hausser's death was described as an accident but connected to the death of Mogens Slotsholm and the money that he had stolen. Neither the press nor the police had any explanation for how or why Hausser had ended up in Copenhagen harbour.

Ravn carefully applied the brush to the wooden hatch. The lacquer was going on very nicely indeed. He was going to give it twelve layers. His head still hurt, and he felt nauseous at the slightest movement. Luckily, nothing was broken. The doctor had merely stitched the two deep gashes on his scalp, and he had gauze wrapped around his head.

Eduardo had forgiven him for sinking his Zodiac. He was kind enough to interrupt his date that night and pick up Ravn on Trekroner with his ketch. The only thing Eduardo was still having a tough time forgiving him for was that Ravn refused to tell him what had happened out there.

And his annoyance grew when Hausser's body washed up—and Ravn still wouldn't spill the beans.

"I need stories like that!" he yelled at Ravn.

"You work for *Information*," Ravn said. "Your paper is still publishing articles about the Cuban Missile Crisis!"

Ravn hadn't spoken to Eduardo since that argument. But he was pretty sure his pal would return once he had cooled down. And Ravn was already on the lookout for a new dinghy for him.

"Looks good," a familiar voice said.

Ravn turned his head to Louise, who was standing on the quay. He put down his brush and smiled. "Do you want to come aboard?"

She shook her head.

He came over to the railing and hopped onto the quay. The movement made his head spin, but the smell of her perfume was enough to make it all go away. "It's wonderful to see you," he said, giving her a brief embrace.

"Thank you, the same to you. Is that table still bothering you," she said, pointing to the bandage.

Ravn shrugged. "Did you get the package I sent you?"

"Yes, thank you, that was sweet of you."

"That's all that was missing."

She smiled awkwardly. "I'm sorry I just disappeared on you. That wasn't very dignified. I apologise."

"Don't worry about it, Louise. You don't have to apologise for anything."

"Yes, I do. There's just been so much to think about, and Mogens's funeral to arrange . . ."

"As I said: You don't have to explain yourself. It was a beautiful ceremony, by the way."

"You were there?" she said, blushing.

Ravn nodded.

"Okay. Well, then you know already," she said, staring at her feet. "We . . . Andreas and I are giving it another try. Does that sound pathetic?"

"No, on the contrary. One must fight for one's relationships, so . . . I understand."

She nodded and her lips formed an inaudible "thank you." "I hope that someday you also . . ."

"Louise, I'm going to be just fine," he said, and took her hands in his. "I am glad that I met you, and that I was able to help a little."

"I think you know how grateful I am for everything that you have done," she said, and pulled him close.

He felt the warmth of her body, closed his eyes, and smelled her hair. It felt safe and a little intoxicating. Then he pulled back and smiled at her. "Want to grab a coffee along the canal sometime?"

She smiled. "Definitely." She untangled herself from his embrace and went back to her little Fiat.

They both knew that it was never going to happen, but it was a nice thought to hold on to as they waved to each other and Louise drove away.

92

"You look like a Hindu with that bandage on your head." Victoria leaned over the billiard table with her cue, trying to concentrate on her next shot. She cocked it up and sent the red ball flying into the pins, which toppled over.

"Doggone it, I can't concentrate with you looking like that."

Ravn chalked his cue, keeping his eyes on Victoria. "Now you know what you subject the rest of us to by wearing that gear every day."

Victoria looked down at her tweed waistcoat and brushed off the blue chalk powder caught in the fibres. "Tweed is an aristocratic material. I'm just trying to add a little class to my environment."

Johnson came into the room with their drinks.

"This round is on the baroness," said Ravn.

"It must be bad if you can't even win against this guy," said Johnson.

"His bandage is putting off my aim," said Victoria.

Ravn put the pins in place and set up for a new game of carom.

"I heard you sank Eduardo's dinghy," said Johnson, removing the empty bottles from their table. "It's been a while. You might want to refresh your sailing license."

Ravn set up for a shot. "Amazing how quickly that story spread along the quay."

Johnson laughed until he caught sight of the man standing in the doorway to the billiards room. "Your quarantine isn't over for quite a while yet," he said.

"Fair enough. But I need to have a word with *him*," Mikkel said, pointing at Ravn.

Ravn straightened up and looked at Mikkel, who was avoiding his eyes like a scolded dog. "Can we talk for a minute?" he said.

Ravn tightened his grip on his cue with both hands. "Do we have much to talk about?"

Mikkel nodded. "Just a minute of your time."

Ravn put down his cue and walked out of the billiards room.

They walked over to the embankment. The wind was whistling in the trees. On the canal, a few kayaks sailed past silently.

"You wanted to talk, so talk," said Ravn.

"I feel terrible about everything that's happened," said Mikkel.

"That's your problem. I don't want to listen to your bawling."

"I know. I was just hoping that we could be friends again someday."

Ravn looked at him and shook his head. "I don't want to bear a grudge, Mikkel. What happened, happened, and I want to move on. But I will never trust you again, so there's no way we can be friends."

"I understand how you feel. I just want to make it up to you, regain your trust."

Ravn shook his head again. "I can't see how. I'm sorry." He'd heard enough, turned on his heel, and headed for The Sea Otter.

"Ravn."

Ravn looked over his shoulder at Mikkel, who was struggling to find the words.

"I came here to tell you that we have instigated an investigation into Kaminsky. Management has given us the green light to stake out his club on Colbjørnsensgade. The tech guys have already rigged his place. We're going to be watching him twenty-four seven."

"Why is Management suddenly interested in Kaminsky's card club?"

"Because a reliable source has told us that a lot more than gambling is going down in there. Kaminsky's place is the command centre for many Baltic gangs operating in the country. And he's deeply involved in drug dealing and human trafficking with Eastern European prostitutes."

"How reliable is your source?"

"It comes directly from Slavros, who's in our custody for nine months. Slavros and Kaminsky have been working together for six years."

"It wasn't friendship between them," Ravn said drily. "But why is Slavros talking all of a sudden?"

"He wants to go home. Do his time in Sweden so that the family can visit him."

"And why are you telling me all this?"

"Because if anyone knows who killed Eva in Christianshavn, it's Kaminsky. The surveillance can lead to information about Eva's murderer."

"Congratulations, I hope you find him."

Mikkel swallowed hard. "That's not what I'm offering you."

"I didn't realise you were offering me anything."

Mikkel cast a look over his shoulder as if to ensure that no one was listening. He lowered his voice. "When I find out who the murderer is, you will be the first to know. Before Management. Before anyone else."

Ravn narrowed his eyes. He could taste the hunger; the one Hausser pointed out. He looked out over the canal. "If Kaminsky gives up a name, you and I are the only people who get to know about it."

Mikkel nodded. "As I said: I just want to win back your trust."

"And I want to know where I can find the bastard."

"I'll contact you as soon as I know anything."

"And not a moment before," said Ravn. He stuck his hands in his pockets, walked back to The Sea Otter, and disappeared into its dark mouth.

ABOUT THE AUTHOR

Michael Katz Krefeld (b. 1966) is one of the most-read Danish crime authors, and his critically acclaimed books have been awarded several fiction prizes. He is best known for his bestselling crime series featuring Detective Ravn, which has thrilled readers across the globe. Having begun his career as a screenwriter, Krefeld tends toward fast-paced and highly unpredictable thrillers. The fight against evil and personal sacrifices made for the greater good are typical recurring elements of his work.

Podium
DISCOVER
STORIES UNBOUND
PodiumAudio.com

www.ingramcontent.com/pod-product-compliance
Lightning Source LLC
Chambersburg PA
CBHW030925120726
47906CB00002B/485